Including *New York Times* Bestselling Authors

MAGGIE
SHAYNE

JEANIENE
FROST

TERRI
GAREY

KATHRYN
SMITH

Weddings From Hell

Finding the right dress was the least of their problems . . .

HARPER
U.S. $7.99
CAN. $8.99

MORE SUPERNATURAL DAYS— AND NIGHTS— TO REMEMBER!

KIM HARRISON

LYNSAY SANDS

KELLEY ARMSTRONG

LORI HANDELAND

Four otherworldly tales of paranormal trysts

Dates From Hell

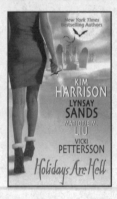

New York Times Bestselling Authors

KIM HARRISON

LYNSAY SANDS

MARJORIE M. LIU

VICKI PETTERSSON

Holidays Are Hell

To love and to cherish . . .
for better or for worse . . .

Years ago, a heartbroken McLellan witch placed a curse on the would-be brides of her family. But Kira McLellan doesn't believe in curses. Then she falls in love with Ian Stewart and is determined to break the spell . . . or die trying.

Maggie Shayne, **TILL DEATH**

To save her brother, Isabella is about to reluctantly walk down the aisle with Mr. Dangerously Wrong . . . unless Chance, a dashing vampire, can derail this wedding of the beauty to the beast.

Jeaniene Frost, **HAPPILY NEVER AFTER**

Nicki Styx sees dead people. Worse, she's a replacement bridesmaid forced to wear a hideously yellow dress. If only the chatty ghost of the original bridesmaid will just leave her alone, Nicki may survive this ceremony yet.

Terri Garey, **GHOULS NIGHT OUT**

Payen Carr has reappeared at a most inconvenient time: on the eve of Violet's wedding. But Payen desperately needs her help, for his immortal life is suddenly at stake . . . and Violet's mortal one as well.

Kathryn Smith, **THE WEDDING KNIGHT**

By Maggie Shayne

DEMON'S KISS • LOVER'S BITE

By Jeaniene Frost

ONE FOOT IN THE GRAVE • HALFWAY TO THE GRAVE

By Terri Garey

A MATCH MADE IN HELL • DEAD GIRLS ARE EASY

By Kathryn Smith

TAKEN BY THE NIGHT • NIGHT OF THE HUNTRESS

MAGGIE
SHAYNE

JEANIENE
FROST

TERRI
GAREY

KATHRYN
SMITH

Weddings from Hell

HARPER

An Imprint of HarperCollinsPublishers

HARPER

An Imprint of HarperCollins*Publishers*
10 East 53rd Street
New York, New York 10022–5299

"Till Death" copyright © 2008 by Margaret Benson
"Happily Never After" copyright © 2008 by Jeaniene Frost
"Ghouls Night Out" copyright © 2008 by Terri Garey
"The Wedding Knight" copyright © 2008 by Kathryn Smith
ISBN 978-0-06-147268-8

First Harper paperback printing: June 2008

HarperCollins® and Harper® are registered trademarks of Harper-Collins Publishers.

Printed in the United States of America

Visit Harper paperbacks on the World Wide Web at
www.harpercollins.com

10 9 8 7 6 5 4 3 2 1

Contents

TILL DEATH

Maggie Shayne

Prologue

It was an ordinary Saturday afternoon. Seven-year-old Kira wore bib overalls of faded denim, a striped T-shirt, and copper-red braid that hung all the way to her butt. Her feet were bare, pant legs rolled up nearly to her knees as she waded in the lake. It was too early, Dad said, to go in for a real swim. But wading in the shallows was okay. The water felt just fine to Kira, and she wondered if she should "trip and fall" all the way into the water. Once she was wet, her parents wouldn't see any sense making her get out.

She glanced at the shore, where dandelions were like yellow polka-dots in the lush green grass. Her mom was spreading a plastic tablecloth on the picnic table. It was red and white checks. Kira thought it was silly to bother with a tablecloth at a picnic, but her mom liked things the way she liked things, so she didn't voice her own opinion on the matter. Probably, Kira thought, there were important reasons to use a tablecloth at a picnic—reasons she was just too young to understand yet.

Her dad was standing at the grill, with a big two-pronged fork in one hand and a long-handled burger-flipper in the other.

"Darlin'?" Mom called, her Scottish accent clear, even in that one word. She'd managed to get the flapping tablecloth to stay put by laying her purse on one end, and Kira's shoes on the other.

Dad turned toward her, and when he caught her eye, he smiled.

"Could ya get the cooler from the car? And while ya do, why not move the car outta the sun, so t'willna be like an oven by the time we're ready to leave."

He looked at the parking lot, just up the hill from where they were picnicking, on the shore of Cayuga Lake. "I don't see any shady spots. Do you?"

"Right there, love, beneath the shading arms of that oak tree," she said, pointing.

He followed with his eyes, and spotted the place she had in mind. "Okay," he told her. "Whatever you say."

Kira grinned, because she heard something in his voice that told her he thought moving the car was about as necessary as a tablecloth on a picnic table. But he would never say so out loud. Mom liked things the way she liked them, and there was no point in arguing.

She had skin like cream and hair the same color as Kira's, but wildly curly where Kira's was straight. Her eyes were green, as green as emeralds, her father used to say.

She'd left Scotland to find a husband, and vowed never to go back. She didn't talk about why not, or what had happened there that had made her so very unhappy. And since Kira didn't like seeing her mom unhappy, she didn't ask. She wondered, though.

Dad moved the car to the spot Mom had dictated, then got out and fetched the giant red cooler full of food from the trunk. It was as he carried the cooler around the car and down the hill, that the car began to roll forward.

It started slowly. So slowly, that Kira wasn't sure it was really moving, at first. Mom didn't notice it. She stood by the table with a roll of masking tape she'd unearthed from the depths of her purse. She tore off one strip and then another and then another, using each of them to hold the tablecloth to the table, tucking the tape underneath so it wouldn't show.

Dad didn't notice it either. His back was toward the car as he strode down the hill carrying the huge red cooler with the white top.

But it was moving. It *was*. It was rolling slowly—then faster, right down the hill toward Kira's parents. She found her voice, shouted, "Mamma! Pappa!"

But instead of looking at the danger trundling toward them, that only made them both look toward her.

"The car!" she cried, and she pointed at it. "Look out!"

Her father turned to look, just as the car rolled past him so close that the mirror on the side knocked the cooler right out of his hands. Mamma turned slowly, and Kira heard her dad shouting her mother's name.

She must have seen it, Kira thought. But not in time.

Kira closed her eyes tight just before the inevitable

happened. And by the time she opened them again, the car's nose was in the water.

She lifted her gaze to see how bad things were, even though she was afraid to look. The red cooler lay on its side, its white lid open, their picnic spilled all over the grass. Macaroni salad and rolls and the chocolate cake she'd helped her mamma frost that very morning, lay ruined and broken. Pappa was on his feet, holding one arm across his chest as if something were wrong with it, even as he stumbled down the hill. He had the most horrible look on his face.

Kira looked for her mamma. The picnic table was crushed. She could see a bit of blue beside it, and that must be her mamma's dress. Kira came out of the water, sloshing step by step.

Other picnickers had come running by now, gathering around, looking and pointing. Someone shouted "Call an ambulance!" and others went running to obey. But mostly they were just looking.

Kira crept around the table. By then her pappa was on his knees beside Mamma. And she heard her mother's voice, weak and slurred.

"It's the curse. It's the curse. Oh, Paul, how could ya?"

"There's no curse. You're gonna be fine," Pappa said.

"I'm dying. You have to tell her, Paul. When she's older, tell her. Before it's too late, warn her. Tell her, Paul."

"Mamma?"

Kira had made her way closer, and stood right beside her parents. Mamma's middle looked almost flattened, and there was a lot of blood on the skirt of her blue dress. Her legs lay all twisted and cockeyed, and they didn't move at all. It was almost like her mamma couldn't feel how messed up they were. Her skin was so white. And her eyes looked far away.

She gazed at Kira. "It isna Pappa's fault," she told her.

"I know." Kira sniffed and wiped her nose. "I should have yelled sooner."

"No, baby. This wasna your fault, either." Weakly, her mamma lifted a hand and touched Kira's cheek.

"Stupid car."

" 'Twas fate, darlin'. An' now I'm goin'. Not 'cause I wanna, but 'cause I've no choice in the matter. But I'll be with ya always, lass. Always my bonny, bonny girl."

"But Mamma, I don't want you to go."

"Like an angel, love. I'll be watchin' over ya like your own guardian angel."

"No Mamma! No!"

But Mamma's eyes fell closed, and her hand, cold and white, fell away from Kira's cheek and landed with a final thud in the grass.

For the first time in her life, Kira heard her father cry. And then there were sirens and more people. Paul Monroe wrapped his little girl in his arms, and carried her a few steps away to let the paramedics have room to work. But Kira knew it was already too late. Mamma had gone. Kira knew it, had seen it and felt it when it happened.

Mamma had gone. And she'd blamed it on a curse. Kira wasn't sure exactly what that meant, or whether it could even be true. All of the grownups who surrounded her for the next several weeks—her grandparents and aunts and uncles—all on her pappa's side, of course—she didn't know any of her mamma's family—told her that there were no such things as curses.

And for a little while, she believed them. But only for a little while. Once Pappa shot himself in the head, she realized that curses were very real, and very *very* bad.

Chapter 1

Present day

Kira answered the telephone without knowing that the call would change everything. She picked it up with a cheery "hello." As if everything was fine.

As if there hadn't been a shadow haunting her ever since she'd been a well-adjusted seven-year-old. As if she hadn't been forcibly ignoring the secrets that were constantly whispering in her mind, beckoning her. *Come find us, Kira. We're waiting for you.* . . .

"Would this be a Miss Kira MacLellan?"

She shivered. His accent was thick and so very much like her mother's had been, that it caused her throat to close up and her eyes to burn. But there was something beyond that. Something familiar, that made her stomach clench up tight. Swallowing with difficulty, she drew a breath. "It's Kira Monroe. My mother was a MacLellan."

"And so're you, as you always will be. But that's neither here nor there, is it now?"

"I . . . have no idea. Who is this?"

"My name's Ian Stewart. I'm a solicitor, calling from Scotland on behalf of your great aunt Iris Mac-Lellan. It's my sad duty to inform you of her passin'. And sorry I am to be tellin' you of it. She was a fine woman."

"I'm sure she was, though I never met her. I never even knew I had a great aunt Iris."

"Ah, you've a raft of relations here in Scotland. An' it's long past time you should be meetin' 'em. Better late than never, I suppose."

"I'm sorry?"

"The viewing will be on Thursday next. We've delayed it a bit to give you time, what with the distance you'll be travelin' ."

"I'm sorry Mr.—"

"Stewart," he said quickly. "But you must call me Ian. I'm practically family myself."

"I'm not going to be able to make it for the funeral."

"Oh, but you have to make it within two days of the funeral, at the very least. The readin' o' the will is to be held then. And it's required ye be present or your inheritance will be divided between those who are."

"*My* inheritance."

"Aye. It's substantial. More than three million pounds."

She blinked. "What's that in dollars?"

"Ahhh, let me see then . . . oh my. At today's rate of exchange, that would be six million dollars, give or take."

She pulled the telephone away from her ear and stared at it.

"Miss MacLellan? Kira? Have ye fainted dead away, then?"

Blinking, she brought the phone back to her ear. "Is this some kind of a joke? Or one of those international scams or something? Are you going to ask for my social security or bank account numbers next?"

He laughed. It was a warm, deep sound that stroked her senses through the shock and disbelief currently taking up most of her attention. "Are you as lovely as you sound, Kira MacLellan?"

"I . . ." Her face heated at the compliment that sounded sincere, though it couldn't be. She hadn't even met the man. He was a stranger on the phone. And yet it felt like more.

"I suggest ye place a call to a solicitor of your own choosin'. Give him my number here. He'll be quite able to verify this is all legitimate."

"I will, believe me."

"And glad of it, I am. Once you've done that to your satisfaction ring me back. I'll help you get your travelin' arrangements in place. All right, then?"

"Sure," she said, not believing it for a minute.

"All right, then. Have a lovely day."

Kira hung up the telephone and the whispers that had long since haunted her called her closer. So she turned toward the bedroom of the small efficiency apartment she rented in the small-town city of Cortland, New York. It was on Main Street, which was convenient, since her job tending bar at Hairy Tony's was only a few steps away, and her classes at the State University of New York were within bicycle distance.

Life was going the way it had nearly always gone. Boring, and slow, and with no real direction, but it was going. She made enough to pay her bills, and take the occasional class, though she had no real goals. It was as if she'd been marking time, or killing it, waiting for something to come along that would tell her what it was she was supposed to be doing. Or, more accurately, not really waiting for that. More expecting it, but not with any sort of excited anticipation or eagerness. She liked her slow, boring life. She'd had enough drama as a child to last her a lifetime.

She stood in front of the closed closet door for a long moment, before she finally worked up the nerve to open it. And then she reached up onto the top shelf and moved things around until she found the shoebox, way in the back. Warily, she pulled the box down, carried it with her to her full-sized bed, curled up with her back against the padded headboard, and stared at it.

Her mother's belongings hadn't amounted to much. Her father had sold most of them in the days following her death, probably in preparation for his own. At his funeral, there had been a woman sobbing as if her very heart had been broken. Kira asked everyone there who she was, but no one knew. She'd stayed in the back of the crowd at the cemetery, and left as soon as anyone ventured near her.

It was only in hindsight, as a teenager, years later, being raised by her father's parents, that she'd begun to understand. Her father had been having an affair. Her mother had known that at the end. She remembered her words, "How could ya, Paul?" All the signs had been there, she'd just been too young to see them.

With hands that trembled, she took the lid off the shoebox, and looked inside. A black velvet box held her mother's wedding band and engagement ring. Another held a favorite gold necklace with a butterfly suspended from its chain. There was a stack of letters and postcards, all bound together with a rubber band, and it was that bundle Kira reached for now. She'd never read them. She'd been afraid to. Something hidden, deep inside her, made her nervous about those letters.

But now, she reached for the rubber band, to remove it for the first time in eighteen years. And just as her fingers touched it, it snapped in two, and she jumped, so startled that the letters fell from her hands, and onto the bed.

She sat motionless, frightened by the way the band had snapped as if on its own, even while she told herself she was being silly. It was nothing. Coincidence.

Without touching the letters that fanned out on the bedding before her, Kira scanned their return addresses. Most of them had come from Scotland. And all of the surnames were MacLellan. She'd never met any of her mother's relatives, had never even heard her mother speak of them.

She didn't know why, but decided it was time to find out. Given that phone call she'd just received, and the constant gut-level curiosity that had dogged her for years, it was time. Her urge to delve into her mother's closely guarded secrets had always been outweighed by the irrational fear of what she might find.

Six million dollars, however, was a powerful motivator. And as much as her practical brain told her it couldn't possibly be for real, her belly told her it was.

Kira picked up one envelope, flipped it over and

paused. It was still sealed. Frowning, she checked another, and then another. None of them had been opened.

What had happened to make her mother turn so completely against her own family?

Because of the curse.

She ignored the voice that whispered in her mind. There was no curse. Her mother had been dying, her brain misfiring, her words coming from some irrational place inside her. She'd asked her father. He'd said there were no such things as curses.

Drawing a breath, she chose the envelope she would open. It was from Iris MacLellan, and the postmark date was April, 1981. Before she had even been born. She slid her thumbnail beneath the envelope's fold and sliced it open, and swore a chorus of breathless whispers spilled out with the sheet of vellum.

For a moment, she went still, looking around the room as if in search of those whisperers. But of course, there was no one there.

Straightening her spine, she unfolded the letter. A scent of lavender wafted from it, touching her face along with what felt like the slightest breath of a breeze. Impossible, of course. Her emotions were heightened, and the long sense of dread and fear of curses were making her imagination play tricks on her.

Adjusting her focus, she read the letter.

My Dearest Mary,

I write you in this, the month you are to be wed, to beg of you, child, do not make this mistake.

Do you not recall how your own ma, my own dear sister, met her end? The way her poor, drowned body washed up on the rocks below the cliffs? And how your Da disappeared, never to be seen again? And never still, not to this day. The curse of the MacLellan brides is real, Mary. You cannot run away from it, even if you run halfway 'round the world. It will find you, lass. And you'll die at your husband's hand. Please, listen to me. Come home, dear Mary, and resign yourself to living the life of a spinster. 'Tis the only way to ensure you'll live at all.

Your loving aunt,
Iris MacLellan

Blinking slowly, Kira lowered the paper to the bed.

Her mother hadn't been hallucinating or out of her mind as she'd been breathing her last. She'd been speaking of something that was real—at least to her it was. Maybe she hadn't believed in this curse of the MacLellan brides before the accident. But once that car had rolled over her body, crushing the life out of it, she must have believed then.

And apparently, she thought the curse would be handed down to her, to Kira. And if that was the case, Kira thought, she really needed to know exactly what it meant. Was every MacLellan woman who married, destined to die by her husband's hand? Could it be true?

Scooping all the letters into a pile, she dumped them

back into the shoebox, shoved on the cover, and stuffed it back into the closet. Then she went to the telephone like she should have done in the first place, called her boss, and asked him for the name and phone number of his lawyer.

Chapter 2

 Three days later, Kira stepped out of the airport in Edinburgh and into overcast weather. There was a heavy mist in the air. It hovered and hung, wet and clingy, like a living fog that attached itself to your face and hair and clothes as if trying to claim you for its own.

Silly thought.

Hairy Tony's legal eagle had been able to verify that Ian Stewart was indeed an attorney in Scotland, and that Iris MacLellan had indeed died. That was enough for her. She'd phoned the man back, and he'd taken care of all the arrangements for her. He'd booked her flight—the tickets had been waiting at the airport as promised. He'd said a car would be waiting to take her to her accommodations. And the entire time his voice had stroked her senses like a lover's caress. It gave her chills, his voice. And she didn't know why.

She peered through the wet air. It was evening, just past sunset, and everything was swathed in shades of gray. But there was a small, boxy black car sitting at the curb, and even as she started toward it, a man got out, and came closer.

"Kira?" he asked.

She nodded, getting a better look at him as he drew nearer, but knowing already who he was. She recognized that voice. It had appealed to her on many levels, from the first time she'd heard it, from its resonance and tone, to its friendly, honest nature, to the accent that so reminded her of her mother, to the feeling it gave her that he was always teasing, just a little.

She was unprepared, however, for the way he looked. He was taller than she'd imagined, and seemed broad in his tan trench coat. His hair was a mass of black curls, all of them wet now where they lay on his forehead. He smiled, and when he did, his velvet-lashed eyes crinkled at the corners and his sensual mouth curved in a way that made her stomach tingle.

"Ian," she said.

"Aye. I'd know ye anywhere, Kira." His eyes, when he said that, probed hers with an intensity that was out of place. He seemed genuinely glad to see her. So glad, she almost expected him to hug her right off her feet at any moment. But he seemed to forcibly restrain himself. "You're a MacLellan, through and through."

"I hope that's a compliment."

"I'll shower you in them, if you like." And then he did hug her. Didn't ask or wait around for permission, just wrapped his arms around her and hugged her hard, as if he'd been doing it for years. Maybe that was the way of things here, she thought. So she hugged him back just as enthusiastically, and she didn't even have to fake it all that much.

And she felt something in that embrace, because it

seemed to change, from friendly and welcoming, to something decidedly more intimate.

When he released her and stepped back, he looked as shell-shocked as she felt. He had to avert his eyes as he took her arm and turned toward the car.

"Oh, my bags—"

"I'll be getting the bags into the boot, lass. You first, though." He didn't slow his pace, then opened the passenger door, which was on the wrong side of the car, and held her elbow as she got inside. He closed her door, and rushed away to get the bags, stowing them in the trunk—er, boot, she corrected mentally.

And then he was back, climbing behind the wheel, putting the car into motion, and turning his high-beam smile on her as he did. "You're about to become a very wealthy woman, Kira MacLellan. And it's not the money alone of which I'm speakin'."

"No?"

"'Tis the heritage of the Clan MacLellan. The family you've never known. The history and the lineage—'tis as rich and colorful as any tapestry you could imagine."

"I suppose it is. But I'll be inheriting more than that, won't I, Ian?"

"Aye, there's the money as well. And some of the holdings, I would imagine. I only know in general the plans your great aunt made for you. My father handled the details."

"Yes, but that's not what I meant. I was speaking about the um . . . the curse."

He jerked the wheel in unison with his head. The car veered as he gaped at her, and then he quickly righted it again, clearly shaken.

"So you know about the curse, then?" she asked him.

"Of course I do. It's surprised I am that *you* know of it."

She shook her head. "I know very little. I have only my mother's dying words, begging my father to warn me about it, and a letter from my dearly departed great aunt Iris, begging my mother not to marry and bring the curse upon herself."

His lips thinned. It was the first time she'd seen him not wearing a smile. "I dinna believe in curses," he said.

"But you know about this one. More than I do, at least."

"Well, now, that would depend on how much you know, Kira."

She shrugged, turned her gaze inward. "I take it that every MacLellan woman who gets married is destined to die at the hands of her husband, in one way or another." Lifting her gaze, letting it roam over his cheek, and battling the way her insides clenched with raw desire as she did, she said, "Is that about the gist of it?"

"There's much more to it, or so they say. But as I said, I dinna believe in it."

"Still, I'd really like to know the rest of it."

He nodded. "I've no doubt o' that. But as it happens, we've arrived." He pulled the car to a stop, and she looked through the windows at a sprawling castle. Not the kind you might see in a fairytale, but more like something out of a nightmare. Its stone was such a dark gray as to appear nearly black in places. There were barred windows in some sections, spikes lining the uppermost walls, towers on either end that stood like menacing sentries.

"Welcome to Castle MacLellan," he intoned as she stared. And then he touched her shoulder. "Dinna look that way, love. 'Tis much nicer on the inside than it seems from without." He got out of the car, came around to her side, and opened her door. "Shall we?"

She got out, and shivered at the cold, wet embrace of the fog. Or maybe it was at the cold appearance of the stone monstrosity in front of her. Or maybe, she thought, it was none of those things. Maybe it was the certainty that she was about to step right into her mother's secrets, and the gut feeling that once she did, there would be no turning back. Not ever. And life would never be the same.

And then Ian took her arm, held her a little closer to his side, and a warmth suffused her, and gave her the strength and courage to walk with him up to the door.

Chapter 3

 The woman who greeted her at the door was fat and pink. Those were the two things most noticeable about her, those and her friendly smile. She'd let her hair go silvery, but still wore it in long curls that tumbled unfettered to her shoulders.

She was dressed in a pewter-colored, quilted house coat, and a pair of what looked like ballet slippers.

She gripped Kira's hands in both of hers, beaming at her. "Lassie! Oh, I'm so glad to see you at long last. Welcome home!"

And then before she could reply, Kira found herself wrapped in soft, squishy arms, and pulled into a bosom that could have housed several small children.

"I'm your aunt Rose," the woman told her. "Your grandmother's youngest sister."

When she could pull her head back enough to allow

her to speak clearly, Kira said, "It's wonderful to meet you too. And thanks for the warm welcome."

"Oh, come with me, child. You, too, Ian! You know we can't get along without you."

Glancing back at her handsome driver, Kira lifted her brows, not quite sure how he fit in to the scheme of things here.

And there was no time to find out, as she was led through a massive entry hall and into some kind of great room that had been filled with modern furniture in the most classic Queen Anne style, everything feminine, delicate, even lacy. The sofas and chairs had curved clawed arms and legs and floral prints. There was a fainting couch, or at least she thought that's what it was. The decor seemed to Kira to be in direct contrast with the architecture, which was big and dark and masculine.

In one of the most elegant of the chairs, a woman sat. She was bone-thin, and her hair was jet black, except for the stark white at the very front. It hung long and straight. Again, unbound.

It seemed strange that women of their age would wear their hair long and loose, rather than cutting it or perming it or pinning it up. Maybe it was a cultural thing.

She rose, the thin one. She wasn't smiling as she extended a boney hand. "Hello Kira. I'm your great aunt Esmeralda."

Kira took her hand and gasped at how cool it was, how frail it seemed, despite the vibrance in the woman's dark blue eyes.

"You don't seem quite as glad to see me as Aunt Rose is," Kira said.

Esmeralda's finely arched brows rose. "You're as frank as your mother always was."

"I don't see much point in being any other way," Kira said. "Would you have preferred I not come?"

"You have every right to be here."

"Is it the money, then?"

The woman just stared at her, as if waiting.

"Well, Ian told me if I didn't show up for the reading of the will, my share would be divided among the other heirs. And it's a lot of money, after all."

"I already have more money than I'll ever be able to spend," Esmeralda said. "We all do."

"Well if it's not the money, then—"

Slow, rhythmic footsteps—high heels crossing the marble floor interrupted her, and she turned to see a third woman. This one was utterly stunning. Her hair was like shiny copper and her figure, hugged in a skin-tight black halter dress, was to die for. Her skin was nearly flawless. Try as she might, Kira couldn't see a wrinkle or a line.

"Hello, Kira," she said. And even her voice was sultry and beautiful. "I'm your aunt Emma. Your mother was my sister."

"You look like her," Kira said, extended a hand.

The beautiful one smiled but it was shaky. "So do you."

"You don't have an accent."

"I've taken lessons to get rid of it."

"I can't imagine why anyone would want to," Kira said. "I love the lilt of the brogue."

"To each her own," Emma said. Then she looked around. "This is all of us, dear. The entire family, or what remains of it."

"Oh." No children. And no men.

"I'll show you to your chambers," Rose chirped.
"Ian, be a dear and bring the bags along." She gripped
Kira's arm, and tugged her through the massive place.
"We could talk with you all the night through, child,
but you'll be wanting to rest after such a journey. And
there's time a plenty before dinner."

She smiled a good-bye to her great aunt Esmeralda
and her aunt Emma, then followed Aunt Rose up a
curving stone stairway and into a vaulted and echoing
hall above. All the way, Ian was right behind her, bags
in his hands. He was oddly quiet now that they'd arrived. Rose threw open a set of double doors, stepping
through them as she did. "And here you are, lass. A
bedroom fit for a princess."

She stepped in and looked around. There was a huge
canopy bed with silky fabric draped all around it. It
was so tall she thought she'd have to get a running start
to get into it. The comforters looked like satin, and
were the color of French cream. They matched the curtains in the tall narrow windows that lined one entire
wall, like a row of soldiers. One of them was open,
admitting a breeze that smelled of the rain, and made
the curtains dance and sway.

The wardrobe and dresser and nightstands were all
made of rich, dark wood. Walnut, she thought. The
floor sported the same kinds of boards, but they only
showed around the borders of the gigantic area rug,
which was pale green in color with cream celtic knot-
work patterns all over it.

On the walls, there were portraits. Family portraits, she realized as she stepped closer to one of
them.

"That was your grandmother, my dear sister Violet, dead these past forty years."

Kira studied the woman's face, an older version of her mother's. And her own. "She must have died young."

"Aye. Far too young. Thirty and five, she was. Left her two dear girls, Mary and Emma, to Esmeralda, Iris, and I to raise."

"Really? Why not their father? My grandfather, I mean. Shouldn't he have been the one to—"

"Now the bath is straight through the door there," Rose interrupted. "That other is a closet, big enough to be a room all its own, I vow."

"Thank you. The room is breathtaking, Aunt Rose, it truly is." She looked back toward the doorway, but Ian had vanished. Only her bags remained.

"I'll send up a tea, lassie. You need a good tea to bolster you after such a journey as you've made." She turned to leave.

"Aunt Rose?"

"Aye, child?"

"I really do want to know about . . . the family history. And . . . and the curse."

Rose pressed a palm to her ample chest and sucked in a breath at the same time. "Then our Mary told you of it, did she?"

"No. She only mentioned it with her dying breath, Aunt Rose. I thought it was the trauma, that she was delirious. But . . . but Aunt Iris mentioned it in a letter she sent to my mother long ago. I only just read it last week. So I know it's real."

Aunt Rose nodded. "Your tea. And then you'll rest. 'Tis na the conversation a lass needs to be havin' without bein' strong, rested, and well nourished. And so

it'll come. It'll all come in due time. An' you've nowhere to go just now, have you?"

"No, I suppose not."

"Patience, then, lass. Patience."

Kira took a nap to help with the jet lag, then an invigo-
rating shower to help her toughen up for the dinner
ahead. She fully intended to confront her aunt and
great aunts and insist they tell her about this alleged
curse of theirs. Not that she believed in curses. Not for
a minute, but still, it was her family history. And she
had a right to know about it.

She dressed as she always did, in a pair of snug-fitting
jeans and a tank top, then pulled a NY Giants sweatshirt over it in deference to the damp chill of this place,
which seemed to seep into her very bones.

She avoided looking at the haunting portrait of her
grandmother, Violet, that hung on her bedroom wall
like a gargoyle. She wasn't ugly—far from it, in fact.
She had been a beautiful woman with raven hair and
deep blue eyes. But there was something menacing in
them, some vague message of doom that seemed to hit
her every time she met those eyes.

Maybe she should ask Aunt Rose to move it to another room. She wondered if that would be out of line,
then put the thought aside at a tap on her bedroom
door.

"Come in."

The door opened with a vague creaking, and Ian
stood there. The rush of emotion that washed through
her at the sight of him was way overblown. And yet
she smiled a welcome all the same. He wore a suit

and tie, and looked incredibly handsome. She got the
creeping feeling that she might have underdressed for
dinner, though. "Rose sent me for you. It's nearly time
for dinner." He met her eyes, briefly, and something
powerful seemed to pass between them before he
averted his.

"Good. I'm not finishing this meal without knowing
the whole story about this curse nonsense."

His all-seeing gaze shot to hers again. "Oh, that's
unlikely tonight. There are guests."

She lifted her brows. "Guests?"

"Aye. My own father, Gregory, the Reverend Mac-
Dougal and his wife, Jane."

Blinking, she let her eyes move from his head to his
feet and back again. "Are they all dressed up like you
are?"

"Your aunts enjoy dressing for dinner," he told her.
Then he looked her up and down. "And while I daresay
you could make a feed sack look like a ballgown, I
might suggest you'd be more comfortable changing
into something a bit more . . . er . . ."

"Fancy?" she asked.

"Just slightly."

Sighing, she turned toward where her suitcases sat,
still packed, on the floor near the bed. One was open, its
contents spilling out from her recent search for the
jeans and sweatshirt. "I don't even think I own
anything—oh, wait, there's a sundress. It's casual,
but—" Dashing to the suitcase, she dug into it, and finally pulled out a pale blue sundress. It was knee length,
with a faint floral pattern to it and a ruffled hemline.
Spaghetti straps and a sweetheart neckline were not going to keep her very comfortable in this oversized re-
frigerator, though.

"Very nice," Ian said, when she held it up for his scrutiny. "An' I've just the thing to keep you warm."

She smiled up into those sky-blue eyes. "I'll bet you do. Tell me, Ian, are you a mind reader?"

He blinked, his face colored, and he cleared his throat. "If I am, lass, it's only since I met you."

They held each other's eyes for a long, tender moment. Then he cleared his throat. "Put the dress on, then. I'll uh—I'll be back momentarily."

She frowned as he left the room, wondering why he seemed afraid of whatever it was simmering beneath the surface between them. Ah, well, whatever. She peeled the sweatshirt off, then the tank top, and then shimmied out of the jeans. The sundress was on a second later, and she was bending over her bags rummaging for a pair of shoes when Ian knocked again.

"It's okay, I'm decent," she called.

She heard him come in, and kept on with her digging. Then she finally found a pair of white sandals, straightened up, and turned.

His face told her all she needed to know. He was turned on. The big fraud, pretending to be all shy and uncomfortable with the attraction she felt between them. Maybe men were different here. Maybe he was just different. But he had *definitely* been checking out her butt just now. And her butt was one of her best features, in her not-so-humble opinion.

She marched up to him, clapped a hand to his shoulder and used him to steady herself while she put on the shoes. When she finished, she looked up at him. They were standing very close. She could feel his breath on her face.

Damn, he was attractive. She didn't know when she'd been this attracted to a man. Maybe never.

He moved his hands toward her shoulders, and for one blissful, exciting moment, she thought he was going to wrap his arms around her and kiss her. But the soft touch of fabric on her skin told her otherwise. He was draping a shawl around her, a deep blue silken thing that felt like heaven.

He adjusted it, and his fingers brushed the skin on her upper arms as he did. She shivered a little, closed her eyes against it.

"It was your grandmother's," he said softly.

And that gave her another chill, but not the good kind like his touch had given her. This one was decidedly unpleasant.

"Most of her belongings remain in her chambers," Ian went on. "I'm sure no one will mind should you wish to make use of them during your stay."

"I think I prefer my own things." That sounded cold. And she didn't want him to think it was because of him, so she added very quickly, "Thank you, Ian. That was sweet of you."

"You're most welcome." Then he turned, and extended his elbow for her.

She hooked her arm through it and let him lead her from the room and through the endless corridors, walking far more closely to his side than was really necessary. He didn't seem to mind it. In fact, his arm tightened on hers a little, pressing it against his side as they moved onward. As they approached the stairs, she smiled up at him. "Tell me, Ian, are you married?"

She saw his Adam's apple move as he swallowed. "No."

"Seeing anyone?"

"No."

"Neither am I," she told him.

"It's glad I am to hear that, Kira." He met her eyes and held them for a long moment as they stood there, halfway down the staircase.

A throat cleared from below, and they broke eye contact, turning at the same instant.

Aunt Esmeralda stood at the food of the stairs, and the look she was sending Ian should have wilted lettuce. "We're waiting, you know," she said, but her tone said far more. It said "Hands off."

Kira bristled at that tone. These women may be blood relatives, but they were also strangers. And they certainly didn't have any right to go meddling in her love life—or lack thereof.

She was going to have to set them straight on that, and soon, she decided. Because, as odd as it was after such a short acquaintance, she liked Ian. And she was drawn to him in a way that went far beyond anything she'd felt for any man before. To make her point to the aunts in the meantime, she snugged her body a little closer to Ian's side, hooked her arm more tightly through his, met her aunt's eyes as they slid to hers, and smiled at her. "I've never been very good at marching to the beat of someone else's drum, Aunt Esmeralda. I'm sorry if I held up dinner, though. From now on, maybe it would be best to just start without me if I'm a little late."

"That is *not* how we do things at Castle MacLellan."

"Then maybe I should find a hotel." Ian's arm clutched hers tighter to his side, as if in warning.

The woman's eyes widened, but held Kira's, and

she met the subtle challenge head on. "There's not one for miles. So I suppose you'll have to adjust, Grandniece. And perhaps show a bit of respect for your elders."

Chapter 4

 Esmeralda was positively icy all through dinner, but the conversation was carried on by Ian's father, Gregory, who entertained them all with stories of the old days when he was a boy and the mischief he used to get into, all in a brogue so endearing that it melted the tension from Kira's shoulders.

The Reverend MacDougal was humorless. He didn't laugh at jokes, and didn't speak unless it was to correct some factual error or add a serious bent to the topic at hand. His wife, Jane, was a meek little mouse, silent and obedient, and she waited on him hand and foot.

Ian's attention was on Kira throughout the meal, though whenever she looked his way, he shifted his gaze. And Esmeralda seemed to be watching them like a hawk, noticing every exchanged glance, bit of banter, or intimate smile they shared. And they shared a lot of those.

"Well, then, the readin' o' the will takes place tomorrow evenin'," Gregory announced. "Nine o' the clock."

"Why so late?" Kira asked.

"'Twas at Iris's request, lass. She left explicit details. I suggest you prepare yourself, though. She was a rather . . . unusual woman." He turned toward his son. "I would suggest, Ian, that you spend the day showin' our new friend about her family's homeland."

"I really don't think—" Esmeralda began.

"I'd love that!" Kira said, cutting her off. "Will, you Ian? My stay isn't all that long, and I'd hate to miss seeing some of the countryside while I'm here."

Ian's father stared at him, and so did Esmeralda. But his eyes never left hers. With a soft smile, he nodded. "Of course I will. It'll be a rare pleasure." And without looking away, he added, "You needn't worry yourself, Esmeralda. You've known me all my life. Your great niece will be perfectly safe in my company for the day."

She didn't argue, but Kira got the feeling Ian was going to hear about this later—and maybe his father would, as well.

"Nothing to fear in these parts, anyway," the minister said. "It's a perfectly safe area. God-fearing folk. Good people."

As the table was cleared, the guests took their leave, Ian and his father pausing at the door. "'Twas a sheer delight to meet you, lass," Gregory said, clasping her hand warmly.

"It was mutual, Mr. Stewart."

"Gregory, please."

She nodded, then looked up at Ian. "Good night, Ian. I'm really looking forward to tomorrow."

"I'll come around for you after breakfast. All right, then?"

"More than all right." He took her hand, and gave a surreptitious squeeze that made her heart flutter in her chest. Seemed he was getting over his shyness, or whatever his issue had been.

Or maybe he was just as much a rebel at heart as she was. Perhaps she owed Aunt Esmeralda a thank you for pushing his buttons.

Kira fell asleep with a smile on her face. But when she heard someone whispering her name, the voice penetrating her girl-with-a-crush dreams, that smile faded. She opened her eyes, blinking in the utter darkness of the bedroom, instantly aware of the chill that hung heavy in the air. This place always seemed cold but this was different. It was bone deep and drew goosebumps on her skin as a shiver rippled up her spine. She tugged the covers higher, hugging them tight.

"Kira . . ." the whisperer breathed. "Kiiiiiiraaaaaaa."

She sat up fast, one hand shooting toward the bedside lamp, then freezing in mid-air as her eyes widened. There, at the foot of her bed, was . . . something. A wisp of fog, in the vague shape of a woman.

"What the hell!" She resumed her groping for the lamp, found it and turned it on.

In the cold light of the sixty-watt bulb, there was no fog. No form. No ghostly apparition looming over her. The chill retreated, too, as the room returned to its normal state of clamminess.

She hadn't been dreaming. She'd been wide awake,

she assured herself of that, even as she lunged out of the bed, snatching up her robe and pulling it on clumsily while heading for the bedroom door.

This was ridiculous. There were no such things as ghosts. And yet she was driven from the room. She needed to find her aunts, demand an explanation. Maybe it was Esmeralda, trying to scare her away. Maybe it was . . . hell, she couldn't think of any other explanation.

She yanked open the bedroom door and dashed into the dark hallway, turned in the direction of Esmeralda's bedroom, and saw it again. That foggy, misty form, floating a few yards down the hall.

"Kira," it whispered.

She turned and ran through the pitch darkness, heading in the opposite direction from the thing, feeling pursued and too afraid to look behind her to find out for sure. She rounded a corner toward the staircase, barely able to see in the pitch blackness of this place. And then it was there, ahead of her again. A segment of mist rose, like an arm, reaching toward her.

The stairs were just to her right, and she turned to race down them, tripped on the hem of her robe, and tumbled headlong. The impact of every stone stair drove screams of pain from her lungs, and when she hit her head at the bottom, she lay there, hurting, dizzy, hovering on the very edge of consciousness.

She forced her eyes open, only to see them, several of them, she couldn't count, but they were floating all around her, reaching toward her, so close now she could feel the iciness of that mist that seemed to embody them, all of them whispering her name over and over.

She screamed, and then she passed out, the scream dying as her eyes fell closed.

"There, there, lass. You're all right now. You're fine."

Kira blinked her eyes open, and stared up at the faces that surrounded her. Her great aunt Rose and her aunt Emma gazed down at her. Rose held a cold compress to one side of Kira's head, her ample rump perched on the edge of the bed. Emma stood on the other side, bending over her, stroking her hair. A little further away, Esmeralda sat in a hard-backed chair. They all wore night clothes, long nightgowns, housecoats, slippers.

Kira closed her eyes, pressing a hand over Rose's, to her head, which ached monstrously. "What happened?"

"You took a tumble, lassie. Right down the stairs. 'Tis a miracle you didn'a break every bone in your wee body," Rose said. "Whatever possessed you to go wanderin' about the castle in the dark like that, bonnie girl?"

She opened her eyes, looking from Rose to Emma, and then spearing Esmeralda with a steady gaze. "I saw something. Someone was whispering my name, and then I saw . . . something."

Rose sucked in a breath. Esmeralda pursed her lips, lowered her gaze.

"I think they were supposed to be ghosts. I think someone is trying to scare me away from here."

"I didna think the ladies would bother you, Kira. Most assuredly not so soon," Rose said.

"The ladies?"

Rose and Emma both looked toward Esmeralda, as

if seeking her permission to speak further. Esmeralda got to her feet, moving to the table beside her, where Kira saw a tea service that hadn't been there before. She poured from a delicate china pot, filling a cup that matched, and then brought it to Kira in the bed.

"I suppose it's time we told her," Esmerelda said. She handed the cup, balanced in the center of its tiny saucer, to Kira.

Kira sat up before taking it, and Emma quickly adjusted the pillows behind her. She took the tea, sipped it. "Don't even tell me they were ghosts. I don't believe in ghosts," she said. And then she sipped some more because the tea was warm and sweet and it felt good going down.

"Aye, they were lass. They linger here. All of them," Rose said.

"All of who?"

"The MacLellan women, the ones who died at the hands of their husbands," Esmeralda said. "Your own dear mother lives among them now. They're trapped between the worlds. We've no idea how to put them to rest, though the dear lord knows we've tried."

Kira pinched the bridge of her nose and squeezed her eyes tight. "Maybe you'd better start from the beginning."

"Aye, perhaps we should," Rose said.

But she didn't speak. Instead, she looked to her sister to do that. And with a deep sigh, Esmeralda began.

"There is a curse on the women of the MacLellan clan, lass. It began more than a century ago, when Miranda MacLellan was wed to the love of her life, Robby Stewart."

"Stewart?" Kira asked.

"Aye, an ancestor of Ian's, just as you've likely guessed," Esmeralda said. "The marriage, it is said, was blissful for her. But her bliss was built upon a lie. For Robby soon found himself in the arms of another woman. And when Miranda returned a day early from a journey to visit a cousin, she found Robby and this harlot, locked in a passionate embrace in her own wedding bed."

Kira closed her eyes briefly. "Men suck."

When she opened her eyes again it was to see her aunts' surprised and somewhat perplexed faces. "It just means they're horrible," Kira clarified. And then she looked at Esmeralda, the elected storyteller. "What happened?"

"Oh, she was devastated, as you can imagine. She raced from the room, crying and hysterical. Robby sprang from the bed, pulling on his clothes to go after her. But he wasn't fast enough. She took the shotgun that hung above the mantel, beneath their wedding portrait. Two barrels, fully loaded. And when he came down the stairs for her, she blasted a hole in his chest. Then she calmly stepped over his body, climbed the stairs and shot the woman, one of her own maids, who was still in bed, shivering and clutching the covers to her chin."

"Some say," Rose put in, "that the woman was also Miranda's dear friend, though we've never heard her name."

Esmeralda nodded slowly. "When her rage was sated, Miranda went to the tower room, bolted herself inside. The noise had roused the servants, but no one could get to her. Inside the room she penned a letter to her descendants, a curse really, for though few knew of it then, many of the MacLellan women were powerful witches. Miranda was, it is said, the most powerful of any of them. She wrote the curse in her journal, her diary, and then she calmly set the pen aside, performed some secret spell that involved, they say, the killing of a dove and the removal of its heart, and when it was done, she threw herself from the tower window to her death on the rocks below."

Kira's throat was tight, her skin, chilled, as she whispered, "What did she write?"

"Read it for yourself." Esmeralda pulled a small, leatherbound book from one of her robe's deep pockets, and handed it to Kira in the bed.

A ribbon marked the passage in question, and Kira opened the book skimming the parts Esmeralda had already related, and beginning on the facing page.

"I would have far preferred he had simply murdered me in my sleep, that I might have died believing in his love. For the pain of his betrayal is a fate far worse than death could ever be. And in the end, he has killed me just the same. For surely my life ended when my eyes beheld the man I adore in the arms of another. And so I leave a gift to my daughters, and to their daughters, and to theirs, and on to every MacLellan woman born to my line. And that gift is this. When you wed, if the man betrays you the way mine betrayed me, you will never learn of it. For I curse him in this manner. I curse him to bring about your death by his own hand, for it will be an act of mercy if you die never knowing the truth. And it will be his punishment to live with his deed for the rest of his days. So mote it be, now and forever more."

Kira blinked and looked up at her aunts. "So anytime a MacLellan woman's husband cheats on her, he ends up killing her before she ever learns of it? That's the curse?"

The three woman nodded sadly.

"It's ridiculous! It's ludicrous!"

"Is it, Kira? Do you not recall how your own dear mother met her end?"

She did. All too well. "It was an accident."

"It often is. It was with your grandmother, as well."

She was almost afraid to ask, but she forced herself. "How . . . how did it happen?"

"Your grandfather was bedding one of the local girls," Esmeralda said, her face a grimace.

"You know that's not what she meant," Emma said softly. She patted Kira's hand where it rested upon the bedcovers. "He took Grandmother sailing. The boat capsized in calm waters and she drowned."

Kira lowered her eyes. Something about Emma's hand on her own brought a tightness to her throat. Memories of her mother's lilting voice and ready smile came rushing back to her. "Did he know about the curse?"

"Aye, but like you, he didn't believe in it. Until it claimed her, at least."

"And what became of him?"

Emma sighed deeply. "He went mad. He's been in an asylum ever since. Doesn't even know his own name, most days."

"The curse is real, Kira. It's the very reason none of us have allowed ourselves to fall in love, to take a husband. To do so is only to invite the curse to take us as well."

"Only if he cheated, though," Kira said quickly. "What if he didn't? What if you could find a man who loved you, one who would be true to you?"

"How could you ever know?" Rose asked softly. "It would be a terrible risk, Kira."

"Love is always a risk. God, wouldn't it be better to take that risk than to live your life alone? Wouldn't it be better to know love once, and die young than to live to be a hundred and never know it at all?"

"No." Esmeralda said it firmly. Emma and Rose, though, seemed wistful for a moment. "Most certainly not. Why do you think the ghosts of our ancestors haunt these walls?"

"I don't know. Did Miranda die here? Is this castle where it all began?" she asked.

"No," Esmeralda said. "They were staying in the cottage, near the shore, at the time."

"Well then why do you think they haunt this castle?" Kira asked.

"To warn us. To make sure we don't forget," Esmeralda said with a firm nod.

It rang false to Kira. Weren't spirits supposed to move on into some Eden-like paradise after death? Weren't ghosts generally believed to be trapped souls, unable to move on due to some sort of unfinished business? She wasn't sure the women of the MacLellan clan would choose to remain in this drafty castle of their own volition. She wasn't even certain they *could*.

But at least she had the answers she sought. She sighed, and lay back on the pillows. "How can I get them to let me sleep?" she asked. "How do you?"

"You get used to their visits. If you ignore them, they stop bothering after a bit," Rose told her.

"I'll try."

"You should. You have a big day tomorrow."

She smiled at Aunt Rose at the reminder of her plans with Ian.

"Nothing is to happen between you and Ian, lass," Esmeralda said. "We don't need another MacLellan woman dying at her husband's hand, and while Ian is a good man, he's also a Stewart. It would be courtin' disaster. And he doesn't deserve the stain of your blood on his hands."

"Oh, for heaven's sake, Aunt Esmeralda. It's one day touring the countryside. I'm not going to fall in love and marry the man." And yet just saying the words made her feel inwardly giddy. Thank God she could spend the day with him tomorrow, and get a break from all this superstition and paranoia.

"See to it you don't."

The women rose, and left the room, Esmeralda flicking off the light and closing the door on her way out.

Kira lay still for a long moment, before she noticed the wisp of luminous mist glowing from a far corner of the room. She sat up in the bed. "Miranda?" she asked. "Are you trying to tell me something?"

There was no sound. No movement, other than the gentle swaying and swirling of the mist.

"You've been trying to tell them, haven't you? But you've given up. Is it because they got the message, or because they just won't listen?"

Again, no words. No movement.

"I think they're wrong," Kira said. "I really think they're wrong. And if there's a way to set your spirits free, and I can find it, I'll do it."

Promise.

Frowning, Kira strained her ears and her mind. Had she just heard the word promise, or had it all been in her imagination?

She thinned her lips. "Yes," she said softly. "I promise."

And just like that, the mist vanished. Gone as if it had never been there. And it had been so thin, so insubstantial, that she might never have truly seen it at all.

But she was pretty sure she had.

Chapter 5

Ian arrived, and made his way into the sunny breakfast room, where Kira sat in a window seat, sipping tea.

She glanced up as he came in and couldn't help the instant smile that spread across her face. "Good morning, Ian," she said, rising to her feet.

"Morning, lass." He clutched her shoulders, and leaned in to kiss her cheek. It was polite and impersonal, that peck. But the gentle squeeze of his hands on her shoulders suggested something just a little more intimate. Something private, just between them.

As he straightened, he frowned, and sniffed. "Mint?" he asked, nodding at her teacup.

She nodded.

"Rose only brews the mint when someone's queasy. Are you ill, Kira?"

"Queasy is a good word for it. I couldn't eat breakfast."

He tipped his head to one side, a sudden worry

clouding his face. "Why are you queasy then? Nerves or jet lag, or have you come down with something more serious?"

"I saw a ghost last night." His brows rose, and he searched her eyes. "Several of them, actually. They kept whispering my name. And like an idiot, I went wandering into the pitch-dark hall to get away from them and wound up falling down the stairs."

He sucked in a breath and his expression shifted from worry to full-blown fear. "And you're all right?" He swung his head toward Aunt Rose, who'd just reentered the room, carrying her china teapot with wafts of minty steam floating from its spout. "Did you phone the physician? Are you sure she's not sufferin' with some hidden injury or—"

"We checked her over quite carefully, Ian. She's fine, I assure you, save for the tummy ache, an' I daresay that's more from stress than anything else. It's unsettlin' the first time you come face to face with the dead."

He looked horrified as his gaze slid back to hers, but Kira only rolled her eyes. "I'm ready to leave if you are," she said. She took a final sip of her tea, and then set the cup on Aunt Rose's tray.

"Should we expect you for dinner, then, Kira?"

"No," Ian answered for her. "We'll return by nine, for the reading of the will. Don't expect us a minute sooner." He met her eyes as if seeking approval. She gave it with a nod and a blatantly grateful smile.

They moved quickly through the castle, into the entry hall, and out the front door. She was nearly running for the car she saw waiting at the end of the drive, and Ian kept pace, opening her door for her and then circling the car to get behind the wheel.

As soon as he got the thing in motion, he looked worriedly her way. "If you're not feeling up to a day on the town, Kira—"

"I am, don't worry."

"Can't help but worry. I've always believed your aunts to be a wee bit . . . well, dotty, where their ghost stories were concerned. I hope you don't mind me sayin' so."

"I don't."

"But you saw them with your own eyes, though?"

She frowned. "I saw . . . mist. Or fog. Vaguely tall and narrow, almost human shaped. It could have been anything. The humidity here, a trick of the light, or even some kind of illusion set up by my aunts."

He shot her a quick look. "They're honest women, Kira."

She met his eyes. "Are you sure about that? I think they're a little bit—how did you put it?—dotty. Who's to say they're not dotty enough to try to prove to me that what they believe is true, and to go to any means to do so?"

"I just don't think they'd do that."

She lowered her head. "Esmeralda doesn't like me."

"Esmeralda doesn't like anyone," he told her.

"Do you think she might be orchestrating all of this to try to scare me away?"

"But why would she want to do that, Kira?" he asked.

"For the money? You said I had to be present for the reading in order to inherit. If I leave, they get my share."

"They've more money than God already, lass. They'll never live to spend it all. They couldn't want for more."

She pursed her lips. He rounded a curve, and pulled

the car into a pulloff alongside the dirt track that passed for a road. Then he shut off the engine and got out, opened her door, and took her hand.

Smiling, she followed where he led, over lush grasses, meandering through a few trees, until they came to the shore of a glimmering blue lake, its surface just as still as glass. "It's beautiful," she whispered.

"Aye, and just the thing to relax you." Taking her hand, he led her closer to the shore, and she saw the little dock, with the rowboat tied to one side. A picnic basket sat in its bow, and oars stood at the ready.

"We're going out on the water?"

"Aye, and I've packed us a lunch as well. I hope your appetite returns to you by midday."

She nodded, and he got into the boat, then held out a hand and helped her board it as well. When he clasped her hand, she caught her breath, and met his eyes. Neither of them had spoken of this—this thing between them. But they were both fully aware of it. She knew he felt it just as much as she did.

She sank down onto the seat. He'd put a velvet cushion atop the hard metal of it. He took his seat as well, facing her, and gripped the oars.

"Did they say anything to you?" he asked.

"Who? The aunts?"

"The ghosts."

She pursed her lips. "I don't believe in ghosts, Ian. And I don't believe in curses, either."

He blinked. "So you finally made your aunts tell you about the curse."

She nodded.

"And you don't believe in it?"

"No."

"How do you explain the way the women of the family have died, then?"

"My mother's death was an accident. A freak accident, yes, but an accident all the same. They happen."

"And your grandmother?"

"Sailing is risky. Or maybe it was murder, did you ever think of that?"

"No, lass, it was an accident. I saw your grandfather after. It was clear as day. He loved her. Now, the death of your great grandmother, Lily, that one may well have been murder. A gun in the hands of your great grandfather, Angus, that went off *accidentally*. He fully expected to inherit her fortune, or so the story goes. But even then a Stewart was employed as the MacLellan women's attorney. My own grandfather. So the will was iron clad, and there were provisions excluding him from a penny should his bride die, even by accident, at his hand."

Kira leaned back on her hands and watched the ripples his oars made in the crystalline water with each stroke. And then she lifted her gaze to watch the way the muscles in his arms did likewise.

"She knew that if she died at his hand, that would mean he had been unfaithful," Kira mused.

"Aye."

"And had he been?"

"Aye. He ran off with the baker's wife, as soon as the courts ruled the will valid, and non-contestable. Local gossip had it they'd been seeing each other all along."

She sighed, her stomach relaxing as she listened to the steady, gentle splash of the oars in the water, and watched the sky slinking slowly past overhead. Blue, blue sky, with puffs of white cloud, fragrant air that smelled of flowers she couldn't hope to name, and the fresh, slightly fishy aroma of the lake. And beneath it all, the cologne he wore, so subtle she only caught faint, tantalizing whiffs of it when the breeze moved just so. She wanted to bury her face in the crook of his neck and inhale deeply.

"Do you know of any others?"

"Others?" he asked.

"Other MacLellan women who've died by their husband's hands."

He nodded. "There were three others. One died in a fire, after her husband rolled over in his sleep and tipped the oil lamp. One choked to death when he fed her a bit of fish that turned out to have a bone in it. One was crushed by a castle stone. She stood on the grounds looking up as her spouse worked on repairs. He knocked the stone free and it flattened her." He shook his head slowly. "And then of course, there was the first one. Miranda, the MacLellan witch who cast the curse."

She nodded. "I can see why the aunts are so convinced."

"I canna' see why you aren't, lass. One or two deaths might be coincidental, but six, since the MacLellan witch penned those words?" He shook his head slowly. "Were I a MacLellan female, I might be more inclined to give it credence, even just as a precaution."

"I feel sorry for them," she said.

He stopped rowing, pulling the oars in and settling them into their brackets along the inside of the boat. Then he dropped a small anchor over the side. "The ghosts?" he asked.

"No, my aunts. Aunt Emma, especially. She's beautiful. She's too young to lock herself away from any possibility of love."

"Aye. Frankly, my father's been pining for her for nigh on ten years now."

Her brows shot up in surprise. "Really?"

"You didn't spot it, then? I always find it so obvious when he's near her."

"I guess I was focused more on his son," she said softly.

He reached out and took her hands in his. "Aye, I found myself quite distracted as well. Have been since I first heard your voice on the telephone, lass."

She smiled shakily, as he held her eyes with his.

"Your Aunt Esmeralda—she's warned me nothing is to . . . transpire, between us."

"Ian," she whispered. "Are you really going to let my Aunt Esmeralda tell you what to do?"

His gaze lowered, focused on her lips. "I donna think I could, even if I tried. An' I've no desire to try, Kira."

"I'm very glad to hear that, Ian."

He leaned closer, and she did too, their faces, their mouths, moving nearer, and still nearer, until at last, they touched. The kiss was tender, barely more than a whisper, at first. And then it changed as his arms crept around her waist, his hands tugging gently. She slid off her seat, and onto her knees, between his thighs. Her arms hooked around his neck, and his tightened around her waist, pulling her against him until the only thing between their bodies was their clothing. And she resented even that thin barrier.

He kissed her more deeply, more passionately, his mouth parting, his tongue dancing and plunging. Her hands buried themselves in his hair, holding his face to hers as she opened to receive him. God, this was good, Kira thought. This was insanely good.

It was as if she'd known him forever.

It was as if she'd been waiting, just for him, all her life.

When they finally came up for air, he stared into her eyes, panting, breathless. Her heart pounded like a jackhammer in her chest, and she was dizzy, giddy, and her skin, she was convinced, had become hot to the touch.

"I've never felt anything this powerful before," she whispered.

His eyes were utterly sincere as they stared into hers, more emotion swirling in their depths than she had ever seen before. "Nor have I. Not ever, lass. And I don't mind tellin' you, I want you so badly right now I can barely contain myself."

"I want you, too, Ian."

He nodded. "I'm . . . I'm not an American, lass. This isna the sort o' thing I take lightly."

"Ian, I may be an American, but that doesn't mean I take sex lightly."

"I didna mean to suggest—I only wanted you to know I'm not like other men you may have known. When I make love to you, Kira, it'll mean somethin' to me."

Her heart was melting in her chest.

"An' it will'na be today," he went on. "We have to give it some time, to be sure this is real. 'Tis far too soon, and far too powerful a feelin' to be treated lightly."

"It's also," she said, staring up into his eyes and imitating his brogue, "far too powerful a feeling to be ignored."

"I won't be ignorin' it," he promised.

She nodded, though she wanted to push a little harder. A little harder, hell, she wanted to push him down in this boat and climb on top of him.

And yet, something held her back. She didn't know

what this feeling was, burning her up from the inside out. It wasn't like her. It was almost as if something beyond her were feeding the fires.

He pulled her across his lap, and snuggled her close in his arms. She nuzzled his neck, and relished feeling more cherished than she ever had. "I can wait for you, Ian. But please don't make me wait too long," she whispered.

"If I wait too long, Lassie, I think I may well die from the wanting." And then he lowered his head and kissed her again.

Chapter 6

 The great room was crowded with strangers. Family, Kira thought, but strangers to her. She wanted to stick close to Ian, would have felt a little more comfortable at his side, but he was at the front of the room with his father.

The aunts had set things up as if this were some kind of a party. Every surface of the great room, all of the ornate tables and stands, were laden with food. Trays of finger sandwiches and hors d'oeuvres of every imaginable sort lined one. A five-tiered silver serving tray held fresh fruits, with dishes of sweetened cream for dipping. Serving platters overflowed with raw vegetables and a variety of dips. Crystal punch bowls with fountains spewing in their centers stood at the room's four corners. The dishes were fine china. The napkins were linen.

They'd dragged in more chairs than had been in the room previously, though there had already been plenty, sofas and love seats and thickly cushioned easy chairs and the like. Now there were several rockers and some folding chairs added to the mix. And there were people in every one of them, and others standing, nibbling from their oversized plates, and sipping from their crystal punch glasses.

The focal point was the fireplace, at the front of the room. Gregory and Ian sat in easy chairs that were situated at angles on either side of a small table. In the center of that table was a large manila envelope.

As Aunt Esmeralda led Kira from one group of strangers to the next, introducing her with lists of names and family connections she would never remember in a million years, she looked his way every little while. Not so much for reassurance—she wasn't the shy type. But more because she so loved looking at him. And every time she did, she found him returning her gaze, his eyes always smiling, the dimples in his cheeks always there. There was more, too, in the way he looked at her—more than just a smile. There was desire, and a tenderness with it that tended to make her throat want to close up a little, and her heart to race a bit faster.

Gregory cleared his throat, and the steady hum of voices fell instantly into silence. "If you would all find a place to sit, we can begin."

People moved, then, meandering around, finding chairs or convenient corners in which to stand, refilling their glasses one last time, or snatching a few more snacks from the offerings to carry with them to their places. Within a few more moments, everyone was quiet again, and still, and all eyes were riveted to Gregory.

He reached for the envelope, tore it open, and extracted from it a sheaf of papers, their length longer than the standard size. He tugged a pair of bifocals from his breast pocket, perched them on his nose, and then looked out over the tops of them. His steady gaze skimmed everyone there, lingered for a long moment on Kira's aunt Emma, but when it finally settled, it settled on Kira herself.

"Being that I was Iris's personal solicitor, I already know the contents of her will. But I am the only one who knows it. She assured me of this." He glanced at his son as he said that, and Kira saw a tiny frown appear between Ian's brows. As if he were suddenly worried.

But why would he be?

"Iris was," Gregory went on, "something of a rebel. I'm sure those of you who knew her are aware of that. She resented some of the restrictions placed upon her by MacLellan family traditions and certain—er—beliefs. And in her final act, she attempted to strike a blow against them."

Esmeralda tensed. Kira saw it from the corner of her eye. Rose and Emma both moved closer to her, standing on either side as if they'd appointed themselves her personal protectors.

"I, Iris MacLellan," he read, "being of sound mind and body, do hereby bequeath all of my worldly possessions, assets and wealth, indeed everything that I have accumulated throughout my lifetime on this planet, to my great niece, Kira MacLellan."

A gasp went up. Every eye turned to Kira. She blinked rapidly, shooting a questioning look from her mother's sister Emma, to her Aunt Rose, and finally sliding her gaze past them both to see Esmeralda. She didn't look shocked or stunned or disappointed. She looked as if she was still waiting. Her face was an impatient, troubled expression of expectation.

"But I thought she was going to divide her assets among all of her relatives," Kira said. "That's what you told me, when we first spoke on the phone, Ian, isn't it?" She met his eyes, saw his solemn nod.

"It's what's always done in the Clan MacLellan," Ian told her. "I had no idea Iris had broken with that tradition."

"It's a sizable bequest, Kira," Gregory said. "Iris owned this castle and all the properties attached to it, which includes more than a thousand acres, much of it overlooking the sea. There are several houses and cottages within the tract as well. Not to mention vacation homes in Spain and Italy. Then there are the other assets. Her bank accounts, stocks, bonds, investments, savings."

Kira pursed her lips and swallowed hard. Then she shook her head slowly. "It's not fair," she said softly. "It's not fair to all the other members of her family." Lifting her gaze again she said, "What if I don't want it? Can I refuse to accept it?"

"Oh, I'm getting to that, lass. There are two stipulations in this will, and they are iron clad. The first is that should you refuse to do as your great aunt requests, in order to accept the inheritance—"

"Do as she requests? What—?"

He held up a hand, "Should you refuse to do as your great aunt requests in order to accept the inheritance, the properties will be sold, the stock liquidated, and the entire estate donated to several charities your aunt has listed within this document."

Stunned, Kira just stared at him, then looked at her aunts. "But it's their *home.*"

"We're not poor, Kira," Esmeralda said softly. "We certainly have accumulated a great deal of wealth on our own, although the deeds and such to our ancestral homes have always remained in the name of the eldest surviving daughter. Still, we would not be destitute." She then shifted her stern gaze to Gregory again. "What is the other condition, dear friend?"

Gregory licked his lips, and tugged at his collar. "I tried to talk her out of this. I vow, I tried. But there was no give in her. Not even a bit." He glanced toward Ian. "I couldn't tell you, son, though it nearly did me in keeping this to myself." With a sigh, he lifted the documents and read on.

"In order to inherit the estate, and thus preserve it for her family, both those who came before her, and those who will come later, Kira MacLellan is required to marry Ian Stewart within one week of the reading of this will."

Ian leapt to his feet, his mouth opening as if he were going to shout something, but no words emerged. Kira felt tears burning in her eyes. No one spoke. And then Esmeralda broke the stunned silence.

"No. It canna happen."

"But Es," Rose began.

"'Twould mean her life," Esmeralda stated flatly.

"I resent that remark, Esmeralda," Ian said, speaking at long last. "You know me far better than to think so little of me."

"Aye," his father agreed. "'Twas Iris's firm belief that the MacLellan family curse could be broken, and she vowed she would be the one to set that eventuality into motion. She's been convinced, for years, that the ghosts who haunt these castle walls do not remain of their own free will, nor as a constant reminder and warning to the women of their line. But rather, that they are trapped here, unable to move on to the heaven they so richly deserve. And that they will remain so until the curse is broken."

He lifted the sheets, read further. "It was the disastrous marriage of the MacLellan witch to a Stewart man that set this curse into being," he read. "Only the successful marriage of another MacLellan to another Stewart can break it. And having set eyes on them both, I've no longer any doubt these two are the ones who can do it. I've watched Kira from afar, kept tabs on her life. She is a good woman, and in possession of the legendary MacLellan beauty. Moreover, she's a strong woman. As for Ian, I've never known a man more honest or true. Should these two wed, should they be ever faithful to one another, should he live out his life knowing only his bride, it is my belief that the curse will be broken. MacLellan women will be free to wed forever more, and the spirits of our mothers and theirs before them, will at last, be set free."

There was stunned silence, but it was followed soon by whispering and muttering that grew steadily louder.

Kira turned her head left and then right, only to see eyes on her. Some of them seemed speculative, curious, nosy. Others appeared hostile. She saw greed in several faces, pity in others. Aunt Rose was one of those who seemed to feel sorry for her. She closed a chubby hand on Kira's shoulder and gave it a gentle squeeze. Aunt Emma was speculative, looking from Kira to Ian and back again, with a tiny frown between her brows.

But it was Aunt Esmeralda who brought silence down hard on the room again with her nearly shouted declaration. "It willna be. I willna have it. And that's all there is to be said on the matter."

"But Aunt Es—" Kira began.

"Gregory, you are to begin seeing to the process of selling the holdings and liquidating the investments. First thing tomorrow, I want it underway. There'll be no more of this nonsense."

"I think that's up to Kira to say, don't you Esmeralda?" Ian asked.

His strong voice drew her eyes to his. He moved through the crowd of relatives toward Kira, and all those present parted to open a path for him.

She held onto the strength in his gaze, locking her own with it and seeing there a steady reassurance. Everything would be all right.

"Ian!" Esmeralda barked. "You canna tell me you intend—"

"This matter is now a very private one." He stood beside Kira, so close beside her that his body touched hers, and the warmth and power of it made her blood heat. "'Tis a decision that will take some time to make, and one that needs to be made in private, between Kira and myself. We'll let you know when we've decided what's to be."

Esmeralda lifted her steely brows and sent him a look that could have wilted a cactus. Rose wrung her hands, and pressed her lips tightly together. Emma, though, tipped her head to one side, looking at them both, exchanging a long glance with Gregory, and then finally, she nodded. "Ian is right. It's no longer our business."

"He didn't mean *that*," Kira said quickly. "Of course it's your business, it's your home. But . . . yes, it really has to be up to *me* now."

She said me, not us, and she hoped Ian picked up on the emphasis she'd placed on the word. She had no intention of letting anyone—not her aunts, and not him—decide her life for her.

"Understood," Emma said. "Now, guests, we have enough food to feed half the township, so dig in. We feast, and then we sleep, and in the morning, things will look decidedly better."

"Things do tend to look better in the morning," Rose muttered.

"Always," Kira agreed.

Ian took her arm, and leaned in close. "I think we should talk. Don't you?"

She met his eyes and nodded once. "Yeah, I guess I do."

[faint mirrored text from previous page]

Chapter 7

 "So, pretty Kira, we've been placed in a hellish situation, yes?"

He'd led her into a small study on the first floor, closed the door behind them, and flipped its lock. She crossed the room, which she'd never seen before, and sank into a soft leather chair. She wished she could keep on sinking, right out of sight.

With a sigh, Ian crossed his arms where he stood, near the door. "I'm sorry this happened, lass."

"So am I," she said softly. "And I certainly don't expect you to marry me just to protect the family fortune."

"Of course you don't expect it. But are you willin' to do it?"

She lifted her head with a snap, and felt her own eyes widen as they found his. "What?"

He moved across the room until he stood just in front of her chair, and then he dropped down onto one knee in front of her. "Will ya marry me, lass?"

"Get up, Ian." She shot to her feet as she said it. "Get up and stop being ridiculous."

He rose to his feet as well, but kept trying to hold her eyes with his. And even though she kept averting her gaze, she found it drawn back to his over and over.

"I donna find it ridiculous at all, Kira. There's . . . somethin' between us. Somethin' more powerful than makes any sense, given the brevity of our acquaintance. You canna deny it."

"I don't deny it. I've felt it too. Hell, it took my breath away from the first time I set eyes on you—I even felt it when we spoke on the phone, but Ian, how will we ever know where it might have led, given time? If we're forced to marry now, our relationship will never have a chance to develop in a natural way."

"It felt pretty natural on the water yesterday, love." As he said it, he slid his arms around her waist, pulled her a little closer, until their bodies were touching.

"It's insane, Ian. No, I can't do it. I'd like to keep seeing you—I'm compelled to. I don't think I could stop if I tried. But we can't get married. Not like this. We barely know each other."

"And yet it feels as if I've known ya forever," he said.

She lifted her head in spite of herself, and he lowered his, kissed her, folded her up in his arms and held her hard as she opened to him, kissing him back as the heat flared between them. Her entire body began to tremble, and she felt an inexplicable, overwhelming rush of emotion that tightened her throat and burned in her eyes.

When he broke the kiss and she melted against him, she felt his heart pounding as rapidly as her own. And she didn't doubt he felt the same mindless need that she did. And yet it made no sense.

"There's no such thing as love at first sight," she whispered, because she was incapable of speaking more loudly than that.

"We've a week, Kira, a week in which to make this decision. I've lived to be near forty, and never felt the likes of this before. I've no illusion I'll be feelin' it again with another woman. But it makes sense to take the time we've been given before makin' any decision. At least, donna refuse me until our time expires."

He stroked her hair, and she clung to him. "I just don't understand any of this. Not what I feel with you, not this curse—"

"I can promise you one thing, Kira. That curse will never harm ya, not if I'm the one you trust to keep ya safe."

She lifted her gaze to his. "I'm afraid."

"Aye, an' so am I. But I've a suggestion."

She stared into his eyes, wondering if the caring she saw in them could possibly be real.

"Try to pretend it's just us, just the two of us, with a week to spend together. Forget the will an' the curse and all the rest of it. An' just focus on the two of us."

"How am I supposed to do that, Ian? How can I, with the aunts, and the castle and all of it, looming over me like a big blade waiting to fall?"

He lowered his hands and clasped both of hers. "Come away with me. Your family owns a cottage on the coast, which they've given my family the right to use at will. It's close enough that you can visit your relatives if you wish it, and yet far enough away to give us time and privacy to . . . to see where this may lead."

She looked down at their clasped hands, and sniffling, she nodded. "I couldn't say no if I wanted to."

His hands tightened on hers. "I'm glad to hear it. I

can think of nothing else but you, and I want nothing more than to be with you."

"I know. I feel exactly the same way. I just wish I understood why."

He licked his lips, lowered his head, and for the first time she had the feeling he was keeping something from her.

"What? What is it?"

He met her eyes again, and shook his head, as if whatever thought had crossed his mind didn't matter. "Go and pack up some things. I'll inform your aunts of our decision."

She did as he suggested, packing a week's worth of things into one small suitcase and snatching up her makeup bag, and then she headed down the stairs to meet him. But as soon as she reached the bottom, the sounds of raised voices caught her attention.

Slowing her pace, she crept nearer to the room, the very study where she and Ian had spoken only moments before.

"You promised me you wouldna get involved with her, Ian," Aunt Esmeralda said, her tone ice-cold and clipped.

"That was before I met her. Esmeralda, what I feel for her—"

"Is exactly what I warned you against. I've feared this very thing, Ian. Do you not see that it's unfolding just as I predicted?"

"Maybe it's supposed to," he said softly. "At least if we spend some time together, we might—"

"Aye, aye, fine. Spend time together. But not there. Not at that cottage, of all places. Ian, it's certain to end in tragedy."

"It willna," he said, his tone grave. "Not this time."

She heard his footsteps coming toward the closed door, but they stopped when Esmeralda spoke again. "If she knew all of it, Ian, she wouldna choose to go there with you."

"Aye, indeed, what the lass needs is more of her spinster aunts' silly superstitions clouding her mind."

"The curse is real, Ian, and it culminates in the two of you. How can you not believe that when you've seen it with your own eyes?"

His hand clutched the door knob, began to turn it. "If that's true, then it's with us the curse will be broken. I would think you'd want that, Emeralda. To finally be free of this dark belief that you've allowed to keep you prisoner your entire life."

"I canna watch her die at your hand, Ian."

"I promise you," he said. "That will never happen. More likely the moon would turn to dust than I would harm a hair on Kira MacLellan's comely head."

The doorknob turned, and Kira backed up rapidly, suitcase in hand, to the bottom of the staircase, and stood there as the door opened. Ian exited the room, and saw her there, met her eyes and quickly pasted a warm smile over the troubled expression on his face.

"Are you ready, then?"

Trembling, and reminding herself that she did not believe in curses, she nodded.

He came closer, and took the bag from her hand, then touched her cheek gently. "You look frightened, Kira. Are you having second thoughts?"

"I just . . . I just have the feeling there may be something you haven't told me."

He glanced back toward the study door. Esmeralda stood there now, watching them. Ian faced her again, and said, "There is something. But I'll tell you all of it, lass, once we're alone, and have time and privacy."

She held his eyes.

"Hysteria and superstition needn't be a part of the conversation," he said. "I far prefer calm and logic to those things."

Kira felt herself nodding. "That makes sense. Frankly, another night here with the ghosts of this place haunting me isn't something I've been longing for."

Esmeralda stomped away, muttering, "And you think the cottage will be better?"

Chapter 8

The "cottage" was bigger than most houses she'd seen. Two stories, with peaks and gables, and a widow's walk, perched on high, looking out over the sea. Its siding was pale blue, its trim white, its driveway a worn dirt track. The grass was higher than it should have been, with tufts of weeds and rushes standing higher than the rest, here and there, waving softly with the ocean's breeze. Beyond it was a rocky beach, and the sea, its waves rolling in endlessly. Seagulls cried and swooped in every direction. The place was beautiful. But dark. Something about it gave Kira a chill right down her spine.

"It's been a while since anyone has used it," Ian said. "The aunts wanted to have it torn down years ago, but my father was able to talk them around. They considered selling it then, but it's been in the family longer than nearly any other holding, besides the castle itself. They couldn't bring themselves to see another owner take possession."

"But they could have brought themselves to demolish it?"

"It didn't make any sense to me, either." He got out of the car, reaching into the back seat for her bag before coming around to open her door.

She opened it herself before he got there, however, and stood staring at the house with the wind blowing through her hair. There was something niggling in the deepest part of her mind, like a word on the tip of one's tongue. It was calling to her, nagging at her to dig around and figure out what it was, but she wasn't certain how.

"I can't wait to show you the place," he said. "Come." Taking her hand, he led her up the walkway, made of flat fieldstones, fitted together like a jigsaw puzzle. There were three steps up to the front door, and they dashed up them, then paused there at the top while Ian unlocked the door. He swung it wide, and she stepped inside and then gasped, overwhelmed with the most incredible sense of déjà vu she'd ever felt in her life. She stood there, almost nauseated with the surreal rush that swamped her. She pressed a hand to her forehead without being aware she was doing it.

"Kira?" Ian dropped her case inside the door, facing her and taking hold of her shoulders. "Are you all right?"

"I just . . . feel so strange." She frowned, and looked around the foyer. The floors were hardwood, narrow boards in rich maple tones. The walls were covered in floral paper, and crown molding painted white gave the place an elegant, antique look. The windows stretched from ceiling to floor, with wide sills, and sheer curtains. It smelled like old wood and the sea.

As Ian led her from room to room, she began to relax. Except when he showed her the room on the third floor, the only room there, in fact. It was a tiny room, that led out to the widow's walk. There were candles and a book of matches upon a dusty table in the room's center.

"What is this place?" she asked.

"I don't know." But he did, she knew he did.

She'd push him on it, later, she decided, as they made their way back to the ground floor and through the kitchen. As they approached the back door, she found herself knowing already what she would see when she got there. A steep, rickety staircase that zig-zagged its way down to the rocky shore far below. And suddenly, as Ian reached for the doorknob she gripped his shoulder and whispered, "I'm too afraid to go out there."

He frowned at her, searching her face.

"The stairs are too steep and they can't be safe, not with the weather and the ocean and all the years . . ."

He nodded. "The stairs were torn down fifteen years ago. There's a deck now, a wide one. Look." And as he said it, he pushed the door open.

Kira peered outside. No rickety, deadly looking stairs sloped dangerously down to the rocks below. A giant redwood deck stretched out instead. At the end of one level, were a few steps down, followed by more decking, and more steps, and more decking. What had been a steep and dangerous descent to the beach was now a gradual walk over the multi-level deck, with only a small set of steps at the end of the final level, that led down to the shore.

Each level had built-in benches and safety railings, some of which were lined with flower boxes, devoid of any growth. It was modern and pleasant, and friendly. The only part of the entire house that didn't give her goosebumps, in fact.

"You see?" he asked, as they walked out over the redwood planks.

"It's wonderful. It's the best part of the house."

"Mmm. Those staircases were treacherous, you're right about that. I argued with the aunts for years to get them to make this change." He led her to a bench that overlooked the beach, and she sank onto it, facing the ocean. "How did you know?" he asked. "About those stairs, that is."

She turned her gaze to meet his. "I don't know."

"Perhaps Esmeralda was right."

Kira held his eyes steadily. "She didn't want you to bring me here."

"No."

"She said if I knew the whole story—"

"You heard that, then?" She nodded and he said, "Aye, I thought you might've. But we've only just arrived, lass. I'd hoped for one happy evenin' together before we turn our minds back to those aunts of yours and their ghost stories."

She sighed. "It feels as if you're putting off telling me something you think will change my mind. Have a little faith in me, Ian. I'm not as easily frightened as you seem to think."

"If you were, you'd have turned tail and run home by now." There was a chiming sound, a doorbell, she realized, and Ian got to his feet. "That'll be the groceries. I phoned in an order before we left the castle. I'll see to it. You just relax."

"All right."

He left her alone on the deck, in the sunshine, and she basked in it. Slowly it burned away the chill that seemed to have settled into her bones from the moment she'd set foot in this country. She closed her eyes, felt the sun's warmth, and in a moment, a smile pulled her lips into its hold, and her mind told her how ridiculous all the rest of it was. Curses. Ghosts. A billion-dollar inheritance. An enforced marriage.

Ridiculous. She didn't have to do anything she didn't want to do. And no curse was going to run her life. It would neither force her into marriage nor keep her from it. And it certainly wouldn't bring about her early demise.

Curses only had the power their believers gave to them. If you didn't believe, they couldn't hurt you. And she didn't believe.

A hand smacked against the window glass from inside the house. The sound was unmistakable, and she sat up, popped her eyes open, and glanced in the direction from which it had come, fully expecting to see Ian smiling at her from the other side of the glass.

Instead she saw her own reflection, only . . . it wasn't her.

She sucked in a breath that hurt her chest as she realized it. The woman with her face wore different clothes, and her hair was up, and her eyes were red as she stared intently through the glass at Kira. And then Kira moved, just slightly, to get a better angle, and the vision vanished.

On her feet now, Kira moved closer to the glass panes. They belonged to a set of French doors that led into a room she hadn't yet seen. "I don't believe in ghosts," she whispered, as she hesitated, then, gathered her courage, and cupped her hands around her face to peer through the glass.

She saw no woman. "Probably just my own reflection like I thought at first." Tricks of light and shadow could explain the differences. Couldn't they?

Within the room, which appeared to be a large living room, she saw no woman. There was a fireplace, a lot of furniture. It was dim inside.

She tried the door handles, and found they gave when she twisted them. Pulling them open, she stuck her head in, looked left and right. "Anyone here?" she asked, feeling silly. Because really, who could possibly be there, besides ghosts, and she didn't believe in them.

Since no ghosts answered her, she stepped the rest of the way inside, but left the French doors open onto the sunny deck. And then, as soon as she spotted them, she moved from window to window, yanking open the heavy, dark draperies that shrouded each of them. Clouds of dust erupted, and as she opened the last set, she brushed her hands against each other, and turned to survey the room in the newly admitted light.

And then she froze, because there, above the fireplace mantel, above the shotgun that was resting on its hooks there, was a huge portrait, as perfect and fresh as if it had just been finished yesterday.

A couple, side by side, his hand on her shoulder, stern faces staring out from the canvas into the room, in that serious pose that was considered appropriate in times gone by.

Her face, Kira realized, was the same face she had seen peering out the window at her. It was her *own* face. Looking at the portrait was like looking into a mirror.

And then she forced her eyes to move to the male subject, and she felt her heart trip over itself in her chest. He was Ian. He was absolutely Ian.

"Kira? Lass, where've you gone?"

She heard him calling to her from some other room in the house, and she walked toward the closed door. "I'm in here," she called, and she closed her hand on the doorknob, twisted, but it didn't give. "I think the door's locked."

He was right on the other side, gripping the knob, twisting. "Odd," he said. "Do you see a way to unlock it?"

"No, just a keyhole. I guess you need a key. That's all right, though, I'll just go back out the way I came in. Meet you on the deck."

She turned and started for the French doors.

They slammed closed so hard she jumped and screeched. Then she dove at the doors, gripping the knobs, rattling and shaking and tugging on them.

Even as she did, the drapes yanked themselves closed, one set after the other. Spinning around, her back to the doors, Kira stared around the room. "There's no point in this," she whispered, as her chest heaved with the force of her rapid breathing. "You can't frighten me—all right, you can, but what good is it going to do? What do you want from me, and how the hell do you expect to get it if you can't even manage to let me know what it is!"

Behind her, the French doors opened, and she almost fell outside as they did, but Ian's arms came around her from behind. He held her, burying his face in her hair. "What happened, lass? What was the noise? You cried out, and doors slammed, and—"

"Look, Ian. Look at that portrait."

From the open doors, the sunlight spilled over the face of the painting. Ian looked, and then couldn't seem to look away. "Aye, it's uncanny, is it not?"

"Then you've seen it before? You knew?"

"I knew. I'd intended to tell you about it before you saw it. In fact, the portrait was in the attic. I put it there myself. I've no idea how it got back down here."

"Someone wanted to make sure I saw it." She turned into his arms, let him hold her as she whispered, "Is that the thing Aunt Esmeralda thought I should know about?"

"That, and her theory. Her ridiculous, outrageous theory that you and I—"

"That you and I?" she prompted when he fell silent.

"That we're," he nodded at the portrait, "them. Reincarnated. Doomed to relive our past."

Shivering, Kira looked around the room. "This is where it happened, isn't it? Where she found him in bed with the maid? Where she killed him?"

"Aye," Ian said. "With that very weapon. I packed away the shotgun in the attic by my own hand. I donna know what's about here, Kira. I donna ken how these items came to be replaced in this room. But you're right, this is where it happened. She shot him, and then she cast the spell, from the tiny room at the top, the room where 'twas said she cast her spells, and then she threw herself from the widow's walk, down the cliffs to the rocky beach below."

"Then I only have one question, Ian."

He faced her squarely.

"Why the hell did you bring me here?"

"Because I donna believe it. Not any of it, Kira. 'Tis a family legend, a superstition that's gained power purely because so many generations have believed in it. That belief is the only power it has."

"You sound awfully sure about that."

He nodded, searching her face. "You said you didna believe in it either, lass."

She nodded, acknowledging her own words. "I'm not so sure anymore. I mean, this place feels so familiar to me. And the ghosts—I've seen them and their antics firsthand." She let her eyes roam throughout the room, and they got stuck on the portrait that looked so much like one of her and Ian, in period costumes. All except for the unbearable sadness in their eyes. "What if it's all true, Ian?"

He moved close to her, clasping her shoulders and drawing her eyes back to his face. "Coming here is the only way to prove that it isn't. An' that's why I brought ya. I feel something for you, Kira, something powerful. I think I might love ya. But we can't know what's between us while this shadow's hanging over our heads, can we now?"

"No. But . . . what if what we feel for each other is just further evidence that all of this is true? What if . . . it's leftover from some past life?"

"What if it's not?" he asked. "What if we responded to each other so readily because we're meant to be together? Soul mates?"

She lowered her gaze. "One doesn't necessarily negate the other."

She shivered a little, and he ran his hands up and down her outer arms, then pulled her into his. "At the very worst, lassie, at the very, very worst, suppose it is true. Then it's up to us to set it right. Here and now. We can put the fate of your family back on track for the countless generations to come."

His whispered words about generations to come made her think of the children she wanted to have one day. A vision of a little girl hovered in her mind. Big blue eyes and dimples and silken curls. She could risk passing along the family curse to that child, putting her through all the angst that Kira herself was suffering right now. Or she could risk everything to ensure that would never happen.

Lifting her gaze to Ian's she met his eyes and nodded once. "All right. I'll stay."

"You'll be safe, I promise."

Kira sat alone in the large living room, staring up at the portrait, and the shotgun. Ian had offered to return them to the attic, but she'd told him to leave them. She wasn't sure why, it had just sort of slipped out and once it had, it felt right.

He was in the kitchen now, preparing dinner. She'd wanted to spend more time in this room, though logic seemed to suggest she should want just the opposite. Maybe to block the doors, and not enter it again for the duration of her stay. But instead she wanted to remain.

Once Ian left her alone, reluctant as he was to do so, Kira bent to the hearth, removed the ornate screen, and began to build a fire. There was a stack of old newspapers nearby, and a tiny pile of kindling beside the circular log holder.

She crumpled papers, positioned kindling carefully over them, and used one of the long matches from the matchholder, striking it on the red brick and watching as it flared to life. Touching the match to the papers, she sat, mesmerized as the fire took hold. Then she tossed the matchstick into the fire, and replaced the screen.

As the fire spread, adding warmth to the chill of the room, Kira sank into a comfortable chair and watched the flames, gradually shifting her focus to the portrait up above. "I want you to stop messing with me, okay? Ian and I need this time together."

The eyes of her ancestor seemed to glare at her.

"I think I love him," she went on. "And I think he loves me, too."

She paused, listening, as ridiculous as that was, for some response. Of course there was none.

"If we can make this work, maybe the curse will finally be broken."

The fire snapped so loudly she jumped out of her chair, and beneath the sound she could have sworn she heard the word "Never!"

Kira swallowed hard, rubbing her arms and looking around the room. "You placed that curse on your family out of hurt and anger and unbearable pain, Miranda. But it was a mistake. You need to recognize that. You made a horrible mistake and your descendents have been suffering for it ever since. But I'm going to be the one to set it right. Since you're not able, or maybe just not willing to do it yourself, I'm going to do it. Ian and I. True love will break this curse of yours. I know it will."

In her mind she heard a heartbroken whisper. *There's no such thing as true love.*

She wondered, later, if Miranda had granted her request to be left alone with Ian. Because she didn't feel the troubling, unsettled presence lurking, and there were no further incidents of flickering lights or slamming doors or snapping flames that sounded like voices.

Ian made steaks, luscious and cooked to perfection, with baked potatoes, mixed baby vegetables, sweet red wine. He suggested they eat on the deck, and so they did, at a small round table on the far end, overlooking the sea.

The wind was cool, but refreshingly stiff, and it matched the pattern of the waves rushing toward the shore below. They ate, and they drank. They talked and laughed, touching on every subject imaginable from religion to politics to the environment to philosophy to favorite foods, colors, and places. She told him in painful detail about her childhood, and the pain of losing her parents. He told her about losing his own mother to cancer when he was barely thirteen, and being raised by his father since then. And he elaborated on how woefully smitten his father was with Emma, but knowing of her firm belief in the curse, he dared not ever let on.

They were still sitting there, sipping the last bit of wine, as the sun sank beneath the horizon, and the skies turned to purple and deepened into blue. Then as they stared out at the darkening sky and the sea below it, a flash of lightning lit the night just briefly.

A second later, thunder rolled slowly across the sky.

"That's close," Ian said. "We'd best get inside before it hits."

She frowned at the clouds that seemed to come boiling out of nowhere, and wondered why she hadn't seen them before.

Ian picked up their plates and Kira took their empty glasses and the bottle and ice bucket. Big droplets began pummeling them before they made it to the door, and she laughed at the cold kiss of the unexpected storm. In the kitchen, she set the glasses and bucket down. Ian deposited the plates in the sink, and turned to face her.

Smiling, his eyes intense, he reached up to brush the wetness from her face. But his hand stilled there on her cheek, and then he was leaning closer, and his lips were pressing to hers.

She opened to him, curling her arms around his neck as the fire he always managed to ignite in her took hold. He buried one hand in her hair, cupping her head and angling her for his invasion. His other hand curled around her bottom, pulling her tighter to him. The heat grew and spread. Her breaths came shorter and faster, and her entire body tingled with longing and need.

He scooped her up into his arms and carried her through the house, still feeding from her mouth, up the stairs, into a bedroom. And then they fell together to the bed as he tugged at her clothes and his own, and she struggled to help.

Naked, at last, tangled in each other, they stopped, suddenly, and Ian backed away just enough to look at her. His eyes devoured her from her head to her toes and back again, and the look in them told her everything she needed to know.

And then he was kissing her again, touching her, rubbing and caressing places that were already thrumming with heightened awareness. Her nipples screamed with pleasure when he squeezed them. And when he kissed and suckled them, it was all she could do not to cry out loud. As he ravaged her breasts, he slid his hand lower, fingers dipping into the hot moistness between her legs, exploring her there, probing and pressing until she thought she'd lose her mind with desire. She touched him in return, shocked at the rigid length of him, that he was that aroused, that throbbingly hard, for her.

"I need you now," she whispered. "Ian, I need you."

"Yes," he muttered, sliding his mouth to her neck, to her ear, nibbling and suckling every bit of skin he encountered. "Yes, lassie, it's been too long."

It was an odd thing to say, and yet felt perfectly natural, as he slid himself inside her, and began to move. And when he entered her, it felt right. It felt like the fulfillment of a longing she'd held forever, yet never been able to name. It felt familiar and perfect.

And as they moved together it was as if they'd been sexual partners for years. She knew what he wanted, what he liked, how to please him. He seemed to read her mind, because he knew all the same things about her. He knew how to push her right to the edge, and let her hover there as he played her, drew it out, made it last, made her want to beg and plead for release. And then he knew how to push her over, into ecstasy, driving into her to keep it going and going.

He even knew how to hold her closer and tighter as she came back down, how to make her feel safe and protected in his strong arms while her body slowly stopped trembling. And he knew exactly what to say to make it absolutely perfect.

"I love you, Kira MacLellan. I love you."

Tears springing inexplicably into her eyes, she whispered, "I love you too."

And as he held her there, it seemed the sky grew darker. Wind she'd been oblivious to before howled and moaned around the corners of the house. The bedroom door smashed open, and an unearthly keening wail filled the room.

Kira sat up in the bed, stunned. And she heard, beyond it all, footsteps, dragging their way up the stairs.

"No!" she cried. Scrambling from the bed, she snatched Ian's shirt from the floor, pulling it on. He was beside her, yanking on his shorts.

"What is it?" he asked. "What the hell is happening?"

And she knew, right to her gut she knew. Miranda had seen them, somehow, seen them making love, and was reliving that night when all of this horror had begun. The night when her heart had been shattered so badly that neither death itself nor the centuries that had passed in between had been able to heal it.

"This isn't your husband!" Kira cried. "This is Ian!"

The windows smashed inward, and the wind and rain surged into the room. Kira gripped Ian's hand as terror clutched her heart, and tugged him with her out of the bedroom.

It was dark, but she sensed Miranda's spirit to her right, near the bedroom door. Dashing past her, pulling Ian in her wake, she headed for the stairs, racing down them as fast as she could manage.

And she sensed it. The pursuit.

"Kira, where are we goin' lass?"

"Out. You have to get out of here. Don't you see, Ian, she's going to kill you!"

He stopped on the landing, gripping her shoulders hard, staring into her eyes in the darkness. "Lassie, it's only the storm. You're in a panic, but I promise you, it's only the storm, and—"

His words cut off mid-sentence, turning into a cry of alarm as he was shoved bodily. He sailed down the stairs, hitting the landing below as Kira turned to stare in shock at the form that stood beside her now. Misty, with a faint glow and the dimmest hint of her own features staring down at Ian.

And then slowly, the ghost's focus shifted to her.

From the corner of her eye, Kira saw Ian move. He was alive, the fall hadn't been a deadly one. She couldn't let Miranda realize that her task was not yet accomplished. So as the woman turned to her, she wracked her brain. In the story, Miranda had murdered the faithless maid as well. And there was definitely murder in her eyes as she stared at Kira.

"My turn now, is it?"

Mist like tendrils extended toward her. Kira bolted up the stairs. "Come and get me, then. Come on, Miranda! You want to do this, let's do it!"

She hit the top of the stairs, glancing over her shoulder to see that the shape was following. And then she tripped over something, and scrambling to her feet, realized it was the shotgun that had hung on the wall above the fireplace, beneath the portrait. Miranda must have managed to bring it with her, but discarded it. Too hefty for mist to manage? Or was it simply unloaded and useless?

It didn't matter. She got to her feet and kept running, even with the chilly essence of the ghost touching the back of her neck. She hit the second stairway, and raced up it, bursting through the door at the top. The door that led to the room where the MacLellan witch had allegedly cast her deadly spell. Kira flipped the light switch, but nothing happened, so she raced to the odd little table at the room's center, and fumbled for the matches she'd seen there earlier. Wooden matches, and God only knew if they were any good. She struck one, struck it again, and again, and finally it sparked and flared. She touched it to the candles on the table, all of them, and she noted there were more than there had been before.

Frowning, she looked at the table in the dancing light of the candles. There were five of them, four forming a circle and one in the center. All black. Dishes of herbs she couldn't identify rested there too, along with a dead dove, three hat pins sticking out of its chest.

Kira caught her breath, stepping backward, away from the table.

And then she felt Miranda behind her, and turned.

Miranda stood there, staring at her. And while she was still translucent, she was also far more fully formed than before. Kira could see the waves of her hair, the tears in her eyes, the greens in the gown she wore.

"Miranda," she whispered.

"How could he? How . . . could . . . he?" the heart broken spirit whispered.

Kira stood there, frozen. "Why . . . don't you ask him?" she suggested.

"I've killed him. I wish he'd killed me instead. I wish he'd spared me this pain. Better he put a knife in my heart than betray me this way. I'll see to it none of my descendents ever hurt the way I do now." She looked at the table.

"No you won't." Kira swept an arm over the table, scattering the dishes of herbs. Then she snatched up the murdered dove, yanking the pins from its poor wounded breast, and racing to the doors that led onto the widow's walk, she flung them open.

"No!" Miranda cried.

Kira hovered there in the doorway with the dove's still warm, limp body in her hands. "I'll toss it unless you ask him yourself, Miranda! I will!"

"How can I? He's dead."

"So are you."

The wraith went silent, her eyes seeming to focus inwardly. She remained that way for a long moment.

"You're dead, too, Miranda. You took your own life, and you died in pain and anguish. But before you did, you cursed your entire family. No MacLellan woman has known love since. The few who've tried have died at the hands of their husbands. The rest are too afraid to give love a chance. You're destroyed your daughters, and theirs after them, for generations to come. And soon the line will die out. All because of your actions that night."

The ghost's brows rose, her eyes lowered, her head moved slowly from side to side.

"Talk to your husband, Miranda. Call out to him. He'll hear you, I know he will."

The winds of the storm raged on. Lightning flashed, and the curtains flew as the rain slashed inward.

"Victor?" Miranda whispered on a broken plea. "Can you hear me?"

To Kira's amazement, a form appeared in the room then. A man's form. He took shape slowly, growing more solid before her eyes. Two of the candles went out as the wind-driven rain spat at them.

"I'm sorry," he said.

"Victor, why? Why?"

"I got very drunk, my love. I was missing you, and drinking, and she came to our room. I took her into my arms, thinking it was you. And even as I realized in my drunken state that she was not my beloved bride, you burst into the room on us. You never gave me a chance to explain."

Miranda's form fell to its ghostly knees, her head lowering, sobs wracking her frame. "But I . . . I k-k-killed you!"

"I forgive you, my love. I forgave you long ago. And I've waited, all this time, for you to forgive me, and yourself, to free yourself of the bondage you created for your soul, and to join me on the other side."

Her head came up slowly. Kira felt tears pouring from her own eyes as it did.

"You forgive me?"

"I love you, lass. It's unendin' what I feel for you. Let it go, my beautiful Miranda." He held out a hand. "Join me, my love. I've missed you so."

Rising slowly, Miranda lifted her hand and took a single step toward him.

"Wait!" Kira cried. "Wait, please. Remove the curse first."

Both heads turned toward her. Miranda nodded slowly, and held out a hand. "Give the dove to me."

Swallowing hard, Kira handed her the lifeless bird, feeling the cold touch, like heavy fog, touching her hand as Miranda took it from her. Cupping it between her ghostly hands, Miranda bent her head close to the bird, whispered something, and then straightening, she moved to the open doors, lifted her hands, and opened them.

The dove soared from her palms, and even as it entered the storm, the winds died. The rain ceased. The lightning and thunder ended. Kira stared skyward as the black clouds skittered away, making a clear path to the new moon that was a thin silver sickle in the sky.

"Thank you, Miranda," Kira whispered. "Thank you."

She turned to look at the couple, but there was no one there. It was over. It was honestly over.

And then she remembered. Ian!

Racing from the room, and down the stairs, she headed through the hallway, and saw him lying on the landing below. Rushing down to him, she took his shoulders, pulling him upright. "Ian, darling, are you all right? Talk to me! Please?"

He lifted his head, blinking at her as she searched his face. "I'm . . . fine. I think. What happened?"

"It's over, Ian. It's over, the curse is broken."

"Thank the Lord," he muttered, and pulling her into his arms, he lay back down, snuggling her close, right there on the floor. "Now let's go back to sleep, love."

Kira frowned, because she wasn't lying on the stair landing. She was in the bed, in the same bedroom where they'd fallen asleep. Ian had rolled onto one side, and was breathing deeply, steadily. Sound asleep.

Kira threw back the covers. She was naked, not wearing Ian's shirt. It was on the floor right where it had been before.

She got up and put it on now, then looked around the room. The windows were not smashed in. There was no rain. The storm outside had abated. The bedroom door was still closed.

She opened it and stepped out into the hall, trying a light switch. It worked fine, flooding the corridor with light. Kira traversed it, seeing no shotgun lying on the floor near the top of the stairs.

She kept going, to the second staircase, and up it, to the spell room at the top. Its door opened easily, its light switch also in working order. The table in the room's center was empty, except for the thick coating of dust, the two candles and the matchbook that had been there earlier in the day. The doors to the widow's walk were closed. But she could see the sliver of moon just as she had seen it before.

Had it all been a dream? Was the curse truly broken?

She left the room, shutting off its light and closing its door, then headed all the way down to the first floor, to the living room. The fire she'd left burning there was only a soft bed of red-orange coals now. Again, she turned on the lights, and again, they worked as they should.

Then she stood, staring up at the gun, that hung right where it should have hung, above the mantel. And above that the portrait was just as it had been before.

Or was it?

Kira moved closer, staring up at the painting. No, she realized, it wasn't the same. The couple—their eyes were different. And their mouths. It seemed they were almost smiling now.

Something tapped the window behind her and she turned quickly, startled.

The drapes were parted, and there on the other side of them, she saw a dove. It stared back at her for a minute, then spread its wings and took flight.

"Darlin'?"

She turned to see Ian in the doorway, looking at her worriedly.

"You had a bad dream, lass," he said. "Is everything all right now?"

"Yes, Ian." She moved into his arms, and felt them close around her. The most incredible feeling of rightness washed through her, and she relaxed against him. "Everything's really all right now. I'm sure of it."

She lifted her eyes to his. "I want to marry you. I'm sure of that too."

His brows lifted in surprise, and then a smile appeared on his handsome face, a smile she loved with everything in her. "But what about the curse?"

"There is no curse, not anymore," she told him. "But

even if there were, I'd marry you anyway. It would be worth the risk. Love is worth any risk, Ian. I understand that now."

He stared into her eyes for a long moment, and then he kissed her, more tenderly, more gently, than he ever had. And Kira knew then, that her life was perfect.

Maggie Shayne

It was a sleepless night spent caring for a sick baby that jump-started *New York Times* bestselling author **MAGGIE SHAYNE**'s writing career.

Now she is the author of more than forty novels, ranging from stories about witches, vampires, psychics, and ghosts to bone chilling, edge-of-your-seat romantic suspense and beyond. Maggie has appeared on the *New York Times, USA Today, Amazon.com, B.Dalton, Booksense, Ingram's, Barnes and Noble,* and *Waldenbooks* (where she reached #1) bestseller lists.

What would she be doing if she wasn't so accomplished a writer? Maggie maintains she'd be equally happy as a rock star. "I have a karaoke machine, and I'm actually damn good," she says. "Furthermore, Sheryl Crow and I are the same age, so I figure if this writing thing doesn't work out, there's still time."

HAPPILY NEVER AFTER

Jeaniene Frost

The old woman glanced at her watch.
Quarter to eleven. It wouldn't be long now.

Across the dark alley, two young men sauntered over
with the sly, exaggerated swagger of teenagers up to no
good. She barely spared them a glance as she tapped
her foot and hummed. Once, *very* long ago, she'd have
sauntered over to them, swinging her hips and mur-
muring promises of pleasure—for a price. But that had
been another lifetime ago.

The youths came nearer, greed and opportunism
glittering in their eyes. The woman knew she looked
like an easy target: a senior citizen standing in a dimly
lit alley wearing an expensive trench coat, a gold watch,
with a bulky purse dangling from her age-skinny arm.
She may as well have added a sign that said "come and
get me!"

"Whatcha doin' out here, grandma?" one of them
singsonged. The other hung back a foot or two, eyes

flickering around to see if anyone was watching. No one was. People minded their own business on this side of South Philly.

At a nod from his lookout, the other punk pulled out a switchblade.

"Give me your money, your jewelry, and your purse. Or I'll cut you."

The old woman smiled. "Do you know what you two are?" she asked in an amused voice.

They looked at each other in surprise, clearly not expecting her lack of fear. Then their scowls returned.

"Yeah, we're the guys robbing you!" the one with the knife snapped.

"No," said a voice from the other end of the alley, an English accent decorating his words. "You're *dinner*."

Before the two could blink, they were dangling by their throats from pale, rock-steady hands. One was yanked close to the black-clad figure. The stranger's eyes changed from brown to glowing green as he dipped his head to the exposed throat. The youth's partner in crime, still hoisted aloft, could only make terrified grunts as he watched fangs pierce his friend's neck.

Then the stranger dropped the now-limp form and latched his mouth onto the other available neck. A minute later the second youth dropped flaccidly to the street. The stranger wiped his mouth with the back of his hand and then pulled the old woman to him.

Instead of struggling, she hugged him as hard as her feeble body could manage. He squeezed back gently, smiling when he let her go.

"Greta, whatever were you thinking by telling me to meet you here? This is no place for you."

She laughed with a hint of her former bawdy cackle.

"I was thinking you'd be hungry, Bones. I knew I'd

have something for you to eat by the time you got here."

He chuckled as well, brushing a strand of white hair from her face. "Same old Greta. Always finding ways to please her blokes."

She felt the warmth of many pleasant memories shimmer through her. Bones' beautiful face hadn't changed with time, and that was a comfort. Time was merciless on so many things, including herself, but it had no power over the blond vampire standing in front of her.

She glanced at the still forms near their feet. "Are they dead?" she asked, more curious than concerned.

Absently Bones kicked one of them. "No, just unconscious. I'll drop these sods in the nearest dumpster before we leave. Serves them right for threatening you."

Which brought her to why she'd called him here. "I need a favor," Greta said.

He took her hand. Once his skin would have felt noticeably cooler, but no longer. *With the meal he just ate and my poor circulation,* Greta thought wryly, *we're almost the same temperature.*

If he thought that as well, it didn't show on his face. Very softly, he kissed her fingers.

"Whatever you need, you know you have but to ask."

Tears pricked her eyes. A long time ago, she'd left the home Bones gave her to marry a man she'd fallen madly in love with. Fifty years later, she didn't regret her decision, but sometimes she wondered how things would have turned out if she'd stayed with Bones instead.

Greta shook off the memories. "It's my grandchildren," she began. "They're in trouble."

Twenty minutes later, Greta was finished detailing their predicament. Bones nodded, a thoughtful expression on his face.

"I can't handle this myself, luv, because I'm focusing all my energy on finding someone, but I'll send a bloke who'll take care of things. I trust him, so you'll all be in good hands. My word on it."

Greta smiled. "That's more than enough for me."

Chapter 1

 Isabella peeked through the slats sectioning off the prep room from the rest of her restaurant's on-display kitchen. Yes, the dark-haired man was still at his table, and yes, he was still staring at her.

Fool, she thought as she jerked out of sight. Hadn't he heard? She was now engaged to Robert "Robbery" Bertini. *Here comes the bride*, she thought with a fresh spurt of anger. Why hadn't she just gone out with Robert the first time he asked? Or the tenth? It was only her repeated refusals that made her stand out from all the other women he had on his expensively clad arm. She'd seen *Goodfellas,* she should have known that saying no to a mob boss, even a relatively minor one like Robert, would only encourage him to go after her. Why had he decided to come to her restaurant every Thursday night, anyway? If he'd never set foot in here, none of this would have happened!

Actually, it could all be blamed on meatballs. Isa gave a nearby pan of seasoned meaty goodness an evil glare. Yep, it was their fault. Damned tasty little bastards had put her late parents' restaurant on the map. Who knew they'd also turn out to be a local mafia boss's favorite meal?

"Isa, table nine wants to see you!" her head chef Frank called out.

She grimaced. That was Tall, Dark and Dumb's table, the new customer with the staring problem. Under other circumstances, Isa wouldn't have minded his fixed attention. He certainly wasn't hard to look at—brown hair falling just above his shoulders, a lean build, and a half-smile that managed to be charming and a trifle devious at the same time.

But today was Thursday, so her fiancé—*for the time being only*, she promised herself—was here with his usual quartet of goons. Isa had already noticed Robert giving a couple of pointed glares to the man for his obvious fixation on her. Soon Robert wouldn't settle for just dirty looks. He'd have the stranger taken out back and his knees broken, if he was in a good mood. Isa didn't want to think about what would happen to the man if Robert was testy tonight.

She made her way to table nine with a polite yet frosty smile on her face. At Spagarelli's, Isa was known for taking time to stop and talk to the patrons, remember the names of her regulars, and even have a drink with some of them. When she'd reopened this restaurant, she wanted to be hands-on with everything, including the customers. Now, of course, it made it impossible for her to refuse Tall, Dark and Dumb's request to speak with the owner. She hoped Robert had chosen now to go to the little boy's room, but he hadn't. Instead, he watched her approach the man's table with narrowed black eyes.

"Isa," he called out, displeasure clear in his gravelly voice.

"Just a moment," she said with false brightness. "I have to attend to a customer."

What she really wanted to tell Robert was to shut the hell up and leave. Permanently. But she couldn't say that, nor could she tell him the other thing that was constantly on the tip of her tongue—that she'd rather marry Al Capone's corpse than him. After all, Frazier was depending on her. Where he was or why she needed to pretend she was going ahead with this wedding, Isa didn't know, but the last time she'd spoken to her brother, Frazier said it was a matter of life and death.

So she played the future Mrs. Robert Bertini, which wasn't easy. Robert had visions of becoming the next Michael Corleone, and to accomplish that, he thought he needed the ideal Mafioso image of being married to a traditional Italian woman. The fact that Isa owned a perfect money-laundering front with her restaurant was just the icing on the cake, she was certain.

Well, Robert had a lot to learn. Anyone who knew her well would have known that trying to blackmail Isa into marriage was a bad idea. Pure-blooded Italian she might be, but a traditional, docile crime-lord wife she was *not*.

Frustration over the whole situation boiled just below the surface as Isa plonked down across from the man at table nine, making sure her back was to Robert.

"Can I help you?" she asked with far less tact than normal.

A slow smile lit his face, making him look even more wickedly enticing.

"Actually, darling, I'm here to help *you*."

Isa was not in the mood for banter. She could practically hear the steam coming out of Robert's ears. This man would be lucky to leave here alive. The longer she talked to him, the less chance he had of that. She couldn't afford to risk his life by playing polite restaurateur.

"The only way I'd need your help is if you were a restaurant critic or a health inspector. Now, unless you have something to say about the wine, since you haven't eaten a bite of food, I really must go—"

"Robbery's got you on a short leash, doesn't he?" the man interrupted. "Yessir, he's been glaring holes into my head for the past hour."

Isa's mouth dropped. So did her opinion of him. If he knew who Robert was, and he'd been eye-humping his fiancé right in front of him anyway, then he had to be the world's biggest fool.

"Are you drunk?" she asked low.

He laughed with a toss of his head. "Nothing like that, Isabella. My name's Chance, by the way. Pleased to meet you."

He held out his hand. Isa shook it briefly and then stood.

"Enjoy the rest of your wine, Mr. Chance."

"Just Chance," he corrected, giving her another appraising stare. "You know, with your black hair and cedar eyes, you look a lot like your grandmother when she was younger."

Isa froze . . . and then sat back down. "How do you know my grandmother?" *Or that she looked like me when she was young?*

Chance cast a glance over her shoulder. "We've got company coming, darling, but suffice it to say my sire's an old friend of your grandmother's, and I *am* here to help you."

Robert's most trusted cohort Paul appeared in the next moment. With his massive size and steamrolling personality, Isa mentally referred to him as Bowling Ball.

"Isa," he rumbled. "Boss wants to see you *now*."

She stood at once, her mind in a jumble. What had her grandmother done? She wasn't even supposed to know Frazier was in trouble. My God, the woman was seventy-five, she couldn't take the stress!

"Next time try the 1997 Cabernet," she said to Chance, tapping on his wine bottle. "In fact, there's a store on Twelfth Street called Blue Ridge Vineyards that sells them. They close at seven on weekdays, so you should be able to pick up a bottle tomorrow."

He inclined his head with another smile. "I'll remember that."

Isa hoped Chance would get the message to meet her there tomorrow night. Whatever her grandmother was up to, it had to be called off. Robert wasn't some average stalking suitor who could be dealt with by filing a restraining order. He practically owned the police, and whatever Chance was—a private investigator her grandmother hired, maybe?—he wouldn't be able to handle the heat Robert would bring.

With an inward sigh, Isa went off to pacify her fiancé.

Chance heard the men following him. Their heavy footfalls, combined with huffy breathing and accelerated heartbeats, made them as noisy as if they were clanging cymbals together. He inhaled, sorting through the bonanza of the evening's scents to filter what was theirs. The one called Paul had recently cleaned the gun in his jacket; the scent of oiled metal was palpable even above the odors of garlic, spaghetti and meatballs. The other one, Ritchie, was less fastidious with his firearms—and his personal hygiene. He smelled like he hadn't taken a bath for days.

Chance didn't quicken his pace from the same leisurely stroll he'd used while leaving the restaurant. Isabella had watched him go, surreptitiously, of course, but he'd caught her eye right as he went out the door. And then she'd blushed as he winked at her.

That blush was what he was thinking about now, far more than the two meatwagons following him to the parking lot. He'd been observing Isabella since he arrived in Philadelphia over three days ago. Familiarizing himself with her routine, marking the places she visited . . . and watching Robert "Robbery" Bertini as well.

Robert was much less interesting a subject, in Chance's opinion, and not just because Isabella was infinitely more attractive. Robert was a typical schoolhouse bully, and all his clothes, money, houses or influence wouldn't change that. His insistence on marrying a woman who didn't want him was just as spiteful as a child demanding a particular toy because some other child had it. As a vampire, Chance had seen Robert's type in one form or another for multiple decades, and his tolerance for his sort hadn't grown with time.

Normally vampires didn't interfere in human's affairs. Humans had their own laws and social structure, and to say they differed from vampire society was to put it mildly. Most vampires had enough to handle within their own group of allies and enemies without adding human trials and tribulations to that.

But in this case, Chance *could* intervene. Isabella's

grandmother, Greta, had once been a member of his sire Bones' line. Time had passed, but Bones' sense of responsibility to her hadn't. Even though Chance was Master of his own line now and no longer under Bones' authority, his sire had asked him for a favor. So Chance could meddle to his heart's content with the wedding plans of the arrogant mobster. Someone who would blackmail a woman into marriage made Chance angry. Power was supposed to be used for the protection of those you cared about, not for selfishness. Apparently no one had taught that to Robert Bertini.

In fact, it was high time someone put the Bugsy wanna-be in his place. A smile tugged at Chance's mouth. *Why not?* he thought. It wasn't what his sire Bones told him to do, which was to simply alter Robert's mind until he no longer believed that he wanted to marry Isabella, but Chance would make sure it still all turned out the same. Well, with just a little well-deserved comeuppance added to it.

And that would mean more time in the lovely Isabella's company. Maybe enough to find out what else would make her blush. Chance already had a few ideas.

"Hey, buddy," the one named Paul growled behind him. "We wanna talk to you."

Chance turned, noting with amusement that they'd picked the darkest end of the parking lot for their confrontation. How unoriginal.

"If you're going to warn me to stay away from Spagarelli's beautiful proprietor or you'll hurt me in various exaggerated ways, save your breath," Chance replied calmly. "I'll be seeing her—and you idiots too, I suppose—there tomorrow night at nine sharp."

Paul's mouth dropped, making him look like a freshly caught blowfish.

"You know who you're talkin' to?" he finally demanded.

"Of course. Spaghetti alla nona, side of extra meatballs."

Ritchie cracked his knuckles as he stepped nearer. "You're in for a beating, dickhead."

"Really? Fuggetaboutit," Chance mocked with a heavy Italian accent.

Ritchie swung. Since he was human, to Chance it looked like he was moving in slow motion. He ducked neatly and at the same time, pivoted Ritchie a little to the right.

That roundhouse punch landed in Paul's face instead.

Paul rocked back even as Ritchie gasped. Chance didn't bother to suppress his laughter.

"Ouch. You owe your friend an apology," he chuckled.

Ritchie whirled around even as Paul began cursing about his nose being broken. From the sudden sweet smell in the air, Chance didn't have to glance his way to know he was correct.

With a snarl, Ritchie came at him again. This time, Chance didn't duck out of the way. He simply moved to the side and stuck out his foot.

Ritchie tripped and went flying, the momentum from his charge making him land with a heavy thud several feet away. More rich, mouth-watering scent filled the air. Ritchie had skinned his knee and his elbow on the asphalt badly enough that both were bleeding.

"Will we be dancing like this for long?" Chance asked.

Ritchie got to his feet slowly, giving Chance a furious look. Paul was still focused on his nose, more red staining the front of his shirt.

"You got fancy moves, pal?" Ritchie asked, drawing a gun from his inner jacket. "Try dodging *this*!"

He fired twice in quick succession, hitting Chance in the chest. The bullets weren't silver, though, so their pain only lasted a few moments. Long enough for him to drop to the ground like a regular person would, clutch his chest (to hide the rapidly healing wounds), gasp out a few breaths . . . and then let his breath rattle out in one last, dramatic exhalation.

Oscar-worthy, if he did say so himself.

"Jesus!" he heard Paul hiss above him. "Ritchie, what the fuck? There's people around here!"

Ritchie's heartbeat was galloping, from the thrill of his presumed kill, or the fear of getting caught. Either way, its sound made Chance's fangs ache with longing.

"Get his keys," Ritchie said roughly. "We'll put him in his trunk, you follow in your car behind me, and we'll bury this fuck before Letterman comes on. Hurry."

Chance felt them tug his car keys from his hand, lift him up with much muttered cursing about being quick to avoid potential bystanders, and then the thump of landing in his own trunk. Mentally he counted off the time. Less than two minutes from shots fired to body hidden, not bad. Clearly this wasn't their first time.

He was jostled more as Paul swung the vehicle out of the parking lot. *Careful*, Chance thought over the squeal of tires. *You dent my new Camaro and I'll shove the steering wheel right up your ass.*

Thoughts of Isabella brightened his mood. She had a beautiful face, a curvy body that bucked today's frightful stick-figure trends, and an ironclad streak of loyalty mixed with bravery. It wasn't every person who would sacrifice themselves to save their undeserving brother, after all. Frazier Spaga had gotten involved with Robert Bertini because of the lure of easy money. Now he was being used as collateral over his sister, and Isabella thought she had nothing but herself to ransom him back.

But you're wrong, Chance mused with a smile. *You just don't know it yet.*

Chapter 2

 Isa walked into Blue Ridge Vineyards fifteen minutes early. She didn't want to run the risk of missing Chance if he showed up. *What a strange name,* she mused. Maybe it was an alias.

Again, she wondered what her grandmother was up to. Isa hadn't bothered to call her and ask, of course. No need to upset her by telling her she was pulling the plug on whatever it was the sweet old lady had put into motion. Chance had said his "sire," which Isa surmised was just a formal word for father, had been a friend of her grandmother's. Despite Isa's inventive lies, her grandmother must have figured out that Frazier was in trouble, which wasn't uncommon. He'd been very rebellious as a teenager and though he'd calmed down in his twenties, he was hardly a stellar citizen. Isa didn't know how Frazier managed to pay his rent every month, since he hadn't held a regular job in years.

Still, when you added her brother's abrupt disappearance with Isa's surprise engagement to a man like Robert, no wonder her grandmother was spooked.

"Hi, Isa," the store clerk greeted her. Since she bought a lot of her wine from this place, she'd been on a first-name basis with most of the employees for a while.

"How's it going, Jim?" she asked.

"Can't complain, who'd listen?" he replied with a friendly smile.

Who indeed? Isa mentally agreed. Certainly not the police. She'd gone to them right after Robert proposed, if that's what you could call him saying, "Good news, Isa. I've decided we're getting married," and cutting off her immediate, sputtering objections with, "Seen your brother Frazier around lately?" with a knowing gleam in his dark eyes. Robert had followed up with, "Yep, I know for a fact you'll see him after our wedding, but if we don't have one . . . well. That brother of yours. He's accident prone, isn't he?"

She'd relayed that to the first police officer she saw at the station the very next day, and Isa would never forget what he did. He looked around, shut his office door, and slid her complaint form back across the desk at her.

"You seem like a nice lady," he'd said without looking at her. "So I'm going to say congratulations on your engagement . . . and don't ever file this form to me or anyone else if you care about your brother. Or yourself."

That's when she knew all the whispers about Robert Bertini were true. He really *did* run the streets, and apparently had considerable clout with the police as well.

She might have tried again. Called the FBI, Homeland Security, *someone,* but later that day, she received a phone call at her restaurant.

"Isa," her brother said as soon as she answered. "Don't say my name, and listen very carefully. I need you to go along with this engagement. Robert thinks he has both of us cornered, but it'll all work out, I promise."

"You're all right?" she'd asked low, trying to look casual in front of her employees.

"Yes. I can't explain, but just hang in there and play along. I'll contact you again as soon as I can, but not on the phone. Robert will probably tap all your phones next."

The line went dead, but Isa said, "Wrong number, no problem," and then hung up like nothing unusual had happened.

It was only later that she'd wondered how Frazier could have said things like "play along" and "Robert thinks he has both of us cornered." As a hostage, Isa didn't think Frazier would have been granted private phone privileges, but it also didn't make sense that he'd say such things in front of one of his captors. Had Frazier somehow managed to get away?

"Hello, Isabella."

Isa had been so caught up in her thoughts, she hadn't even heard the store's door open. Yet there Chance was, standing behind her with a faint smile on his face. Under the harsh fluorescent lighting, his hair looked to be deep brown instead of the darker shade it had seemed last night, and his skin was surprisingly pale. The eyes she hadn't been able to guess a color on before turned out to be an intriguing mix of gray and blue. *Like the ocean,* she thought. *Right before a storm.*

She was staring. With a shake of her head, Isa brought herself back to the present.

"Jim, do you mind if I show my friend the new stock in the back?" she asked, flashing a smile at the clerk.

"Sure thing," he responded with a lazy wave. She bought in bulk and she always paid on time. Jim would pretty much let her do anything.

Isa walked toward the back, glad that Chance followed without argument. When they were away from any prying eyes, Isa started right in.

"Whatever my grandmother hired you for, I'm telling you the job's off. If she owes you any money for your time, I'll pay it. Just tell her you didn't find anything or that everything's okay. She doesn't need this kind of stress at her age."

Chance regarded her with open curiosity. "You think I'm someone she *hired*? You mean your grandmother hasn't told you anything about me?"

"No," Isa said, impatient. "But whoever you are, you don't want to be mixed up in this. Trust me, pal. It goes way over what any pay scale can cover."

He continued to stare at her like she was speaking a foreign language. Isa tapped her foot. Maybe Tall, Dark and Dumb had been an accurate way to describe him after all.

"Has your grandmother ever mentioned the name 'Bones' to you before?" Chance asked in a very careful voice.

"Who?"

Chance inhaled. From her scent—and the thoroughly blank look on her face—she was telling the truth. She had no idea he was a vampire. Odds were, if her grandmother hadn't told her about Bones, Isa had no idea that vampires even existed.

This would make things more complicated.

"The only name that matters here is Robert Bertini," Isa went on. "You already seem to know what he's involved in, so I shouldn't have to spell out how hazardous it would be to your health if you continue to mess around with him."

Chance laughed. "You'd be amazed at all the things my health can handle, darling. Your little Robbery doesn't scare me, and as I told you last night, I'm here to help you. It's not a matter of money, so you can keep your bank account as it is. It's a matter of honor."

"Honor?" Isa couldn't stifle her snort. She had enough to handle without anyone meddling in this. "Right. Do me a favor. Go away before you make things worse."

It would be so much easier if she knew what he was, Chance mused. Still, it wasn't his place to enlighten. Not yet, anyway. Maybe there was a reason for Greta's secrecy. Perhaps Isabella was one of those humans who couldn't handle the knowledge. She didn't strike Chance that way, but then again, this was only his second time talking to her.

Chance smiled. "Thanks for the wine recommendation," he said, and walked away.

Isa watched him go, gripped with the uneasy feeling that she hadn't seen the last of him.

At nine o'clock sharp, Isa's premonition was confirmed when a familiar dark-haired man slid into table twelve at her restaurant. She almost groaned out loud in frustration. Talk about not taking a hint!

Chance even had the nerve to wink at her as he took his seat. What was it with men lately? Didn't the phrase "*No* means *no*" translate to them anymore?

She didn't even wait for the waitress to approach his table before she marched over.

"Whatever you want, we're out of it," Isa announced crisply.

Chance pushed his menu aside with a lazy grin. "Doesn't matter. I'm only here for you, darling."

Isa clenched her fists. She may not be able to throw Robert out on his ass—yet—but that didn't mean every male around could ignore her wishes in favor of their own!

"Get out, and by the way—calling a woman 'darling' when you don't even know her is sexist and demeaning. Got that, *sugar lips?*"

She stressed the endearment as a taunt, but it didn't have that effect. A light appeared in Chance's eyes. If Isa didn't know better, she would swear they seemed to be turning green.

"Sugar lips . . . mmm. I confess I'd like to find out."

The way he was looking at her mouth made Isa want to wipe it, but not in disgust. To see if it had suddenly turned into dessert, since that was the only way she could justify the intensity of Chance's stare. For someone who said he wasn't here for food, Chance looked very, very hungry.

"You have to leave. Now."

Isa said it with none of the internal tremble that had taken up inside her. The last thing she needed was another complication in her life, and a stubborn, sexy-as-hell private eye would definitely complicate things.

Then again, so would Robert's two goons Ritchie and Paul, and they just swaggered in the door.

"Oh, hell, it's Smelly and Bowling Ball," Isa muttered.

Chance began to laugh. "Is that what you call them? How appropriate."

She gave him a fraught look. "Are you *trying* to get killed? Leave! Before they see you!"

But it was too late. Paul glanced their way . . . and stopped so abruptly, one of her waiters crashed right into him. Spaghetti alla nona decorated the front of him, but he didn't even seem to notice.

"You!" Paul exclaimed in a voice much higher than usual.

Chance inclined his head. "I see you're wearing your favorite meal. Now if you can only bash into someone carrying meatballs, your ensemble would be complete."

Isa's eyes closed. *Good God, he was a dead man.*

Ritchie, oddly enough, didn't fly into his usual hair-trigger temper.

"You can't be here," he almost squeaked. "We—"

"You what?" Chance interrupted. "Shot me? Put me in a trunk, drove me to an old warehouse, wrapped me in plastic, and buried me around the back?" Chance let his words sink in, and then he smiled, perfectly cordial. "How preposterous. If that's what you did, then I wouldn't be sitting here, would I?"

Everyone in the restaurant had stopped eating to watch this exchange. Isa was torn between the ingrained urge to keep her business running smoothly—and the new, unhinged desire she had to bash plates over Paul's, Ritchie's, and even Chance's head.

Her business sense won. Isa laughed like a joke had been told and then approached Paul and Ritchie with a fake, warm smile.

"Let's get you guys to your favorite table. Lauren, bring something to help clean Paul up. And Ritchie, you look like you could use a drink."

She politely dragged them across the room under her effusive hostess pretense. Both of them went like they were dazed while still staring at Chance. Isa didn't know what he'd meant by his bizarre little imagining of what Ritchie had been about to say, but damn it, this was her restaurant! Not some criminal macho show-boating ring.

Paul stiffened. "Uh . . . we gotta go, Isa," he said. "Gotta check something out."

"You think Kevlar?" Ritchie whispered with a glance in Chance's direction.

"Must've been," Paul muttered.

Isa didn't care what they were babbling about as long as they didn't cause any more disruption.

"Don't worry about him, he's on his way out," she said low.

Paul looked at Chance and grunted. "Uh huh. We thought that last night, too."

What?

Ritchie grabbed Paul's arm. "Come on, let's roll. Boss needs to hear about this."

With a last look at Chance—and the mess on his Armani shirt—Paul left with Ritchie in tow. Chance gave them a cheery wave that made Isa want to smack him again. Thankfully, it was obvious Robert's two thugs had pressing business elsewhere.

Chance stood, stretched, and brushed his hand across Isa's cheek.

"Some things we need to talk about, but not here. I'll see you later, darling."

"No you won't, nut muffin!" she replied as low and fiercely as she could.

He laughed at that, giving her a lingering glance. "Yes, I will."

Chapter 3

 Robert came in right after closing. All the patrons were gone and it was just her, a few servers, and her head chef Frank tidying things up.

"Isa," he said, without acknowledging any of her staff. "Brought you your wedding dress."

Frank and the others left the main room, used to Robert's rudeness by now. Paul obediently approached Isa holding a garment bag. Isa stared at it for a moment before taking it. Even holding the dress in her hands filled her with panic. *Frazier better call again soon,* she found herself thinking, *because I can't fake this much longer.*

"Um . . . thanks." She couldn't manage to say anything more enthusiastic.

"It was my mother's, God rest her soul," Robert replied, crossing himself. "My sister made an appointment for you to get it fitted. She'll call you tomorrow with the date and time."

No consultation, no consideration for her schedule.

Isa hadn't even participated in the decision of where or when her wedding was going to take place. Robert's sister had showed up at Isa's restaurant a week ago and told her what church to be at on what date. It was a good thing Isa had no intention of actually marrying Robert, or she would have been pissed about how someone else was planning her wedding.

"The boys tell me that dark-haired mook's been hangin' around you again," Robert went on. "They warned him to stay away last night, but they said he was back again tonight. I don't like that, Isa. It's disrespectful to me."

She had to tread carefully. Chance might be asking for trouble, but Isa didn't want to serve him up a big plate of it.

"He's just a customer, Robert. I wouldn't even remember him, except Paul and Ritchie made such a stink when they saw him earlier."

Robert gave her a hard stare, but Isa schooled her face to show only innocence. If Catholic nuns couldn't make her admit to cheating on a test in high school, then Robert had no chance of breaking her with his gaze.

Finally he shrugged. "Good. Then you won't mind if the boys keep this troublemaker from bothering you in the future."

"If I see him again, I'll tell him not to come back myself," Isa said with complete honesty.

Robert moved closer. It took all of Isa's willpower not to flinch when he touched her face.

"Still . . . maybe you should come home with me. This guy could be a real whack job. I don't want anything happening to you."

Isa hardly knew Chance, but already she surmised

that out of the two of them, the true whack job was the man in front of her.

"That's okay, Robert. I'll be fine. If I see him again, I—I'll call you so you can deal with him."

A complete lie. She'd chase Chance away herself, true, but she'd never turn him over to Robert.

Robert trailed his fingers down her arm. "Maybe that's not the only reason I want you to stay with me," he said in a husky voice.

Oh, shit. Isa steeled herself to stay where she was, instead of running away screaming, "*hell* no!" like she wanted to.

"I told you before, Robert—I'm an old-fashioned Catholic girl. That's one of the things you like about me, remember? Well, in my family, we don't have sex until our wedding night."

Another bunch of bullshit. Isa hadn't been a virgin since nineteen, and while she hadn't racked up the notches on her bedpost, she'd had a few lovers in her time. None since she moved back to Philly three years ago, however, which is why Robert didn't know about them and believed her claims of chastity. And while she couldn't speak for her grandparents, Isa was pretty sure her parents hadn't abstained from premarital sex either.

But just in case Robert needed more convincing than her supposed desire to wait until their wedding night . . .

"Besides," Isa whispered, waving Robert closer. She unzipped her purse and held it open so the contents were visible. "It may not be a good time right now."

Robert peered inside at the multiple tubes and then picked one up curiously.

"Vagisil," he read the label, his mouth twisting down. "For treatment of acute feminine itching and discharge—argh!"

He threw the Vagisil across the room as if it had grown into a hairy cockroach. Isa bit her lip to contain her laughter from the horrified look on Robert's face.

Ritchie gasped before dropping his gaze below her waist.

"What kind of nastiness do you *have* down there?"

Robert stalked over and punched him straight in the face. "That's my future wife you're talkin' to!" he snapped, though he also gave a look of dread at Isa's lower half.

She spun around and zipped her purse back up as if indignant. It helped that none of them could see her expression, because her lips couldn't stop twitching.

"It's not nastiness, it's a yeast infection," she informed them in a prim tone. "They're very common. After another week of treatment, it'll be gone, or so my doctor tells me. You remember the doctor's appointment I had last week, right, Robert? Well, this is what it was for. My doctor even put me on antibiotics to help ensure that the bacteria doesn't spread and turn into a urinary tract infection as well."

Lie number three. Isa *had* gone to the doctor and gotten antibiotics, true, but that was for the sore throat she'd claimed to have. Then she'd bought every kind of over-the-counter yeast infection treatment available and stuffed it all in her purse, just waiting for the moment when Robert might try this.

"You . . ." Robert didn't seem to know what to say. Isa turned back to him, biting the inside of her cheeks hard to keep from grinning. Robert gave one more disgusted glance at Isa's purse before he continued.

"Get yourself fixed up, and call me if that mook comes back. I'll see you, uh, in a couple days."

Ritchie and Paul hurried after him. Only when Isa heard Robert's car pull away with a squeal of tires did she allow herself to break into a smile.

Her head chef Frank came out of the prep room. From his smile, he'd heard every word.

"You're one sadistic chick," he said admiringly.

Isa's grin widened. "Never underestimate the power of a woman." Then she patted her purse. "Or Vagisil."

Isa came out of her bathroom, toweling the wetness from her hair—and froze.

Chance was in her bedroom, one hand resting on her end table while the other stroked the fabric of the overstuffed chair he was sitting in.

"You don't lock your windows," he said chidingly.

Unbidden, her gaze went to the window and then back to him. She was on the fifth floor of a brownstone condo, and the fire escape had long been broken. How in the world . . . ?

"Are you a freaky cat burglar or something? Well, sorry, because everything I've got is tied up in the restaurant."

He ceased stroking her chair with a half-smile. "I'm something, but it's not a cat burglar."

It occurred to Isa that the proper thing to do was call 911. Or scream for help. Or run into her bathroom and lock the door while doing all of the above. After all, this was a man she'd just met two days ago. He could

be a mass murderer for all she knew. Maybe her grandmother had gotten him involved, but that didn't mean
he was safe.

"So what are you?" she asked instead, tightening her
robe around her. Good thing she hadn't just strolled out
naked. That would have made this even more discon-
certing than it already was.

Chance gave her a very serious look. "You're not
ready to know what I am, so don't ask me that question when you don't really want a truthful answer
to it."

Arrogant man. Where was her purse full of
testosterone-repellent when she needed it?

"I could have you arrested for breaking and entering," she said, dropping the towel from her head.

Chance shrugged. "Go ahead, but then Robbery will
hear I was in your house and he'll *insist* you stay with
him. I don't think you want that, do you?"

Clever jerk. That's exactly what would happen, and
no amount of Vagisil in the world would stop it. No, Isa
didn't want that, and for some strange reason, she didn't
think she was in any danger from Chance, so she wasn't
going to call the police.

"All right. What do you want bad enough to break
into my home for?"

"A chance to talk to you," he replied instantly. "It's
so much nicer when—what did you call them?—Bowling
Ball and Smelly aren't around to interrupt us."

A gorgeous, mysterious man broke into her bedroom
because he wanted to *talk?* Isa rolled her eyes. Yep,
that sounded like her luck.

"Well, Chance, it's two A.M. and I'm tired, so make it
quick."

He stretched, rippling his muscles from shoulders to

knees in one sinuating motion. Isa just stared. Wow. That was something she'd like to see again.

From the new tug at his mouth, he'd guessed her thoughts. Oh well. Isa was sure she wasn't the first woman to find that impressive.

"I'm going to stop this wedding and get your brother back unharmed," Chance said as mildly as if he were commenting on the weather. "But I'll need you to keep up your pretense of being Robert's fiancée in the meantime."

Yet another person to tell her that. Isa hadn't liked hearing it from her brother over two weeks ago, and it didn't sound any more enticing now.

"Of course you are. Then you're going to give me multiple orgasms and pay off my mortgage too. I saw this movie, pal. It was in the fantasy section."

The grin he flashed her was decadent. "Do I get to pick the order in which these things will occur? Because I do have a preference, Isabella."

There was that hint of green in his eyes again. It made her heart speed up, and when he gave her a slow up-and-down appraisal it made her feel warm all over. Like she was being caressed.

Chance inhaled with a long, deep breath that somehow seemed as intimate as a kiss. Self-consciously, Isa brushed her hair back from her forehead. Yes, it was definitely getting warmer in here.

"And just how are you going to get my brother back without getting him—and possibly me—killed in the process?" she asked, to distract herself from counting how long it had been since she'd had sex. Ugh, if she counted *good* sex, then she'd have to break out more of her old calendars than she cared to count.

"I'm going to find out where your brother is, and once I get him safely away, then I'm going to convince Robert that it's in the best interest of his health never to bother you or your family again."

Isa snorted in a very unfeminine fashion. "How? Are you a world-renowned hypnotist?"

Chance didn't laugh. "Something like that."

She stared for a different reason this time. He was serious. Good Lord, maybe he *was* a dangerous crazy person. Where had her grandmother dug him up from, anyway?

"You should go now," Isa said slowly. "And once again I'm going to tell you to stay out of this. You don't understand what Robert's like if you think you can hocus-pocus your way around him. He'll kill you. He'll bury you right next to Jimmy Hoffa and no one will ever find your body, got it?"

Chance sighed. "Would a demonstration make you feel better?"

Demonstration? "Um, of what, exactly?"

"My hocus-pocus abilities, as you call them."

Isa shifted. This was getting weirder by the minute. "Look, why don't you just go . . ."

"You can open your eyes now."

Isa blinked—and then jerked back in shock. She was on the chair with Chance. On his *lap*, to be more precise, with her arms around his neck and her mouth mere inches from his. Holy shit, how the hell did *that* happen?

Chance watched Isa scramble off him, her knuckles white as she clutched her robe. She backed away several feet, looking around her bedroom as if expecting to see someone else there.

"What did you do to me? How did I end up on your lap?" she demanded.

It would be so much easier to tell her the truth. To *show* her the truth, since once he said, "I'm a vampire," she'd just insist on proof anyway. But the suspicion in her gaze stopped him. Well, that, and the simple fact that he wanted Isa to get to know him better before she found out what he was. Chance had lived long enough to recognize what was stirring in him—and to appreciate that it didn't happen often.

Sure, he'd been attracted to her since the first night he watched her, then he'd grown to like her for her spunk and bravery, but that wasn't what was rare. It was the additional feeling she inspired. The one of connection, like she was someone who *should* be part of his life. Some people called it chemistry, others called it infatuation, some even called it fate. Chance didn't care what name was stuck on it. He only knew it was real.

And she felt something for him, too. He could smell it in the way her scent changed around him, the way her heart beat faster when he stared at her, and the way her body leaned toward his even as her eyes were rimmed with caution. Oh, part of that was just the attraction of a compatible woman to a compatible man, but there was more as well. Chance intended to find out how much more, and then he'd show her what he was, because he wasn't going to hide himself from her for much longer.

"I used my hocus-pocus and hypnotized you," he replied. It was mostly true. He just wasn't going to elaborate that his power was derived from being a vampire.

"You hypnotized me?" she repeated. "With what?"

He shrugged. "My gaze and my voice." Again, true enough.

Isa began to pace. "This is too weird. You're some kind of wacko David Copperfield and my grandmother hired you to abracadabra my brother safely back?"

"I told you this wasn't about money," Chance corrected.

"Whatever!" Isa said. Then her gaze narrowed. "You didn't do anything perverted while I was on your lap, did you?"

Chance folded his arms across his chest. "If you think I'm some lowlife scum who'd coerce a woman into doing something sexual against her will, then I suggest you *do* call the police. I had you come over to me because it proved that I can do what I claim I can do. You certainly wouldn't have perched on my knee of your own inclination just then, would you? But that was all you did, Isa, and my hands remained at my sides the entire time."

He locked his gaze with hers until she looked away, but the suspicion had left her eyes. There was still confusion, yes, and a healthy dose of wariness . . . but no more angry accusation.

Isa flounced on the side of her bed. "So . . . you can walk up to Robert and um, hypnotize him into telling you where Frazier is?"

"Yes," Chance said simply.

She chewed her lip. It had been over two weeks since her brother last contacted her. Even if he *had* managed to sneak away to make that phone call, maybe he'd been caught and dragged back. All the uncertainty over her brother's fate made Isa reckless. She couldn't just sit back and accept Robert's assurances that Frazier was okay. If all she had on her side right now was a trespassing honor-bound hypnotist— well, She'd just have to make the best of it.

"Assuming you can do that, Frazier's got to be guarded. You're pretty good with your little trick one on one, obviously, but up against several mini-gangsters with guns? You'd get shot before you even got near Frazier. Or the two of you would get shot before you managed to get away. We need to coordinate when this is going to happen. Robert's house is huge, and he likes to keep things close to him, so you should check for Frazier there first. I can go over to Robert's and leave a door open or something. Then I can, um, distract him while you sneak up on him and try your David Copperfield act."

"Isa . . . that's very brave of you, but it's not necessary. I can get in Robert's house with very little effort, and neither he nor his men will be able to keep me from leaving."

"Your arrogance could get my brother killed!" she snapped. "Excuse me if I'm not comfortable with that!"

He met her gaze very steadily. "I've done this before. My sire trusts me. Your grandmother trusts me. You're going to have to trust me as well."

She gave him a hard look. One that said she wasn't used to trusting anyone but herself. Chance could appreciate that. He'd lived with it as his credo for most of his human twenty-seven years.

"Look at it this way," he urged her next. "Where are

you now? Dependent on Robert's very questionable mercy that he won't kill your brother, that's where. You're using the only bargaining chip you have—yourself—to ensure Frazier's safety, but Robert still holds all the cards. You need to have an ace up your sleeve that Robert won't expect. Well, Isabella, I am that ace, and you can trust that Robert will never expect me at all."

"I'm doing okay," she replied with obvious defensiveness. "I didn't see *you* at the restaurant earlier deflating Robert's hard-on!"

A grin touched Chance's mouth. "Ah, yes. Your galloping yeast infection. A very clever move. I'm sure Mini-Mob won't be able to get it up for days."

"Mini-Mob?" Isa laughed. Chance enjoyed seeing her face light up with it. "An Austin Powers fan, are you?"

"Guilty as charged."

"Wait a minute." Isa's laughter cleared at once. "How did you know that? You *weren't* there. How could you possibly know that?"

Because I'd been on the roof of the building across the street, listening to you all night. And I almost swooped down and ripped Robert's balls off with my bare hands when I heard him suggest that you were going home with him. Robert should thank his lucky stars you had your fake yeast infection as a shield, or he'd never become a father.

But Chance couldn't say that, of course. He couldn't tell Isa that he'd been watching her long past what his initial reconnaissance had required. Or that while she'd been in the shower earlier, he'd lain in her bed just so her scent could wrap all around him.

Yes, whatever word applied to Chance's condition, he had it bad.

"I was following Robert for a chance to get him alone," was what Chance settled on. "So I was near enough to the restaurant earlier to hear what happened. None of them ever knew, and neither did you. I've had some practice with this, Isabella. You can trust me."

He so very much wanted her to trust him, because his deliberate vagueness and these multiple unfinished sentences were wearing. If there was one thing he'd learned in his century-plus of living, it was that honesty was a cornerstone in a relationship. Women would forgive many things, but lies were at the top of their list for unpardonable sins. If Isa demanded more direct answers from him, Chance would give them to her. No matter if she was ready to hear them or not.

She chewed on her lip again. Chance watched her and wanted to do the same.

He might be having that "so I'm a vampire," conversation sooner rather than later with her. Inhaling the fragrance of her arousal earlier had almost outed him from his coffin, because he'd felt his eyes start to change and fangs press lustfully against his gums of their own accord. Even now, his blood wanted to rush to a particular place, and Chance had to concentrate to send it elsewhere. He pitied human men who had no control over that. The ability to direct his blood where he wanted it to go was just another perk of being a vampire. It beat the hell out of walking around trying to conceal a hard-on, and on the flip side, no vampire *ever* had to worry about impotence.

"Okay," Isa said finally. "I'll let you try to work your

mojo on Robert to locate my brother, but if you find out where he is, you *call* me, understand? Because if something goes wrong—"

"Nothing will," Chance interrupted her firmly.

She gave him that look again. The one that said plenty of things had gone wrong in her life. Chance remembered reading that her parents died in a small plane crash while vacationing in the Bahamas when Isa was just thirteen. Her grandmother had been the one to raise her and Frasier. Yes, Isa would have learned young that life promised no happy endings, but in this case, Chance could at least promise he wouldn't make any mistakes with Frazier.

If he was even still alive.

Chance pushed that thought away. He'd assume Frazier was alive until he was shown his dead body. The fact that Ritchie and Paul hadn't known where he was when he asked them the other night—not that they remembered the body they'd wrapped in plastic had sat up and interrogated them, of course—concerned Chance. He would have thought Robert's top two meatheads would have been privy to that information, but maybe Robert played things closer to the vest. It would be smart of him, considering how weak-minded Smelly and Bowling Ball were. Robert himself was made of sterner stuff. Chance figured he'd have to drink his blood first to get what he wanted out of him, whereas Ritchie and Paul only required the light in his gaze to spill their secrets.

"Nothing will go wrong," Chance repeated, and meant it. If Frazier Spaga was still alive, he'd bring him back that way to his sister. If he was already dead . . . then Chance would see to it that everyone who'd had a part in his demise met the same fate as well.

Isa gave him a level look. "I'm going to hold you to that."

Isa sat across from her grandmother and watched as she made tea. It was their Saturday afternoon ritual that Isa would have gladly done herself, but her grandmother was still fiercely independent and wouldn't hear of it. Her only capitulation to Isa's concerns about her health was to wear the LifeCall alert Isa had gotten her. Isa noted her thinness and the translucence of her flesh that was common with advanced age, and had to blink back tears.

She'll be gone soon, Isa thought with a stab of grief. It was doubly hard, since her grandmother had been both mother and father to her since Isa was thirteen, and Frazier even younger at nine. Then a mere five years after her parents had died, Isa's grandfather passed as well.

Some people would be broken from grief, but Greta Spaga dried her tears after her husband's funeral and said that death was simply part of life. That prolonged mourning only stole the good memories of the person who was gone. Isa doubted she'd have the same strength.

Now, over ten years later, Frazier was missing and Isa would have agreed to almost anything to keep her grandmother from facing another crushing family loss. The old woman might be strong as steel emotionally, but there was still only so much one person could take.

There was only so much Isa could take as well. Robert never said the words directly, but Isa knew that her brother wasn't the only collateral he was holding against her. She'd seen Paul and Ritchie drive by her grandmother's a few times when they knew Isa was there to spot them. Their actions screamed that more than Frazier would pay if Isa refused to do what Robert wanted.

"Here you are," her grandmother said, setting down Isa's cup of tea.

"So tell me about Chance," she said, trying to distract herself and genuinely wanting to know more about the sexy oddball.

Her grandmother smiled as she set her own cup down with more of a clatter.

"Downright tasty looking, isn't he?" Greta asked slyly.

Isa almost choked on a swallow. There was no mistaking the wicked note to her grandmother's voice.

"I meant, where'd you meet him? What does he *do* for a living? And how long have you known about Frazier, while we're at it?"

"Hmm, where'd I meet Chance? A long time ago in Louisiana. What does he do for a living?" Greta paused to cackle. "He doesn't do anything for a *living,* dear. How long have I known about Frazier? Since he didn't call me on Tuesday three weeks ago to check in. Frazier always calls me on Tuesdays. He hasn't missed one in the past five years."

Isa's mouth dropped. Her brother Frazier, who couldn't remember anyone's birthday and who hadn't held a steady job since *Melrose Place* was a hit, called their grandmother faithfully every Tuesday?

Greta tsked. "Don't look so shocked. Frazier's a bit high-strung, but so was I at his age. He's settled down a lot, Isa. You shouldn't judge him so harshly."

Now Isa did choke on her tea, lightly spraying herself with it. Once she'd regained her breath, she was glad it happened. Or she might have shouted, "High-strung? Associating with crime lords is a bit more than *high-strung!*"

But her grandmother didn't need the added worry of learning about how Frazier had cozened up to Robert these past few months. Hell, Isa had Frazier to thank for the fact that Robert had even stepped foot in her restaurant in the first place. Sure, Frazier tried to dissuade Robert once he saw the interest Robert immediately took in her, but by then, it had been too late.

"Tell me more about Chance," Isa managed. Anything except how Frazier was a misunderstood softie.

Her grandmother stared at her without speaking for so long, Isa repeated the question, thinking maybe her hearing was finally slipping.

"Oh, I heard you the first time," Greta said, still studying her. "You've always been such a serious child. Why, you stopped believing in Santa Claus *way* before your other friends did, and once your parents died, you stopped believing in a lot more things, didn't you?"

"What does this have to do with Chance?" Isa asked, squirming under that too-knowing pale brown gaze.

"A lot," her grandmother replied sharply. "Once your parents were dead, you stopped believing in people themselves. That's why you withdrew from all your friends. That's why you've never let any of your boyfriends get close to you, and that's also why I haven't told you certain things that otherwise, you would know by now."

Isa stood, looking at her watch with a fake expression of regret. Yes, she'd wanted to find out more about Chance, but not at the price of ripping open wounds she'd tried so hard to forget were there.

"Sorry I can't stay, but I'm supposed to open the restaurant today. That's right, Frank . . . Frank said he had an appointment. I have to go."

Her grandmother snorted, as eloquent as a twenty-minute dissertation on how Isa was full of shit.

"Fine, go. But before you do, I'll say one thing about Chance: Don't think the world contains only what you've been taught at school. Oh no, my dear. That's just the first layer of it."

Isa gave her a kiss and then got out of there as fast as possible. It would have been easier if her grandmother was wrong, instead of all too accurately nailing her with observations Isa would just as soon not acknowledge.

Chance was outside waiting for Isa when she locked up later that night. He saw her start in surprise when she spotted him leaning against the far side of her restaurant's building, and then the tension left her shoulders.

"You scared me," she said accusingly.

He cast a meaningful look around at the almost empty parking lot and the deep shadows where the streetlights failed to penetrate.

"As well you should be wary. You're a beautiful young woman walking without an escort at one in the morning. Why doesn't one of your staff at least see you to you car?"

"Because they're not sexist pigs who think women are incapable of taking care of themselves."

Chance rolled his eyes. "This has nothing to do with feminism. I'm all for gender equality, but the fact remains that women are targeted for more specific crimes than men, and the perpetrators of those crimes often look for circumstances such as these to attack."

"See this?" Isa pulled something dark and oblong out of her purse. Chance's mouth twitched.

"Turbo Vagisil?"

"No, it's a taser!" Isa said indignantly. "I can take care of myself, Chance. I've been doing that just fine for the past twenty-nine and a half years *before* you showed up, remember?"

He'd forgotten how hard it was to start a relationship. Casual dating, casual sex, or casual bloodletting was easy, but this? Chance figured it was a good thing he wasn't growing any older.

"Of course," he said, reminding himself that what was once considered polite concern for a lady's well-being was now obviously cause for insult. "But if it's all right with you, I'd like to walk you to your car. I mean no disrespect and I am fully aware that you can take care of yourself. May I?"

Isa hesitated, then nodded. "Okay."

Chance took her arm when she drew even with him. She looked like she might pull away, but then she relaxed and kept it curled around his. Now he could feel her pulse speed up as well as hear it, and he found himself staring at her profile. Her black hair had been up in a neat twist at the beginning of the evening, but now it was coming loose with long pieces falling over her shoulders. She was chewing on her lower lip again, worrying it faintly between her teeth as they walked. Chance's tongue traced his lower lip as he watched, imagining it was hers instead and wondering how she tasted.

Isa stopped next to her vehicle. Instead of letting her arm go, Chance held on and faced her.

She met his eyes—and quickly looked away. "No luck on, ahem, speaking with Robert?"

"No. He's meeting with several guests who flew in this morning. They're staying at his house and they have their own entourage of guards as well, so it's not an opportune time."

"Probably the Salucci brothers," Isa murmured. "They're another lovely criminal family vying for that oh-so-coveted 'made man' status. They're rivals of Robert's, too, if what I've overheard about them is true. I don't know why they'd stay with him. They don't like each other."

"Probably because to refuse is to admit fear, and then that gives Robert the upper hand. Don't worry. I listened in on them and they'll be gone tomorrow. That means tomorrow night, I'll have my talk with Robert."

Isa shivered. "So many things could go wrong . . ."

"They won't," Chance said.

She gave him a jaded look. "Sure, you managed to get me to perch on your lap like a kid visiting Santa, but doing that and getting a mobster to spill his secrets is worlds apart. Not to mention that you're the one with the greatest threat of repercussions if you failed. Robert might make things unpleasant for me or Frazier if you can't pull off your hocus-pocus routine, but he'll *kill* you. You know that, right? Really, I don't understand why you're doing this to begin with."

"I told you it was a matter of honor," Chance replied.

A sharp bark of laughter escaped Isa. "Honor. Who knew anyone still cared about that nowadays?"

Chance didn't reply. Yes, it was true honor was an undervalued commodity according to modern human standards, but in the vampire community, it still had strong merit. Bones had asked him for a favor and Chance had promised to grant it. That meant whatever the risks, he'd take them.

Of course, since he'd spent time with Isa, he knew he'd take those same risks regardless of his sire. He felt drawn to her in ways he hadn't felt for anyone in a long time. In order to see where it led, there were a lot worse dangers Chance would take on than a spoiled-brat mobster.

"I wanted to thank you," Isa said at last, meeting his eyes squarely. "Guess I never have gotten around to doing that. You're taking a huge risk, and whatever your reasons, I really appreciate it."

He smiled. "You're more than welcome, Isabella."

Chance heard her heart begin to thump with an irregular, advanced rhythm. Her gaze flicked to his lips—and stayed there.

His hand was still on her arm. There was less than

a foot between them. Isa shivered, but it wasn't cold out. No, the luxuriant new scent drifting from her said she was feeling anything but cold at the moment.

Chance's hand tightened on her arm as he moved closer. Now there wasn't a foot between them, but mere inches. Her pulse sped up even more as he leaned down.

Right before his mouth brushed hers, however, Isa turned her head. Chance didn't follow the movement, but let his lips caress her cheek instead. *So soft and warm.* It was all he could do to keep his tongue from flicking out and tasting her.

Isa gave a shaky laugh. "I must be *really* tired. Here I am, engaged to Robert Mini-Mob Bertini, and yet about to make out with a virtual stranger in a public place. For my next idiotic trick, maybe I'll call Robert and dare him to kill Frazier."

Chance's fingers played with the skin on her arm. "Is being in a public place your only objection? Because that can be remedied."

Another sweet wave of scent came off her even as she backed away.

"I-I have to go," Isa stammered, not answering his question. "You'll call me after you speak with Robert, right?"

Chance made no move to stop her. He just stared at her as she got into her car and shut the door a little too hard.

"I'll speak to you as soon as I'm done with him, yes."

"All right." Isa paused, looked like she was about to say something else, then put the car in gear. Chance heard her mutter under her breath, "I must be crazy," right as she pulled away.

He smiled to himself. *No, darling, you're not crazy. You're just fighting your emotions—something I learned long ago will always win in the end.*

Chapter 5

 Isa dreamed her restaurant had turned into a breakfast diner. Frank was whipping up bacon, eggs, hashbrowns, and assorted omelets while coffee brewed from multiple pots. The smell of freshly baked bread permeated the air as Isa hurried from table to table, making sure every customer had what they needed, rotating the order of the tables for the wait staff, and checking food supplies. Meanwhile, she was so *hungry*. All the sights and smells from the kitchen teased her, making her stomach knot with need. Still, she didn't stop. The responsibilities of the restaurant came first. Once the breakfast rush was over, she'd have Frank fix her a large plate, but until then, there was work to do.

"Isabella."

She turned to see who'd called her name, but all the faces in the diner seemed to blur out of focus.

"Isabella, wake up."

Her eyes snapped open. She was in her house. In her

bed, and there was no breakfast diner, no rush of hungry customers to attend to, and no staff to oversee.

So why was it that she could still smell bacon, bread, and coffee?

"Am I going to have to come in there and wake you?" a voice she now recognized asked.

Isa stiffened, pinching herself to make sure she wasn't still dreaming. No, she definitely felt that, and yes, once again, Chance was in her home.

Her gaze went to the window. Had he gotten in through there again? Or did he go through the front door this time, because maybe he was an expert lock-picker as well? More importantly, why wasn't she angry? Why was she getting out of bed, smoothing her hand over her sleep-tousled hair, and wondering if she should put on something more appealing than her long cotton pajamas with their constellation pattern?

She heard a clatter of pans. "I know you're awake. Come on out, your breakfast is getting cold."

"Nothing comes before the bladder," Isa muttered under her breath, surprised when she heard him laugh a moment later. He couldn't have heard her . . . could he?

She walked into the kitchen five minutes later, too proud to change out of her pajamas, but conceding to brush her teeth and run a wet towel over her face. As far as her hair—well. It was hopeless, as it always was in the morning.

Chance was in the middle of her kitchen, looking far better than what was in the array of pans on her stove. He had on a light blue shirt that complimented his pale skin and deep brown hair, plus a pair of darker blue, loose-fitting jeans. His feet were bare, and Isa found herself momentarily fascinated by them. They seemed at once so completely masculine and yet so . . . cute.

She stopped staring at his feet to sit on one of the stools across from her counter.

"You're a regular repeat offender with the breaking and entering, aren't you?" she asked flippantly.

Chance grinned. "You skipped dinner last night. One would think since you owned a restaurant, you'd get around to eating, but apparently not."

She *had* skipped dinner last night, but how did he know that?

"Aren't you supposed to be spying on Robert, not me? Or better yet, breaking into *his* home, not mine?"

He heaped generous portions of bacon, eggs, and hashbrowns onto a plate before sliding it across to her.

"Robert's later tonight. You're hungry now. I'm just going down the line of priorities, darling."

"I told you not to call me that," Isa replied automatically, though she didn't mean it now. Truth be told, she rather liked the caressing way he said "darling."

And the look in his eyes when he said it was even better.

Oh, shit. She was *so* in trouble. Last night after almost kissing him, Isa had berated herself for hours about the stupidity of getting involved with some pseudo-magician whacko—albeit a smolderingly sexy one—when she still had to find her brother *and* get out of marrying a career criminal. Yet here she was now, getting all starry-eyed over something as benign as Chance's feet, for crying out loud.

That was it. She was getting a vibrator. Clearly she was in need of sexual healing, and right now a battery-operated device had the least amount of complications.

The timer on her oven went off. Chance turned around with a graceful spin and then lifted out a pan of wonderful-smelling bread. Isa's mouth watered even though she'd just taken a bite of food.

"You'd make a great chef," she said once she'd swallowed. "Ever think of leaving the honor-bound, criminal-interrogating hypnotist society to try your hand at that?"

Chance sliced her a steaming piece of bread, an odd smile on his face. "I can never leave the society I'm part of, Isabella. Once you become a member, you stay that way forever."

"Then I hope they have a hell of a retirement plan," she quipped.

That made Chance grin, highlighting the dimple on his chin. "The best there is, I assure you."

He took the stool next to Isa, but didn't bother getting himself a plate. Isa gestured with her fork at all the food spread out in front of her.

"Are you going to eat anything?"

His lips were parted, so Isa could see his tongue flick out to caress the tops of his teeth.

"Later."

There was something in the purr of that single word that made Isa suddenly lose her appetite. Her appetite for *food,* to be more specific. Another appetite reared its long-neglected head and began screeching to be satisfied.

Chance reached out, gently brushing her hair back from her face. His hand was cool against her cheek, like silk made into flesh. Isa drew in a breath, noting with curious detachment that it was uneven. Funny, the more she stared into Chance's eyes, the more she became convinced they were turning green.

"Back away, Chance. We need to keep things professional between us."

She made herself say it, because even if it wasn't true, it made sense to utter those words. Chance was practically a stranger, and a peculiar one at that. So what if she was drawn to him in ways she'd never felt before? So what if he fascinated her with his unusual mix of courtliness and utter disregard for the law? Getting Frazier back safely was her top priority, period. That meant canoodling with a local crime boss who thought she was going to marry him, *not* making out with an out-of-town hypnotist who might get killed with his next act.

Chance leaned closer, so that the breath from his words fell directly on her lips.

"You don't want to."

Boy, was he right about that. Keep things professional? Hardly. All Isa wanted to do now was press her mouth against his and rake her tongue inside until she couldn't taste anything but him.

Chance's nostrils flared. He closed his eyes and took in a deep, slow breath.

Isa closed her eyes as well. If she tilted her head even the *slightest* way in either direction, his lips would brush hers. Chance was that close to her. Yet she couldn't do it, and she instinctively knew it was what he was waiting for.

"Why are you fighting this so hard?" he whispered.

The question startled Isa into opening her eyes and sitting back, putting a safer distance between them. She ran a trembling hand through the same part of her hair Chance had smoothed away moments before.

"Because I want it too much."

Her honesty surprised her more than his question had. Chance took in another deep breath, his eyes still closed, and then he leaned back as well. Now there were a few feet of distance between them. Isa couldn't help but feel disappointed, even though it was her own fault.

Chance opened his eyes. They didn't look green-tinged anymore, and somehow that made Isa realize how serious he was.

"After I get back from speaking with Robert, you and I need to talk. I've lived too long not to recognize what a rare thing this is between us, but there are certain things about me you need to know before we go further."

"Are you married?" Isa asked at once, dread in her belly.

A soft snort escaped him. "No."

"A CIA agent? Illegal alien in search of a green card? Wanted criminal?"

"Nothing like that. Stop guessing, trust me, you wouldn't pick it at random, and as I said, I'll tell you later. After I've discovered what's going on with your brother."

Frazier's predicament did come first. Wasn't that why she'd stopped him earlier, when it looked like he'd been nanoseconds from kissing her? So why was she feeling, oh, bereft now?

"I have a feeling I won't like whatever it is you're going to tell me."

Chance gave her such a penetrating look, Isa wondered if mind reading was also part of his skills. It seemed like he was seeing into her fears and weighing them against whatever it was he intended to tell her.

"Either way, you will hear it. And then you'll decide what you want to happen between us."

If she was braver, she would have insisted on hearing it now. But Isa didn't think she could take her uncertainty over Frazier, her fears that her grandmother would be the next person Robert used against her, and whatever tidbit Chance would reveal about himself all at the same time. At least let her have closure on one of those things, then she'd handle the bad news Chance threw her way, because Isa doubted he had something as mundane as unpaid parking tickets to tell her about.

"You're going to Robert's tonight?" was all she said.

Chance nodded. "And afterward, I'll come see you with what I've discovered . . . and to talk."

That clenching in her stomach returned, but Isa forced herself to ignore it.

"Then I guess you'd better get prepared. You have a big day ahead of you."

He slid off the stool, moving like his body was somehow absent of bones and made entirely of coiling muscles instead.

"I'll see you later."

Isa hoped so. She also hoped Frazier was with him. In fact, she couldn't remember when she'd hoped so hard for things she wasn't taking care of herself. *Leaning on another person.* It was so unlike her, yet it was what she was doing now.

"I'm counting on that."

Chapter 6

Chance watched the men below him. The Salucci brothers seemed to be pretending to be Joe Pesci in *Casino*. All bada-boom, bada-bings, and just looking for ways to get insulted. Robert, surprisingly enough, conducted himself with more finesse, though he also seemed to be doing a bad acting job. Any moment now, Chance was sure Robert would lower his voice to a scratchy whisper and make the Salucci brothers an offer they couldn't refuse.

Chance had been around enough genuinely frightening people to know all this bluster and showboating for the camouflage it was. When someone was truly deadly, human or otherwise, he or she didn't waste time trying to convince people about it. No, he or she just killed everyone around them who had a dissenting opinion. *That's why you'll always be a bridesmaid and never a bride*, Chance thought while looking at Robert. *You think if you kill a few people,*

*bribe a few cops, dress in Armani suits and have a
cookie-cutter Italian wife, the real mafia will welcome you into their fold. But you're wrong. They can
smell a poser almost as well as I can smell my next
dinner.*

Still, at least this grandiose dick-measuring contest
between the Salucci brothers and Robert afforded
Chance an easier way of grabbing him. Robert had
even picked the Penn station docks along the Delaware
River at midnight for their powwow. The clichés were
so thick, Chance was almost choking on them.

"You're makin' a mistake," the older Salucci brother
told Robert before he turned with a dramatic swirl of
his trench coat. He stalked off, his younger brother and
bodyguard in tow. They got into the black Bentley that
had been running the entire time, and the driver peeled
off with a squeal of tires.

"Finally," Chance muttered. He gave Paul's jugular
a caressing glance. Paul had eaten about a dozen
doughnuts before this meeting, Chance knew, because
the heavy smell of fried sugary goodness wafted up
to him even from his light pole perch. Chance licked
his lips. *Mmm, dinner* and *dessert, all at the same
time.*

Chance dropped down from the tall broken street-
light. It never ceased to amaze him how some humans
could be so oblivious to their environment—especially
ones who prided themselves on being cunning. If Robert, Paul, or Ritchie had even *once* looked up, they
would have noted that the south street light was signifi-
cantly taller than the ones around it. They might not
have been able to see what—or who—was perched on
it in the darkness, but they could have realized that
something was there.

Instead, they just gaped at him when he appeared behind them with nothing more than a faint rush of wind to announce him.

"Nice night, isn't it?" Chance remarked.

Robert was the first to recover. His hand slid inside his jacket and he pulled out his gun.

"Yeah, it is. Paul, Ritchie? You gonna stand there, or are you gonna pull your pieces and maybe point them at this asshole?"

Chance watched with amusement as they scrambled to obey, replacing their formerly amazed expressions with tough ones.

"You just don't fucking learn," Paul breathed. "We do, though. Ritchie, pat down this joker and make sure he's not hiding any more bulletproof vests. Or wires."

Chance spread his arms out obligingly as Ritchie came closer. The other man was wary, no doubt remembering how Chance easily had dodged his attempts to pummel him before. *Don't worry*, Chance thought coolly as Ritchie gave him several quick, thorough pats. *If I wanted you dead, your blood would already be warming my stomach.*

"He's clean," Ritchie announced.

Chance wrinkled his nose with mild distaste. "Can't say the same about you. Really, man, soap is nothing to fear."

Ritchie reared back like he was going to punch him, but Robert grabbed his arm.

"Did I tell you to hit him?" he asked in a dangerous undertone.

Ritchie gave Chance a hateful glare before facing his boss. "No. Sorry."

Robert clapped him on the shoulder. "All right."

Then he turned his attention to Chance. "They told me you had a smart mouth. Okay, smart mouth, we're going to take a walk. And then we're going to take a ride. You got a problem with that?"

"If I did, I suppose Bowling Ball and Smelly would just shoot me again," Chance drawled.

Robert shook his head. "Not them. You know what they say. When you want something done right, you gotta do it yourself."

Chance let out a bark of amusement. "My thoughts exactly."

They led him at gunpoint to the far end of one of the finger piers where a boat was moored. Robert waved, and a man on board waved back, powering the craft to life.

Chance was rather impressed that Robert had arranged to have another getaway from the docks. The Salucci brothers hadn't had that foresight. They seemed more brute muscle than operative brains. In a straight physical fight they might win, but if it was a matter of strategic planning, Robert would prevail. Not that Chance cared. The lot of them could drop dead and society would be far better off. In fact, he'd probably be helping society very soon when it came to that. Just not before he had his questions answered.

Chance went aboard the boat, surmising that this was an excellent opportunity to get Robert to himself *and* dispose of Paul's body, if he did decide to indulge and eat him. When the four of them were clustered around the back of the boat, the driver sped off without much consideration for the waterway's "no wake" zone.

Ritchie and Paul gestured with their guns for Chance to sit on the aft bench, which he did, stretching his legs before settling down comfortably.

After about twenty minutes of glaring at him while the boat navigated the waterway, Robert spoke.

"So, what's your name?"

"Chance."

Robert grunted. "Bullshit. What's your *real* name?"

"Ask your men. Didn't they find any identification when they rummaged through my pockets the other night?"

"You know fucking well you didn't have a scrap of ID on you that night. Plus, Paul and Ritchie tell me you must've been wearing Kevlar, on account of you bein' here instead of resting in plastic under six feet of dirt. What I want to know is, what kind of a man walks around with no ID while wearing Kevlar? Seems pretty paranoid to me."

Chance shrugged. "If you say so."

Paul leaned in and shouted in Chance's face. "Answer the question, asshole!"

"Quit pissing me off," Robert said in a more mild tone. "In my current mood, I have no intention of letting you off this boat alive, so you're gonna need to work to change my mind."

That was meant to scare Chance, but he found it ironic instead.

"I can personally guarantee that I *won't* be getting off this boat alive," he replied.

"He's insane," Ritchie said in wonder. "Look at him. Thinks he can smart-mouth his way out of anything."

Paul held up a length of chain. "See this?" he asked,

rattling it for effect before he began to wrap it around Chance. "We bought this in case things went south with the Salucci brothers. This is fifty pounds of steel. I'm going to tie you up with it and then lock it around you."

Chance glanced down at the chains as Paul began carrying out his threat. If it made them feel more secure . . . and the more time they wasted trussing him up, the further along the river they were getting. *How convenient.* He wouldn't have to worry about anyone overhearing screams.

"You're tryin' my patience," Robert growled. "Now, I'm gonna ask you again, and you'd better cut the shit. What's your name? Your *real* name?"

Chance did have another name, of course. The one he'd been born with well over a hundred years ago, but even though it would be of no use to Robert, he still refused to utter it.

"Chance is the only name you're getting out of me."

Robert jerked his head at Ritchie, who left his position looming over Chance to go around the side of the boat. When he came back minutes later, he was wheeling a large bucket on a dolly filled with something gray and grainy.

Chance closed his eyes, but only so the others didn't see him roll them with annoyance. Couldn't they do *anything* original?

"Cement," Robert supplied, though Chance already knew that. "You keep it up with your smart mouth and that bucket's gonna be your new pair of shoes. There's no getting out of this one. You talk, or I'm gonna shove your chained, cemented ass off this boat. Hell, I'll even let Paul shoot you in the head first, 'cause I know he's itchin' to."

Chance winced. Head shots hurt like hell, silver or no silver. He knew he'd have a terrific headache for about ten minutes while everything knit back into place. *Damned melodramatic mobsters*, he thought irritably. He was eating every last one of them before this whole mess was finished!

But first things first.

Robert watched him with an inscrutable expression. "There's only one thing that'll stop all this unpleasantness from becoming a reality." He leaned forward until his nose was almost touching Chance's. "Tell me where Frazier is, and I'll let you live."

Chance's eyebrows went up. *Well*. He hadn't been expecting that.

"You're the one using Frazier to blackmail Isabella into marrying you, and yet you're telling me you don't know where he is?"

Robert whipped him across the head with the butt of his gun. Chance's fangs nearly popped out on their own accord with the desire to bury themselves into Robert's oh-so-deliciously close jugular, but he controlled himself. As soon as he got off this boat, he'd find a nice tasty person to score a pint off of. Hell, maybe even *two* nice tasty persons. After all, he'd owe himself a treat after getting his brains rearranged.

"Don't fuck with me," Robert said in a menacing tone. "Right after Frazier went missing, you showed up in town shadowing Isa. No one knows you, you don't have no record, no ID, no nothing. It's like you're a fucking ghost. But I don't believe in ghosts, so you know what I think? I think you're some kind of loose-cannon mercenary the Salucci brothers hired to break Frazier out. Isa's a bit shy, so she needed a little persuading to agree to marry me. But if her brother's on the loose, it's a potential issue for me. Makes me look bad, which then means the Saluccis get the syndicate support, and I don't."

"That's an interesting theory," Chance noted. "Go on. I'll tell you if you're getting warmer."

Robert glared at him but continued. "I figure you got greedy. Began playing both sides, since if the Salucci brothers had Frazier, they would have taunted me with it every time they'd been around me. Guess you thought you could drive up whatever price they'd agreed to pay you, because you thought you was holding all the cards. Well, guess what? I call your hand, and you got *nothing*. In fact, you're about five seconds away from a horrible death, and the only thing that's gonna save you is if you tell me where Frazier is. Otherwise, I'm gonna to let Paul shoot you in the head, and then we're gonna throw your dead ass off this boat. You'll spend the rest of eternity rotting on the bottom of this river, understand? So what's it gonna be? Life or death?"

Chance met his gaze with absolute coldness. "Even if I knew where Frazier Spaga was, I would never tell you, so you may as well have your man shoot me and stop wasting my time."

Robert straightened. "You stupid fuck. Those were just your last words."

Chance let a smirking Paul finish wrapping the chains around him before securing them, as promised, with a solid lock. Then he let them press his feet into the cement, piling the gray substance up until it encased his lower calves. He let them lead him to the edge of the boat, the three of them supporting him, since he couldn't very well walk with his feet immobilized in the bucket.

"One last chance," Robert said, pointing at the churning dark water before them. "You talkin' or what?"

Chance smiled icily. "I'll talk the next time I see you, and that'll be sooner than you think."

"Stupid mook," Robert muttered. Then he nodded to Paul, who grinned as he placed his gun to the side of Chance's temple.

"Fuck you," Paul said, and pulled the trigger.

The resulting explosion made Chance unaware of the exact moment when they shoved him in the water. He came to with his feet—still in that bucket, of course—on the river's bottom with his head hurting just as much as he knew it would.

Oh yes. He was going to eat *every last one* of them and use their veins as dental floss!

But first things first . . .

Chance kicked free out of the bucket and ripped the lock off his chains with one hard tug. Then, after a few minutes of unwinding and shaking the last of the cement globs from his feet, he began to ascend toward the surface.

If he had his choice, he'd swim after Robert's boat and drink them all until his stomach bulged, but there were more pressing matters at hand. Someone else had Frazier Spaga. Could Robert have guessed correctly? Was it the Salucci brothers, and they hadn't bragged about it because they were more disciplined than Robert realized?

There was only one way to find out.

Robert's boat was moving at a good clip. None of the men were on the aft side anymore, thus they missed seeing Chance's head pop out from the waves as he began to swim back toward the city.

Isabella looked up as the door to her restaurant banged open. Her heart sank when she saw it wasn't Chance. She'd stayed up all night, but there had been no word from him. Her stomach seemed formed into a perpetual knot of anxiety, and the look on Robert, Paul, and Ritchie's faces as they strode inside only made it worse. It was just a few minutes after two. Her place didn't open until five. Whatever they were here for, it wasn't dinner.

"Frank, Steven, Ed, get outta here," Robert ordered.

Her three chefs gave her an apologetic look as they exited out the back. Isa straightened her shoulders, trying to calm her sudden onslaught of fear. *Where was Chance?* God, had something happened to him? Had he gotten caught trying to get Frazier away? What if they'd both been hurt—or worse?

"What's going on?" she asked, glad her calm voice belied the lurch in her stomach.

Robert smiled as he came across the room. Ritchie

and Paul took up flanking positions on either side of the restaurant's entrance. Robert gave her a kiss on the cheek, and it was all Isa could do not to wipe it away with her butter-smeared hands.

"Just wanted to see my wife-to-be, is all. Nothin' wrong with that, is there? You workin' hard, baby? Not for long. Once we're married, you're quitting this job, but don't worry. Paul's taking over runnin' the place, so you won't have to slave here anymore, but your family's restaurant will still stay in business."

Anger blossomed in her. Oh, she could just imagine how Paul would take over the running of this place. More laundering would get done here than across the street at the dry cleaners. If Isa would have had a gun at that moment, she'd have shot Robert where he stood.

"This is *my* restaurant, and I'll work here as long as I want to."

Robert slapped her. It wasn't a hard blow, but enough to make Isa's cheek sting.

"You listen to me," he said, voice low and resonating as he seized her shoulders and pulled her near. "I've been real patient with you, Isa. A true gentleman, because a man needs to be considerate of the future mother of his children. I let you work here when you should be with my sister planning our wedding. I let you tell me we're not having sex until we're married. I let your miserable brother live when by all rights, I shoulda put a bullet in his head when I caught him snooping around my house. I let all those things happen, but I will *not* let you disrespect me in public. You got spirit, kid. I like that, but there's a time and a place. Don't make me remind you again."

Isa touched her cheek, almost abandoning her promise to Frazier right then, because she would not, *could* not pretend to be this man's fiancée—his *property*—a single moment longer. She even opened her mouth to say the words, but then a voice stopped her.

"Take your hands off her."

Relief flooded through Isa. *It was Chance! He wasn't hurt, thank God, and . . . why did Paul just drop his gun?*

"You're dead," Paul breathed. His face was stark white, and his hand shook as he made the sign of the cross. "I shot you in the head and threw your weighted-down body in the river!"

Isa's eyes bulged at that.

"I am dead," Chance agreed calmly behind her. "And yet I'm still standing here. Makes you wonder how, doesn't it?"

Ritchie seemed equally shaken. He crossed himself too, and Isa heard him mutter the familiar Latin incantation: *"In nomine Patris, et Filii, et Spiritus Sancti . . ."*

Even Robert looked like he'd seen a ghost, which sent a chill up Isa's spine. No one was denying Paul's statement that he'd shot Chance in the head. That wasn't something you'd walk away from afterward, but here Chance was, announcing that he was dead and yet he *still* wasn't going anywhere. Could he have hypnotized them into thinking Paul had shot him? Was such a thing even possible?

Isa swung around to look at Chance, and there was something in his gaze that froze her. She remembered the cool feel of his skin on hers, the way his eyes seemed to change colors, and how he'd gotten into her five-story-high home through the window when there wasn't any fire escape. There was only so much skill or hypnotism could account for. So if it wasn't that . . .

Chance met her stare levelly, as if he knew what was brewing in her mind—and wasn't denying any of it. Once again, her grandmother's words rang in her head. *Don't think the world contains only what you've been taught at school. Oh no, my dear. That's just the first layer of it* . . . Or Chance himself, when she'd asked him what he was. *You're not ready to know what I am, so don't ask me that question when you don't really want a truthful answer to it* . . .

Robert drew out his gun. "Fuck it, I'm shooting you until you *stay* dead!"

Isa heard multiple *pops*, saw a blur of motion . . . and then she was swinging from Chance's grip. Noises seemed to coalesce into one loud murmur, and her stomach felt oddly hot though the rest of her was chilled. She tried to look down, but Chance's arms blocked her. He had them pressed to her stomach even as she realized with shock that they were somehow outside. On rooftops. Moving at speeds that defied any logical explanation.

Then there was a jarring suddenness as they stopped. Chance loomed over her, his face very close . . .

Oh God, his face*!*

Isa screamed. Or tried. It only came out as a wheezing cry of denial. Chance ignored that, whipping a knife out from somewhere on him. *Those glowing eyes, his fangs . . . he's some kind of devil*, she realized dully. Cold slithered further up her limbs. *In nomine Patris* . . .

Chance stabbed her in the side. Isa did scream this time, a high-pitched wail of agony that wrenched out of her soul. There was another horrible, spine-bowing pain as Chance wiggled the knife, and then mercifully, gray encroached her vision. The pain started to fade even as the cold increased. Isa could barely make out Chance's transformed face as he slashed the blade across his wrist next, and then pressed the cut to her open mouth.

Chance took Isa to her grandmother's. It wasn't far, considering he traveled in a beeline by leaping from rooftop to rooftop. Up here, traffic definitely wasn't an issue.

Isa hadn't spoken a word to him since he'd made her drink his blood to heal her gunshot wound. Digging that bullet out of her side had filled Chance with rage, regret, and fear. He hated hurting her that way, but if he hadn't, her flesh would have knit back over the wound soon after she swallowed his blood. Drinking that small amount wouldn't turn her into a vampire—Chance would have needed to mortally drain her first, and then have her drink far more deeply from him—but it would heal her internal and external damage from the gunshot wound. He wouldn't risk her life by taking her to a local hospital; the bullet had torn through her liver. *So close to losing her forever.*

As soon as she was safely at Greta's, Chance was going to hunt down the two shooters and kill them. They wouldn't live out the next hour, either of them.

Chance didn't bother going to the front door, in case Greta was being watched. He leapt from the top of the roof down to the side window with Isa clutched in his arms. To anyone casually looking up, he'd appear as nothing more than a hazy blur. Vampire speed defied human ability to track with the naked eye, so he wasn't worried about 911 calls about a rooftop-jumping superman.

One hard jerk broke the lock on her window. It slid up and Chance maneuvered them inside with one fluid motion. Isa blinked at her surroundings for a second, as if she couldn't believe where she was. Then she shoved against Chance's chest. Hard.

"Let go of me."

She had more force behind the push than she normally would have. Her head bobbed around, listening to noises she wouldn't have heard an hour ago. His blood had done more than just heal her. In the quantity he'd given her, almost a half pint, it had also heightened her strength and senses.

Chance let her go. She backed away from him at once, her gaze flicking around like she expected him to attack. For the tenth time, she rubbed her stomach, feeling the smoothness where there had so recently been a bleeding hole.

"I'm not going to hurt you, Isabella," Chance said quietly.

She let out a derisive bark that stated she didn't believe him. Meanwhile, Chance heard Greta stir in the other room. She must have been taking a nap.

"You were shot," Chance told her, knowing with the instant shock her body would have gone into, she might not have realized that. "I had to dig the bullet out. That's why, with the knife . . ."

Isa backed up until she was almost to the door of the living room. "Who shot me? Robert?"

Chance's mouth tightened. "No. But Robert pulling his gun distracted me from seeing the other two men outside who were taking aim. Apparently the Salucci brothers got tired of negotiating with Robert, and decided a drive-by shooting would be much more efficient instead."

"Those were the pops I heard," Isa murmured, as if to herself. Then she gave Chance a repelled look that pierced his heart. "You're not human."

This wasn't the way he'd intended her to find out, but there was no turning back. Even though he could erase the knowledge from her if he bit her and used his power, Chance refused to manipulate her that way.

"No. I haven't been for a long time."

"What's going on?"

Greta came around the corner, her eyes wide at seeing Chance and Isa in her living room. Hearing the old woman's heart start to beat irregularly, Chance hastened to reassure her.

"It's all right, Greta. Isabella was hurt, but I healed her."

"Isa, what happened?" Greta exclaimed, giving her granddaughter a hug.

Chance saw that while Isa gripped her back, she never took her eyes off him.

"Grandma . . . he's not human. I'm not crazy and I'm not making this up, but Chance isn't *human!*"

Greta tssked. "Well, of course he's not, dear. He's a vampire. I wouldn't have gotten him involved if he'd only been human. He wouldn't have been much use then, would he?"

Isa's mouth dropped. She looked back and forth between Chance and Greta like she expected one of them to suddenly yell, 'Surprise, you're on candid camera!'

"You *knew* this?" she finally managed.

Before Greta could respond, Chance held out a hand. "I have to leave you both now. Greta, don't open the door for anyone, and if there's trouble, call me at once. Isabella, you know how to use a gun, yes?"

"I, um, it's been a long time . . ." she sputtered.

"Good," Chance interrupted. "If anyone but a trusted friend shows up here, you shoot first before you open the door. There shouldn't be more trouble, but it's better to be safe than sorry. I'll be back as soon as I'm done."

"Done doing what?" Isa asked, taking a step toward him before stopping herself.

Chance let his fangs slide out while vampiric green lit up his eyes. Their glow highlighted Isa's face, and she gasped.

"Killing the Salucci brothers," he said, and vaulted out the window.

Chapter 8

Her grandmother stared at Isa, not speaking. Isa didn't know what to say either. So many things had happened, she felt like her entire world had been pulled out from under her.

"So," her grandmother said at last. "You didn't know Chance was a vampire until I told you, but you knew he wasn't human. How'd you figure that out?"

Isa brushed past her into the kitchen, a brittle laugh coming out of her throat. "Let's see, I started to suspect something wasn't right when Paul almost fainted at seeing Chance, because apparently, last night Paul blew Chance's brains out and sank him to the bottom of the river!"

To Isa's surprise, her grandmother began to laugh. "Oh, I wish I'd been there to see the look on Paul's face when Chance walked in. He must have pissed himself!"

"That's not the point!" Isa said harshly, which made her grandmother sober. "The point is that Chance is a vampire, for God's sake! And it's like you don't even care. How did you ever get mixed up with a *vampire*, grandma?"

"Sit down, Isa."

Her tone brooked no refusal. Her grandmother might be as frail as a cobweb physically, but there was still a strident note of command in her voice that said she was a force to be reckoned with nonetheless.

Isa went back into the living room and sat on the couch, scowling. Her grandmother rummaged in the kitchen and then came out with two glasses. Instead of her normal tea, she poured herself a whiskey. And then poured one for Isa as well, handing it to her with a look that dared Isa to refuse it.

"Do you know how old I am?"

Isa blinked, not expecting that question. "Uh, of course. You're seventy-five."

"Wrong," her grandmother said flatly. "I'm a hundred and twenty-six. I was born August second, 1882, in New Orleans, not Yonkers. When my mother ran off before my sixteenth birthday, I had no way to support myself except one—prostitution." She ignored Isa's gasp. "I started off on the streets, but then worked my way up to a nice room on Basin Street where the high-class 'soiled doves' lived. Prostitution was legal in an area of New Orleans back then that the locals called The District. Later, it became known as Storyville.

"One evening, a young man walked in and told the madam he wanted six girls for the entire night. Well, you can imagine how we laughed to ourselves at such a boast. But he paid, so we went upstairs with him." She paused to give Isa a knowing look. "Let me tell you something about vampires. With their stamina, six women for an entire night is simply a healthy start."

"Grandma!" Isa interrupted, shocked beyond further words at the thought of her grandmother being a paid participant with the *undead* in a ménage-a-whatever seven people consisted of.

"Oh, hush," her grandmother said casually. "The man who came to the bordello that night was a vampire named Bones, and he was looking for permanent residents for one of his houses. He showed all of us what he was, and to the three women who panicked, he erased that knowledge with the power in his gaze. To the three of us who didn't, he offered a new life living as his blood donors. We went with him, and he set us up in a beautiful house. Had tutors sent to teach us reading, writing, arithmetic, history, culture, anything we desired. And he gave us the most precious gift of all—the ability to stop aging, for a while at least."

"How?" Isa whispered, her mind reeling at everything she was hearing.

"Blood. Vampires don't age, one of the few things about their legend that's correct, and if you drink blood frequently enough from a vampire, your own aging will slow as well. I lived quite happily with Bones and the other girls for over forty years until I met your grandfather. Then I fell in love, but he had a very closed mind when it came to the supernatural. I either had to choose him and turn my back on everything I'd come to take for granted, or say no to true love. I chose love, Isa, and I haven't regretted it. Following your heart is always the right choice, no matter the circumstances."

Isa drained her whiskey in a gulp. Her grandmother's lips twitched as she sipped more daintily at hers.

"So is that how you met Chance?" Isa asked after a long silence. Then, "Good God, he's not the same vampire you lived with, is he?"

"Heavens, no. I only met Chance once, very briefly when Bones came to visit me after I'd married your grandfather. Then not again before two weeks ago."

This felt like a dream, sitting across from her grandmother discussing vampires, of all things. If Isa hadn't seen Chance's inhumanly glowing eyes herself—not to mention his *fangs*—she'd swear her grandmother was senile by relaying such a story. Still, there was nothing imaginary about a bullet hole in her stomach that wasn't there anymore.

"But Chance has been walking around in the daylight!" Isa suddenly exclaimed. "I thought vampires couldn't do that?"

"Really, dear, if you were an intelligent species that managed to hide your existence from mainstream society for thousands of years, wouldn't it make sense to plant some red herrings along the way? You know, like fake weaknesses such as a deathly aversion to sunlight or crosses? Then, when people saw you strolling around at high noon holding your rosary beads, they'd think, 'Well, that *can't* be a vampire,' because they believe the propaganda that's been deliberately mixed with the legend?"

Isa eyed her empty glass before going into the kitchen and pouring another stiff one. No one should have to process this information sober.

"So they're not all monsters who lie in wait to feed off the blood of the innocent?" she asked hesitantly.

"Some of them are," her grandmother replied with utmost seriousness. "But most of them are decent people who only feed enough to live and don't kill their donors. Most people who've given blood to a vampire don't even remember it afterward. Their gaze is very powerful, and they have the ability to manipulate both behavior and memories. But being a vampire doesn't make them a monster, Isa. They'd have to choose that route for themselves."

So that was how Chance had hypnotized her before. So much for his being a freelance magician.

"And apparently shooting a vampire and sinking him to the bottom of the river doesn't kill one, so what does? A wooden stake through the heart?"

"*Silver* through the heart. Or decapitation, but a vampire won't hand you his or her head. Nor will one stand still and let you poke his heart with silver, either. Never try to battle against a vampire, Isa. They can kill you before you even blink."

Isa remembered how fast Chance had moved at the restaurant earlier. She hadn't even really seen him, he'd only been a blur. Yes, it was easy to believe how deadly vampires could be. Fangs. Mind control. Incredible speed and strength. All of it was very frightening.

. . . with their stamina, six women for an entire night is simply a healthy start . . .

Isa jerked her mind out of the gutter. Okay, so maybe it wasn't *all* frightening.

"You got Chance involved because of me and Frazier," she said at last. "I guess it makes sense. What's scarier than a mobster, if not a creature of the night? Well, why hasn't Chance just . . . eaten Robert, then? It would be no great loss to the world, in my opinion."

"I'm not sure myself," her grandmother replied slowly. "At first I thought it was because he wanted to make sure Frazier was safe. Then I wondered if he was waiting for some sort of backup from Bones. You know, if Chance intended to clean Robert's entire gang off the street, he'd get a few more mouths together to feed off them? But I spoke to Bones today, and he was very surprised to hear Chance still hadn't wrapped things up. So I'm guessing it has to do with you."

"Me?" Isa burst. "What about me?"

Her grandmother sighed. "Youth is truly wasted on the young. Come now, dear. Don't be stupid."

Isa stared at her. Her grandmother stared right back, unblinking. The thought formed in Isa's mind, hitting against wall after wall of uncertainty and anticipation.

Could Chance have been stringing along Robert just to spend more time with her? If so, what was she going to do about that? Scream and grab lots of garlic?

Or meet him with her hair up while wearing a low-necked gown?

Isa shook her head to snap out of her mental meanderings. Frazier was out there somewhere, and whatever she did or didn't feel for Chance, her brother's safety took priority. If Chance had been deliberately slow about bringing this situation to a conclusion, then she would have to speed him along. After all, if she had a vampire on her side to use as a weapon against Robert, then she was damn well going to point and fire him at the would-be mafioso.

"Do you think he was serious?" Isa asked at last, her gaze sliding toward the still-open window. "About killing the Salucci brothers, I mean?"

"Oh, Isa. With how angry Chance was, in all likelihood, they're already dead."

Isa looked at her grandmother and wondered how she had ever, ever thought this woman was a straight-laced Italian housewife. That cold glint in her grandmother's eyes belonged more to a shylock than the gentle old lady who'd raised her.

But as Isa had been reminded via a bullet cut out of her torso by a man who happened to be a vampire, looks were very deceiving.

With everything that happened, Isa never expected to fall asleep. But after being awake all last night, drinking multiple shots of whiskey while she waited for Chance to return, and then lying down on her grandmother's couch, she must have dozed off. A soft touch on her cheek made her eyes flutter open. Chance was kneeling next to her, the room cast in shadows. It was dusk. He'd been gone for hours.

"The Salucci brothers?" she asked quietly.

Chance dropped his hand from her face. "You won't have to worry about them again."

There was a hard satisfaction to his voice that said Isa wasn't the only one who wouldn't have to worry about them. Neither would anyone else on the planet. She supposed she should be aghast that Chance had murdered them so easily, but she could only muster up the faintest feeling of . . . caution.

"What about the police? I'm amazed they haven't come by yet. With holes shot into my restaurant and my staff telling them I'd been there, I thought for sure they'd come to my grandmother's asking about me."

"They won't. I took care of them," Chance replied.

That *did* make Isa uneasy. "Um, the permanent way?"

Chance smiled faintly. "No. The mind-altering way. After I was done with the Saluccis, I went back to your restaurant and pulled aside the lead detective there. He now believes he's spoken to you and that you didn't see who fired the shots. I can't imagine Robert would say anything to contradict that, whenever he surfaces again."

"So Robert wasn't hit earlier? He's okay?"

"For now."

There was that coldness to Chance's voice again. Isa shivered. The man—no, the *vampire*—kneeling just a foot away from her had admittedly killed two people today, and from his tone, he wanted to up that number.

"Robert struck you," Chance said, as if reading her thoughts. "You think I'd let him live after that?"

"Robert's done much worse to a lot more people," Isa countered. "If you're going to kill him, kill him for them, not for me."

Chance shrugged. "Dead is dead, darling. I suspect those other people will care more about the end result than my motivation."

"I care about your motivation," Isa said sharply.

Green began to swirl in Chance's blue-gray eyes. "Do you?"

It seemed like he caressed those two words, as if they had a taste he enjoyed. Isa shivered again, but for a different reason this time.

"Why didn't you show up last night?" she asked, mostly because she was worried about Frazier, but also to cut the growing pull she felt toward Chance. "Was it because of what Paul did to you? I mean . . . did it take a while, to, ah, heal?"

Chance must have seen her refusal in her gaze, because he stood up and walked to the other side of the room.

"No, my head healed very quickly. That's how it is for vampires. Why I didn't show up was because Robert confessed he didn't know where Frazier was. He thought I'd stolen him away, that I was someone the Salucci brothers hired to make him look incompetent. So I paid them a visit last night. An all-too-kind one, as it turned out, since I should have just killed them once I'd gotten what I needed to know out of them. Nevertheless," Chance waved his hand curtly, "that's been remedied."

He hadn't killed the Salucci brothers last night when he could have. She wasn't upset by that, though it had ended up almost costing Isa her life. In fact, she was relieved, because it reinforced her grandmother's claim that vampires weren't random killers despite their vicious legend. Chance had killed the Saluccis today out of necessity. She didn't need him to tell her how violent a power struggle between two competing crime lords could be. She still had the evidence smeared around the hole in her shirt, in fact. If they were alive, the Saluccis would have only become more dangerous. They'd know Robert would retaliate, and anyone caught in the crosshairs would end up as collateral damage. Like she nearly had.

"Did they know anything about Frazier?"

"I'm sorry, no. They truly believed Robert still had him. In the gangster world, Robert holding your brother hostage to ensure you'd marry him isn't the shameful act of cowardice it should be, but just a strong-minded way to get a woman to behave."

The scorn dripping off Chance's words echoed Isa's own anger. All right, now she didn't feel the *slightest* bit bad that they were dead. In fact, she hoped it had hurt.

"This does complicate things, however, since the two most likely sets of suspects in Frazier's disappearance are innocent," Chance went on. "Is there anything about your brother you haven't told me? Anything at all that might shed light on where he could be?"

Isa got up as well and began to pace. "I have no idea where he is. When he called me a couple weeks ago, he just told me to play along being Robert's fiancé and that he'd contact me again, but he hasn't."

A low sound came from Chance. "You neglected to tell me that."

Isa swung around, shooting him an accusing glare. "Oh, don't *even*! If you want to talk about withholding information, I'd say you, Mr. Vampire, are far more guilty than I am!"

Chance inclined his head. "Touché. However, I intended to tell you about that. Remember when I said yesterday we had to talk? It wasn't to discuss a new dish for your menu, darling."

"Yes, well, I don't think *artery d'jour* would go over big with the locals, anyway," Isa muttered.

"You might be surprised. There are more of us than you realize. No doubt you've served several vampires in your establishment already."

"You're the only person who's sat there for two hours without eating," Isa replied, rattled by the thought of the undead mingling among her patrons without her knowing it.

"We can eat solid food, and we can drink liquids aside from blood. It just doesn't nourish us, but if we're out with humans and we're trying to blend in . . ." Chance lifted his shoulder. "When in Rome, as they say."

It still seemed unbelievable to Isa that he wasn't human, because he looked so *normal*. Well, aside from being pale, but then most people were this time of year in Philly.

"Does your heart beat?" she found herself asking.

Chance stared at her. "Come and find out."

She walked over to him, her own heart rate accelerating with every step. It sounded so loud to her, Isa knew Chance had to hear it too. Did it make him hungry? Was that why his eyes began to tinge with green whenever she got close to him?

"Do I need to worry about you eating me?" she joked when there was less than a foot between them.

There was a bright flash of emerald in his eyes. "Not the way you're thinking of."

Her hand froze in mid-reach to his chest. Chance caught it, pressing her palm inside his shirt over where his heart was. Cool, hard flesh met hers, but there was no throb of life underneath. Just stillness.

"You see?" Chance almost whispered. "My heart doesn't beat, I don't breathe, I will never age in appearance, father children, catch diseases, or die of natural causes. I am a vampire. Nothing will change that."

Isa's hand was still on his chest. Chance dropped his hold on her and backed away, letting her fingers slide off until he was out of reach.

"Why are you telling me this?" she asked, equally hushed.

A small, despairing smile curled his mouth. "Because I want you to know everything I am . . . and accept me regardless. My feelings for you have gone far past mere friendly accord. In fact, these are feelings I haven't had for anyone in a very long time. I want you in my life, Isabella, so I'm telling you what that life consists of. Whether you choose to be a part of it is up to you."

Isa glanced down, oddly enough, at her hand. She'd felt no revulsion when it had been pressed to Chance's skin. Yes, he was cooler than she was, but how important was temperature, really? Was it enough to risk the first true tug on her heart she'd experienced? Okay, Chance was a vampire, and that was undeniably a large relationship hurdle. But did it mean she shouldn't even try? Was she going to always run from people because of the pain she'd felt when those closest to her, her parents, had been taken away? Wasn't it time she risked getting hurt again, instead of just accepting the numbness of never letting anyone in? If she kept going on like that, then the real dead person in the room was her, not Chance.

Well, not anymore, Isa thought, and stepped toward him.

Chapter 10

 Chance watched her approach. He didn't move, because he was afraid the slightest unexpected motion from him would stop her. She paused when she was a foot away, reaching out to slide her hand around his neck, and then pulled him down to her.

Chance closed the space between them, wrapping his arms around her and—*at last*—covering her mouth with his. Her lips were soft and she parted them at once, letting his tongue penetrate into the warm sweetness of her mouth.

She tasted like whiskey and honey, so intoxicating, and Chance inhaled through his nose to absorb the waves of desire coming from her. Her heartbeat was a rapid vibration against his chest, the race of blood through her veins like singing, and Chance moaned as he pressed her closer. *I need you,* he thought with a surge of lust so strong, it made his hands itch to tear her clothes from her body. *Give yourself to me.*

Chance didn't dare utter the words aloud, let alone

open his eyes to look at Isa. This was where the power of vampiric mind control could cross unintended lines. With how aroused Chance was, there was no controlling the light in his gaze that would take Isa's decision away from her. He wanted her, yes, so badly—but never enough to steal what should only be given.

Isa's fingers curled into his hair as her head fell back. Chance followed the motion, letting his lips slide to her neck. Her pulse pounded so strongly against his mouth, it seemed to be begging him to bite it. Chance licked it instead, swirling his tongue around the throbbing apex and hearing Isa moan with pleasure.

He wanted to hear her moan again, but louder, and while he was licking a different part of her. The thought of her scent surrounding him while he filled his mouth with her juices made his blood nearly scream to travel elsewhere. Chance let it, directing the flow, feeling himself thicken and harden as it flooded his cock. Isa must have felt it too, because she pressed herself there in a long slow rub that almost ripped Chance's control away entirely.

He'd grasped her hips and ground himself against her before he could form another thought. Isa let out a strangled noise, then her hand was ripping at his shirt while the other one tangled in his hair.

"Chance," she gasped. "I want you."

A blaze of exultation made his words choppy. "Not here. Come."

Chance picked Isa up and went swiftly to the guest room, not knowing or caring if Greta would object. Once there, he kicked the door closed and rent Isa's shirt from her with one hard tug. Her pants met the same fate, as did his clothes, until at last his bare skin pressed against hers. She blinked at the speed of his actions, but Chance didn't give her an opportunity to be bashful. He dropped to his knees, pulling her underwear down with him, and buried his mouth between her legs.

Her whole body shuddered. She would have fallen, but Chance gripped her thighs and held her as he took long, greedy licks into her wet hot depths. Her nails dug into his shoulders while gasping cries reached him above the pounding of her artery, so deliciously close to his mouth. She tasted salty and sweet, not unlike blood. The deeper Chance penetrated his tongue inside her, the more Isa shuddered against his mouth, until her cries became sobs of ecstasy. Chance licked her harder, faster, glorying in the rich scent of her lust and the fiery wetness slicking his mouth.

She ceased clawing at his shoulders to push on them instead.

"Now, Chance, *now*. Fuck me."

Something primal flared in him hearing Isa say that word for the first time. In response, he lifted her up and set her on the side of the bed, his tongue still thrashing deep within her.

A groan that ended in a roar came from her. "Damn it, for once, do as I say!" And she yanked at his head hard enough to pull out a clump of hair.

Her mouth flew open in horror as Isa stared at the dark strands around her fingers. Chance just laughed, fiercely delighted with her impatience and burning with the need to be inside her. He pushed her back along the bed until they were both stretched out, and then settled his hips between her legs.

His eyes met hers in the instant before he thrust forward. Her mouth was open, breathing in short rapid pants, and her hair was a dark tangle framing her wide cedar eyes. Chance groaned, wanting to tell Isa how beautiful she was, or that he'd never forget how she looked at this moment . . . but a more powerful need took over than the one to talk. He pushed inside her even as she arched up against him—and then he couldn't think anymore. There was nothing aside from the hot sweet embrace of her walls, the indescribable rapture of plunging deeper and faster within her, her sweat clinging to his skin, their scents merging into one . . . and the twisting spasms of her orgasm that seemed to squeeze his cock with a thousand tiny hands.

Chance knew he should have let himself climax then, too. After all, if he were thinking, he'd remember Isa was tired and she'd had a difficult day from being *shot,* for God's sake. But he wasn't thinking. He only knew he didn't want to stop, so he didn't. He held her and kissed her, sucking on her breasts or between her legs to tease her into a fevered state of excitement, before he'd plunge inside her over and over again. He finally allowed himself to come when he realized Isa was close to exhaustion. She was drenched in sweat, and her cries had a distinctively hoarse note to them.

Chance held her as tightly as he dared while his release rippled through him. It felt like his skin was splitting, the pleasure was so intense. Then a sensation of pure contentment settled into him, making him realize he couldn't remember the last time he'd felt that post-orgasm. It was wondrous, and yet also faintly terrifying. *What if Isa didn't feel the same way for him? What if she woke up tomorrow and said this had all been a mistake?*

Chance pushed those fears aside. Isa didn't seem the type to jump lightly into things, and she'd offered herself to him knowing full well what he was. There were no guarantees in life—or undeath—so Chance had to take things with Isa as they came. When was the last time he'd been so nervous/exhilarated over the future? Wasn't that worth the cost of a little fear?

Chance rolled them until they were lying on their sides. Isa was still gasping, her heart rate a constant staccato in his ears. He took her hand, kissing it, and her fingers stroked his cheek.

"Do you know what I'm going to do, first thing tomorrow?" she asked when she caught her breath.

He felt a grin tug his mouth. "Can I put in a request?"

She swatted at him with no strength. "I'm going to call every man I've ever had sex with . . . and demand an apology."

Chance laughed even as a surprising dart of jealously pierced him. *It doesn't matter what happened before*, he reminded himself. *She's with you now.* "Thank you, I think."

"Believe me," she said, settling closer to him. "Thank *you*."

Isa had been sound asleep, but Chance shaking her shoulder woke her. She blinked in the darkness of the room, barely seeing Chance put a finger to his lips.

"Someone's circling around the back," he whispered.

She glanced at the clock on the nightstand. It was almost three in the morning. Definitely not time for a social call.

Chance got up in a pale blur of flesh and was soundlessly out the window before Isa could even react. She had a second to be glad no one should be awake at this hour to wonder why a naked man was streaking around her grandmother's house, when a cut-off yelp made her vault out of bed. She didn't take time to hunt for clothes, but just wound the bed sheet around her and darted down the hall. Her grandmother's gun was in the living room where Isa placed it earlier. Sure, it didn't have silver bullets, but Robert or his goons would go down with plain old lead.

The back door opened and Chance appeared. At least Isa assumed it was Chance, not being able to see his face clearly in the dark. But really, how many other naked men coming in her grandmother's house at this hour could there be? Especially ones dragging a half-struggling form with him.

"Be still," Chance snapped, his gaze blazing emerald. The form quit moving at once.

"Is it Robert?" Isa asked, debating with herself on whether she needed the gun or not.

"No," Chance said, holding the other person's head up by their hair. "I believe this is your brother."

"Frazier!" Isa exclaimed.

"Don't turn on the light," Chance warned her as she was about to flip the nearest switch to verify that it was indeed her brother. "Close all the drapes first, you never know who might be watching this house."

Isa quickly went around and yanked all the down-stairs drapes closed, then she nearly fell over in relief when illumination did reveal that it was her brother. Frazier was here, alive and unhurt—except for the dull glaze in his eyes as he looked at Chance.

"Er, can you snap him out of that?" she asked.

Her grandmother came out of her room right as Chance muttered something to Frazier that had her brother instantly back to himself and leaping away.

"Frazier, it's okay!" Isa said at once, catching Frazier's arm. "He won't hurt you . . . and where have you *been*?"

Her brother continued to back away from Chance. "Isa, who is this guy? What's some naked stranger doing at Nana's?"

"He's a naked, um, magician, and he's my new boyfriend," Isa stammered, flushing as Frazier eyed her very tousled hair and the sheet she kept dragging up around her.

Her grandmother just laughed, a bright tinkling sound. "Frazier, I'm so glad you're all right! I expect we'll all want to hear where you've been the past few weeks."

"I can't really say . . ." Frazier started to hedge.

Isa's fingers dug into her brother's arm. "The hell you can't! I've been forced to play fiancée to Mini-Mob Bertini this past month, because you told me it was a matter of life and death, so now you are *damn* well going to explain why."

"I can't," Frazier snapped, trying to tug away and surprised when he couldn't. "I only came here to make sure you were all right, I heard Spagarelli's got shot up earlier—"

"No thanks to you," Chance cut him off in a menacing tone. "If your sister hadn't been playing her role, then Robert wouldn't have been near her and the men trying to kill him wouldn't have shot Isa instead."

"You were shot?" Frazier blurted. "How? I heard you weren't even there!"

"She was shot *at*," Greta interrupted smoothly, with a knowing look at Chance. "Her presence wasn't revealed to the local police in order to keep her out of danger, since then the shooters would know a civilian might be able to identify them."

You go, Grandma, Isa thought with admiration. *A hundred and twenty-six, and you're still quick on the draw.*

But Frazier was shaking his head. "Don't need to worry about the shooters coming after Isa, Nana. They're dead. The Salucci brothers *and* their three top enforcers were found with their heads half ripped off outside a warehouse a couple hours ago. Bertini's being questioned now by the FBI, but the son of a bitch actually has an alibi . . ."

"How do you know all this?" Chance cut Frazier off. "This isn't information you'd get off the news."

Isa had gone pale upon hearing the description of how the Salucci brothers and their backup had been found, but Chance's question pushed that aside. *How* did *Frazier know all that?*

"You mind putting on some pants, buddy?" Frazier asked, glancing at Chance and then quickly away. "I gotta say, this isn't decent."

Greta tsked. "Frazier, you're such a prude. Still, Isa, Chance, he's not going anywhere, so you have time to find your clothes."

Isa didn't miss the steel in her grandmother's tone when she said Frazier wasn't going anywhere. Her brother didn't miss it either. He gulped.

"Nana . . ."

"You *so* don't want to upset me by arguing, dear," she said with a coldness that had Chance grinning at her. "Now, stay right there. Or I'll have Isa hold you at gunpoint until you tell us everything we need to know."

Isa smiled nastily at her brother. "Try me."

Frazier sighed. "Go on, get dressed. I guess I'll be waiting here."

Chapter 11

 Three weeks later, her grandmother adjusted the veil over Isa's face. Isa stared at her reflection and smiled. *Here comes the bride.*

Agnes, Robert's sister, frowned. "You shouldn't have altered my mother's dress. Robert isn't going to like that."

"I'm amazed your mother was able to breathe, what with how it buttoned all the way up to her chin," Isa responded tartly. "Plus, this is *my* wedding. Not hers."

Agnes muttered something about how soon Isa would learn respect, which only made Isa's smile widen. *No,* she thought. *Robert will.*

Her grandmother handed Isa her bouquet. It was a beautiful arrangement of white and pink flowers that trailed to the ground in a tear-drop shape. "You look radiant, dear. Are you ready?"

Isa nodded. "Oh, yes."

Greta gave her a pat on the arm. "I'll see you in the front."

Isa watched her grandmother and her would-be sister in law leave, then she turned to the mirror again.

"So, how do I look?"

It popped out of the wall and was set to the side as Chance came out from the recently made alcove behind it. He took one of Isa's gloved hands and kissed it.

"Breathtaking."

She grinned. "Easy for you to say, you don't breathe."

"Sometimes I do." And he leaned into Isa and took in a slow, deep breath that was as intimate as a kiss. Chance had told her often over the past couple weeks how he loved breathing in her scent, even though certain times when he did it, it made her blush.

"You don't have to do this," he whispered, his mouth touching the veil near her ear.

"I've earned it."

And then some. Continuing to play docile fiancée while Robert informed her what her life was going to be like now that he'd finally attained his coveted "made man" status? Yeah, Isa had earned this.

Ironically enough, it was Chance who'd ensured Robert's acceptance into the unhallowed halls of the mafia. After Chance's gruesome eradication of the Salucci brothers and their three henchmen, Robert was welcomed into the syndicate fold. No one else had stepped forward to claim credit for their murders, so it was assumed Robert had done it as retaliation for their attempt on his life—and gotten away scot-free. That sort of clever ruthlessness was just what the big boys of crime were impressed with. In fact, two of the East Coast's most dangerous criminals were among her wedding guests. A gangster wedding wasn't an event one turned down attending, it seemed. There were just a few more guests here than Robert was aware of.

Chance glanced down at the bouquet in her other hand. "If you insist."

Isa's fingers tightened on it even as she gave him a grim smile.

"I do."

Which was the only time today she intended to say those words.

Everyone in the church stood up when Isa appeared at the doorway, and she began to descend down the aisle alone. One of Robert's friends had offered to give her away, but she'd refused, and in this, Robert hadn't pushed. He hadn't been the soul of capitulation over much else, though. Every detail of the wedding had been planned by him and Agnes. They'd wanted an impressive event, considering Robert's newly exalted status, and Isa's wishes weren't something to be concerned with. Robert's only other acquiescence was that Isa stayed with her grandmother in the weeks prior to the happy occasion. Robert thought it was because Greta had been feeling poorly. It was actually because she had a ground-floor house with a basement, which made it so much easier for Chance to come and go without being seen by Robert's spies. Robert still hadn't known what to make of Chance being there that day at Isa's restaurant. The last she'd overheard, he figured Chance must have had a twin brother.

Well, if you didn't believe in ghosts or vampires, Isa supposed that was the next logical explanation.

She smiled at Robert as she walked down the aisle. Not because she was happy to see him, but at how his face darkened when he saw the alterations she'd made to his mother's wedding dress. The once high-necked collar had been slashed to reveal generous cleavage instead, and the long fitted sleeves had been cut off at the shoulder. It gave Isa far greater range of motion with her arms, plus of course, it also gave the dress a sexiness that was well at odds with the prim virgin-Catholic bride she was supposed to be. Really, it was Robert's own fault for believing that. Who thought a modern woman would still be chaste at almost thirty?

She reached the dais and Robert held out his hand, glowering at her. Next to her, Agnes, as Isa's imposed matron of honor, reached for her bouquet so Isa could take Robert's hand. The older priest gave Isa a prodding look when she just stood there, not moving. Robert's frown turned menacing.

"Isa . . ." he said low and dangerously.

She smiled at him. A beautiful smile filled with all the joy over what she was about to do. And then she yanked the flowers off the top of her bouquet to reveal a .357 Magnum.

"Robert, dear, I *don't*," Isa said clearly, pointing the gun at him.

At that moment, the doors to the church burst open and multiple SWAT team members fanned inside. Her brother Frazier appeared behind them, shouting, "Justice Department, nobody move!" even as several of their guests at once attempted to disperse.

Isa only saw that from her peripheral vision, however, because she didn't take her eyes off Robert. A seething anger filled his gaze as he looked from Frazier back to Isa.

"Your brother's a fuckin' pig."

Isa smiled. "Yep, he's an undercover officer. Who

knew? I just thought all that moving around meant Frazier couldn't hold a job. Thanks for inviting your mob buddies to our wedding, by the way. Do you know how hard it is to get them all under one roof, apparently?"

Robert's fist swung toward her, but Isa didn't flinch. With the blood she'd drunk last night as a precaution from Chance, it seemed like Robert was moving in slow motion. Isa fired, hitting Robert in the thigh. He fell to his knees as Agnes let out a cry.

"Hold fire!" Frazier yelled, but the members of the SWAT team had already been briefed to know Isa was one of the good guys. It was easy to pick her out, after all, being as she was the only one wearing a wedding dress.

"Fuckin' bitch . . . I'll kill you for this," Robert gasped.

"Ma'am, put the gun down now," one of the black-clad SWAT members said to Isa as Robert was quickly surrounded.

"You won't see me again," Isa said, lowering the gun only after Robert had been handcuffed. "In fact, you'll never see Paul or Ritchie again either."

Which had been something Chance refused to negotiate on. Isa already had a hell of a time convincing him that Robert needed to live in order to stand trial for the multiple murders, racketeering, embezzlement, and bribery Frazier had spent three years gathering evidence on. But Ritchie and Paul? Small potatoes.

Or, as Isa surmised right about now, dinner. They'd been assigned to watch the church's exterior in order to ensure that nothing unexpected happened. Like, oh, a few dozen SWAT team members barging in. But they'd mysteriously disappeared right before Isa entered the chapel. Chance hadn't wanted to leave Isa's side during Robert's takedown at the altar, but Isa flatly insisted. She'd been pushed around by Robert for too long, so he'd know, in the end, exactly who helped put him in jail.

She wondered if Ritchie and Paul knew, in their last moments, that they were merely Chance's consolation prize. Still, dead was dead, as Chance had once stated. Guess the end result really was more important than the motivation behind it.

Several of the men being handcuffed from the groom's side of the church gave Isa very cold glares as they were led away. Mentally she shrugged. Frazier told her that she and her grandmother would need to be sequestered by Witness Protection until after all the trials, but Isa had other ideas. Ones that involved the very gorgeous vampire with a lot of friends in grave places. Chance would keep her and her grandmother hidden far more effectively than any government relocation program, and a lot more enjoyably, too. Isa doubted Witness Protection could provide the same kind of extracurricular perks that Chance did.

He came out from the back of the church, shouldering though the throngs of people and flashing the special ID Frazier had given him. His face looked more flushed than usual, and when he reached Isa's side and kissed her, his lips were almost warm.

Oh yeah. Bye bye, Paul and Ritchie.

"Are you ready to go?" he asked softly.

Isa nodded. "Big, fussy weddings were never my style, anyway."

Chance laughed. "I'll have to remember that."

Frazier came up to them then. "Isa, you're going to

have to come back with us and give a statement. Plus, uh, I'm sure nothing will happen because it was self-defense, but you're going to have to be booked for shooting Robert."

"Right," Chance snorted. "Come here for a moment . . ."

He put an arm around Frazier in a friendly way, ignoring her brother's stammering about procedure. Then when Chance had him mostly concealed by the tall cross behind the altar, Isa saw his eyes go green. A moment later when they walked back out, Frazier had stopped talking.

"We have five minutes before he snaps out of it," Chance said to Isa with a wicked grin. "I didn't think I should leave your brother mentally asleep for longer, considering his current circumstances."

"How are we supposed to get past all," Isa's hand swept out to encompass the multitude of SWAT team members, FBI, and police officers, "*this?*"

"Never underestimate the resourcefulness of a vampire, darling," Chance murmured. Then he led her quickly to the nearby confessional box, squeezing them both inside.

The panel slid open at once on the priest's side, and a pale blonde head appeared next to the privacy grill.

"What are your sins, my child?" a smoothly accented English voice asked.

Chance laughed. "Too many to list, Bones, and so are yours. If you don't mind, I'd like to add to them."

"Indeed. Desecration of the confessional, coming up straightaway."

There was a tear of metal, and then the grille separating them was gone. Bones—*this* was the vampire her grandmother spoke about?—gave a hard tap at the wall behind him and it fell away, revealing an exit had been recently cut but then dry-walled back into place.

"The rectory," Bones supplied, crawling through. "Let's not dawdle."

Chance and Isa climbed through the space as well. With all the commotion, there should have been sufficient sound coverage to muffle their escape, but soon people would notice that the gun-toting bride was nowhere to be seen.

Once inside the rectory, Bones gestured to the window. "Your car's across the street. I'll stay here and delay anyone who might have a mind to come after you. Best get moving, or Greta may take off without you."

"You let a hundred and twenty-six-year-old woman drive my Camaro?" Chance asked in disbelief.

Bones laughed. "You're older than she is, who are you to throw stones?"

"How old are you?" Isa gasped. Okay, so she hadn't gotten around to asking some things.

"One hundred and forty-three," Chance supplied, giving her a quick kiss. "But don't worry, darling. I don't feel a day over the century mark."

"Nice meeting you, luv," Bones called out as Chance swept Isa in his arms. He vaulted through the open rectory window at full speed, making everyone they passed look like no more than a haze of colors.

Across the street, Greta revved the engine of the Camaro. Chance dove in the open passenger door and Greta took off without waiting for him to close it, swinging the car into the street with a squeal of tires.

"Where are we going?" Isa asked, her head firmly

clasped to Chance's chest. He had the seat reclined to avoid them being spotted—or so she guessed.

"Anywhere you want," he replied. "We have time."

Isa looked over at her grandmother, who was wheeling the muscle car around, and she smiled. *Following your heart is always the right decision,* Greta had said, and Isa agreed. That's what she was doing, so it didn't really matter where they went. Besides, Chance was right. They had time. All the time in the world, if she wanted.

"Surprise me," Isa said, and kissed him.

JEANIENE FROST lives with her husband and their very spoiled dog in Florida. Although not a vampire herself, she confesses to having pale skin, wearing a lot of black, and sleeping in late whenever possible. And while she can't see ghosts, she loves to walk through old cemeteries. Jeaniene also loves poetry and animals, but fears children and hates to cook. She is currently at work on her next paranormal novel.

To know more about Jeaniene, please visit her website at *www.JeanieneFrost.com*.

GHOULS NIGHT OUT

Terri Garey

Chapter 1

 "I look like a giant pineapple," I muttered. "Put a bowl of fruit on my head and I could give Carmen Miranda a run for her money."

How many ruffles did one dress need? Ruffles from waist to ankle—in shiny yellow taffeta, no less.

"I'm Chiquita Banana and I'm here to say, bananas need to ripen in a certain way . . ."

If I craned my neck just right, I could see in the mirror how the giant bow on my butt made my ass look at least four sizes bigger. The waist was too big, and the flat bodice and off-the-shoulder sleeves squashed my boobs down to nothing.

Not like they were big to begin with, but they were usually *something*.

And this particular shade of yellow was so not my color—it didn't go with the pink streaks in my hair.

"How are you doing? Need help with the zipper?"

I whipped the curtain to my dressing room back with a rattle.

"Oh," the saleslady smiled, clearly blowing smoke up my newly huge ass. "You look lovely."

"Are you sure this is the dress Debbie picked out?" I asked hopefully. "She said she was going to keep it simple." The stiff tulle of my underskirt rustled as I stepped forward—walking in this thing would be a nightmare, and I was going to have to do it in front of witnesses, with a smile pasted on my face.

The woman actually looked disappointed. "Don't you like it? All the other bridesmaids loved it."

That's because they're all morons, I thought to myself. *Redneck morons.*

Though to be fair, only half of the Hathaway clan were morons, the rest were idiots. Debbie and her three sisters would welcome the chance to dress up like a Brazilian bombshell in pineapple season, particularly if there were hats or ribbons involved.

Cousins on my mom's side, the Hathaway sisters made me glad I was adopted. But I knew my mom would've wanted me to do the right thing, and when Debbie called me out of the blue and begged me to be in her wedding, it had been Emily Styx's voice I'd heard in my head. "Family is everything, Nicki," she'd have said. Besides, as cousins go, Debbie had always been my favorite—I couldn't erase the mental image of the little tow-headed girl who used to follow me around at family reunions.

Which is why I'd driven an hour into the middle of nowhere to be fitted with one of the ugliest bridesmaid dresses I'd ever seen.

Taking my silence for consent, I suppose, the grimly cheerful saleslady ushered me up onto a pedestal in front of a wall of mirrors. I stared at myself in dismayed silence as she fluffed a few ruffles and tugged at the sleeves.

"And here's a lovely hat to complete the ensemble," she said, fake smile firmly in place.

I watched in horror as she held out a floppy yellow concoction, dripping with ribbon.

"You're not serious," I said, unable to muster even a pretense of politeness.

"Oh, but I am, dear," she answered, nodding. "It's your cousin's day, after all, isn't it?"

Her day. Her beautiful, precious, I'm-getting-married-and-you're-not day.

"No bride in the world is going to let a bridesmaid outshine them on their wedding day, dear," the woman said, not unkindly. "Now put your hat on and stand up straight. Time to break out the measuring tape if we're to have this dress ready by Saturday."

Ten minutes later I was still standing there, waiting impatiently while the hem was pinned; it was going to have to come up at least an inch and the ruffles made the pinning difficult. The shop door opened, and a woman came in. She was in her early twenties, dark hair in a messy ponytail, and stopped short when she saw me standing in front of the mirrors.

"That's my dress," she said, clearly surprised to see me in it.

The seamstress, whose name I'd learned was Bebe, looked up. "I have to get that door fixed," she said absently. "It keeps blowing open."

"Who are you?" the dark-haired girl asked me, "and why are you wearing my dress?"

Bebe ignored her, rising to her feet with a relieved sigh. "That's it," she said to me. "Be careful of the pins when you take it off."

"Hell-ooo," said the girl, obviously exasperated. "Cat

got your tongue? I know you can see me. You're looking right at me."

My heart sank to the level of my newly pinned hem.
Not another one.

I glanced at Bebe again, hoping against hope that the
seamstress saw the dark-haired girl, too.

Bebe gave me a quizzical look. "You okay, hon? You
look like you've seen a ghost."

*Ghosts, spirits, phantoms, spooks—call them what
you like, just don't call them too loudly.*

They might hear you.

Trust me. I know what I'm saying.

My life had changed in an instant a few months ago;
one minute I'd been lying on the couch with what I
thought was heartburn, the next minute I'd woken up in
the hospital after being declared legally dead. In between I'd been to the Other Side—Heaven, Nirvana, or
whatever it was. I thought of it simply as the "Light."
The incredibly beautiful, amazingly wonderful Light,
where I'd known everything, seen everything, and understood everything.

Until I'd regained consciousness.

And unfortunately, I'd brought a little extra something back from the Light with me: lifetime instructions to "do unto others as I would have them do unto
me," and the ability to occasionally see and hear
spirits.

And boy, did they wanna be heard.

"Yoo-hoo," said the dark-haired girl sarcastically,
waving her arms in the air. "What the hell is going on?
I've been in here three times today and every time she's
acted like I'm invisible. If this is Debbie's idea of a
joke, it's really getting old."

I shook my head, numbly, but didn't answer her. Instead, I spoke to Bebe. "Um, was someone else supposed to wear this dress?"

Bebe's eyebrows rose. "Well, yes . . . I thought you knew. In fact," she gestured vaguely toward the main counter, "when she was here for her fitting the other day, she left her cellphone in the dressing room. I don't suppose you know how to get hold of her? The only number she left me was the cell."

"Aha!" said the dark-haired girl. "So that's where my cellphone is. And I told you it was my dress!"

Bebe was beginning to look vaguely uncomfortable. "Your cousin Debbie called me that same afternoon and said Michelle had pulled out of the wedding. She said you'd be coming by, and asked me to refit the dress for you."

Great. Being a replacement bridesmaid made looking like a pineapple in public even more appealing.

Particularly when the girl I was replacing was dead.

And apparently, she didn't even know it.

The dark-haired girl must've read something in my eyes, because hers went wide.

"What the hell is she talking about? I never pulled out of the wedding. I just talked to Debbie a couple of days ago, right before I—" She stopped, brow furrowing. "Right before I—" Her image wavered, began to fade. "Oh, shit," was the last I heard, before she disappeared completely.

"You look a little pale, dear," Bebe said, touching my arm. "Why don't you sit down?"

"I just need to get out of this dress," I said faintly, and let her steer me toward the dressing room. As soon as the curtain closed behind me, I buried my face in my hands, knowing Debbie's upcoming wedding was going to be a wedding from hell, in more ways than one.

"How did I let myself get sucked into this?" I wailed into the phone. "I'm a replacement bridesmaid, and the dress is hideous! It makes me look like a giant fruit salad. With a hat." I deliberately didn't tell Evan that the bridesmaid I was replacing was dead. My best friend and business partner, Evan *lived* for fashion, and I knew it was easier for him to talk about that than my dubious "gift" of being able to see and talk to the dead.

"What did you expect, Nicki?" Evan wasn't the least bit surprised about the ugly dress. "You're lucky Debbie didn't stick you with a tube top and Daisy Duke shorts."

I sighed. "Yeah. At least there were no sequined flip-flops."

"Don't be in the wedding if you don't want to do it—come down with something contagious or something."

"I have to do it," I said glumly, finding myself, once again, in the position of having to explain why I was doing something I didn't want to do, for someone I didn't want to do it for. *Do unto others, Nicki, as you would have them do unto you.* "Debbie needs four bridesmaids to balance out the groomsmen, and she's only got three sisters." Darlene, Diane, and Donna. Or as I privately thought of them: Dumb, Dumber, and Dumbest.

It wasn't their fault, really—the gene pool was obviously tainted. Debbie was okay in a clueless sort of way, but her sisters were another matter. Prickly as sandspurs, and just as irritating.

"Those cousins of yours are walking advertisements for birth control," Evan said, echoing my thoughts exactly. "Didn't your aunt know that she was supposed to swallow the pill instead of trying to hold it between her knees?"

"Well, since Uncle John never seemed to learn the alphabet past the letter 'D,' I imagine birth control was a foreign concept. They probably think oral sex means talking about it instead of doing it."

Evan laughed, and I felt a little better. A girl deserved to be snarky when she was going through an ugly bridesmaid dress crisis.

I stared out the window of my car at the parking lot of Bebe's Bridal. There was only one other car, a dusty old Camry that obviously belonged to the saleslady.

"I can't wait to get home. Joe promised to be waiting with a bubble bath and a glass of wine."

Evan made a purring noise. "Ooo, I need to get your hunky boyfriend and my hunky boyfriend together to talk about how to treat a lady."

"Forget it, you fairy," I said good-naturedly. "If you got your greedy little hands on Joe I'd never get him back."

I heard the distant tinkle of the shop bell through the phone, and knew that a customer had just come into Handbags and Gladrags. Our store was the coolest vintage shop in Little Five Points, Georgia, and Evan was manning it while I was out in the boondocks fulfilling family obligations.

"Push the Led Zeppelin t-shirts," I said, "we're over-inventoried."

"Climbing the Stairway to Heaven as we speak," Evan answered gaily. "Drive carefully."

He hung up, and I snapped the phone closed and dropped it on the passenger seat. Gripping the steering wheel in both hands, I let my head fall forward until it rested there, too. I closed my eyes and tried to think positively—I was doing it for Mom. Aunt Nadine was her only sister, which is how I'd ended up with such a dorky middle name.

Nicholette Nadine Styx, sucker extraordinaire.

"Don't be such a drama queen," my mom would've said, if she'd lived past my twenty-second birthday. *"It's only one day. You can handle one day, can't you?"*

"Yes, Mom," I replied dutifully, though there was no one there to hear it. Then I buckled my seat belt (another lesson from Mom), and started the car. As I was backing out of my space, I happened to glance at the saleslady's Camry again, and this time I noticed that someone had used their finger to write a message in the red clay dust that coated the passenger side door.

"Help Me," it said.

"Wash Me" would be more appropriate.

Making a mental note to run my little red Honda through the car wash when I got back to Little Five Points, I pulled out of the parking lot, already dreading my return visit to pick up the newly altered Carmen Miranda dress.

"Don't let her do it," came a woman's voice from the back seat.

"Shit!" I jumped, swerved and nearly drove myself into a roadside ditch.

"Don't let her," the voice repeated.

I slammed on the brakes, heart pounding. Afraid to turn around, I checked the rear view mirror.

Nothing.

Gathering my nerve, I swiveled my head to look, glad there was currently no traffic in Hogansville.

The back seat was empty, but there was a dark spot on the upholstery—it looked wet.

"What the hell?"

Thoroughly spooked, I sat there, engine idling. You'd think I'd be used to this sort of thing by now—the girl in the bridal shop wasn't the first spirit I'd ever seen, and somehow I knew she wouldn't be the last.

"Hello?" *Speak now or forever hold your peace, Spirit.* "Don't let who do what?"

No answer.

"Great," I muttered. "Just great." Hoping the spot was just water and nothing more ominous, I headed home.

If I checked the rear view mirror a little more frequently than I needed to, nobody knew it but me.

"You're really tense tonight, babe." Joe's fingers were working magic on my shoulders. The Cure's "Just Like Heaven" was playing on the CD player, and the lights were low.

"You would be, too, if you had to wear an ugly yellow dress like the one Debbie picked out."

He leaned down and nuzzled my ear. I could smell the clean scent of recently showered male, felt the brush of dark hair on my cheek. "It wouldn't make me tense. It would make me a cross-dresser."

"A tense cross-dresser," I said stubbornly. "In an ugly dress."

Joe laughed, using his thumbs to dig in deeper. "It's just one day, Nicki. You can handle one day, can't you?"

I shot him a look over my shoulder. "Have you been talking to my mom?"

The rubbing stopped. The magic fingers were removed. "You told me your mom passed away. You're not saying . . ."

I sat bolt upright. "No! I was kidding! Just kidding!" That would be way too weird, and my mom would *never* do that to me.

Joe sighed with relief. He knew all about my little problem with dead people, and more about my other problems than was probably good for him. But since he hadn't run away screaming into the night—yet—I dared hope he might be able to cope with them. "You haven't seen any ghosts for a while, Nicki. Maybe that part of your life is over."

It was my turn to sigh. "No such luck," I said. "I saw one today."

"What? Why didn't you tell me this sooner?" Joe came around the couch and sat down next to me, a look of worry on his handsome face.

I hated seeing it—he worried enough about his patients without having to constantly worry about me. Joe was an E.R. doctor at Columbia Hospital in Atlanta, which is how we'd met. He'd been the doctor who'd declared me dead, and the one who'd been there when I'd come back to life.

"Don't worry," I said, reaching to push his dark hair out of his eyes. It felt like silk under my fingertips. "Nothing happened. A girl came into the bridal shop, that's all."

Joe quirked an eyebrow. "That's all?"

He knew me too well.

"Evidently she was a friend of Debbie's who was supposed to be in the wedding." I grimaced. "Debbie didn't bother to mention that I was a 'replacement' bridesmaid. Anyway, whatever happened to her must've happened pretty quick—she hadn't yet realized that she was dead. Once she understood what was going on, she just faded away."

"One of your cousin's bridesmaids just died, and she didn't mention it to you?" Joe looked pretty skeptical.

"We're not exactly close," I said. "We'd see each other a few times a year when my mom was alive—holidays and stuff like that—hardly at all since my mom passed."

"And that's it? This girl, this spirit—she's gone?"

"Well, I thought I heard a voice coming from my back seat, but there was nobody there. It looked like there was a wet spot on the upholstery, but by the time I got home, it was dry. I could've imagined that part."

Joe made a disgruntled noise, leaning back against the cushions. "I don't like it."

Our romantic evening was heading downhill, and I wasn't about to let that happen.

"You men never like wet spots," I teased. "That's why we girls always end up sleeping on them."

A reluctant grin curled one corner of his lips. "Don't try and distract me."

I leaned over, resting my weight against his arm and bringing my lips closer to his. "Who said anything about *try?*" And then I kissed him, letting my tongue do the talking, without words this time.

His arms came around me, and before I knew it Joe was stretched out full length on the couch, with me on top. The growing bulge beneath my hip told me the evening was once again looking up.

The phone rang, but I ignored it; that's what answering machines were for.

"Hi, Nicki!" The volume was loud enough for Joe and I to hear the message being left. "It's your favorite cuz,

Darlene. I cain't believe it, but Diane says she forgot to send you an invitation to Debbie's bridal shower—it's tomorrow at one, at the house." The "house" would be Aunt Nadine's rambling old place out in Hogansville. "She's registered at Target." Darlene pronounced it "Tar-jhay," like pretending to say it in French made it haute couture or something. "Oh, and could you pick up some beer on the way over? Donna's supposed to, but I know she'll forget. See you then."

Click.

Somewhere in the middle of the message, Joe'd begun to smile. By the end, he was chuckling, despite the fact my lips were still glued to his. I opened my eyes to see his were open, looking straight into mine.

"Beer at a bridal shower?" he asked.

I sighed. "You don't know my relatives."

"I'm not sure I want to," he laughed.

Chapter 2

"Nicki!" Aunt Nadine enveloped me in a huge hug, smelling of hairspray and roses. "You look pretty as a picture, girl!" She pulled away to hold me at arm's length, her eyes roving over the pink streaks in my hair, taking in the three earrings in one ear and the necklace of black beads I was never without. "Always the fashion plate . . . and running your own business at your young age, too! Your mama would be so proud of the way you turned out."

Some of the tension eased from my shoulders. Aunt Nadine had always been sweet to me; it wasn't her fault she'd married into a family of rednecks.

"Is that Nicki?" boomed my Uncle John.

Speaking of rednecks.

"What'd you do, girl, fergit to wash the paint outta yore hair?" Another huge hug, this time smelling of cigarettes and beer.

"Hey, Uncle John," I said weakly, trapped against a husky plaid shoulder. "How are you?"

"I'm as nervous as a fox in a henhouse, that's what I am," Uncle John chuckled, letting me go. "Women everywhere I look today, and that's a fact."

"Get on outta here, John," Aunt Nadine said affectionately. "We hens got some cluckin' to do." She shooed him off with her fingers and he went, but not before chucking me under the chin, just like he'd done when I was a kid.

"You always were a wild one, girl," he said with a smile. "Pink hair and piercings—got any tattoos?"

"Go on, now," Aunt Nadine repeated, "and don't overdo it at the Moose Lodge or you'll be nursing a hangover come mornin'."

He grabbed her around the waist and whispered something in her ear, making her giggle and blush like a schoolgirl.

I couldn't help but smile. Then he gave me a wink and was gone, the screen door slamming behind him with a bang.

"Look who's here, girls," Aunt Nadine called out. "It's your cousin, Nicki, down from Atlanta." She ushered me through the living room toward the back of the house, where a big family room overlooked the side yard, complete with an above-ground pool and an old swing set.

A squeal of joy came from the direction of the couch, barely enough warning to brace myself before Debbie's hug nearly knocked me over. Petite and blond, Debbie was the youngest of the Hathaway girls, and had always been the most bubbly. "You're here! You're here!" she cried. "Now we can get this party started!"

Judging by the amount of gaiety and laughter I'd interrupted, the party had started a long time ago. I hugged Debbie, Diane, Darlene, and Donna in turn, then went through a dizzying round of introductions to people I'd never met and would never remember. There were other relatives, too, but I barely knew them: Great-Aunt Ida, who was eighty if she was a day; second cousins Gina and Margaret; Darlene's little girls, Amber and Brittany.

"Sorry this was so last minute," Aunt Nadine said. "We waited until all the family could make it to town before we held the shower."

"Did you bring any beer?" Darlene whispered.

Aunt Nadine's introductions kept me from having to answer. "This is Alice, and her friend Bernice."

"Her *partner,*" Darlene added as a murmured aside. "That's what we're supposed to be callin' it these days."

I smiled until my cheeks hurt, hugged everybody who needed hugging, then collapsed into a folding chair. The babble of voices around me continued without a pause, and I was glad to no longer be the center of attention. Luckily, Darlene had moved on to annoy someone else near the buffet table.

"Don't put that bowl of potato salad there," I heard her say irritably. "Put it at the other end, near the hot dogs."

"You must be the new girl." Alice's friend Bernice was sitting next to me. She had short, graying hair, and wire-rimmed glasses.

"The new girl?" For a moment, I had no idea what she was talking about.

"Oh, you know," Bernice said, waving a chubby hand negligently. "That other girl was gonna be one of the bridesmaids, but I guess that ain't gonna happen now."

Ah. Keeping my voice low, I asked, "Yeah, I wondered about that. What happened to her?"

Bernice shrugged. "I dunno. She and Debbie had a fight or something."

A fight?

"Well, I'll be damned," came an indignant voice. "They don't even know I'm dead."

I turned my head, and there was the dark-haired girl from the bridal shop standing next to my chair. Unlike the last time I'd seen her, this time she was soaking wet, hair plastered to her head, clothes plastered to her body. "Here they are, partying along without me like nothing happened." She cast a scornful glance toward the buffet table. "Darlene didn't even get the decorations right. Those balloons were supposed to go on the mailbox so people could find the house."

"Go away," I whispered. "I can't talk to you now."

"I was here first," Bernice said, obviously offended. "Go sit over there if you got a problem with me."

Mortified, I felt heat rising to my cheeks. "I'm sorry," I said, "I wasn't talking to you."

Bernice gave me a skeptical glare, and then gave me the cold shoulder. She turned toward the woman on the other side of her, dismissing me.

The dark-haired girl gave a heavy sigh. Water dripped from her shirt onto the carpet. "I was supposed to make my special three-bean salad for this shower. My name's Michelle, by the way. What's yours?"

Refusing to answer, I shot her a warning look.

"Okay, okay," she said. "Not a good time. I get it."

"How you doing, Nicki?" My cousin Donna plopped into the chair on my other side. She'd gained quite a bit of weight since I'd seen her last, and her mousy brown hair could use a shampoo.

When I glanced back toward the dark-haired girl, she was gone.

"Fine, Donna. Good. Great." I forced a smile, glad my cousins were far enough apart in looks to keep their names straight. Debbie was the cutest, and the only blonde. Darlene was tall and red-haired, with a face like a hatchet; Diane and Donna both had brown hair, but Diane had always been skinny, and Donna had always struggled with her weight.

She was obviously fighting a losing battle, though the plateful of macaroni and cheese she was clutching was a clear indication why.

Potato salad, beer, and hot dogs with macaroni and cheese; Debbie's bridal shower was Carb Central, the hillbilly way.

Forcing myself to be sociable—Donna was my cousin, after all—I asked, "How are the wedding plans coming? Is Debbie nervous about the big day?"

Donna shrugged, eyeing her much younger, much prettier sister. "She's handling it pretty well, I think. At least she was, until that bitch Michelle pulled out on her."

I heard an outraged gasp behind me, and knew that my ghostly friend hadn't left the party just yet.

"Good thing you agreed to fill in as bridesmaid," Donna went on. "Debbie was ready to throw a full-fledged conniption fit, but toned it down to just a hissy when you said yes."

Anyone who's grown up in the South knows the difference between a hissy fit and a conniption fit; a hissy fit usually ends in tears, while a conniption fit can easily end up in a trip to the emergency room.

"What happened?" Might as well get the inside scoop.

"I'm not sure. Debbie said they had a fight a couple of days ago, but that's nothing unusual. They've been fighting and making up on a regular basis since junior high school. Anyway, Michelle up and drove back to Augusta in a huff."

That explained why nobody knew she was dead. If everybody thought she'd left town because she was mad at Debbie, nobody would be looking for her.

"That's a pretty sweater," Donna said. "Come from your store?"

Unlike Debbie's choice of bridesmaid dress, my cotton candy pink sweater looked great on me, and I knew it. The beaded black butterflies on the left breast and jet buttons down the front were the perfect touches.

"Yes," I answered, surprised Donna had even a passing interest in fashion. "Nineteen fifties, hand-knit."

Donna took a big bite of macaroni and cheese, speaking around it.

"Got any in my size?"

Um, no, we don't carry "ever-increasing."

"Vintage doesn't work that way. All of the stuff in my store is unique, one-of-a-kind. That's what makes it special."

"Well, la-dee-dah." Donna swallowed, then put down her fork and took a swig of whatever was in the cup she was holding.

Before I could respond, she got up and walked away, heading back toward the buffet table. "Ma," she called out, uncaring that a room full of women heard her, "looks like Buster peed in the house again. There's a wet spot on the carpet."

I closed the bathroom door behind me with a sigh of relief. The sound of laughter was muffled, but I could still hear Debbie's high-pitched giggles over the see-through nightie Great-Aunt Ida had given her. "If that don't get you some sugar, nothin' will!" the eighty-year-old had declared.

Since Debbie had been opening her gifts for some time, I'd felt safe enough to slip away for a few minutes. There were only so many crock pots one could "oo" and "ah" over, after all.

"Michelle?" I whispered. "Are you still here?"

"Yes," someone said morosely. The voice came from the bathtub.

The shower curtain was closed, so I very gingerly pulled it aside just enough to peek behind it, visions of the movie *Psycho* going through my head.

There was Michelle, slumped in the tub, fully clothed, and still very wet. "I figured this was the safest place to sit," she said, "since I'm dripping all over everything."

"Why are you wet?" I asked her. "You weren't wet when I saw you at the bridal shop yesterday."

"Beats me," she answered. "I was hoping you knew."

"How would I know?" I pulled back the shower curtain so we could see each other better and looked around, making sure the toilet seat was down before I sat.

"Well, you see dead people, don't you?" Michelle sat up in the tub, pushing damp hair behind her ears. "You obviously have some special powers or something. What am I doing here? What happened to me?"

Oh, crap. How was I supposed to help her pass on if she didn't know why she was still hanging around?

"Okay, look—what's the last thing you remember?" A detective I was not, but I'd give it a shot.

Michelle sighed, resting her elbows on her knees. "Debbie and I went to the bridal shop, and then we went shopping in Peachtree City. We were looking for something cute to wear on her honeymoon." She frowned, remembering. "We stopped at some Mexican place for lunch—we both had a couple of Margaritas. I made the mistake of asking her one too many times if she was sure she wanted to get married, and she got really pissed off."

Interesting.

"Why would you ask her that at this late date?" I was just trying to get a feel for things.

Michelle gave me a look. "Have you met Dale, the guy she's marrying?"

I shook my head. "No."

She sighed. "Debbie could do so much better. She could've stayed with me in Augusta, gotten a job, gone to school—gotten out of this dinky little town. They practically roll the sidewalks up at night around here."

Now *that* was something I could relate to. "Hogansville has sidewalks?"

Michelle smiled a little at that.

"You're her cousin Nicki, right?"

I nodded, thinking.

"I should've known when I saw the hair," Michelle said. "Debbie told me you were all Goth and everything. I didn't expect you to be so pretty."

"Um, thanks." What *did* she expect—the Bride of Frankenstein? Just because I liked to play with my hair and makeup didn't make me some kind of freak. A little extra eyeliner never hurt anybody.

"Debbie really likes you," Michelle said, almost wistfully. "She always thought you were cool. Thanks for filling in for me."

"You don't sound like you're mad at her," I said. "Must not have been much of a fight."

Michelle shrugged. "We've been best friends for

years, even after I moved away. We've had a few spats, but we always make up." She looked away, tears filling her eyes. "Guess we won't be making up this time."

Oh, man. I was never good with tears—I usually left the tea and sympathy up to Evan, but Evan wasn't here. Making a game effort, I snagged a piece of toilet paper and offered it to her.

She tried to take it, but her hand went right through it.

"Damn," she said, "that keeps happening. I can think about being somewhere and then find myself there, but I can't touch anything or make anybody hear me." Michelle looked at me, swiping the tears from her eyes with her fingertips. "Except you."

"Can you . . ." I hesitated, finding my own thoughts a bit creepy. "Can you *think* yourself back into your body?"

I'm not sure how a ghost could actually turn pale, but that's what she did.

"I don't want to," she said, shaking her head.

"But if you did, you could come back and tell me where you are, and then I could go find you."

Convoluted logic, anyone?

Michelle shook her head again, harder this time. "No. It's dark, it's scary—"

A knock at the door made me jump. "Hello? Anybody in there?" The doorknob rattled.

"Just a minute," I called, jumping to my feet like I'd been caught doing something wrong.

When I glanced back toward the tub, Michelle was gone.

"Michelle?" I whispered.

No answer.

Just a damp bathtub and a racing heart.

Chapter 3

"You're not leaving, are you?" Debbie came up to me as I was telling Aunt Nadine what a lovely time I'd had (otherwise known as lying my ass off). "It's Girls Night Out after the shower! We're going to the Long Branch—they just got a karaoke machine!"

Oh goody. Can we go by Sizzler first?

"Gee, Debbie, that sounds like fun but I've got a long day tomorrow. My partner's taking the day off and I need to be there early to open the store."

Her face fell. "But I thought . . ."

"Why don't you go, Nicki?" My Aunt Nadine gave me a reproving look, instantly reminding me of my mom. "It's Debbie's last night of fun before she gets married."

"Gosh, Mom, you make it sound like getting married means I'll never have fun again!" Debbie griped.

Aunt Nadine smiled at her, touching her hair. "Oh, you'll have fun, sweetie. Just a different kind, and maybe not as much. Once the babies come, everything changes."

Debbie wrinkled her nose. "Babies? Who said anything about babies?"

"Yeah, really." I grinned at Debbie, sharing a moment of understanding. "Dale's not one of those 'keep 'em barefoot and pregnant' types, is he?"

Debbie laughed, shaking her head. "Dale's in no hurry to start a family, thank the Lord." She grabbed my arm. "Say you'll come out with us, Nicki. It'll be so boring otherwise. Darlene acts like a pickled prune until she gets a few beers in her, and Donna and Diane will probably just bicker with each other all night."

"Sounds like fun," I said weakly.

"It will be," Debbie said, "I promise."

"Bad news, baby," I said into the phone. I was standing in Aunt Nadine's front yard, waiting for everyone to pile into her Dodge Caravan. Aunt Nadine was taking no chances with her girls, and had given Debbie strict instructions about either calling her or calling a cab when girl's night out was over. "I've been roped into going to Debbie's bachelorette party." I, of course, was taking my own car—I was hoping to slip out after a beer or two, and wasn't going to need a designated driver.

"That's not so bad," Joe said. "For a minute there I was worried you were going to tell me that you'd seen another ghost."

My silence told him all he needed to know.

"Crap, Nicki."

"Well, it wasn't *another* ghost, exactly. It was the

same ghost." I realized I was chewing nervously on a cuticle and gave myself a mental slap. "The girl from the bridal shop. Her name's Michelle. She doesn't know what happened to her."

"And you're determined to find out, aren't you?" Joe didn't sound too happy at the prospect.

I gave a sigh, not bothering to deny it. "You know as well as I do how this usually goes, Joe. The spirits who come to me don't leave me alone until I help them, so I might as well get it over with. But that's got nothing to do with tonight." *I hoped.* "Aunt Nadine pulled the guilt card, and put me on the spot about going out with the girls. I'm just gonna have a beer or two, then slip out. The Long Branch Saloon doesn't really sound like my kind of place."

"The Long Branch Saloon? Where are you, Dodge City?"

"Might as well be," I complained, watching as my cousins came down the front steps toward the van. "Hogansville apparently doesn't boast much in the way of night life. Country and western karaoke . . . yee-haw!"

It was Joe's turn to sigh. "Be careful, Nicki."

"I will."

"Call me when you're on your way home, okay?"

"Maybe you could wait up for me." I lowered my voice to the level of a sexy tease. "Beer and rednecks get me hot."

Joe gave a short bark of laughter. "Right. In that case, I'll break out the Pabst Blue Ribbon and greet you at the door wearing nothing but a John Deere cap."

I kept teasing. "Who knows? Maybe the Long Branch has a mechanical bull. You know what they say about mechanical bulls."

"No, what do they say about mechanical bulls?"

"I don't know, but I'm sure it's something sexy."

"It would be if you said it."

Awwww.

"How about I just give you the ride of your life when I get home instead?" I asked, as a reward for the compliment.

"Yeehaw!" Joe crowed through the phone, making me burst into laughter. "Ride 'em, cowgirl!"

When my cousins and I walked in the door of the Long Branch Saloon, the jukebox was blaring "I Beg Your Pardon, I Never Promised You A Rose Garden," which should have been my first clue to get the hell out of there. The smell of stale beer and cigarettes nearly knocked me over, and I immediately stepped in something sticky.

All I could do was be grateful I'd worn ankle boots instead of sandals.

The room seemed dark after the brightness of the late afternoon sun, but the earliness of the hour didn't seem to inhibit business much—the place was packed. It was obviously happy hour in Hogansville. A sea of cowboy hats and trucker caps turned in our direction as seven women spilled through the door.

"Hoo-ee," I heard a guy at the bar say, "the night is looking up."

I followed the pack of women—four cousins and two second cousins—to a pair of tables that had been cordoned off with rope. Real rope, not your average velvet-covered stuff, very classy. All the way there, I wondered how it could be physically possible to *feel* a roomful of rednecks eyeing your ass. Darlene untied the rope from one of the chairs and let it fall to the floor. Donna kicked it under the table, and we all took our seats.

The waitress, a tired-looking woman with big hair, came over. "First round is on me," Darlene said. "Long necks for everybody!"

Unimpressed, the waitress nodded and moseyed on back to the bar.

"Anybody up for some pool?" Diane asked hopefully.

"I am!" said second-cousin Margaret.

"Me, too," said Donna, and the three of them headed for the back, where two battered pool tables were currently in use by a couple of good ol' boys. Seeing the way Diane took her time choosing a cue, it was obvious she'd done this before. Margaret went straight to flirting with a guy who was waiting on his shot, and I knew it wouldn't be long before they'd have a game going.

"Mmm, mmm," Gina said, "I think I've just laid eyes on my next husband." Gina was round and short, with curly auburn hair and freckles. I was pretty sure she'd been married a couple of times already, but she wasn't wearing a ring.

"Which one?" Darlene asked, craning her neck to see who Gina was ogling.

"The one at the bar, in the blue plaid shirt."

Oh yeah, that narrowed it down.

"I like that one," Darlene said, pointing. "The one with the black cowboy hat. Reminds me of Tim McGraw."

"Darlene!" Debbie giggled, pretending to be scandalized. "What would your husband say?"

Darlene shrugged her thin shoulders. The sparkly green top she was wearing actually suited her; her red hair gleamed like flame, taking attention from her not-so-pretty face. "Married ain't the same as dead, Debbie. You'll find out soon enough."

Right on cue, I looked up to see someone who really did know what it was like to be dead. Michelle, Debbie's former bridesmaid, stood against the wall, watching us with an envious expression on her face.

Though what she had to be envious of, I had no idea. I'd gladly have traded places with her, if I didn't have to be dead to do it.

"So you got a boyfriend, Nicki?" Gina turned her attention from the guy at the bar long enough to make small talk.

I nodded, tearing my eyes from Michelle. She looked so lonely standing there. "Yes, his name is Joe. He's a doctor at Columbia Hospital."

"A doctor?" Gina leaned back, obviously impressed. "Good for you."

The comment irritated me. It wasn't like I'd chosen him because of his profession—I'd chosen him because he was a great guy.

A great, *hot* guy.

"Is he coming to the wedding?" Debbie had no idea her best friend was standing in the shadows, watching her. She was so caught up in her own fantasy of happily-ever-after that it hadn't occurred to her some people might not be.

Living happily ever after, that is.

"He's coming," I said.

"Eight long necks," said the waitress, sliding a tray onto our table. "You girls want me to run you a tab?"

"Hell, yeah," Darlene said. "We got some partying to do; my baby sister's getting married!" She snatched up her beer and gestured for us to do the same. "To

Debbie and Dale—may they share everything, including housework!"

"Amen!" said Gina, as we clinked our long necks.

The beer tasted good, and I tried to look on the bright side. A couple of these and I was out of here.

Gina and Darlene put their heads together, sizing up all the different men at the bar, while Debbie turned her blond head toward me.

"Do you think you'll ever get married, Nicki?" She took another swig of her beer while she waited for my answer.

I hesitated, and that seemed answer enough for her.

"Probably not, hm? Why should you? You've got your own business, your own house . . ." Her voice trailed off, and she took another sip. "You don't need a man to take care of you."

"See what I mean?" Michelle's voice made me jump. She slid into the empty seat beside Debbie, watching her friend closely. I couldn't help but notice she was dry again, looking much the way she had when I'd first seen her in the bridal shop.

Debbie, of course, didn't see her.

"She doesn't want to get married—she's just doing it because she doesn't think she has a choice," Michelle said.

"Everybody has a choice about whether or not to get married," I said.

Debbie, thinking I was talking to her, answered, "I know. But I love Dale—really I do." Her voice sounded a little wistful, and she didn't meet my eye.

"Methinks she doth protest too much," said Michelle. She leaned back in her seat, crossing her arms.

I ignored the dead girl, and spoke to the live one.

"You don't have to go through with it if you don't want to, Debbie," I said softly.

Debbie shrugged. "You sound like my friend Michelle."

"Wasn't Michelle supposed to be in your wedding?"

Debbie shot me a guilty look. "Well, yeah. But she got mad at me and drove home to Augusta. She hasn't returned any of my calls."

"She's been calling?" Michelle sat up.

"I think she's just jealous," Debbie went on. "She claims she never liked Dale, but I think she has a crush on him."

Michelle gave a gasp of outrage, but Debbie didn't hear it.

"Why would you say a thing like that, Debbie?" Michelle seemed to have momentarily forgotten that Debbie couldn't see or hear her.

"Um, why would you say a thing like that?" I asked, on Michelle's behalf.

Debbie took another swig of her beer. "I don't know—just the way she looks at him sometimes. Michelle doesn't seem to have a lot of luck with guys. She goes for the flashy type, frat boys with money or football jocks with big shoulders and big egos. A couple of dates, and then they dump her. Dale's not flashy, but he's solid."

"Oh, he's solid all right." Michelle was disgusted by Debbie's assessment. "About as solid as a block of wood." She leaned back in her chair, crossing her arms. "And just as exciting."

"I think in her heart she wants a guy like Dale." Debbie looked thoughtful, staring down at the battered tabletop, marred by years of spilled beer and cigarette burns. "Somebody to depend on. Somebody to grow old with." She shrugged, toying with the label on her beer bottle. "Dale's not perfect, but who is? Nobody's perfect."

The jukebox seemed to be eavesdropping on our conversation, because right then Tammy Wynette started singing "Stand By Your Man"—an annoying song I'd always hated. If my man ever cheated on me, I wouldn't be standing by him; I'd be standing *on* him, preferably while wearing a very sharp stiletto heel.

"Michelle's always been my best friend," Debbie said. "I can't believe she's not here to help me celebrate." Her lower lip quivered as she raised the bottle of beer again. After a few healthy swallows, she set it down empty.

"I—I think I need to tell you something, Debbie." I had no idea how I was supposed to explain to my cousin how I knew her best friend was dead, but things couldn't go on like this.

"No." Michelle interrupted me. She leaned toward me, shaking her head emphatically. "You can't tell her yet."

I looked at her, raising my eyebrows in question.

Michelle shot Debbie a glance, then sighed. "She's about to get married. I don't want to ruin her wedding. Tell her afterward."

"And what about you?" Was I supposed to just let this poor girl's unquiet spirit just hang out until the "I do's" had been said?

"I'm fine," Debbie answered my question, thinking it was meant for her. "But I could use another beer."

Darlene chose that moment to lean in and say to her sister, "Well, look who's here." She tipped her bottle toward the door, and we all swiveled our heads to look. "I knew that man wouldn't be able to resist crashing the party."

Two guys had just come in, both of them standing tall

and scanning the room, obviously looking for someone. The better-looking of the two saw us first, his face splitting into a broad grin. He nudged his friend, nodding in our direction, and they made their way over to our table.

"Dale!" Debbie stood up, reaching up to hug her fiance even as she scolded him. "You're not supposed to be here! This is my night to let loose and have a little fun, remember?"

"Oh, I remember," Dale said, grinning. "And I'm not stayin'. I'm just here to let all these yahoos know you're already taken." He grabbed her around the waist and pulled her against him, raising his voice to be heard above Tammy Wynette's whiny singing. "Listen up, fellas!" Dale looked around the room, making certain he had everyone's attention. "This here's my future bride, so don't any of you bone-heads be getting any ideas! I'll kick the ass of anybody who tries anything!" The idiot grin on his face made it hard to take him too seriously. "Her friends are fair game,"—to my horror, he nodded toward the table where Gina, Darlene, and I still sat—"but I done got me the pick of the litter!" Then he swooped down and bent Debbie backwards in a big, sloppy kiss, while his friend—and everybody else in the bar—looked on.

"Woo-hoo!" Somebody shouted, "Get 'er, Dale! Show the little lady who's boss!"

"Yeah!" shouted somebody else. "It's the last chance you'll ever get! After Saturday, she'll be the one wearing the pants in the family."

Dale broke off his kiss long enough to raise his head and shout back, "Fuck that! After Saturday, ain't neither of us gonna be wearing pants for a while!"

The room erupted into laughter, while I cringed

inwardly at his crudeness. Debbie buried her face in Dale's shirt, embarrassed but laughing.

I looked for Debbie's ghostly friend Michelle, but she was gone.

"Hoo-ee," said Dale's friend, a skinny guy with a buzz haircut and a belt buckle the size of a small hubcap. He was eyeing me like I was a prize heifer at the county fair, and I didn't like it. "Who's your friend, Debbie?"

"This is my cousin Nicki," Debbie said, turning to face me. "She's gonna be one of my bridesmaids. Isn't she pretty?"

"She sure is," Buzzcut said, leering. He pulled out Debbie's chair without asking and took a seat at the table next to me. "Nice to meet you, Nicki. My name's Randy. Do you believe in love at first sight, or should I walk by again?"

"Oh by all means, Randy," I answered sweetly. "Then keep on walking."

Randy and Dale burst out laughing like that was the funniest thing they'd ever heard, and I got my first real whiff of whisky breath. These two guys had been partying long before we girls had even started.

"C'mon, darlin', don't be like that. Lemme buy you a drink."

"I've got one, thanks." I looked away, taking a sip of beer to prove it. Maybe if I ignored him, he'd leave me alone.

"You're one of them dead girls, aren't ya?"

That got my attention. "Excuse me?"

"You know, one of them girls that's all into death and doom and gloom. Crosses and seances and all that shit." Randy waggled his fingers in what was supposed to be a spooky way, I guess. "I hear dead girls are easy—so why you making it so hard, baby?"

The way he was leering at me made it clear he thought his little double entendre was very clever.

"You're drunk, Randy," Debbie said flatly. "Leave Nicki alone."

I appreciated Debbie's effort, but I could take care of myself. I looked Randy in the eye and asked, "Are you always this stupid, or is today a special occasion?"

Dale let out another whoop of laughter, causing heads to turn our way yet again. "Randy's got a real way with the ladies," Dale said to me, when he'd stopped laughing. "You better watch yourself."

"Great idea," I said sourly, rising from the table. "I think I'll go look for a mirror."

"You going to the little girl's room, Nicki?" Darlene stood up, too. "I'll go with you."

I didn't answer, having to squeeze by a too-close-for-comfort Randy and a still-entwined Debbie/Dale sandwich before I could even start looking for the restroom.

"It's over here," Darlene said, with a tilt of her red head toward the back.

I followed her, weaving my way past tables full of blue-collar guys with shit-eating grins on their faces. Women seemed to be scarce at the Long Branch, or maybe they were just all at home with the kids while their husbands whooped it up over a cold brew.

Not that there was anything wrong with blue-collar men, mind you—as long as they weren't blue-collar jerks. But I had a feeling that the jerk factor in this particular bar was pretty high.

Darlene led the way down a narrow corridor toward two doors marked "Bulls" and "Heifers," and pushed open the door to ladies room. It smelled like cheap perfume and sour vomit—exactly what I'd expected. A coin-operated vending machine hung on the wall, displaying condoms, tampons, and breath mints.

Prerequisites in a place like this, I suppose. One never knows when one will be kissing, cramping, or canoodling with the redneck of your dreams.

"That Randy is such a creep. He thinks he's a real stud," Darlene said, heading into one of the stalls. "Don't let him get to you."

"Thanks," I said, glad my initial impression had been confirmed, "but I think you just insulted a horse."

I could hear Darlene chuckling through the stall door. "You got spunk," she said. "I'll give you that."

Since I'd only come into the bathroom to get away from Randy, I put my purse on the counter and started digging for my lipstick. When I glanced up, my heart nearly stopped at what I saw reflected in the mirror.

Michelle was standing behind me, soaking wet again. Her lips looked blue, and her skin had taken on a waxy tone.

"You have to get out of here," she said, "or you'll be next."

"You are creeping me out," I answered, frozen in place with a tube of lipstick in my hand.

"What?" Darlene's voice came from the stall. "Did you say something?"

Flustered, I stuck my lipstick back in my purse. "I said Randy creeps me out," I lied, loudly.

"Yeah, I know what you mean. He's been sniffin' around Debbie like a dog in heat ever since high school, but she ain't never give him the time of day. Don't know how Dale can stand hanging around a low-life like him, but there ya go."

The toilet flushed, and Darlene opened the stall door.

"Must be a guy thing, I guess, or else Dale's just used to it. They work together at the garage."

She came over to the sink to wash her hands, narrowly missing walking right through Michelle, who didn't bother to move out of the way.

In fact, Michelle looked lost in thought, and very, very sad. Her gaze had turned inward, and she paid no attention to Darlene whatsoever. Water dripped from her clothes and hair.

Stalling, I fumbled in my purse again, this time bringing out a tube of eyeliner along with the lipstick.

"Don't you get tired of getting all glammed up everyday?" Darlene eyed me curiously in the mirror as I touched up my lips. "It takes me forever to put on makeup and strap myself into a push-up bra."

I shrugged, not understanding women who didn't want to make the effort to look good. "It doesn't take me that long." Which was true. "Besides, I deal with the public all day. It pays to look good when you sell fashion for a living." Then I paid her an honest compliment. "You look great, by the way—however long it took you tonight, it was worth it."

Darlene looked surprised, but pleased. "Thanks. I guess it don't hurt to get fixed up now and then." She eyed herself in the mirror and stood up straighter, drying her hands with a paper towel. "Well, I'm going back out. You comin'?"

"In a minute. You go ahead."

"Well, hurry up," Darlene said as she left. "Karaoke starts in five minutes."

Gee, I can hardly wait.

"He's here," Michelle said, before the bathroom door had even swung shut. "You have to go."

"Who's here?" I turned to face her, doing my best to

control a shudder of distaste. Michelle looked different every time I saw her, but this time was definitely the worst.

She looked . . . well . . . dead. Really dead. As in several days dead.

"When I saw him, I remembered," Michelle said, twisting her hands together nervously. The memory obviously upset her. "He followed me from the restaurant after the fight I had with Debbie—he must've seen me in the parking lot or something. I should never have pulled over."

"Who followed you?"

Michelle kept glancing toward the door as if she was afraid whoever she was talking about was going to walk in any minute.

"Randy. It was Randy—he was waving and flashing his lights—I thought there was something wrong. When I pulled over he got out of his car and told me my rear tire was almost flat. Offered to fix it for me." Michelle was shaking now, very agitated. "I was so stupid; I should've known better than to trust him. I thought since he was a friend of Dale's it'd be okay."

The bathroom door swung open to the sound of giggles and the blare of country music. Three women I didn't know spilled into the room, laughing at something someone had just said.

"Ew," said one. "It smells like somebody died in here."

"Yeah," said one of the others, wrinkling her nose, "and watch out—there's a puddle of water on the floor. Don't they ever clean this place?"

Michelle's face twisted, and she started crying, tears lost on her already wet cheeks. She faded away to nothing as I watched, powerless to say or do anything to stop her.

"You two go ahead," said the third girl, stepping gingerly toward the sink. There were only two stalls in the ladies room, and not much room at the sink, either.

Since I didn't feel like standing there like an idiot, I snatched up my purse and left the bathroom.

"Fire on the mountain; run, boys, run; the devil's in the house of the rising sun." Charlie Daniels singing about how the devil came down to Georgia sounded weirdly appropriate at the moment, and the urgency of the song fit my mood.

I needed to get the hell out of the Long Branch Saloon, for more reasons than I cared to think about.

Unfortunately for me, Debbie and her sisters had other ideas. I had to sit through an excruciating round of karaoke music, which included a very tipsy Debbie mangling Madonna's "Like A Virgin," and a tone-deaf Diane singing "Hey, Good-Lookin'" to the guys playing pool.

Luckily, Randy and Dale were nowhere to be seen, and I could only assume they'd moved on to do their drinking elsewhere. The whole time my ears were being assaulted, my brain was working—how could I accuse some guy I just met of murdering somebody? Where was Michelle's body? Where was my proof?

Darlene did a passable version of Shania Twain's "I Feel Like A Woman," but by the time Gina got up to sing "I Will Survive," I'd had enough, and pulled the old fake phone call routine, scrabbling in my purse for a phone that wasn't ringing.

"Hello?" I put a finger in my ear like I was having trouble hearing the person on the other end. "The store alarm?" I glanced at my watch, pretending to care what time it was. "No, it's after closing. Nobody should be there at this hour. Okay, Evan, I'll meet you there."

Darlene gave me a sour look across the table, which told me she wasn't buying it, but Debbie was working on her fifth beer and singing along with Gina, so she wasn't paying attention anyway.

"That was my partner, Evan," I said to Darlene. "There's an emergency at the store. I gotta go."

Darlene merely shrugged and took another sip of beer, but as soon as I stood up, Debbie grabbed my arm. "Where ya goin', Nicki?" Her voice was definitely slurred, but her face was flushed and happy. "The party's just getting started."

I looked down at her, knowing why her friend Michelle wanted me to keep quiet until after the wedding, but not liking it. Still, I knew she was right—Debbie deserved to have a little fun before she married Dale and gave birth to a litter of little rednecks.

And there was no saving Michelle, because what happened to her had already happened.

"I'm sorry, Debbie, but the alarm's going off at the store. I have to go."

She looked disappointed, but a wild whoop from the direction of the stage distracted her long enough not to argue. Instead, she rose to her feet and threw her arms around my neck in a farewell hug. "Bye! See you at the church on Saturday!"

"Hoo-ee," somebody shouted, "girl-on-girl action! When's the wet t-shirt contest?"

"In your dreams, buddy," I muttered, returning Debbie's overenthusiastic squeeze. Then I waved a good-bye to the rest of my cousins and headed toward the door.

Chapter 4

 The parking lot was full, and so was the moon. It hung low in the sky, reminding me that the evening was still young. If I drove fast, Joe and I would have plenty of time to rustle up some *real* fun when I got home.

I'd just slid my key into the door of my car when I heard a man's voice say, "Mmm, mmm, mmm."

I whirled, gasping, and saw a shadow disengage itself from a pickup truck parked nearby.

"You are one fine-lookin' woman." The shadow raised a hand, and I saw it was clutching a bottle—too big to be a beer bottle. "Ready for that drink yet?"

The man took a step forward, while I shrank closer to my car. The moonlight gleamed on a big, shiny belt buckle.

Randy.

I took refuge in bravado, though my heart was pounding so hard I was afraid he'd hear it. "What the hell are you doing out here? You scared me shitless!"

"I've been waiting for you, baby." Randy took another step toward me. "No need to play hard to get—ain't nobody here to see. Just you and me and the moon." Waving the bottle toward the sky, Randy threw back his head and howled drunkenly, like the beast he was.

If Michelle was telling the truth—and I had no reason to believe she wasn't—this guy was a murderer. And he was here, alone with me, in a dark parking lot.

"You're drunk," I said flatly. "Leave me alone."

"Hell, yeah, I'm drunk," he said, grinning widely. "Drunk on *loooove,* baby. Don't you feel it?"

I fumbled with my car keys, twisting then pulling as I tugged on the door handle.

Randy came up behind me so fast I couldn't avoid him. In two seconds he had me pushed up against the car, his body pressed hard against me, pinning me in place. "I said, don't you *feel* it?"

Problem was, I did. His erection pressed against my hip, frightening me more than I cared to admit.

Without thinking, I elbowed him, hard.

His breath left him with a *whoosh,* drowning me in the sour smell of whisky. He stumbled back, but not far enough. There was a sloshy *thud* as the bottle he'd been holding hit the ground.

I barely managed to get the car door cracked open before he slammed me against it again.

"Oh, you're gonna pay for that, bitch." His breath made me want to retch, and this time he wrapped his arms around me, tight. "Think you're too good for old Randy, don'tcha?"

I squirmed and twisted, trying to break free, but I had no room to maneuver. One short squeal was all I managed before Randy's hand clamped over my mouth. The scent of oil and gasoline rose from his skin.

"Uh, uh, uh," he said, breath rasping in my ear. "You city bitches are all alike." Then he laughed, and my blood ran cold. "But you're all the same under them fancy panties."

"Let her go!" Another man's voice, saying words I'd never been so glad to hear in my entire life.

Randy barely even flinched. He didn't even bother to turn around, just spoke over his shoulder. "Mind your own damn business. This is between me and the little lady."

"The hell it is."

A sudden wrench as Randy's shoulder was grabbed and pulled in the direction of the newcomer. I twisted and squirmed even harder than before, managing to raise a foot against the car and kick backward. Randy stumbled back, but didn't loosen his grip, keeping me pinned with my arms at my sides. Frantically, I flailed my legs, feeling my heels connect against his feet and ankles.

Damn cowboy boots.

Desperate, I jerked my head backward, hearing Randy's grunt of pain as my skull connected with his chin. Despite the sudden flare of stars, it was worth it to know I'd hurt him.

Then I felt myself ripped from Randy's painful embrace, and pushed away. Shaken and unsteady, I fell to the ground a few feet away.

"You okay, babe?" A little distance and some moonlight showed my rescuer clearly. His face looked like thunder, and his eyes were trained on Randy.

"Joe," I whimpered, hating how shaky I sounded. *Thank God.*

Further conversation was impossible as Randy launched himself at Joe, tackling him to the ground. I rose to my feet, heart racing, as the two men rolled and grappled in the dirt of the parking lot. One second Randy was on top, then Joe would get the upper hand. I wanted to cheer when Joe's fist connected with Randy's ribs, and cry when Randy's return blow drew a grunt of pain from Joe. Then Joe kicked himself free of Randy's grip and gained his feet, cracking Randy a good one on the chin on his way up.

Randy fell backward, momentarily stunned. Between the liquor he'd obviously consumed and the blows he'd taken, his head had to be spinning.

"You sorry bastard," Joe said, breathing hard. "Attacking defenseless women in dark parking lots. Is that the only way you can get a date?"

"Defenseless, my ass," I said. To prove it, I snatched up the discarded whisky bottle at my feet and wielded it like a club. I was shaking with fear and rage, but the fear had definitely lessened since Joe showed up. "He just caught me off guard."

"I'm gonna kick yore ass," Randy moaned, twisting to the side to push himself up.

"Bring it on, Cornpone," Joe taunted, clearly furious and ready to go another round.

I'd never seen Joe like this—his job was to heal people, not hurt them—but he obviously had no trouble inflicting pain when he needed to.

A teeny part of me was thrilled. *Okay, a big part of me was thrilled.* If anybody needed some pain inflicted, it was Randy.

My gloating was short-lived. Randy had gained his feet, swaying slightly. Moonlight glinted on something he held in his hand, and with a sinking heart, I shouted, "He's got a knife!"

Joe didn't hesitate. He lunged forward, grabbing

Randy's wrist with one hand, his shoulder with the other. Another brief struggle, until Joe's knee came up and caught Randy right where it hurt.

Randy froze, eyes bugging, his agonized wheeze bringing joy to my heart. Joe was still moving, twisting Randy's arm behind his back before giving him a hard shove. Randy went down face-first, and Joe stood there alone, holding the knife.

Randy curled into a ball, drawing his knees up tight. The next sound we heard was retching as he emptied his stomach in the dirt.

I hoped he'd choke on his own vomit.

Joe threw the knife into the bushes that ringed the parking lot and came over to gather me in his arms. "You okay? Did he hurt you?"

Not taking my eyes from Randy, I held on to Joe for all I was worth. I was still clutching the empty whisky bottle, not ready to let it go yet. "I'm okay." I was shaking like a leaf, dammit. "Where'd you come from? How'd you find me?" Not that it mattered—Joe was here, warm and solid, breathing hard but thankfully breathing.

"Google Maps," he muttered into my hair. "You told me the name of the bar, and I had a bad feeling." He turned us a little so he could keep an eye on Randy, too. "Beer, rednecks, and my gorgeous, fiesty girlfriend; not a good mix."

I couldn't help but laugh a little. "You know me too well."

"Not nearly well enough," Joe said softly, letting me bury my face against his neck. "But I'm working on it."

Randy moaned, drawing our attention. He dragged himself to his knees, then pushed himself to his feet, stifling another groan. Without another word, he staggered toward his pickup truck, bent over and holding his belly.

Joe started after him, but I tightened my fingers in his shirt. "Let him go," I said. "Let him crawl back into his hole."

"Nicki," Joe clearly didn't like that idea. "He pulled a knife on me; who knows what he would've done to you if I hadn't shown up."

"Oh, I know what he would've done." I couldn't help the involuntary shudder that rippled through me, and remembered what my mom always called that particular feeling: *somebody just walked over my grave.*

"I'm calling the cops," Joe said grimly.

The truck's engine roared to life.

"Not yet."

Clearly frustrated, Joe looked from the truck to me. "Why not?"

Another shadow moved in the parking lot, one I'd known had been there all along. Michelle stepped into the ring of light beneath the single lamppost, staring at me silently.

"Because we have to follow him," I said.

Chapter 5

 The One-Stop Body Shop was a dump, but it was a dump that sent a chill down my spine, and not just because of the name.

It was a garage like many other garages, a run-down building with three big dented and rusty steel doors closed and padlocked against thieves, a small office with glass windows overlooking a dirt parking lot that held four cars and one pickup truck.

Randy's pickup truck.

What sent a chill down my spine was the big retention pond in the field beside it, and the way the moonlight glistened on the slick, oily surface of the water. Once there'd been a chain-link fence surrounding the pond—now there were just a few sections left, sagging and covered with kudzu vines.

It hadn't been hard to follow Randy here. We'd had a guide, after all. Now that Michelle's spirit knew and remembered what had happened to her, she had no trouble directing us down the main roads to the One-Stop.

I was worried about her, though. Other than a few sparse words telling me when to turn and where, which I'd relay to Joe, she said nothing. Her eyes looked haunted, which was weird, considering she was the one doing the haunting.

"This is it," Michelle said, as we drove slowly past. "He has a room in the back."

I looked at Joe, nodding, and he pulled over to the side of the road beneath some trees a few hundred yards away.

"This is a really bad idea, Nicki." Joe put the car in park a little harder than he needed to. He glanced in the back seat, which to him must've appeared empty. "I mean, what are we gonna do, go in and make a citizen's arrest or something? We have no proof this guy did anything except assault you in the parking lot; no proof he murdered anybody." He checked the back seat again, a little self-consciously. "I mean, I'm sorry for your friend Michelle, but we're out of our league here."

"If we find Michelle's body, that's all the proof we'll need," I argued.

"You won't find me," Michelle said hollowly. "Not without scuba gear."

I was trying hard not to look at Michelle any more than I needed to—ever since she'd seen Randy at the bar she looked more and more like a corpse, and less like the college girl she'd once been. Her dark hair hung in damp rat-tails, and her skin had taken on a greenish tint.

"She's in the pond," I said to Joe. "Maybe we can find her car or something, get the police to come out and investigate."

Michelle spoke up again, sounding more despondent

by the minute. "The car's in the pond, too. Everything's down there." She was staring out the window, toward the garage.

"We have to do *something*." I was beginning to get annoyed with her attitude. Here we were trying to help her, and she was giving up before we'd even begun. "Do you want him to get away with this?" I would've reached out and given her a good shake if she'd been real. "Do you want him to do it to someone else? Darlene said he was always sniffing around Debbie—what if he decides to go after her next?"

That got her attention. "Debbie," she said, almost as though she'd forgotten her best friend. "That's why he did it, you know." The circles beneath her eyes made them look sunken, which I supposed they were. "He's mad because he can't have her. They went out a couple of times in high school, but now she's marrying Dale and he has to stand up there in a monkey suit and watch while it happens." The way Michelle recited the words told me they came from memory. "She thinks she's too good for him; I think I'm too good for him." *He'd said the same words to me.* "We fucking bitches are all alike."

"Stop it!" I couldn't listen to it anymore—Randy's foul words coming from the mouth of a dead girl—a girl he'd murdered with no more thought than squashing a bug. And for what? Unrequited love? Jealousy? Revenge?

"Nicki." Joe's hand on my knee brought my attention back to him. "I say we call the police and report the guy for assault. They'll come out here and talk to him, and maybe they'll find something."

"Or maybe not." I didn't have a whole lot of faith in the local police—this was rural Georgia, not New York

City. A town like Hogansville probably had two depu-
ties, tops. And they were probably off having fried
chicken at Popeye's or something. "Besides, it's my
word against his."

"*Our* word against his, remember? At the very
least, it'll rattle his cage," Joe insisted. "He won't like
having cops snooping around if he's been up to no
good."

"Don't worry," Michelle said, though Joe couldn't
hear her. "*I'll* rattle his cage. He'll be *begging* for the
cops when I'm done."

I turned back to her, glad to see that the empty light
in her eyes had been replaced by something else. Anger, and a calculated gleam that should've made me
nervous, but instead made me optimistic.

"What do you have in mind?" I asked, ideas of my
own beginning to percolate.

Michelle glanced out the car window again. "You
can see me," she said, obviously thinking out loud. "If
you can see me, maybe we can make *him* see me, or at
least make him *think* he sees me."

I grinned, liking the way this was going.

"We both have dark hair," Michelle said, "and we're
about the same size."

Joe was watching me, and when he saw my face
light up, he began to shake his head. "No, Nicki. Whatever it is you're thinking, the answer is no."

I leaned over and gave him a quick kiss on his non-
responsive lips. "That's not what you said last night."

He wasn't in a playful mood. "This isn't a joke. The
guy's a murderer!"

Michelle and I looked at each other, and I knew I
couldn't just walk away.

"Yep." I nodded. "And he's about to be one very freaked-out murderer."

The bad part about this plan was that I had to get wet; the good part was that Joe had a plain white t-shirt in his gym bag, so I didn't have to ruin my pretty pink sweater. I mean, I wanted to help and all, but one-of-a-kind, designer vintage that fit me like a glove was hard to come by.

The t-shirt was perfect—way too big for me, so it fell nearly to my knees. The extra fabric made it look like a shroud. And I didn't have to go near the scummy, oily pond; there was a hose on the side of the building furthest from the office, so I gritted my teeth and let Joe hose me down.

The whole time, Joe was grimly silent, but I knew I was gonna hear about this later. I even suspected he took some satisfaction in dousing me with freezing water from the hose, but I couldn't really blame him. It was a measure of how much he cared that he was there to begin with, and I didn't want to lose sight of that.

I'd make it up to him. I'd *enjoy* making it up to him. If we lived through this night, Joe had a lot of hot monkey love to look forward to.

Mud squelched beneath my toes (I wasn't going to ruin my leather ankle boots, either), so I reached down and scooped up a couple of handfuls. With a silent grimace, I smeared some on my legs and arms. My suspicions about Joe's satisfaction were confirmed when he did the same to my face without asking.

He looked at me critically. "Too pink," he whispered, and glopped some into my hair.

I cringed, making a moue of my lips, and he promptly smeared those, too.

I got him back, though, planting a big, muddy kiss on his nose before he jerked out of range.

"You be careful," he whispered fiercely. "Wait until I draw him out, and then I'll be just a few feet away, behind the vine-covered fence."

Nodding, I put all joking aside and got ready to get down to business.

Together, we skirted the parking lot, keeping low and weaving between the parked cars just in case Randy happened to look out. Then we were on the office side of the building, between it and the pond. Michelle's restless shade was nowhere to be seen, but I knew she was still there somewhere.

I was counting on it.

The night was quiet—just the *chirrup* of frogs and the faint whine of a mosquito as it buzzed past my ear. There was no traffic on the road—the nonexistent Hogansville sidewalks were already rolled up for the evening in favor of primetime TV. The grass was cool beneath my feet, and I hoped fervently there was no broken glass or sandspurs to worry about.

Then I was in position, crouching behind the bushes closest to the pond.

Joe's arm was around my shoulders, his face close to mine, so I couldn't miss the heavy sigh of resignation he gave. "You are a lot of trouble, woman," he murmured, directly into my ear. "If we make it out of this alive, I'm going to turn you over my knee."

I leaned against him for a moment, letting him take my weight. "Promises, promises."

He kissed my wet, muddy hair, giving me a final squeeze. "Stay put until I'm in position," he reminded me sternly, then he was gone, heading back toward the parking lot.

I lost sight of him for a few seconds, but when he came back I saw he was carrying something in each hand—a couple of rocks. He looked in my direction to make sure I was keeping low, then hefted the one in his right hand. I thought he was gonna throw it, but he didn't—he walked over to Randy's pickup truck and smashed one of the headlights, then did the same to the other one. The tinkle of breaking glass was loud, but not nearly as loud as the smashed sound the front window of the shop made when Joe turned and heaved the rock through it with all his strength. He started running the instant it hit, lobbing the second rock for good measure just before he ducked behind a saggy section of vine-covered fence.

"What the fuck?" Randy's bellow of rage, coming from somewhere inside the body shop, made me cringe. For an instant, I wondered if I could go through with the plan. I looked toward Joe, and there, standing in the grass right between us, was Michelle. She was wet and shivering, staring toward the garage with a fixed expression that told me something: even in death, she was afraid of the man who'd killed her.

So I took a deep breath and let it out slowly. If this poor girl could face down the monster, so could I. If he got away with what he'd done to Michelle, he'd do it again to some other girl, I had no doubt.

And then there he was, bursting through the front door with a sawed-off shotgun in his hands.

Oh, shit. Why hadn't I thought of this? He was a redneck who lived in the back of a garage in rural Georgia—*of course* he'd have a sawed-off shotgun.

"Where are you, you fuckin' rat bastard?" he shouted, scanning the parking lot with his furious gaze. He cocked the shotgun, the *cha-chick* noise it made sounding like certain death. "I'm gonna blow your fuckin' head off!"

I looked at Joe—he was motioning with his hand and mouthing the words, "Stay down."

Like he needed to tell me that.

"Don't worry about the shotgun," Michelle said calmly. "That thing is old, and he didn't take care of it. His first shot will blow it to pieces—I dropped an extra shell down the barrel."

I was dying to know how she'd managed that when she hadn't even been able to take a piece of toilet paper from my hand earlier in the day, but now was hardly the time to ask.

"Anger gives me strength," she said, as though reading my mind. "I didn't know it earlier. I went to his room while you were getting ready, and when I saw him passed out on the bed where he—" she paused, obviously reluctant to finish that particular sentence. "I wanted to kill him." She looked at her hands. "I couldn't pick up the gun, but I saw the loose shotgun shells laying there on the table. I had to concentrate really hard, but I managed to pick one up and drop it down the barrel." She looked at me, and her face was hard. "My granddaddy taught me about guns. That one is a rusty piece of crap."

All I could do was stare at her, dumbfounded. And hugely relieved.

"I couldn't let him hurt you," she said.

"Come on out, you motherfucker! I know you're here!" Randy pointed the shotgun toward the sky and fired. There was a deafening explosion, then Randy screamed and fell backward, clawing at his face. The shotgun fell to the ground. The stream of obscenities that poured from his lips would've made the devil himself blush.

I couldn't help but smile with grim satisfaction, and when I looked at Joe, he was doing the same.

Randy's foul language slowed down some, and I watched as he tentatively lowered his hands, staring at the blood on them, then touching the skin of his cheek gingerly.

"Shrapnel from the barrel," Michelle said. "I hope it hurts like hell." Then, to my surprise, she walked toward Randy.

He, of course, couldn't see her, and he was so focused on the injuries to his face that I doubt he would've noticed if he could.

When she got closer, she kicked out at the shotgun. To my surprise, and to Randy's, the gun actually moved several feet away.

Randy eyed it warily, keeping a hand to his cheek. To him, it would've appeared to move all by itself. He moved toward it, reaching out slowly to pick it up.

Michelle kicked it again, sending the shotgun skittering across the dirt parking lot, and Randy jerked his hand away.

He stood up straight, scanning the parking lot nervously.

Michelle walked behind him, entering the open door of the garage. Within seconds, it slammed shut, causing Randy to flinch. He swiveled, reaching for the door handle. The *click* it made as Michelle locked it from the inside was loud in the stillness.

Unless Randy wanted to climb through the broken front window, he was locked out, and he knew it. What he obviously didn't know was *how* he'd been locked out. He scrubbed a bloody palm over his buzz-cut hair, clearly unnerved.

Now it was my turn.

From my hiding place behind the bushes, I let out a breathy sigh, as though I'd just run a marathon and was exhausted.

"Who's there?" Randy pivoted in my direction so fast it startled me.

Steeling my nerves, I let out another sigh, adding a slight moan on the end for good measure.

"Goddammit, I said who's there?" he roared, taking a few steps toward the pond.

Instead of answering, I dropped to my hands and knees, breathing hard, and began to crawl backward toward the pond.

I was afraid to look at Joe. We hadn't discussed the particulars of what I'd do to convince Randy that I was the spirit of Michelle, but my instincts told me that the more freaked out Randy was, the better.

What would freak out a guy who'd drowned somebody more than seeing that somebody come crawling out of the water? I prayed that between the freak-out, the darkness and the mud on my face, I'd look enough like Michelle to fool him.

Not that I was going to get all the way into that nasty black pond, of course—that would be too gross—but being all wet and muddy and having my feet in the water would give the illusion that I was dragging myself onto the bank.

And it worked.

Randy took a few more steps toward the pond, and then the bushes were no longer in his line of sight.

I was.

He staggered, visibly shocked. I wasn't sure which one of us looked scarier—him with his blood-streaked face, or me with my mud-covered one. I borrowed a page from all the bad zombie movies I'd ever seen, and twisted my lips into a sneer, glaring at him beneath my lashes. Saying nothing, I let my eyes do the talking as I started crawling slowly toward him, digging my nails into the muddy grass surrounding the pond.

Chapter 6

 "Wha . . . wha . . ." Randy was momentarily speechless. His fear did my heart good, and almost made up for the scrapes I was gonna have on my knees.

"Randy," I whispered hoarsely, giving my voice a coarse, guttural quality that strained my vocal cords. I drew out his name as I kept crawling, very slowly. "Raaaannnndddyyy . . . did you miss me, lover?"

"You're not real." Randy started backing up, away from me.

"He raped me," Michelle said. I hadn't seen her reappear since she'd slammed and locked the door, but my eyes had been trained on Randy. "He had me follow him here to the garage, saying he'd patch my tire, but when I got out of the car he dragged me in the back and threw me down on the bed. I screamed and cried, but there was nobody here to hear me."

"That was so sweet of you to offer to fix my tire," I rasped to Randy, not having to fake the hatred I was feeling. I didn't want to come any closer to him, so I slowly stood up, never taking my eyes from his. Joe's formerly white t-shirt clung to me, hanging to my knees, heavy with mud and water. "Did you like the way I screamed when you raped me?" I bared my teeth in a ghoulish grin. "Was it good for you?"

Randy was paler than any ghost. He shook his head, wordlessly, eyes as big as saucers.

"When he was done he got off me, and told me to get dressed," Michelle's voice was shaking. "I thought he was going to let me go—I was so stupid!" A sob broke from her throat.

I didn't dare look at her, but every word she said left its mark on my heart.

Poor girl. Poor Michelle.

"I'm never going to leave you, you know," I rasped maliciously to Randy, wishing I had a shotgun of my own. "Real men like you are so hard to come by."

"I turned toward the door, and he hit me in the back of the head." Michelle hadn't finished her story. "Everything went black. I dreamed about being back in my car and watching it fill with water—I thought it was just a nightmare, a horrible nightmare, until that day at the bridal shop."

Oh, how I hated being the one who'd woken Michelle from her nightmare. Sometimes the spirits I met knew full well they were dead, sometimes they didn't; it was definitely easier if they knew, but either way, it was never any fun for me.

But I had more bad news to deliver, and this time I didn't mind it so much.

"You're the man of my dreams, Randy," I lied, holding out my muddy arms. "Now we can be together forever."

A wet stain appeared on Randy's jeans, just below

his giant belt buckle. I'd never known how satisfying making someone pee his pants could be. I didn't have much time to enjoy it, though, because Randy turned and ran for the parking lot.

"Raannndddy," I rasped loudly, taking a few steps in his direction. "Don't leave me here, Randy!" I looked frantically at Joe, where he crouched behind the section of tumbledown fence. My vague plan had been to get Randy to confess his crime, but if he took off, this whole muddy episode would have been for nothing.

Joe stood up, but it was too late—Randy's pickup rumbled to life, and he tore out of the parking lot like a bat out of hell, leaving nothing but a spray of dirt and a plume of reddish dust in his wake.

"What do we do now?" I asked Joe plaintively.

Joe shook his head, walking toward me along the wet, muddy bank of the pond. "I don't think he'll get very far on these dark back roads without headlights," he said.

And sure enough, there was a squeal of tires followed by a huge thud, then the tinkle of broken glass.

"Holy shit," I breathed. "I thought *I* played rough."

There was a hard light in Joe's eyes—one I'd never seen before. "The bastard put his hands on you," he said flatly. "And he murdered that poor girl. He's lucky I didn't kill him."

"You may have done exactly that." I was shocked; my gentle, playful lover had a dark side all his own.

Joe shrugged, pulling out his cellphone. "He deserved it," he said. "I hope he burns in hell."

Unfortunately, hell was going to have to wait. We could hear Randy's shouts and groans long before we made it to the pickup, which hadn't gone very far.

Joe called an ambulance on his cellphone, telling the police dispatcher there'd been an accident in front of the One-Stop Body Shop, then very reluctantly stopped to get his emergency medical kit out of the trunk of his car.

Then we went toward the truck, which, from all appearances, had kissed a tree pretty hard. Branches from the tree covered the crumpled hood and rested on the roof. The one front tire I could see looked pretty mangled—that truck wasn't going anywhere unless it was on the flatbed of a wrecker.

"Help!" Randy called, from inside the cab. His voice was weak, thready. "Somebody help me."

Joe took his time, putting his medical kit on the ground and opening it without saying a word. He pulled out a pair of surgical gloves and put them on, a sour expression on his face.

I hung back a little, not wanting Randy to see me. I was still wet and mud-covered, though I'd slipped my half-boots back on when we'd reached Joe's car.

"Is somebody there?" Randy asked weakly. "Anybody out there?"

I was tempted to stick my head in the broken window and give him another good scare, but I restrained myself. For the time being, I'd let Joe handle it.

"This is Dr. Joe Bascombe from Columbia Hospital in Atlanta," Joe said, in a clipped tone. "An ambulance is on the way."

"Oh, thank Gawd," Randy moaned. "I think both my legs are broken."

"I sincerely hope so," Joe murmured. Then he went to the driver's side door and peered in the window, which was shattered. "Are you injured anywhere else?"

"My chest hurts," Randy moaned. "I think I hit it on the steering wheel."

Joe frowned. "Are you having any trouble breathing?"

"No. But it hurts like a motherfucker. Can you get me out of here?" he whined. It was obvious that Randy either couldn't see Joe very well in the dark, or just didn't recognize him as the man he'd been brawling with in the parking lot of the Long Branch Saloon.

"Unless you're bleeding heavily or having trouble breathing, it's best not to move around too much. You may have spinal or internal injuries and I don't have the equipment here to handle the level of care required. The ambulance will be here soon."

Another groan was Joe's answer.

"I'm going to open the door and check your vitals. Try and stay still."

I watched while Joe reached in and did something to Randy; I couldn't see the murdering asshole from my angle, and that was fine with me.

"Your pupils look good. How's your head?"

"It hurts, man . . . cain't you give me something for the pain?"

Joe shook his head. "Nothing until the paramedics get here." His expression was pure doctor, dispassionate and intent. "Pulse is steady, that's good. How many fingers am I holding up?"

"Two," Randy groaned. "My legs are killin' me."

It was like Randy had used the magic word. Joe stepped back, then looked at me. There was a gleam in his eyes that warned me he was up to something. "Yeah, I'll bet they are. Can't move, can you?"

"Hell, no. Where the fuck is that ambulance?"

Joe didn't answer. Instead, he raised his eyebrows at me in an unspoken question, and like a flash, I knew what he was up to.

My nod and my smile gave him the answer he needed. With the flick of a finger, he motioned me to stand behind him, then turned back to Randy.

I got into position, staying back while Joe distracted Randy with more doctor talk.

"That's a nasty cut on your cheek. Might need some stitches. I've got some bandages right here in my first aid kit." Joe moved away, leaving me with an unobstructed view of Randy, and him with a clear shot of me, framed in the open door of the truck.

"AAAAAHHHH," Randy shrieked, jerking backward on the front seat. He didn't get very far, though, his legs like two dead weights dragging him down. His face was pale and blood-streaked, and a bruise was beginning to darken his chin.

I gave him my best ghoulish grin, delighted to be able to terrify the murdering bastard without having to worry about him coming after me.

"Get her away from me," he hollered, sounding like a little girl frightened by a spider. "Get her away."

Joe stepped in front of me, his expression unconcerned. "Calm down, big fella. Get who away from you?"

Randy raised a shaking finger and pointed. "Her! She's right behind you! Get her away!"

Joe turned and looked, but didn't acknowledge me in any way. "I don't see anything. There's nobody here but you and me."

"I'm tellin' you, man, she's right behind you!" Randy's eyes were popping out of his head with fright.

I raised my hand and gave him a little wave, smiling all the while. "He can't see me, Randy," I rasped, "or hear me. Only you can see me. And you're going to see me every day for the rest of your life, unless you tell the nice man where to find my body." I moued him a kiss.

To my surprise, Randy's eyes rolled back in his head, and he fell over in a dead faint.

"Coward," Joe muttered. "Not so brave now, are you, Cornpone?"

I heard a girl's laughter, and it wasn't mine. Michelle was still with us, and given the circumstances, I was glad she was enjoying the show.

Joe sighed, and went back to his medical kit.

"Is he okay? When I said I wanted to scare him to death, I didn't mean *literally*." I couldn't help but be a little nervous—unlike Randy, I was no murderer. I didn't want anybody's death on my conscience.

"He's fine," Joe said. "His pulse is good, he's alert and talking, no dilation of the pupils. Unfortunately, I see this all the time in the E.R. When a person is drunk, like Jethro here, their reactions are slower, so the body doesn't have time to tense up before impact, which often results in fewer injuries." Joe shook his head, disgusted. "I'm willing to bet this jerk's got nothing wrong with him but a couple of bruised ribs, maybe a broken leg. But I think he needs a little more convincing to do the right thing." He ripped open a packet of something—ammonia, I guess—and held it under Randy's nose.

Randy's face twitched, eyes fluttering. When he opened them, his expression was dazed. "Wha . . . what happened?"

"You passed out, buddy," Joe said, faking a doctorly concern. "And right before that you were hallucinating. Must be a head injury—if that ambulance doesn't get here soon I can't be held responsible for what happens to you."

"What do you mean?" Randy's face showed fear of a different kind than I'd inspired earlier.

"Subdural hematoma," Joe intoned. "Bleeding on the brain. It could be very serious."

"What?" Randy's voice cracked on the word. "Am I gonna die?"

Joe hesitated, and I stepped up, coming where Randy could see me over Joe's shoulder.

"Oh, I hope so, lover boy," I said, smirking. "Then we can really be together forever."

Randy gasped, eyes glued to me. He seemed, for the moment, speechless.

"I'm a doctor, not a priest," Joe said, as if I hadn't spoken. "But if you have anything you'd like to get off your conscience, now might be the time to do it."

Randy's Adam's apple worked as he swallowed. His eyes moved back and forth, from Joe to me.

"Tell him," I hissed, deciding to get tough. "Tell him what you did to me, and how you put my body in the car and drove it into the pond." I was improvising as to the details, but I knew it had to be something like that. "Tell him where I am so my soul can be at peace." Giving Randy my fiercest glare, I threatened, "Do it, or you'll never have a peaceful night again as long as you live."

It was my sincere hope he'd never have one anyway, but I had only one night—this night—to convince him of it.

"You're not looking so good, buddy," Joe said to Randy, completely ignoring me. "Stay with me, now."

"Everywhere you look, you'll see my face," I rasped. "Every time you close your eyes, you'll hear my voice." I raised my hands, curling my fingers into claws for good measure. "Every time you touch a woman, you'll feel my cold, dead flesh instead of hers. Your dick will . . ."

That did it. I didn't even get to finish my sentence before Randy blurted, "I killed somebody. I didn't mean to, I swear I didn't!"

I glared at him, knowing a lie when I heard it, but he couldn't look at me anymore.

He grabbed at Joe, babbling a confession. "It was an accident—I panicked and tried to hide the body. I put her in the front seat of her car and drove it into the pond." He was frantic now, beginning to blubber, crocodile tears mixing with the blood on his cheeks.

"Are you telling me you killed someone? A woman?" Joe's voice was very calm. The wail of sirens came from somewhere far away.

"Michelle. Her name was Michelle." His gaze flicked to me but didn't linger. He stared at Joe, holding tight to one of Joe's wrists.

Joe drew back, pulling his arm from Randy's grasp.

"You gotta help me, man," Randy pleaded.

"You need a lot more help than I can give you, *man*." Joe's tone was grim, and so was the look he gave me.

The wail of sirens was a lot closer now, strobe-like red and blue lights flashing through the trees.

Randy saw them, too. "Thank Gawd," he moaned in relief, closing his eyes and letting his head fall back against the seat.

Joe jerked his head toward the trees, and I took the hint, ducking low and threading my way into the bushes surrounding the truck.

I was expecting an ambulance, but it was a sheriff's cruiser that reached the scene first. Only one deputy, and a pretty hefty one at that. His gut led the way as he got out of the car, settling his hat over a nearly bald head as he emerged.

"You the guy called nine-one-one?" The deputy took Joe's measure pretty quickly, eyes flicking over the open medical kit on the ground and the stethoscope Joe wore around his neck as he walked toward the truck.

Joe nodded an affirmative. "I'm Dr. Joe Bascombe from Columbia Hospital in Atlanta—I came upon the scene and was able to offer medical assistance."

"Looks like Randy Catlett's truck—he in there?"

Joe nodded again. "He's in there. He's banged up, but he'll survive."

The deputy peered in at Randy, while more sirens sounded in the distance. "What kind of trouble you got yourself into now, Randy? Didn't that DUI you got last month slow you down none?"

In a town the size of Hogansville, it made sense that Randy and the deputy knew each other.

"It weren't my fault, Dwayne." Randy's tone was whiny now. "My headlights weren't workin'. Get me outta here, would ya?"

Deputy Dwayne turned away from Randy, muttering under his breath. "Stupid shit. Only a matter of time before something like this happened."

The ambulance was in sight now, sirens wailing noisily as they came up the road. The deputy flagged them over with a raised arm, as though they couldn't see the truck wrapped around the tree or his cruiser sitting there, lights flashing.

"It gets worse, Deputy," Joe said. "This man just confessed to me that he murdered someone. A woman."

That stopped Deputy Dwayne in his tracks. "That

so?" he asked, shooting Randy a glance. I couldn't help but notice the skeptical tone in his voice. "We don't get many murders around these parts."

The ambulance rolled to a stop and turned off the siren, leaving blessed silence in its wake.

"Well, you've got one now," Joe answered the deputy firmly. "Just before you got here he confessed to murdering a woman named Michelle."

From my hiding place in the bushes, I watched as Randy's eyes got big. Now that help had arrived, he was obviously having second thoughts about his confession.

"I—I don't know what he's talking about, Dwayne," he shouted, still trapped in the truck. "What kind of crazy talk is that?"

Shit. What was I supposed to do now? I couldn't step out from the bushes and terrorize Randy in front of the deputy and the paramedics, who were already out of the ambulance and on the way over.

Joe's face reflected my thoughts. One quick glance in my direction before he looked away, but I knew he was warning me to stay put.

"I'm telling you the truth, Officer. This man told me he murdered a woman and dumped her body in a pond. I'm willing to swear to it in a court of law."

Deputy Dwayne didn't answer. His jaw worked, but I was willing to bet it wasn't gum he was chewing on. He confirmed it when he leaned to one side and spit. No self-respecting Georgia lawman would be caught without his chewing tobacco.

The paramedics had reached the truck, an older man with a crewcut and younger guy with a mullet. The older guy eyed Joe and his stethoscope, and Joe spoke to him automatically, though he kept his gaze trained on the deputy. "Broken or bruised ribs, possible fracture of the right tibia. No sign of chest compression, concussion, or spinal injuries."

"You mean I ain't gonna die?" Randy's face showed his relief. He even ventured a weak half smile, while my heart sank.

Surely he wasn't going to get away with this . . . surely this whole muddy, messy, dramatic evening hadn't been for nothing . . .

A blast of music startled me, making me jump. It startled everyone else, too, and masked the rustling I'd made in the bushes. It was the radio in Randy's truck.

Music and voices blurred into a solid stream of noise, as though the radio was scanning through stations, very fast. Everyone stood frozen, listening, until the scanning stopped.

Clear as a bell, loud in the stillness, came a familiar voice, singing a familiar tune that raised the hair on my arms.

"Every breath you take, every move you make, every bond you break, every step you take, I'll be watching you."

Sting, singing "Every Breath You Take."

Randy looked like a deer in the headlights, staring at the radio as if he expected it to bite him.

"Every single day, every word you say, every game you play, every night you stay, I'll be watching you."

Michelle was still here. I knew it, and Randy knew it, and the knowledge proved too much for him.

"All right, all right!" he shrieked. "I did it! I killed her!"

The older paramedic drew back, looking first at Randy, then at Deputy Dwayne.

"You got somethin' you need to get off your chest, boy?" Dwayne asked Randy, shooting Joe a glance before he moved toward the truck.

"Michelle," Randy babbled, still staring at the radio. "Her name's Michelle. I don't even know her last name—she's a friend of Debbie Hathaway's. She's in the pond back at the body shop."

I breathed a silent sigh of relief, and looked at Joe. He flicked his eyes toward where he'd left his car, and I got the message; time for all good ghouls to hit the road.

I wanted to celebrate, to throw my arms around him and kiss him to thank him for helping me, but now was not the time. Instead, I ducked down and scrambled away as quietly as I could. Once I was far enough away, I stood up and took off at a run toward the One-Stop Body Shop.

Joe could handle it from here, I had no doubt.

But the evening wasn't over yet. I was at the hose, quickly wiping the mud from my face and arms with Joe's newly rinsed t-shirt when Michelle showed herself one final time.

Or tried to show herself, anyway. Her form was hazy, indistinct, and I couldn't help but be a little relieved; she'd been looking pretty bad since she knew she'd been murdered, and I didn't want to see any more. I'd had enough of a creep show for one evening.

"Something's happening to me," Michelle said. Even her voice sounded fuzzy. "I feel like I have to be somewhere, but I'm not sure where it is."

I smiled, knowing the place Michelle was being drawn to was a good place. "It's okay, Michelle." I kept my voice gentle. "It's time for you to go now. Just close your eyes and let go, and all of this will seem like a bad dream. Only this time, when you wake up, it will be to a better place."

It would be in the Light, which was a very good place, indeed. I wasn't sure I had the words to describe it, but I didn't really need to. Michelle would find out soon enough. I couldn't believe that the innocent victim of such a horrible crime would go anywhere else.

"Nice trick with the radio, by the way," I added.

"Thanks."

I could hear the smile in her voice, and it made me happy.

"Could you do me one final favor?"

Repressing a tired sigh, I answered, "Sure."

"I don't want Debbie thinking that I died mad at her," Michelle said. "I know her . . . if we leave things on a sour note, she'll blame herself for what happened to me. If I told you what to say, would you say it?"

Great—how was I supposed to do that? Walk up to Debbie at her wedding and tell her I had a message from the "other side"? Par for the course, I suppose. How ironic that in a family of rednecks, *I'd* managed to become the one everybody considered strange.

Hell, I'd figure something out.

With a shrug, I said, "What do you want me to tell her?"

"Calm down, Debbie," Darlene said. "Just because that idiot Randy had to get himself busted up and in the hospital right before the wedding doesn't mean the wedding's ruined." She shot me a look over Debbie's head as she was adjusting her sister's veil.

Darlene was the only one who knew the truth about why Randy wasn't here. I'd called her yesterday and asked her to meet me for coffee—then I'd told her what happened in the parking lot of the Long Branch Saloon when Randy'd attacked me. I'd fudged about why Joe and I had followed Randy to the One-Stop Body Shop, claiming it was because he was so drunk we were worried about him causing an accident, but I'd told the truth about how Randy, afraid he was about to die, had confessed to murdering Michelle. I'd appealed to Darlene's sisterly instincts, getting her to agree that Debbie didn't need to know the dirty details about Michelle until after she and Dale got back from their honeymoon.

Truth be told, I'd done it more for Michelle's sake than Debbie's—it had been Michelle's last wish to not ruin her best friend's wedding, and I'd done my best to honor that.

Darlene had surprised me; she'd shed a few genuine tears for Michelle before she'd blistered my ears with some well-deserved names for Randy, a few of which I'd never heard before. Then she'd picked up the phone and taken things one step further—her defensive instincts had kicked into high gear, and she wasn't about to let her baby sister's wedding be ruined. It turned out that she used to date the Hogansville Chief of Police, and she'd called in a favor by asking him to keep news of Randy's arrest under wraps until after the wedding. Hard to do in a small town like Hogansville, but the now-married chief didn't stand a chance against a determined Darlene. As far as Debbie and everyone else knew, Randy was in the hospital after wrapping his truck around a tree, period. Anybody who spilled the beans about Michelle's murder before the wedding was going to have a pissed-off red-haired spitfire on their hands.

Darlene was still breathing fire a day later in the dressing room in the back of the church, though she'd used up most of it on the florist, who'd showed up late to decorate. To Debbie, however, she'd been nothing but sweet, helping her dress and fussing over her like a mother hen.

"But now the procession is ruined," Debbie fretted. "There's four bridesmaids and only three groomsmen; even if Nicki walks down by herself, the ceremony will end up lopsided, and so will the pictures afterward."

I seized my chance. "I don't mind not being in the wedding, Debbie. If I dropped out, the wedding party would be even again." I waved a hand toward the pink sundress and sandals I was wearing. "I'm not even dressed yet, so it's no big deal." I'd put off wearing the ugly yellow dress until the last possible second, and it looked like it might pay off.

Darlene shot me a sardonic, knowing glance, but kept her mouth shut.

Unfortunately, Aunt Nadine, who'd been fussing over the bridal bouquets, was not about to let me off the hook. "Of course you're going to be in the wedding, Nicki. You're family. I only wish my sister Emily had lived to see this day." Aunt Nadine's lip quivered, and I knew I was sunk. "All five of our girls together, sharing this joyous occasion."

Crap.

Easy for Aunt Nadine to talk; she looked pretty in rose-colored silk, while I had to wear one of the most hideous bridesmaid dresses I'd ever seen. "You'd better get moving, Nicki; the wedding starts in ten minutes."

The atmosphere in the tiny dressing room at the back of the church was hectic—it was crammed to the gills with women in various stage of undress. Aunt Nadine bent to help my niece Brittany, who made a cute flower girl, while Donna and Diane bickered over whose hat belonged to who.

"Everything will be fine, Debbie," Darlene said, sliding home the final hairpin that held her sister's veil in place. The yellow bridesmaid dress I hated looked surprisingly good on her, which tipped me off as to who'd picked it out. The yellow hat brought out the auburn in her red hair. "Everything's going to be fine."

"Can somebody zip me?" whined cousin Donna. "I don't think Bebe got my measurements right."

"If you'd put the Twinkies down once in a while she

wouldn't have had to keep letting it out," Diane snipped, turning her sister around in order to oblige.

"At least I ain't a bean pole," Donna snipped back. "Men like a woman with a little meat on their bones."

"Would you two just stop it?" The bride's nerves were obviously frayed, and her sisters' squabbling wasn't helping. "You're ruining my big moment!"

"Huh," Diane muttered. "Only thing big around here is Donna's butt."

"I heard that," Donna shrilled. "Mama, did you hear what she said to me?"

"Now girls," Aunt Nadine began, but I tuned them out, resigned to my fate. With a sigh, I grabbed the hanger that held my dress and went down the hall to the ladies' room to get dressed.

Forget the bride. Right now *I* was the one who needed a moment.

The wedding went off without a hitch, if you ignored little Brittany bursting into tears halfway down the aisle and throwing her basket of flower petals on the carpet. Darlene took it in stride, catching her daughter by the hand and dragging her along to one of the front pews to be snagged by an elderly woman who shushed her with hugs and kisses. By the time I started down the aisle, bringing up the rear behind my three cousins, Brittany's tantrum had subsided to sniffles, barely heard above the processional music.

The church was packed. It looked like the whole town had turned out for Debbie's wedding, and I was glad. It was her big day, pineapple dresses, flowered hats and all.

There was Joe, smiling at me from a pew, tall and

handsome in a pinstriped suit and the vintage Hermes tie I'd given him for the occasion. I tried not to look at Evan, knowing he'd make me laugh, but couldn't help but notice how fabulous he looked in a untucked fitted buttondown and gray silk blazer. His boyfriend Butch stood next to him, bald head gleaming, muscular shoulders straining the fabric of his coat, a single daisy pinned to his lapel.

Then I was at the front of the church, taking my place next to Diane. Silence for a moment, broken only by a final sniffle from Brittany, and the wedding march began. Despite my desire to be somewhere else, wearing something else (*anything* else), I felt my heart swell along with the music.

Nicholette Nadine Styx, romantic sucker extraordinaire.

A shuffle of feet as everyone rose, and all heads turned toward the rear of the church. All heads except Joe's, that is. He was looking at me. I gave him a wink, and was rewarded by the way his smile deepened, warming me to my toes. I might look like a pineapple piñata in a borrowed dress, but Joe didn't seem to mind.

Debbie was glowing, trembling on the arm of my Uncle John as he walked her down the aisle. I shot a glance at Dale where he stood at the altar, a band of white showing on his forehead where his hat usually rode. The pants of his rented tuxedo were hemmed too short, and the sleeves too long, but he was beaming as he watched Debbie come toward him.

The church organ was only slightly off-key. I risked a glance at Evan, not surprised to find him clutching at Butch's arm, a bit dewey-eyed as he watched the bride. I was quite familiar with his fairytale visions of me in white and him in Armani—we'd talked about our ideal weddings since we were kids in junior high school.

Evan caught me looking at him, but he just arched a blond eyebrow, then turned his gaze back to the altar.

A lump rose in my throat as Uncle John said the words that gave Debbie away, placing her hand in Dale's.

My dad would never get a chance to do that. He and my mom had died together on that wet stretch of road seven years earlier. It was my only comfort, knowing they'd died as they'd lived, together.

I missed them so much.

And then it was time for the vows, which I only half-listened to. My attention was distracted by a shaft of light that came through the stained glass window over the altar. Dust motes sparkled, twisting and spinning, and then there she was—though no one could see her but me.

Michelle, dry and smiling, come to watch her best friend get married.

Her form was vague, indistinct, wavering like a mirage in the beam of light that carried her. I knew what it must cost her to fight the pull of the Light, to anchor herself here for however long it took to see Debbie wed.

But she did, and when it was over, when the "I do's" had both been said, she turned to me with a smile and mouthed, "Thank you."

To my eyes, Michelle looked like she did that day in the bridal shop, before she knew she was dead—young and carefree and smiling. I gave her a little nod, then jerked my chin toward the stained glass window, trying hard not to cry.

Time to get going, ghoulfriend.

Then she was gone, and the recessional march was playing, and we all stood up to watch Debbie and her redneck prince leave the church in triumph.

The reception was held right there at the church, in a big meeting room right off the kitchen. Dale and Debbie danced their first dance to "Can You Feel The Love Tonight," and the funny thing was, I did. The way they looked at each other was really sweet, and I even dared hope that they'd be happy together.

Maybe their particular litter of little rednecks wouldn't be so bad.

My Aunt Nadine and Uncle John were both beaming; flower girl Brittany had forgotten her tantrum and was being chased around the tables by her sister Amber; Donna and Diane squabbled amiably over how much rum was needed to thoroughly spike the punch.

"Aren't you going to introduce me to your friends, Nicki?" Darlene had stopped by our table with a plateful of food from the buffet. She'd already met Joe—I'd introduced him after he'd waited patiently in the front pew during our interminable post-wedding photo session. Now she was eyeing both Evan and Butch with interest.

"Yes, this is my partner, Evan Owenby," I said, patting Evan fondly on the arm. "And this is *his* partner, Butch." I leaned in toward Darlene, remembering what she'd said to me at the shower, and stage-whispered, "That's what we're supposed to be calling it these days."

To her credit, Darlene just cut her eyes at me and laughed, extending a hand to Evan and Butch in turn. "I'm Darlene," she said, "Nicki's favorite cousin."

"Have a seat, Darlene." Joe rose, pulling out a chair for my cousin like the gentleman he usually was. "Join us."

And to my surprise, she did. We were laughing and chatting with surprising ease, when Debbie came over to our table, flushed and happy.

"I have *got* to sit down," she said, fanning herself with a hand. "I need to catch my breath."

Evan leapt up before Joe did and pulled out a chair for her. "You sit right next to me," he said gallantly, "and tell me *all* the details about your bee-*yoo*-tiful wedding. *Love* the dress. Who did the catering?"

I saw Butch's arm move toward Evan, and knew they were holding hands beneath the table. Both men listened, spellbound, as Debbie held court, while Joe and I exchanged smiles.

Barely a minute passed before my Aunt Nadine came bustling over. "Don't get too comfortable, sweetie. It's almost time to cut the cake," she said to Debbie. Glancing around, she added distractedly, "I can't believe Michelle isn't here. Even if you two had a little spat, surely she could've made it to the reception."

"It's okay, Mom," Debbie said cheerfully. "She's with us in spirit."

Darlene froze, fork halfway to her mouth, but I bit back another smile, knowing what was coming.

"I got a text message from her last night," Debbie went on. "She was really sorry for acting like such a bi—" Debbie caught herself, shooting her mother a guilty glance. Apparently getting married didn't change the normal mother/daughter dynamic. "Like such a twit. She apologized, and we're cool, but she was too embarrassed to face everybody after bailing on me at the last minute."

Darlene couldn't help herself. She lowered her fork and asked, "Are . . . are you sure it was Michelle?"

"Of course it was her; my cellphone has caller ID. Besides, who else would it be, silly?" Debbie grinned at her sister. "Michelle was probably worried that *somebody* might make a scene."

Darlene gasped in outrage, ready to spit fire, but she just happened to catch my eye, and subsided. Instead, she took a big bite of potato salad, chewing determinedly, a fixed look on her face.

"Well," Aunt Nadine said, sounding doubtful, "I'm just surprised, that's all. It's not like Michelle to miss something as big as this—she's your best friend."

"It's okay," Debbie said, rising to her feet with a smile on her face. "Michelle and I are good. We'll kiss and make up in person when Dale and I get back from our honeymoon. Now let's go cut the cake."

Darlene waited until Debbie moved away, then swallowed her potato salad hastily. She leaned over to hiss, "How could Debbie have possibly gotten a text message from Michelle last night?"

I shrugged. "Who knows? Maybe she sent it earlier and the message was delayed or something. I imagine the cellphone service here in Hogansville can be pretty spotty."

Darlene eyed me narrowly, sensing bullshit when she heard it, but there was nothing she could do about it. Donna called her name, urging her over to the cake table, and she went, but not without shooting me one final glance over her shoulder.

"Text message, hm?" Joe murmured in my ear. "Aren't you the clever one? How'd you manage that?"

Bebe of Bebe's Bridal had been all too happy to turn over Michelle's cellphone when I'd gone back to the store to pick up my dress. I'd told her Michelle asked me to get it for her (which was true), and that was that.

As to the actual message, I knew it by heart, since I was the one who'd typed it:

SRY 4 BEING SUCH A SHIT, G/F. PLS 4GIVE ME. SRY TO MISS WEDDING, BUT WILL BE W/U IN SPIRIT, I PROMISE. LUV U 4 EVAH! BFF, CHELLE

"Don't you worry about how I managed it," I said to Joe, teasingly. "I have my ways."

"You certainly do," he answered, with a gleam in his eye. "By the way, I've really enjoyed seeing you in that pineapple dress," Joe murmured.

I shot him an incredulous look.

"And I'm going to enjoy it even more when I rip it off," he said, smiling.

Drawing him even closer, my breast against his arm, I eyed him beneath my lashes.

"My hero," I sighed.

Terri Garey

A Southern girl with an overactive imagination, **TERRI GAREY** grew up in Florida, always wondering why tropical prints and socks with sandals were considered a fashion statement. She survived the heat by reading in the shade, and watching cool shows like *The Twilight Zone* and the classic gothic soap opera *Dark Shadows*. Born too late to be a hippy and too early to be a Goth, Terri did the logical thing and became a computer geek.

Balancing a career with marriage and motherhood convinced her that life was too short to rely entirely on the left side of her brain, and quirky ideas about life among the undead began to replace the dry logic of computers. Deciding imagination was her best weapon in the war against reality, Terri dove even deeper into the world of the unexplained and started writing her own demented tales from the dark side. Her debut novel, *Dead Girls Are Easy*, was released in September 2007 and will be followed by the sequel, *A Match Made in Hell*, in July 2008. She still lives in the Sunshine State with her husband and three children and still refuses to wear tropical prints or socks with sandals.

Visit Terri Garey on the web at *www.tgarey.com* or *www.harpercollins.com/TerriGarey*.

THE WEDDING KNIGHT

Kathryn Smith

Chapter 1

London, 1879

"And of course you know that Violet is to be married next week."

Payen Carr froze, a large bite of rare steak halfway to his mouth. He raised his head to smile pleasantly—falsely so—at the elderly woman across the table. "Who?"

Lady Verge fixed him with a vaguely chiding expression, as though she thought him deliberately obtuse—which, of course, he was. "Violet Wynston-Jones, the Earl of Wolfram's ward. You do remember dear Violet, do you not?"

Payen shoved the steak into his mouth and chewed thoughtfully, savoring the rich juices as they embraced his tongue. Remember "dear" Violet? Damn it all, he couldn't seem to forget her. She was the reason he had left England five years ago, and now on his first night back in the city, she was the first subject he heard spoken of. He began to cut another slice of meat.

Married. Good. At least she hadn't been sitting

around pining for him as he'd feared. Not pining at all if she had met someone she liked the look of enough to marry. Enough to share a bed with.

"Payen."

Who was she marrying? Some rich young buck, no doubt. Handsome, he'd wager. Human—that went without saying. And probably hung like a stallion.

"Payen!"

He looked up just as his dinner plate shattered. He had driven his knife right through the fine china. Oh, hell. Shame-faced, he met Lady Verge's wide blue gaze. "Sorry, old girl. Wasn't paying attention."

"I'd say it is safe to assume that you *do* remember Miss Wynston-Jones after all."

A gentleman should remember the women whose beds he shared, especially the virgins. Especially those named Violet.

"Of course I remember the girl."

Lady Verge watched him with a gimlet gaze, her eyes unnaturally bright in her pale, English rose complexion. He had met and befriended Lord Verge some forty years past and remained a friend right up until the man's death eight years ago. The most painful drawback of immortality was watching one's friends age and die. Once, Payen had determined to never befriend a human again. That resolve hadn't lasted more than ten years—a damn sight longer than most vows he made.

One vow he took very seriously was his promise to look after Margaret—Lady Verge—not that she needed his assistance. She was one of the few humans who knew that he was a vampire. At first she'd been a little afraid of him, and more than a little disgusted, but once she'd realized that he wasn't some undead fiend, preying on children, and came to know him as a person, she accepted him as her husband's friend, and her own. Payen had never bothered to tell her that he was part demon, turned that way by willingly drinking from a chalice that contained the essence of the Vampire Queen, Lilith. He had done so to protect that same chalice from others who would use it for some unknown dark purpose, but that didn't change the fact that as a "child" of Lilith he had been cursed to walk in darkness by the Almighty. It was a long story, as most of the good ones were, and he really didn't want this church-going woman thinking he was an affront to her God.

"I take it that you have not been invited to the happy occasion?"

"Must have gotten lost in the post."

"Yes," she agreed politely. "It must have, indeed."

Appetite now lost, his plate in ruins, Payen placed his knife and fork neatly together across the ruined china and dabbed at his mouth with his snowy white napkin. "Miss Wynston-Jones's fiancé, is he a good man?"

"He is." Damn it all, that wasn't sympathy in her eyes, was it? Because it shouldn't be there—wouldn't be there if she knew that he had robbed Violet's soon-to-be husband of his wedding night prize. And no one knew that he and Violet had shared a bed one glorious night. No one but the two of them.

"They had their photograph taken for the engagement. Perhaps after dinner you would like to see it?"

No. He'd rather eat this broken plate. Rather stick this fork into the soft, squishy part of his eye. "Of course."

After a dessert he barely tasted—it might have been

dirt for all he knew—Payen followed his hostess to her favorite parlor—the one dripping in lace and painted the most nauseating shade of powdery pink—and sat while she poured them both a glass of sherry. His mind remained focused on the same topic during the entire ordeal.

His Violet was getting married.

That meant she wasn't *his* anymore. That was supposed to be a good thing. It was. It was a bloody good thing.

Margaret—he was never to call her Maggie, or worse, Peg—joined him on the sofa a few moments later with a glass of sherry, which might as well be water as far as the effect it would have on him—and a small framed photograph. Despite the wine's lack of potency, he took a drink before looking at the picture.

Black, white and gray did nothing to capture the essence of Violet, yet there she was all the same. A kick in the chest would have affected him less. In a tightly fitting gown with a demure square neckline and lace at the elbows, and her thick hair piled up on top of her head, she looked every inch the proper young woman. Only he knew there was nothing demure about her, nothing at all. But where was the gleam in her eye that he so adored? Why wasn't she smiling and turning her cheeks into little apples he so loved to nibble upon? She looked so serious, so mature. He may as well be looking at a stranger with black hair, gray eyes, and pale gray skin, garbed in yet more gray. This was not his vibrant Violet.

And he blamed the equally colorless man seated in front of her.

The fiancé—he didn't even know the boy's name, and didn't care to—was just that, a boy. He might have been five and twenty at best—just a few years younger than Payen had been when he drank from the Blood Grail, taking his oath to protect both it and the world from the forces of evil more than seven centuries ago.

Anyone under the age of 90 was youthful as far as he was concerned. Which was why he had no business taking such an interest in Violet's affairs.

"Her fiancé is Rupert Villiers," Margaret remarked with forced neutrality. "Handsome, isn't he?"

Payen shrugged, his gaze never leaving the gray girl in the photograph. "I wouldn't know the current taste in good looks." He looked at the boy—Villiers—once more. He had a tolerable enough face. "Is he French?"

"Heavens, no!" Margaret was one of those Brits who retained a great disdain for the French, no matter how many French dishes she served and French fashions she wore. "His family has been in England for many generations."

Payen smiled, enjoying egging her on. "But they were French, once upon a time. De Villiers, I would imagine."

Margaret sniffed and extended her hand for the photograph. "He's a lovely young man. He went to Oxford."

"So did I," He replied. His gaze settled on the photograph one last time, and as his old friend tried to take it, his fingers tightened on the frame. The hand-carved wood groaned. "Jesus H. Christ."

"Ouch!" Margaret shook her hand as Payen snatched the photograph from her.

Payen ignored her. Normally he would have apologized immediately—he was nothing if not polite—but the roar of his own blood in his ears robbed him of all thought of decorum. He was on his feet, staring at the tiny detail that had somehow managed to grab his attention.

He wouldn't have seen it if Villiers hadn't chosen to place his hand over the one Violet set on his shoulder.

On the forefinger of the boy's right hand was a ring. Its brightness told Payen that it was silver, but he would have known that regardless from the signet on the top. Were he human, he probably wouldn't be able to see the detail, but he hadn't been human since before the Villiers family stopped being French.

The boy wore the mark of the Order of the Silver Palm. It had been so long since Payen had seen it, that at first he almost hadn't recognized it, but there it was—a reminder of why he had become what he was. A reminder of betrayals that managed to enrage him even now.

The Silver Palm had been formed by men who were once Templars—men who were supposed to be deserving of the title "knight." It was the Order that he had vowed to protect the Blood Grail from, and it was the Order that had betrayed the Templars by spreading those horrible rumors started by King Philip of France. Because of them, many had suffered unjustly. Jacques de Molay, the last Grand Master, had been burned alive. Payen had lost many friends and sometimes, he still felt that old guilt at having survived. The Blood Grail was gone—under the protection of others now—but still he existed, because he had made a promise, and as long as the Blood Grail existed—as long as there was the slightest whimper from the Silver Palm, he would go on.

So long. And it chilled him to the bone to see evidence of the group he had started to hope no longer existed. Stopped his heart to see a member of that order holding his Violet's hand.

"Payen, my dear, whatever is the matter?" Margaret didn't hide her concern, she never had.

He glanced at her, knowing that she had hoped to get a reaction out of him when she told him about Violet's marriage—and that he hadn't given her the one she wanted. "When's the ceremony?"

"Tomorrow morning. I'll be leaving at eight. Payen? Where are you going?"

He gave her the photograph. He had to hurry. He had to get there before dawn. Had to get there in time to speak to Henry and Liza, Violet's guardians.

"Have my things sent on to Hertford, would you, Old Girl? And I shouldn't worry about getting up early tomorrow morning." He smiled grimly. "There isn't going to be a wedding."

A girl should be happy on the eve of her marriage, Violet Wynston-Jones thought as she gazed around the crowded ballroom of her guardian, the Earl of Wolfram's Hertford Mansion. A young lady should be ecstatic that all her friends and family had gathered to witness her wed a highly suitable and handsome young man.

So why wasn't she happy? Why was she struck by this persistent anxiety? The answer was as obvious as the longing in her breast every time she gazed at the door.

Payen wasn't there. He wouldn't be coming. Even if he somehow managed to arrive in time, he could never risk the sunlight to watch her get married. He didn't love her enough.

Sunlight killed vampires.

Straightening her shoulders—her too-broad shoulders, she often complained—she forced herself to stand as tall as possible, which with the heels on her shoes and high pile of her hair, put her somewhere close to six feet. Sturdy. That was what her father used to call her before he died. Strapping. Solid. *Robust*.

Losing a full stone over the past two months hadn't changed that opinion of herself either. Every time she looked in the mirror she saw a woman better suited to hard labor than the life of a lady. Though she was dressed in the height of fashion in a slim gown of violet satin that came down low over her shoulders with a tiny, ivory lace ruffle, clung to her torso and hips to froth around her legs in little frilly layers, and cascaded out behind her in a small train from a delicate, gathered bustle, she still felt every inch the same large awkward girl who had first come to live with the earl and countess—Henry and Eliza—after her parents' passing twelve years before.

The only time she had ever *not* felt like that girl was when Payen Carr looked at her, and she hadn't laid eyes on him since that fateful night five years ago.

Lifting a glass of champagne to her lips, she allowed her gaze to drift about the ballroom until it landed on the tall, pleasing form of her husband-to-be. Rupert was possessed of thick, wavy hair, bright blue eyes and a smile that could charm the devil himself. He also had a good sense of humor and an inquisitive mind, which made conversation with him a treat. With any luck, he'd be one of those men who didn't know a virgin from a dishrag and wouldn't notice that his bride wasn't innocent.

Then again, after five years, maybe her hymen had grown back. She'd heard Eliza and several of her friends joking about such a thing once.

As if sensing her gaze, Rupert turned his face in her

direction. His gaze locked with hers and he smiled, raising his own glass of champagne in salute before having his attention called by his aunt, Lady Gantley.

"You have the look of a morning bride," came a familiar voice at her elbow. It was Eliza, the woman who had become a mother to her.

"Do I?" Violet took a sip of champagne before she could say anything else—such as beg the older woman to save her from her fate. Nerves. It was just nerves.

"Yes." Since Eliza was smiling, Violet took this to be a positive thing. "Your cheeks are flushed, your eyes are bright and your hands are trembling. Premarital jitters."

"Yes, you must be right. I am feeling rather . . . anxious."

"It's all very normal, my dear." Eliza slipped a slender arm around her. At just over five feet, she was a tiny little pixie compared to Violet's gargantuan self, with glossy blond hair and pale green eyes.

"I'm pleased to hear that." Was it normal to keep hoping the vampire who stole your heart and then abandoned you would walk through the door insisting that you were making a terrible mistake? Was it normal to hope that he then would sweep you into his arms—because a man that strong could tote you around like a rag doll—and whisk you off to some dark, gothic ruin where he would ravish you for a fortnight before finally making you his forever? Because that didn't sound normal for a bride to be thinking—not when the vampire wasn't the man she was about to marry.

"The night before I was set to marry Henry I tried to run away," Eliza confessed in a conspiratorial tone, with a smile that said she was glad she hadn't succeeded. "I fashioned a rope out of my bed clothes and tried to climb down from the balcony."

Violet turned to her in surprise, closing the space between them so as not to be overheard by nosy guests. "What happened?"

Narrow shoulders formed a tiny shrug. "I made it to the garden gate. Who do you suppose was waiting there?"

"Your father?"

Eliza shook her head, diamond and emerald earrings swaying with the gesture. "Henry."

"He knew you were running away?"

"No. He was running away. He just came to say good-bye." At Violet's gasp she continued, "He could stand his mother's interference no longer and had resolved to leave for France that night."

"What happened? Obviously you got married." She knew the outcome, but it was the in between that fascinated her.

"We did. We realized that what we were running away from was our families and their plans and expectations. We eloped to Gretna Green—I grew up but a few miles from there in Cumbria, as you know—and returned in time for our English wedding, already married."

Grinning, Violet shook her head. "Why? You eloped, why go through the ceremony the next day?"

Eliza smiled broadly, like a delighted child. "Because we owed it to our parents who had gone through all those arrangements—but we were able to stand against their heavy-handedness as man and wife. Knowing that we were already married made the rest of it cease to matter."

Violet had met Eliza's parents—Henry's too—and could only imagine the row that must have resulted. "Your mother must have wanted to paddle your backside."

"She did, but there was nothing she could do. I wasn't her concern anymore."

They shared a chuckle, and when Eliza held out her arms, Violet went into them without hesitation, accepting the embrace and all the love that came with it.

"Trust your heart, my dear," the older woman whispered in her ear. "It will never steer you wrong."

Violet's good humor faded, but she kept a smile pasted on her face. That was exactly what worried her. Her heart was telling her to get the bloody hell out of there and run as far away as she could.

As Eliza left her to return to her duties as hostess, Violet glanced around once more, panic building in her chest. There had to be a way to escape. A way out without disappointing everyone.

And then, as though God saw and took pity on her, the door to the ballroom was flung open. The small string quartet playing in the upper corner stopped their music, and the dancers with it. Everyone turned their attention to this new guest, who stood just inside the door, his hair mussed by the wind.

Violet's heart stopped cold. "Oh no," she whispered, casting a disbelieving glance heavenward. "Why did you have to answer *this* prayer?"

It was Payen, looking no older than he had five years earlier when he'd left her. Oh his hair was a little different—a little shorter, neater, but just as thick and golden. His eyes were the same sherry color she remembered, his lips just as exquisitely perfect, and almost too feminine. He was beauty personified— Apollo come to life. Over six feet tall, he wore evening attire in a manner that would have made angels weep. As he swept into the room, black cloak swirling behind him, he kept his attention fastened on one person—her.

Violet shivered under the force of that gaze and the intensity behind it. Whatever his reasons for being there—they were not to wish her happy, of that she had no doubt.

Eliza and Henry intercepted him when he was mere feet from her. And Rupert, realizing something strange was afoot, came to stand by her side. The ballroom was silent, save for the whispers circulating. *Who was he? What was he doing there?*

"Carr," Henry greeted warmly, if not a little cautiously. "What a pleasant surprise."

"I'm not here on a social call, Henry," came the low, rasp of the vampire's reply. And he looked like a vampire tonight—a predator from the darkest shadows. And God help her, Violet would let him ravish her right there in front of everyone if he asked.

"We're celebrating, Payen," Eliza said softly. "Perhaps you didn't know that Violet is to be married tomorrow."

He spared her a glance, brief but so electrically charged Violet felt it in her toes. "I know. I've come to stop it."

Chapter 2

Payen's announcement caused a bit of a commotion. This was, of course, in comparison to the Crusades, the measure for all his confrontations.

"Damnit, Payen!" That was Henry. "What is the meaning of this?"

Eliza joined in. "Stop the wedding?"

The whole room was in an uproar, and the groom—the little tosser who Payen had no choice but to call handsome indeed—was saying something to Violet, practically yelling in her ear.

Violet wasn't talking. Like him, she was the only silent person in the room. In fact, Violet didn't seem to be listening to her fiancé either. She was staring rather intently at Payen, who was staring rather intently right back. She looked . . . hopeful.

She also looked damned beautiful, even more so than the girl he remembered. More than that colorless girl in the photograph.

So tall. With those shoes and that mass of sable hair

she was almost as tall as he. She had lost weight, but that only called more attention to the magnificent bounty of her breasts, framed delectably by the square neckline of a gown the color of her name. She was a Junoesque woman—a true Amazon. Her face, just a tad too round to be a perfect oval, was the most fascinating composition of features—large, hazel eyes, high cheekbones that appled when she smiled, a little slender nose, slightly tilted, and sweet, berry lips that seemed designed to curve naturally into a smile.

She wasn't smiling right then.

"Why would you want to stop my wedding, Mr. Carr?" Her voice, soft as it was, was enough to make him want to drop to one knee and promise her the moon.

Several hundred reasons came to mind, but only one mattered at that moment. He raised a finger and pointed at Villiers. "He is the spawn of Satan." Not exactly accurate, but he didn't have time to get too detailed.

A collective gasp filled the room. Violet's jaw dropped and Henry colored up like a gin blossom on a drunk's nose. "You forget yourself, sir!"

Henry only called him "sir" when he was royally pissed. Payen turned an expressionless gaze toward him. "I assure you, my dear Lord Wolfram, I forget nothing."

His friend frowned, obviously realizing then, that he was deadly serious.

"I don't know who you are," Villiers informed him, stepping in front of Violet as though to shield her. "But you are fortunate, sir, that duels are illegal."

Payen raked the little miscreant with a bored gaze. "Indeed. I hate spilling blood."

The deeper meaning of his words was not lost on Violet, whose eyes widened as she peered around Villiers at him. Villiers, meanwhile, flushed a rich scarlet. "You do not know me, yet you insult me."

"Yes, that is badly done of me." Payen sketched a bow. "Payen Carr, Mr. Villiers." He reached out and snatched the other man's hand, lifting it to the light even as he tried to pull free. "And *this* is an insult to me." He was careful not to touch the silver that would burn his flesh like open flame.

Villiers scowled at the signet on his finger. "My ring insults you?"

"I am disgusted by what it stands for, and those who support it."

Henry, perhaps the only one who remembered they had an audience, came between them, forcibly breaking the grip Payen had on Villiers. "Gentlemen, perhaps we should discuss this somewhere more private."

A disbelieving bark of laughter broke from Villiers' throat. "My lord, surely you don't believe this madman?"

Henry, God love him, sent the boy a grim look. "My study. Now."

Payen, Eliza, Violet, and Villiers fell into step behind him. Payen would rather not turn his back on the Silver Palm disciple but he trusted that the bastard would not risk exposing himself by attempting to cause Payen bodily harm.

He walked beside Eliza, ignoring the curious stares and whispers as they cut through the crowd. He glanced around the ballroom instead, noting the salmon color on the walls and the cream trim. "You've redecorated," he commented absently.

"Yes," Eliza replied. "Two years ago."

"I like it. Much easier on the eyes than that awful blue it was last time I was here."

"You have a lot of nerve returning this way, my friend," she murmured for his ears alone.

"She can't marry him, Eliza." He could tell from the startled light in her eyes that she knew he meant it—and that he would do everything in his power to keep the wedding from taking place.

"Oh dear."

Behind them, Payen could hear Violet and the miscreant talking. Their voices were low, but not so low that he couldn't listen in—selective hearing was one of the perks of vampirism. Most of the time he could keep the world out, but when he wanted, he could hear mice scurrying in the attic above.

"Who is this idiot?" Villiers demanded.

"He's a friend of Henry's," Violet replied. Payen might have smiled at her defensive tone, were it not for the fact that she hadn't argued the "idiot" remark.

"What is he to you?" Ahh, now this was interesting. Villiers was jealous—not as dumb as he looked, obviously. But Payen knew that looking dumb didn't exclude a man from being dangerous.

Violet sighed. "Right now, I'm not certain."

Fair enough. After all he shagged her and then walked out of her life five years ago and never once tried to get in touch, but that didn't stop his chest from pinching at her bewildered reply. Some part of him expected her to know that he was motivated by nothing more than a desire to protect her. He would rather walk out into the middle of Hyde Park on a Sunday afternoon and fry like an egg than see her influenced by the Order of the Silver Palm, a group who would think nothing of destroying a sweet thing like her.

Henry led them downstairs, to a back corner of the house where he kept his study. Years ago, when

Henry and Eliza had barely made this house their own, Payen had christened that room Henry's sanctuary. It was far away from the dining room and the drawing room his wife liked to use for entertaining, and it was large enough to contain a billiards table, a sofa and several chairs, a card table, and a massive oak desk. This room, he was pleased to note, had not been redecorated.

And then, of course, he wondered inappropriately if Violet had changed anything about her bedroom, and if she still had that demure nightgown she'd worn that sweet, hot night.

This close to her, with the scent of her engulfing him like a face full of lilacs, it was so hard to keep the memory of that night at bay. Images of the two of them entwined, desperate and damp, tender and trembling, flooded his mind. His gums itched with fangs ready to extend, the urge to feed almost as strong as the urge to mate. He had done both with Violet, and that only whetted both appetites all the more.

Once they were all inside the study, each of them drifting away from Payen until he stood in the center of their haphazard circle, the questions began.

"What the devil do you mean, coming into my house and causing such a scene?" Henry demanded. "Deuce take it, Payen! I would expect better of you."

Payen gave him a quick nod. "You're right to have such expectations. I wouldn't have come at all were it not important." Was it his imagination, or did he see Violet wince out of the corner of his eye?

"Perhaps you should explain," Eliza suggested, when no one else seemed inclined to speak. They all just stood there, staring at him with varying degrees of curiosity and antagonism.

Payen focused on Henry, who he had known since he was a babe. Payen had been friends with his father, and his grandfather before that. A long time ago, a Rexley—Henry's family name—had been a Templar the same as Payen, and they had been friends. That relationship had led to a connection with the family that had followed almost every generation since. The Rexleys were the only people he ever revealed himself to, except for a handful of others over the countless decades.

Stephen Rexley had been killed by a man wearing a ring just like the one on Villiers' hand.

Remembering that made it easy for Payen to look Henry in the eye as he jerked his head in Villiers' direction. "He belongs to the Order of the Silver Palm."

Understanding drained the heightened color from Henry's dusky cheeks. "Are you certain?"

"His ring proves it."

"What the devil are you about?" Villiers demanded, breaking the circle by taking several angry steps forward. "How do you know about the Order? And what business is it of yours if I belong?"

Payen turned his head, stopping the young man dead in his tracks with a simple look. "I know more about the Silver Palm than I wager you do. It was your people who helped fuel King Philip's distrust of the Templars. The Order has been involved in every sinister plot known to man since Judas betrayed Christ."

Villiers stared at him, blue eyes wide with fear—and complete bafflement. How could he seem so innocent and wear that ring?

"You think Violet shouldn't marry me because of something that happened more than five centuries ago?"

De Molay had *burned*.

"Six," Payen corrected. "October thirteenth in the year

of our Lord thirteen-hundred and seven." He remembered as though it was but a handful of years ago. "And no. I won't allow you to marry Violet because you are part of a vile organization that should have been slaughtered out of existence a long time ago."

If Villiers hadn't thought him mad before, he certainly did now. Payen could smell his fear, his disgust. There was anger there as well—defiance.

"You go too far, sir. Whom Violet marries is not your decision, and there is nothing vile about the Order. I would explain that to you were I not sworn to secrecy by our ancient laws. Every male in my family for generations has been a member, and none of them have ever broken any laws or betrayed any confidences."

Payen smiled—coldly. "Not to other members at any rate. But your family wealth is tainted by the blood of good men, Mr. Villiers. Men who were murdered so that your precious Order might thrive."

Villiers turned his attention from Payen to Henry and Eliza, then Violet. "The three of you cannot believe this?"

"Not of you, Rupert," Eliza said softly.

"But of my family?" He shoved his hands through his hair, laughing almost hysterically. "I can't believe this! Vi, you don't believe him, do you?"

She stared at him. "I don't want to, Rupert, but I know that Mr. Carr has reason to feel as he does, and if you belong to such a despicable group . . ."

"Despicable? Good God, listen to yourself! You would judge as such an order you know nothing of? An order to which I, the man you are supposed to love, belongs?" His hands came down on her shoulders. "I would never harm anyone. You know that."

She nodded. "I know."

Payen watched the confusion and indecision play across her features. He hated doing this to her. Any satisfaction that came from preventing her marriage to this bastard dissolved in the wake of her pain. He knew then that Villiers was going to press her, and that she would give in out of guilt. Then what would he have to do—steal her away? Because he would, if that's what it took.

Time for more underhanded measures.

"Did Violet ever tell you about me?" he asked, his tone conversational—convivial even.

Villiers shot him a scowl. "No."

"Hmm. That surprises me." Violet shook her head at him, face pale as she realized exactly where he was going. He hoped she could see the regret in his gaze.

"Why would that surprise you?" The younger man couldn't keep the sneer from his voice or his face. "I don't see how you are of any significance."

Arsehole. "But I am," Payen informed him, squaring his shoulders. "You see, five years ago, Violet gave me a wonderful gift."

Violet pressed a hand to her lips. "Payen, no."

Villiers took another step toward him, still scowling. "Why should I care?"

Payen smiled grimly. "Because the gift she gave me, Mr. Villiers, was her heart. You see, Violet cannot marry you because she's in love with me."

She could kill him. Would that someone give her a sword so she could take his smug head right off his divinely broad shoulders.

Instead, Violet was forced to stand there, impotent and humiliated as her fiancé and her guardians stared at her. And Payen, she noted, didn't look all that smug after all. In fact, he looked rather ashamed. He should, the bastard. Of course, it might have been worse. He could have mentioned that matter concerning her virginity.

Why of all reasons did it have to be the Order of the Silver Palm? She'd heard enough to know why he hated them and agree that he had every right, but why did that have to be the basis for his objection to her marriage? Why couldn't he have professed undying love for her instead of reminding her of how she had declared her feelings for him that night? Did he know that he was the only man she had ever loved enough to give herself to? Was he so stupid he couldn't see that she loved him still?

"Is it true?" Rupert demanded, his voice hoarse, his face white.

She stared at him helplessly before turning the same gaze to Eliza and Henry. Henry looked as though he could cheerfully murder Payen himself. Too bad the vampire could take on all four of them and not even break a sweat.

"Come," Eliza said sharply, directing a glance at both Payen and her husband. "We are going to leave Violet and Rupert alone to speak."

"I'm not leaving her with him," Payen growled. "No goddamn way."

The little blond woman glared at him. Softly, so that only he and Violet heard, she murmured, "You do as I say, Payen Carr, or I'll make sure the drapes in your room get opened just before noon."

Payen's jaw tightened, and those perfect lips thinned, but he didn't argue. He shot one last contemptuous glance at Rupert before following Henry and Eliza to the door. Violet didn't feel one ounce of sorrow toward him for the confrontation he was about to have with her adopted parents.

She was, however, feeling a great deal sorry for herself.

The door clicked shut, leaving her alone with her fiancé, a wonderful man she never meant to hurt. A man whose attention she had felt lucky to have, if she were truthful, having come to believe that no one but Payen could ever find her attractive.

Rupert lifted his gaze from his shoes, which he appeared to have been contemplating. His hair was disheveled and his eyes were bright with disappointment and hurt. Before she had thought him handsome, now he simply looked like a boy to her. Handsome meant nothing after Payen's overwhelming beauty.

"I don't deserve you," she said softly, not just because it was true, but because it was all she could think to say.

"Is it true?" He demanded, brow knitting. "Do you love him?"

She hesitated, and knew from his expression that she shouldn't have. He knew there was more now. "I did." Do.

"Did you . . . make love with him?"

That phrase made her want to giggle. Make love? She had thought so at the time, but what she had done with Payen . . . it had been crude and sweet at the same time, so wrong and yet so right. It was nothing so banal as making love—love had already been made long before she let him into her bed.

She could lie, tell him what he wanted to hear, but that wasn't fair to him. She had been looking for an out and she had been handed one. It was time to be an adult and face her mistake—face the man she had wronged. "Yes."

Rupert closed his eyes, but not before she saw the anguish in them. "Why didn't you tell me?"

"I didn't think it was any of your business." Perhaps that was a little too honest.

"None of my business?" Anger replaced hurt, easing the guilt that pierced her chest. "How was it none of my business that my fiancée had spread her legs for another man?"

This was a side of him she had never seen before. It made it easier for her, and she took advantage of that, as shameful as it was. "Have I asked you if you've been with other women?"

He looked affronted. "That's different."

"Because you're a man?"

"Of course. Men are expected to be experienced, just as a wife is supposed to be a virgin to ensure the legitimacy of the first born."

Violet laughed. She couldn't help it—this really was so ridiculous. "It was five years ago, Rupert. I think you could safely claim any children as your own."

His face was a mask of disgust. "With no guarantee that you had not lain with someone else before or after our vows."

He had every right to be angry, Violet knew and accepted that, but that she would not be spoken to in such a manner. She would not have what she had shared with Payen turned to a defect of her character.

"Yes," she agreed. "Perhaps you should make sure I haven't shagged the priest—or better yet, your groomsmen."

He flushed. "A lady doesn't use such language."

"You've already established that I'm no lady, Rupert, at least not in your eyes. I made a youthful mistake and you would punish me for it, despite the fact that I know that you went to that brothel, Maison Rouge, last time you were in London."

His mouth fell open. "How did you . . . ?"

"I overheard your friends Halpert and Gibbs talking about it that night we went to the theater. I forgave you because I thought you deserved one last indiscretion before settling down. Tell me, how does knocking boots with a whore make you better than me?"

His mouth worked, but no sound came out. He looked around the room, like a drowning man desperately seeking purchase.

"It doesn't," she answered when he remained silent. Any guilt she felt was gone now. She hadn't expected his forgiveness, nor his understanding, but by God, she would not tolerate this kind of treatment—not from a man who claimed to love her when he asked for her hand in marriage.

If he had loved her, he would have seduced her rather than going to a brothel. If he had loved her, he never would have gone to a prostitute at all.

Payen would never have done such a thing. He had his faults, but lack of loyalty was not one of them. After all, he had just destroyed her engagement out of some archaic need to protect her. As angry as she might be with him, as hurt and disappointed, she was also a little grateful.

"I think you should leave now, Rupert." Shoulders back, she stood straight and still, not caring if she was as tall as he, not giving one fig about how she looked or how large she was. Even if this was the only chance she ever had at marriage, she would not beg *this* man to have her.

She might not be perfect, and she had too many faults to list—but she deserved to be respected by her husband. She deserved love, loyalty, and compassion. It was no less than she would give.

He looked as though he was about to speak, and she had heard enough. "I'll tell our guests that the wedding has been canceled and I'll see that all the gifts are returned, you needn't worry. And the wedding breakfast will be given to the less fortunate in the village."

"You've got it all sorted out already." His tone was a mixture of disbelief, hurt, and contempt.

"I suppose I've been giving it some thought these last few days." Let him stew on *that*.

He didn't disappoint her—the astonishment on his face gave her at least a bit of satisfaction underneath the guilt that threatened to crush her once more. Ending their engagement was for the best—for both of them.

"I had no business accepting your proposal in the first place," she told him. "And for that I am truly sorry, but for anything else I might have done—for whatever transpired between myself and Payen—I refuse to apologize, to you or anyone else. You know the way out."

And then she pivoted sharply on her heel and swept from the room with all the dignity she could muster. It wasn't much, but indignation and a certain amount of relief spurred her on.

Now she was going to find Payen and have a little chat, because if that vampire thought he could breeze back into her life, muck it up, and then walk away again he was in for a big surprise.

She wasn't about to let him walk away. Not this time.

Chapter 3

Henry and Eliza were hard on him, but no more than he expected. Regardless of his friendship with them both, he had just ruined their ward's wedding and possibly her reputation. It was badly done of him, and he'd do it all over again if he had to.

All he had to do was focus on the here and now and not spend too much dwelling on how Violet's declaration had terrified and thrilled him five years before. And how it had lit a fire under his heels. He had seduced her and left her.

Damn it, she had seduced him.

The earl and his countess at least understood his motivation. They knew about Stephen Rexley—a man who had been Payen's best friend before his death. They knew of the vile nature of the Order of the Silver Palm and understood that Payen would not want to see Violet drawn into such an affiliation. What they didn't understand is how someone as "good" as Rupert Villiers could be part of such an organization.

Personally, Payen didn't care, but he offered a suggestion to ease their minds—he wasn't totally cold-hearted. "The family connection would bring him in without him having to prove himself," he told them. "But now that he's in, he'll have to undergo tests and trials similar to an initiate. They'll want to know what he's capable of, and whether or not he's worthy of being a true Disciple."

"Then there's hope for him." Eliza didn't bother to disguise her own hopefulness. "He may not be the villain you believe him to be."

Payen slid her a sharp glance. "Are you willing to wager Violet's life on whether he will remain innocent?"

She frowned, looked to her husband. "But . . ."

Payen didn't relent. "For him to have been given a ring based on name alone, his family has to be in very deep, Eliza. They wouldn't let Villiers in unless they were certain he would bow to their traditions and do exactly as they want."

"It's been centuries, Payen," Henry tried to reason with him. "Surely the Order that exists today is different from the one you fought."

He had to force himself to remain calm, to remember where their doubt stemmed from. They were not intentionally trying to fight him, they simply wanted to make this all go away.

"If I walked into one of their meetings right now and announced what I was—Templar or vampire, I would be lucky to walk out alive. And anyone associated with me would be in danger."

Something sparked in Henry's eyes. "You suspect Villiers' interest in Violet is because of you?"

"My God," Eliza breathed, pressing her palm to the

breast of her green silk gown. "This can't be happening."

Payen shrugged. Actually he hadn't thought of that, but now that the idea was in his head . . . "It's possible. Has he ever asked about me?"

"No," Henry replied. "Until tonight I don't imagine he's ever heard us mention you." His expression turned uncomfortable, even apologetic. "Violet was so upset after you left the last time that we got into the habit of not discussing you in front of her."

Eliza's gaze was cooler than her husband's. No doubt she guessed that Violet hadn't declared her love without provocation. "I suppose we know why she was so upset now, don't we? How could you, Payen?"

"Yes," came a voice from behind him. "How could you?"

He had heard the door open, of course. Heard her soft footfalls and short, angry breaths. Let her make her entrance, let her think she caught him unaware.

He turned, brow arched, face perfectly composed. Still, the sight of her with her cheeks flushed, her eyes glittering, took his breath away. She looked as though she could gladly run him through—and if he had a sword he'd be tempted to give it to her just to see her try.

Women with weapons had always been a weakness of his.

Their gazes met and locked, and it seemed to Payen as though sparks literally danced between them. He grinned. "What took you so long?"

She didn't return the smile. In fact, her thickly lashed eyes narrowed as she glared at him. "I had a wedding to cancel." It was meant to wipe the smile from his face, but it didn't—not totally.

Eliza said something in sympathy, but Payen wasn't

listening. He kept his attention focused on the Amazon before him, noting the softness of her cheek, the lush curves of her breasts straining against the neckline of her gown. To him, Violet was like a ripe, succulent peach just begging to be plucked, bitten, and sucked.

Knowing that he had kept Villiers from being the man to do just that didn't bother him one damn bit. Knowing that he might have broken Violet's heart . . . well, that was another matter.

"I think Violet wants to speak to me alone," he said, tilting his head in the direction of his friends. His gaze never left the woman whose touch haunted his dreams.

"I'm not leaving her alone with you." Eliza's voice rang with conviction. "Not after what you did."

To Payen's surprise, it was the lady herself who interjected. She swung that hazel gaze to her adopted mother and said, rather calmly, "It's all right, Eliza. I would like to talk to Payen alone."

Ignoring Henry and Eliza, Payen carefully studied Violet as her attention slowly drifted back to him. There was a confidence to her that hadn't been there before—not in her physical appearance, but in her inner self. She was not a timid little thing like her namesake. Pride warmed the inside of him. Had there ever been such a woman as Violet? As a girl she had captivated and seduced him. As a memory she had haunted his every turn. And now, as a woman, she had him ready to drop to his knees in fealty before her.

When the door clicked shut behind her guardians, she raised her chin, her gaze locking with his once more. "I should despise you for what you've done."

He nodded. "Yes."

"You deliberately betrayed a private moment—a

private declaration—between you and me just to get your own way."

A moment he would never forget. "Yes."

"You've ruined my wedding."

Did he really need to answer any more of these rhetorical questions? He straightened his shoulders. "Don't expect me to apologize, because I'm not sorry."

Her face softened. "Thank you."

Payen blinked. Shook his head. "Excuse me?"

Violet came toward him, fists clenched loosely at her sides. "Thank you for doing what I didn't have the courage to do myself." She smiled ever so slightly—sweetly. "You always were my knight in shining armor."

And then the damnedest thing happened. Instead of demanding to know what she meant—why she hadn't wanted to marry Villiers (had the bastard been forcing her into marriage?)—Payen took a step forward, pushed by an invisible hand. Violet moved as well and then she was in his embrace, her arms wrapped around his shoulders, fingers in his hair as his mouth fastened over hers.

Christ, she tasted sweet. Her lips were so pliant, so lush beneath his as they opened for him without coaxing. Her tongue met his with a passion that shook him. No woman had ever responded to him like Violet—no woman had ever elicited such a response out of him. He was hard already, ready to take her right there, standing in the middle of his friend's study. He could do it too, support her full weight as she wrapped those strong legs around his waist, hold her as she slid down the length of his cock.

He groaned into the moist heat of her mouth, and wrapped his arms around her more tightly. She didn't struggle, didn't whimper in discomfort. In fact, she pulled at his hair, clutched at his shoulder, digging her fingers into the fabric of his coat until he felt the five points of pressure on his skin. So strong, his Violet.

He lifted his head just enough to nibble on her full lower lip. His fangs had partially extended, eager for a little nibble of their own. He ignored that hunger for now. At this moment, in Violet's intoxicating presence, he was more man than vampire.

"I missed you," he heard himself confess, breathless and hoarse against her lips. "Vi, I missed you so damn much."

She pulled back, smiling at him. For a second he thought she might echo the sentiment, but she didn't. Then he thought maybe she was going to shove her knee into his crotch, but she didn't do that either.

She might as well have, so surprising were her words, "You didn't come here because of Rupert and the Silver Palm."

"No?" He questioned dumbly, still thinking with an organ much lower than his brain.

Her smile grew. "That was just the excuse you needed to stop my marriage. Ask yourself, Payen, why you needed to do that. Then, maybe I'll forgive you for making me wait five years."

"Violet—"

She cut him off, shoved him away, and he let her. "Lie to yourself if you want to, but after all this time, don't you dare lie to me. You owe me that at the very least."

And then she left him standing there, hard and horny, feeling every inch the idiot.

Because she was right.

Payen Carr was in love with her, Violet was certain of this.

What wasn't so certain was if Payen himself knew it.

Oh, he had reacted to her in all the right ways, but she had no doubt that in his mind, he had truly destroyed her wedding out of hatred for the Silver Palm.

"Bollocks," she said aloud, punctuating the silence as she set a prettily wrapped present in a pile of others to be returned.

Her friend, Sarah looked up in surprise. "What was that?"

They had been working all morning, affixing tags to gifts so that the footmen would know where to deliver them, and sorting them according to location. The London ones, and those farther abroad, would have to be delivered by post, of course.

"I said bollocks." Violet flashed a tight smile.

Sarah blinked, wide blue eyes bewildered. "Any particular reason why?"

"Because men are rubbish." She jotted down an address on a tag. "Do you know that Rupert actually got into a huff over Payen? It's fine for him to go to a brothel, but one indiscretion and I'm a slut."

Blond curls tilted as Sarah pondered the statement. "Bollocks," she chirped, drawing a chuckle from the both of them.

"Do you regret it?" Her friend asked after their laughter faded.

"Regret what? Kicking Rupert out?" Violet attached another tag. "No, I do not." She didn't either. She wasn't going to admit to having wanted a way out of the wedding, because that was too cold, and even as good a friend as Sarah might not understand, but she had no ill feelings about showing Rupert to the door after what he had said to her last night.

"No." Sarah leaned down, as though there was a

chance of someone overhearing. "Do you regret being . . . *intimate* with Mr. Carr?" Of course she knew. Violet had cried on her shoulder after Payen left.

Violet stilled, considering the response that had leapt readily to her tongue. "Not at all." It felt good to admit it to someone other than herself. "I've tried to make myself think of it as a mistake, but now I think it was the only right thing I ever did. The only thing that was ever truly for myself, with no consideration given to anyone else."

Her friend sighed, resting her elbow on a large floral-wrapped gift as she tucked her chin into her hand. "Mr. Carr is so very lovely." She arched a fair brow. "Does he look as lovely naked?"

"Lovelier," Violet quipped and they laughed once more.

A few moments passed once more in comfortable silence as the two of them worked. Somewhere in the house a clock chimed out the hour.

"Ten o'clock." Violet lifted her head as the last note faded. "We would be at the church right now." Despite her certainty that it was good that her engagement had ended before this hour, she couldn't help feel a little twinge of sorrow for the loss of her wedding day.

And all these presents.

Sarah sniffed as she peered outside at the gray and misty morning. "Bah. It's not a very cheery day for a wedding. Although, it would have been much more romantic if Mr. Carr had barged in during the ceremony rather than the party last night."

It would have been much more illuminating as well, what with Payen bursting into flames in the daylight.

"I suppose, but then Payen would have humiliated me in front of Vicar Carlson and all those guests."

Sarah shot her a concerned gaze. "At least he waited until it was just the five of you to make such an announcement."

"Yes," she murmured, but she had no illusion as to what would have happened should the situation not have followed that particular direction. "Payen would have announced it in front of everyone if it meant keeping Rupert and myself from marrying."

Damn the man, she didn't know whether she wanted to kiss him or kill him.

A sigh drifted across the room. "He must love you very much."

Violet nodded. "I think so, but he'd deny it if I asked."

"Why?"

"He claims he stopped the marriage because of something he learned about Rupert."

Sarah's nose wrinkled. "I can't imagine Rupert ever doing anything as exciting as getting himself involved in scandal—until now, of course."

"Of course." Violet's lips curved. "I'm not at liberty to discuss the details—after all, I don't know that Payen's information is true, and it's Rupert's concern, not mine. Not anymore."

"But still, Mr. Carr must care about you if he went to such lengths."

"I would hope so."

"Are you going to marry him?"

"He hasn't asked."

"But if he did?"

Smiling, Violet set yet another package aside. "If he asked, I would say yes."

An exuberant bark of laughter broke from Sarah's throat, brightening her eyes and cheeks as she clapped her hands in delight. "How wonderful! Do you think he will?"

Her smile faded. Violet tried very hard not to lie to herself and she wasn't about to start now. "No."

All the joy drained from Sarah's face. "Oh, Violet."

"Never fear, dear. I'm not too proud to ask him." That brought the light back to her friend's eyes. She didn't like seeing pity in Sarah's expression—not for her. Not when she had been raised by two wonderful sets of parents, had a fortune of her own and friends who loved her. Sarah didn't have nearly as many creature comforts as she, and yet she never complained. She never compared their circumstances. She had simply shown up on the doorstep one day when Violet first came to Hertford, and asked if Violet would be her friend. Violet had taken one look at the skinny little girl who was a head shorter than her and at least two stone lighter and thought that yes, she would.

"You would, wouldn't you?" As always, Sarah never seemed to know if Violet was jesting or not. "You'd ask him?"

Violet nodded. "I would." And she just might—if she could screw up the courage. She knew from Henry that Payen would be staying for a few days—something about wanting to make sure there was no backlash from the Silver Palm. His presence would add to the scandalbroth, but the worst of it had surely already happened.

She had a pretty good idea of what his answer would be too—some idiocy about him being a vampire and her a human. Sweet God, wasn't that easy enough to remedy? All he had to do was make her a vampire too—the fool.

The door came flying open and in burst Eliza, her face flushed and her eyes wild. She hadn't even removed her hat or gloves. "I'm going to strangle Payen Carr!"

Violet arched a brow. "You've been to town, haven't you?"

Her guardian nodded, still trying to catch her breath. "I have."

"Even though Henry told you expressly not to go. Eliza, you went looking for trouble, and found it, didn't you?"

"It found me," the older woman replied defensively. "I was at the glove shop looking for a new pair of gray gloves when Mrs. Randall approached me—that vile wretch of a woman."

Sarah's eyes widened at the venom in Eliza's tone, but Violet forced a small smile. "She couldn't wait to say something, eh?"

Eliza shook her head as she tugged at her hat pin. "Gossiping busybody."

Folding her arms over her chest, Violet braced herself. "So what's the word from town? Am I ruined?"

Eliza's arms crumpled to her side like a rag doll's. Defeated, she sank into a chair next to Sarah, holding her hat in her lap. "Yes." Her gaze locked with Violet's. "I'm certain Rupert had nothing to do with it, but given Payen's untimely arrival and the fact that he had left so abruptly five years ago . . . The gossips are convinced you were lovers and that Rupert cried off because of it. I'm so sorry my dear."

Ruined. The word sounded so strange in Violet's head. Ruin was what happened when something was soiled beyond repair. She didn't feel soiled.

Eliza was beside her now. "We'll go to France, or

Italy. You'll meet someone there, or at least let the scandal die down."

Violet shook her head. "I'm not leaving. Not yet."

"But dearest—"

"No, Eliza." Her tone was sharp, brooking no refusal. "Last time I checked, it took two people to bring about a woman's ruination. Payen Carr owes me. I let him get away five years ago, but he's not going to run away this time."

Eliza obviously didn't like the look in her eye. "Violet, what are you planning?"

"Payen is mine, and I'm his," she replied, her conviction taking the melodrama out of her words. "And it's about time he figured that out. I'm going to marry that va . . . man, if it's the last thing I do."

Chapter 4

That Eliza hadn't made good on her threat to open the drapes in his room was the first thought that occurred to Payen when he woke late that afternoon.

The second was the kiss Violet had given him the night before, the taste of it burned into his memory for all time.

Why would a woman whose wedding had just been interrupted—to put it mildly—kiss the man responsible? And the things she had said, the questions she asked. What the hell was her reasoning for that?

Ask himself why he came back, indeed. He had come to keep her from marrying a man who was part of a great evil. Did she think he took pleasure in ruining her wedding?

God, he hoped not, because he had taken pleasure in it. There had been more pleasure in preventing Violet from marrying Villiers than there had been in the last five years of his life.

Pathetic, that was.

And he resolved not to think on it any longer. He knew when he left Violet last time that there could be no future for them. As much as he adored her, the years had tossed one too many capricious women in his path. The years had taken one too many away as well. He'd been betrayed, devastated, endangered, and made a fool of one too many times.

The laughable part was that none of it had hardened him against women or love, but rather it had made him a coward, reluctant to risk his heart—or anyone else's—when there was such an overwhelming possibility of having it broken.

He listened in the darkness, concentrating on the sounds of the house until he found the one he sought. Violet. She was talking to Eliza, asking if Payen had given any indication as to how long he planned to stay.

Long enough to make sure she was safe. Then, he would leave again, but he had made arrangements for Eliza and Henry to have use of his properties in France or Venice should Violet decide to go abroad until the scandal died down. He hadn't heard anything yet, of course, but a canceled wedding always caused talk.

Once he knew that Villiers was no longer a threat to Violet or the Rexleys he would move on, and it would be a long time before he returned—if at all in their lifetime. It was better for all involved if he stayed as far away from Violet as possible.

Tossing back the covers, he slipped out of bed and walked naked across the darkened room to the attached bath. He washed and dressed and then lit a lamp and sat down to read for a bit. Reading quieted his mind, and helped whittle away the remaining hours until the summer sun began to sink into the west. Almost as though he had set an internal clock, he knew exactly when it was safe to leave the room and go downstairs.

And when he did, Violet wasn't there.

"She decided to take a tray in her room," Eliza told him. The look she gave him left no question as to who was responsible for her unsociability.

There was nothing he could say to make his friend less angry with him. Nothing he could say to make everything better. He could only hope that Eliza, and especially Violet, learned to forgive him.

Although Violet hadn't seemed all that upset with his actions last night. In fact, she had thanked him. So why was she avoiding him now?

The question ate at him all through dinner. He ate because it gave him a sense of normalcy and habit, not because it gave him sustenance. That he would find elsewhere later this evening, when he could sneak out without anyone realizing he was gone.

But before he went, he was going to have to speak to Violet. As the evening wore on, Payen grew more and more agitated. What if something was wrong? What if Villiers had tried to contact her? Or what if they planned an elopement?

It was ridiculous of course, because Violet had seemed so relieved the night before. However, he had been duped by other seemingly "honest" women in the past. If Violet's behavior had been meant to throw him off, she had succeeded.

Damn it all, if she ran off with Villiers he would chase her to the ends of the earth to bring her the hell back. And he'd take Villiers' head off with his own bare hands.

The thought of her running away increased his agitation. Images of her laughing with Villiers, kissing him, letting him touch her flittered through his mind, torturing him more than any adversary ever had, until he was pacing the parlor like a caged beast, ready to pounce at even the smallest prey.

Watching him warily, Eliza announced around eleven that she and Henry were going to bed. Henry opened his mouth, but one glance from his wife shut it. His friend shot Payen a sympathetic glance. "Good night, Old Boy."

Payen didn't have to force a smile. He couldn't remember a time when someone in that family hadn't referred to him as "Old Boy." "Good night, Henry. Eliza."

She merely nodded her head at him. And then, as she followed her husband from the room, she turned and fixed Payen with a gaze that could have frozen fire itself.

"She asked me not to say anything, but I thought you should know. Your little spectacle last night has damaged Violet's reputation irrevocably. The gossips have the two of you pegged as lovers, and regardless of how true that might have been once, she is going to suffer for it now. I hope to God you were right about Rupert, because she is ruined, Payen. Worst of all, you could fix it, but I know you won't. And so does Violet."

She left then, with those bitter words stinging like a thousand angry wasps. Payen stared at the empty doorway, bathed in shame, and worse—regret.

No wonder she hadn't come down to dinner. Whatever kind feelings she'd had for him the night before, were surely destroyed now.

It was better this way. It would be easier when he left, knowing that she despised him. She would go on with her life and he could finally get on with his.

Easier be damned. He could not spend the rest of eternity knowing he had hurt her so badly. The last five years had been hell, he couldn't take hundreds more. Couldn't let Violet live out the rest of her days thinking the worst of him.

He was halfway up the stairs before he even realized he had left the parlor. Violet's room was at the far end of the hall—far enough away from Henry and Eliza's to give her privacy. Unfortunately, he had to pass the Rexleys' chambers to reach Violet's. Luckily, he had been sure and soft-footed as a human, and was damn near cat-like now.

He didn't knock. Couldn't risk anyone hearing. Wouldn't risk her turning him away. He turned the knob, was surprised to find it unlocked, and opened the door, letting himself into her private quarters without so much as a "please."

She was sitting by the window, bathed in moonlight and the soft glow of a lamp, wearing a flimsy little nightgown and wrapper. He could see the soft pink of her thigh through the thin satin, the flush of a hard nipple.

Christ.

Violet looked up from her book, not looking the least bit surprised to see him, or that he had barged into her room.

"Good evening, Payen." Rising from her chair, she cast the book aside, and stood before him, thick, glossy hair rippling around her shoulders, the faint musk of arousal clinging to her flesh. "Close the door, will you. I don't want us to be interrupted."

It wasn't victory that thrilled Violet to her toes, but rather the realization that Payen could no more resist her than she him, the knowledge that she was not alone in this instinctual need.

She'd spent the evening waiting for him, knowing that he wanted her as much as she wanted him, that he would come to her, unable to stand being apart any longer.

God, how she loved being right.

She moved to him. Standing before him, their gazes locked, fused together by this shared heat, she loosened the ties on the front of her robe and shrugged the thin satin from her shoulders. It fell down her arms with a whisper and pooled around her ankles with a gentle caress.

Payen's sherry-hued gaze fell upon the heaviness of her breasts beneath her nightgown. Violet's breath caught, sharp and raw in her throat as he cupped them with his hands. His fingers were warm and firm as they massaged her needy flesh, his thumbs brushing the peaks with brutal tenderness. Her nipples hardened, tightening with every stroke. Sparks of pleasure ignited between her thighs, deep inside her in that place that ached to be filled by him.

Locking her gaze with his, Violet lifted her hands. Hooking her fingers beneath the straps of the gown, she pulled them down over her shoulders. He lifted his hands so that her nightgown fell to the floor on top of the already discarded wrapper. Naked, Violet stood stock still beneath Payen's gaze. Such an intimate appraisal would normally make her uncomfortable and too self-aware, but there was none of that with him, because she knew that in his eyes, she had no flaws—at least not physical ones. He seemed to love the full curves of her body, the width of her shoulders and hips.

"So beautiful," he whispered, the tips of his fingers skimming the pale roundness of her belly, up to her breasts again. "My sweet warrior queen."

Violet shivered at the caress of both hands and voice. She was trembling now, and he'd barely touched her. "Undress."

He grinned, a slow, seductive spreading of his lips. "Make me."

How could she resist such a challenge? Satisfaction rippled through her as she pulled his coat down his arms and tossed it aside. His cravat and waistcoat followed, and all the while, he stood there beneath her hands. He never once lifted a finger to assist her—his fingers were busy elsewhere, touching her anywhere he could, raising patches of gooseflesh on her sensitive skin.

As she pulled the tails of his shirt free from his trousers, Violet thrummed with anticipation. Her body seemed hot and prickly, parts of her heavy with need and others tight with desire. Her breasts brushed Payen's torso, the linen of his shirt scratching her flesh, making her gasp as it rasped against her nipples.

She pulled his shirt up. He grabbed the hem and pulled it over his head, tossing it to the floor.

His gold and faun hair was mussed, standing up in little spikes that made her hands itch to slip through the silky strands. The lamp lent hollows beneath his high cheekbones and accentuated the rippled muscles of his chest and abdomen.

Her mouth dry, Violet raised an eager hand. She touched the warm, smooth skin of his shoulder, her fingers caressing, gliding over the sleek muscle and knobby bones. Then down, her hand went, over the firm, satiny flesh of his chest. His pectorals were defined and separated by a slight indent that ran down to his stomach, where a fine trail of silken hair disappeared beneath the waist of his trousers.

"I think you're beautiful," she murmured, sliding both hands over him now. "Like a golden god." She didn't care if it sounded silly, that was how she saw him. She traced the indent of his navel with her finger, smiling as he sucked in a quick breath.

"It would take a god to resist you," he told her, his voice slightly hoarse.

Briefly, Violet met the heat of his gaze and saw the truth and desire there. Her heart caught and squeezed. She had to look away. Her gaze slid lower, to the bulge in the front of his trousers. Reaching down, she cupped him with her hand, smiling at the groan that escaped his lips as she rubbed the hard length of him with her palm.

"I've been told," she whispered, leaning close to his ear, "that a man finds it very pleasurable when a woman takes his erection into her mouth."

Beneath her hand Payen's erection twitched. He chuckled softly, fingers trailing down her spine to caress one buttock. "It's true. Are you going to take my cock into your mouth, Vi?"

Pulling back, she met his gaze without shame or embarrassment. "Would you like that, Payen?"

"Christ, yes."

Fingers fumbling, she unfastened the falls of his trousers, her gaze never leaving his as she slid the fine wool down the lean firmness of his hips and thighs. Kneeling, she removed his shoes and pulled his trousers over his feet. She tossed them aside and sat back on her calves, taking a moment to revel in his nakedness.

She rubbed her cheek against his thigh, feeling the springy hair there and warm, firm flesh. Then, turning her head, she admired the proud jut of his erection, the length and size of him. She was responsible for that—his desire and readiness.

For a moment, she doubted herself, and then she reached out and wrapped her fingers around his thickness. His body tensed in response. "That's it," he muttered. "Touch me. Lick me."

Violet needed no more encouragement. His words seemed to strike right at the very center of her sex, intensifying the hot ache there. She could feel dampness on her thighs, cool air on her slick, heated flesh. She kissed the tip, ran her tongue along the smooth, silky head, all the while stroking with her hand.

Payen groaned.

Smiling coyly, Violet lifted her head to gaze at him. Another lick. "Do you like it?"

His lips parted on a small gasp as she took just the head inside her mouth and sucked gently. "Christ, yes. More. Please." His head fell back as she applied more pressure. "Suck it."

She did. Violet bathed him with her tongue, savoring the saltiness of his skin. She took him full into her mouth so that the head filled her throat as she stroked him with her tongue, then withdrew to torture him with licks and nips, while pumping him with her hand. He held her head in his hands, holding her in a way that allowed her to move, but not to release him. As if she would.

This power was intoxicating. Grasping him by the flanks, Violet bobbed her head up and down, sliding her mouth over the slippery length of him until his fingers tightened in her hair.

"Vi," he gasped. "Violet . . . oh." Then he stiffened and shuddered, groaning aloud as release came upon him.

Releasing him, she rose to her feet. He was leaning

back against her vanity for support, head back as he gasped for breath. He was absolutely beautiful.

"You're incredible," he told her as he straightened. She preened under the praise. "Now, it's my turn to taste you. It's been too long."

He was right. Just the thought of what he meant to do to her had Violet practically racing for the bed. Climbing onto the mattress, she leaned back against the pillows and spread her thighs. Could he smell her dampness, her arousal?

Payen followed her onto the bed, kneeling between her spread knees with a seductive smile. "Eager?"

"Yes." What would be the point in lying. "I want your mouth on me, your tongue inside me." He had done that to her before and she'd thought she'd died, it felt so good.

She didn't have to ask twice. Braced on his forearms, Payen lowered his head to the heated valley of her thighs. The first stroke of his tongue made her hips jump in response, jolting her senses into supersensitivity.

He was ruthless with his tongue. He licked her, sucked on her until she thought she couldn't take anymore, filled her with his tongue. And then, he slipped a long finger inside her, stroking a place deep inside that had her writhing and gasping beneath him as his tongue found that tight little spot that ached with the promise of incredible pleasure. And then she came in a great flood of heat that had her shuddering and stifling her cries with her hand.

Payen didn't give her time to recover. He couldn't. He was hard again, tight and heavy with the need to be inside her. Holding her knees apart, he positioned the head of his cock against the soaked entrance to her body, and slowly slid inside. She was so tight, so wet as she stretched to accommodate him. It damned near killed him to go slow, but Violet's coo of delight gave him all the restraint he needed.

Leaning down, he trailed hot, wet kisses along her neck. He nipped gently with his teeth—just the barest scrape of fang. She gasped, arching her hips upward so that he was fully buried within her. He wasn't going to bite her. As good as it would be for both of them, he didn't want anything to interfere or diminish this moment.

It had been too long since he'd felt this completeness. Too long since Violet showed him what it felt like to be home. Her arms and legs were wrapped around him like ivy, holding him so tightly he could feel it in his chest—in his heart.

His mouth went to her breasts, licking and sucking each nipple until they stood tall and distended, red and puckered. Violet gasped and moaned, undulating beneath him. Her fingers caught at his hair, dug into his scalp as she held him to her breast. "Harder," she begged. "Oh, Payen, harder!"

He bit her. He didn't mean to—only wanted to nip at the sweet pebble of flesh in his mouth, but his fangs were fully extended and they pierced the delicate flesh around her aureole. Violet's back arched, giving herself up to the bite as little keening sounds slipped from between her lips.

Payen let the taste of her fill his mouth as he plunged inside her. Hot and wet, Violet thrust against him, every stroke bringing him closer to the edge, as she quaked and moaned beneath him.

Payen's movements quickened. He was going to come. Every lonely moment of the last five years, every empty night had been worth the pleasure of having Violet wrapped around him, pleading with him to make her climax. He would literally smash down mountains for this woman, the only one who had ever accepted him without question.

She terrified him, and yet there was nothing so perfect as the peace he felt in her arms. She belonged to him. And God help him, he belonged to her.

Then it hit. A ragged cry tore from Payen's throat as he plunged himself down upon her. He stiffened as his climax rocked him, pounding his hips against hers as she arched, crying out her own release against his shoulder.

It wasn't until moments later, when he was lying beside her, enjoying listening to the slowing of her breath, that Payen felt the first twinge of regret.

Chapter 5

 Violet knew what the expression on Payen's face meant. She had seen it five years ago, just before he walked out of her life.

"Say you are sorry and I will neuter you," she growled in a voice strange even to her own ears.

Payen jerked, guilt lighting his eyes. "Violet, I . . ."

"I mean it, Payen. I have a silver letter opener in my desk."

A sad smile curved his lips. That he didn't seem to take her threat seriously wasn't nearly as much of an insult as the fact that he didn't take her giving herself to him—on what should have been her wedding night to another man—as seriously as he ought. He was the only man she had ever had sex with—the only man with whom she had ever shared a bed. The only man to whom she had ever given her heart.

She would not allow him to make her feel soiled for having chosen him.

His hand braced on the mattress, Payen angled his

body toward her. The muscles in his arm bulged beneath the taut gold of his flesh. The slash of his ribs drew her attention to the sheets pooling around his lean hips. He was a beautiful distraction, making her forget her heart's demands with the temptation of his body.

Almost.

"You want to run away," she murmured, drawing her gaze upward to his face, which was no less breathtaking than the rest of him. "Just like you did five years ago."

He reached across the scant distance between them to cup her cheek in his palm. His thumb stroked her flesh softly as he stared into her eyes with a gaze so sweet it broke her heart. It hurt so much—so very much—to know that he wouldn't allow himself to be with her. "As fast as I can," he replied.

She couldn't hate him, as angry as he made her. "Why?"

Warm fingers whispered over her lips—a fragile caress, one that made her breath catch with its simple, light reverence. "You know why."

"Say it." The words came out as a hoarse whisper, made rougher by the tightness of her throat. Violet clutched the sheet to her chest, not to shield her nakedness, but to somehow create a barrier between him and her heart. It didn't work, of course, but it made her feel stronger, kept her from turning her face to his hand, and burrowing there like a needy housecat.

In the faint light his gaze was brilliant as a polished tiger's eye. "I'm a vampire."

"I know what you are." Did he think her a stupid child? She had known what he was for years—long before giving him her virginity. Long before she fell in love with him. Shortly after coming to live with Eliza and Henry, they'd been out for an evening ride and her horse had bolted, spooked by a rabbit. Payen had caught her horse—on foot. If that hadn't been proof enough that he wasn't human, the fact that he looked no different now than he had more than a decade earlier certainly was.

His hand fell away from her cheek, but he didn't move away. He didn't have to; he'd already put more distance between them than physically possible. "And you are human."

A moot point and they both knew it. "That's remedied easily enough." When he began to protest— obviously she knew it wasn't *that* simple—she cut him off. "You'll have to do better than that."

He spoke so readily she knew the response had been planned—perhaps even rehearsed. "I swore an oath when I drank from the Blood Grail never to change another person."

"That was a long time ago, Payen." So long it was beyond her realm of understanding. He was beyond her realm of understanding, but she didn't care. She could live to be one hundred and still know only a fraction of his life, and it didn't matter. She loved him.

"I gave my word."

Brushing back the hair that tumbled over her shoulder, Violet pinned him with a sharp gaze. She wasn't a girl anymore and she wasn't going to let him get away from her as easily as he had before. "Who are you trying to convince that we can't be together? Me? Or yourself?"

"You," he replied without hesitation, without malice. Then, with the hint of a smile, "And perhaps I need a reminder myself."

The words came rapidly, without thought—without care. "Is a seven-century-old promise worth a chance at happiness?"

He almost said no, she could see it in his eyes. Stubborn, stupid man. He wanted her as much as she wanted him. Perhaps—and she daren't let herself believe it—he loved her as much as she loved him. "I made a vow."

"And prevented me from saying my own." A cheap shot, but who cared?

"You thanked me for that." His expression, his posture, and his tone were defensive. This time he did pull back. "You wanted me to tell you not to marry Villiers."

He wasn't going to turn this on her, make her somehow to blame. "Because I had hoped that you harbored some feeling for me." She had nothing left to lose—he had already taken her innocence and her reputation—her heart and soul. What else could he do?

"I do." It was a low blow and they both knew it. And it answered her question, obviously he had the power to still do a lot to her. He spoke so smoothly, held her gaze so carefully that only the tiniest flicker of emotion came through, but she saw it.

He wanted to play, did he? She threw back the blankets and slid from the bed. "Obviously, not enough."

"Damn it, Vi. It's not that simple."

"I think it's amazingly simple." Snatching her robe from the foot of the bed Violet slipped it on and tied the sash tight around her waist. "Either you love me or you don't, Payen."

The color drained from his face, and Violet's heart shattered into thousands of sharp, jagged shards.

Not enough. She fought the pain, tucked it inside her. "That's what I thought." But dear God, she had hoped. She had almost believed.

In a flash he was out of the bed. Gloriously naked, and comfortable with it, he came after her. He stopped just short of touching her. He was very careful not to touch her. "You don't understand."

Violet stood her ground. Toe to toe they stood. She wanted to hit him, wanted to shake him and kiss him. Wanted to climb him and take him inside her. She poked him in the chest instead. "Then make me."

"My feelings for you are inconsequential." Payen shoved a hand through his hair on an exasperated sigh. "I knew what I was doing when I became a vampire. I lost everything I had or could have had to become what I am."

She watched him for a moment, the subtle flush in his cheeks, the shuttering of his gaze. Why hadn't she seen it before? Had she been too young to see it—or just blind? "What was her name?"

His expression closed down completely, but not before she saw the truth there. "What makes you think there was a woman?"

She spoke plainly, her battered heart slightly buoyed by this new revelation. "Because men are seldom as stupid with anything else as they are when a woman is involved."

"You do not think very highly of your own sex."

"On the contrary, I think women capable of almost anything. That men are so easily duped by us is what gives me pause." She placed a hand over his heart, felt the slow—too slow to be human—beating there. "Tell me."

"Alyce," he replied, his gaze clouding with a mixture of memory and regret. "And she's the reason Stephen Rexley died."

The annoyance on Violet's lovely round face gave way to bewilderment before comprehension dawned in her eyes. "Henry's ancestor?"

Payen nodded, turning away from her as he did so. "He was my friend." He wasn't going to tell this story naked. He found his trousers on the floor and pulled them on. He needed all the armor he could get.

Fortunately, or perhaps unfortunately, Violet was patient enough to wait for him to dress before he continued. He pulled on his shirt but didn't tuck it in and sat on the edge of the bed, regarding her with a tired gaze as he tugged on his shoes. It wasn't a pleasant story, but one she deserved to hear. He owed her that at the very least.

Maybe then she'd understand, but he doubted it. Damn, she was so young. To talk of love and promises— what did a girl her age know of either? No doubt she thought him some kind of romantic figure—a white knight—her hero. He was neither.

She was still waiting patiently, in her thin robe that left little to his imagination—not that he needed imagination to know every delectable curve and hollow.

He sighed. "We were both Templars charged with protecting the Blood Grail from the Order of the Silver Palm. I had just drunk from the cup and become vampire to better serve our cause. Stephen was uncertain whether or not he could also commit himself to an eternity of standing between the Silver Palm and the power they sought." He smiled, both sad and amused. "I rushed at the chance to pledge myself."

And when the cup was taken by Philip's men, he tracked the six new vampires for a century, waiting for a chance to steal the chalice back. They did not abuse its power, although they certainly abused their own, but that changed when one of them committed suicide by walking into the dawn. The remaining five turned to the church, and learned that the Blood Grail was safe once more.

Violet was watching him, her expression strangely unreadable. Normally she was an open book to him. "I imagine you did. You loved Alyce?"

Impatient minx. But she kept him from dwelling too long. "Yes. She was a girl in the town where Stephen and I lived at the time. We met her through her brother, a young man we would sometimes drink with at the local ale house." His jaw tightened at the memory of that young man. "I loved her with all the foolishness a young man can. I didn't know it but so did Stephen."

She didn't seem the least bit bothered by his confession, wise enough to not be jealous of a woman long dead. Perhaps she was less of a girl than he gave her credit for. "Which one of you did Alyce love?"

Payen chuckled proudly—and a little bitterly. Not a stupid one, his Violet. "Above all, I'd say herself, but that might not be fair. Between the two of us, I think she loved Stephen more. Regardless, she was only interested in one thing from either of us."

"Let me guess." Violet crossed her arms beneath her generous breasts, unknowingly pushing the generous swells of flesh upward like an offering of worship just for him. "Alyce belonged to the Silver Palm."

Perhaps he should be surprised that she figured it out, but it did sound like the plot out of a gothic novel or some moral tale against the sin and evils of woman that seemed so popular these days. "Not quite. Her brother did. Back then the Order hadn't realized that women could be as useful to their organization. That came a little later." He wasn't going to think of those women now.

"So how did she betray you?"

So transparent. The depth of the story was either lost on her, or he had made too much of it in his own mind. "I did it to myself. I revealed the truth about myself to her."

Hazel eyes widened. Was that hurt in the bright depths? Surely she had to know there had been women before her. So many women.

But never one like her.

Violet's long fingers clutched at the front of her robe, twisting the silky fabric. "She betrayed you to her brother."

For a moment, Payen wanted nothing more than to take her into his arms and kiss her senseless—forever. The words were said with such horror, such disgust. Perhaps it was because she had no blood relation left to have such loyalty as Alyce's. Or, perhaps it was because Violet would never betray a man she claimed to care for.

Which meant she didn't care for Villiers—not really.

"Yes. She confessed what she had done to Stephen, why I don't know. The idiot came to warn me, a hero till the end."

"He was killed in the fight? Henry told me he was killed in battle."

Payen flinched before meeting her gaze. "That's what I told him. In truth, the battle didn't start until after Stephen died. He was killed by Alyce's brother, who had already murdered his own sister for her disloyalty."

Violet frowned. "That must have been horrible for you."

"I had my vengeance." He wasn't about to tell her what he had done to those men. He didn't want to think about it, but even after all of these centuries, he could smell their blood in the air, feel the stickiness of it on his hands.

And his shrewd little Vi, so much sturdier and stronger than her namesake, looked at him as though she too smelled what he smelled and felt what he felt. She would have been right there beside him, a sword in hand.

She would kill for him, he realized with a sudden jolt—one that hit straight in his heart.

She also wasn't about to let him off with a story of old betrayal. "So you don't want to be with me because I might hand you over to the Silver Palm? You don't trust me?"

"That's not it at all."

A sharp dark brow shot up against the pale flesh of her forehead. "You didn't think I'd reveal you to Rupert? Perhaps he and I are in league already."

Payen scowled his offense. "You would never do such a thing." And he knew she wouldn't. Had never once thought she might.

"Then you haven't cast judgment against all women based on the actions of one?"

"Of course not." He was beginning to lose his patience.

"But because of this, you and I cannot be together."

"Damnit, Violet!" Drawing a sharp breath, he rose from the bed and walked toward her once more. He cupped her shoulders with his hands, feeling the supple strength of her beneath his palms. "People I love die."

Her dimpled chin lifted defiantly. "People die, Payen. Whether you love them or not."

"You don't understand." Sadly, he knew of no other way to make her see.

"I understand perfectly." She tilted her head. "It's a little pathetic, frankly."

His hands dropped. "Excuse me?" Surely he couldn't have heard her right.

"I never would have thought you such a coward."

He had heard her right. Indignation—anger—swelled within him. "I've killed men for less than such an insult."

Violet practically sneered at him. "You'd never physically hurt me and we both know it."

But he heard the thinly veiled barb in her words. He had hurt her emotionally. "I am not a coward."

"When it comes to your heart, you are," she insisted. This time it was she who lifted her hands, placing one on either side of his face. Instinct demanded that he pull away, get himself to safety, but his pride held him still. He would not prove her right.

"You love me." Conviction rung in her words, made him frown even deeper.

"I've never made any such declaration," he insisted pompously.

Her smile was one of serene indulgence. "You love me, and I love you. But I don't have the luxury of being able to wait forever, Payen. If you wait too long to realize what it is your heart wants—what *you* need—I'll be gone. Ask yourself which you'd rather have, your vow, or me by your side for all eternity."

Payen pulled away, shocked and silenced to the depth of his very being by her words. She loved *him*? Loved *him*? No, she couldn't. Yet, there was nothing but truth in her guileless gaze. Nothing but sadness and certainty. She loved him, and she believed that he loved her.

Christ, what had he gotten himself into?

He had to get out of there. Had to go. Had to be somewhere she wasn't. Somewhere far away.

He backed toward the balcony.

"Go ahead and run," Violet said softly. "But if you're not back here by sunrise, I'll come looking for you, Payen Carr. I'll hunt you till the day I die."

She would too. He could see it. "Why?"

Her smile was sad yet determined. "Because I'd rather spend the rest of my life chasing you than missing you."

That was it. He could hear no more. He stared at her for what felt like a lifetime, but in reality was but a few seconds, and when his heart could bear the sight of her no more, he turned and fled through the French doors. He vaulted off the balcony and into the sky, shooting frantically toward an unknown destination.

And from the darkened garden below, Rupert Villiers watched in astonishment.

Chapter 6

 Payen did indeed return by dawn. Violet heard him on the stairs—and knew whatever noise he made was for her benefit.

When he came to her door, he was silent and stealthy once more. Violet felt his presence rather than heard it, but she knew he was there, separated from her by nothing more than a slab of wood that wasn't even locked. What good would a lock do against a being who could crush rock with his bare hands? But more to the point, why would she ever lock her door against the man she loved?

The only thing that kept Payen from coming into her room was himself, and that took some of the shine off what pleasure his return gave her. She lay in her bed, still and listening. She wasn't sure exactly when he walked away, but eventually she realized that he was no longer near. Perhaps she imagined the entire thing. Still, Violet didn't close her eyes and attempt to sleep again until the first pale light of dawn crept through her bedroom window. She could rest now, knowing that Payen was her prisoner at least until sunset.

When she woke a few hours later, it was with a renewed sense of hope. She wasn't certain how one engaged in a battle of wills with a centuries-old being, but she was spoiling for the fight, regardless.

His loyalty—outdated as it was—was admirable. Violet hadn't any concerns that he would be just as loyal to her. His feelings for her weren't the problem. The problem was in his head, in his thinking that he couldn't love her, be with her, and still keep those ancient vows.

Surely the people who gave him those vows never intended that Payen should not have happiness in his life? Surely they didn't mean that he couldn't turn his mate into a vampire if he so chose? If they had, then they were wrong.

Her convictions and determination firmly in place, Violet rose and rang for her maid. Then, she washed, slipped into her undergarments, and stood still while her maid laced her into her corset. The fine boning nipped her waist in a flattering manner, but lifted her breasts far too prominently. Unfortunately, there was nothing to be done about it.

Payen seemed to like them. He had practically worshipped them the night before with his mouth and hands. Ah, the feel of his hot, wet tongue against the sensitive ache of her nipples . . .

"Are you all right, miss?" Her maid questioned. "You look a little flushed. Are your stays too tight?"

Mortified, Violet shook her head. "I'm fine, Anna. Thank you." No more thinking of Payen and the pleasure he gave her. But a little shiver raced down her spine at the thought of being able to enjoy that pleasure forever.

Immortality didn't frighten her, although it must be terribly lonely for someone who spent their nights alone. She wouldn't allow Payen to continue that way.

A rose and cream striped morning gown came down over her head, interrupting her thoughts, and Violet slipped her arms into the snug sleeves. It was a new gown, very pretty and feminine. It was stylish, but without a lot of the frills and trimmings that were so popular these days. A woman her size didn't want ruffles around her hips and derriere—a bustle was bad enough. Still, Violet had to concede that the colors were very flattering to her complexion and that the high neckline took the emphasis off her bust. She couldn't change that she was tall and statuesque, but this dress—part of her wedding trousseau—made her feel pretty and almost delicate.

Perhaps Payen might rise early enough to see her in it.

It must be awful to be the only vampire amongst a house full of humans. Not only because of the obvious temptation, but it had to be terribly lonely. Ostracized from company because of the sun's deadly light, forced to walk the night when most country folk were asleep in their beds.

Payen needed someone to share the night with— someone who accepted him for what he was, and had no misconceptions about how different life at his side would be. Someone who understood what it was to be alone.

Violet hadn't been so young when her parents died that she didn't remember them. She remembered them vividly and with great love and sorrow. Henry and Eliza had been very good to her, but they had never presumed to take the place of her parents—and they had their own children, both of whom were married now and about to make the earl and countess grandparents.

The Rexleys had never made her feel unwelcome, just the opposite, but Violet was old enough to miss what she once had, and always feel as though she didn't quite belong.

Until Payen. She belonged with him—as surely as the moon belonged to the night. She just had to make him admit it. No, she had to make him *accept* it.

It was with this thought in her head, this determination in her heart that she went downstairs to face the bright light of day and the scandal that her canceled wedding had become.

The papers tended to sympathize with Rupert, despite most of the accounts having been written by women. They just couldn't understand why Violet would jilt such a lovely man.

Then again there was one writer who cheerfully announced that she'd leave her husband for a man who looked like Payen as well.

"If Payen doesn't marry me I'll never be able to show my face in London again," Violet surmised, not without some bitterness, as she lifted her cup of coffee.

Eliza watched her over the rim of her own china cup. "Do you want to marry Payen?"

"I've had no other ambition since I was sixteen years old." She took a sip of hot, rich coffee. "He loves me, Eliza. He just won't allow himself to be happy."

Her guardian—her friend—didn't look convinced. Did she think Violet too young? Too foolish? She might be four and twenty years old, and perhaps her experience of the world was limited, but she knew her heart.

And she knew Payen. In fact, she'd wager that she knew the vampire better than Henry himself, who had known Payen since he was a boy.

Henry didn't know the truth about Stephen Rexley's death. That little reminder to herself took the sting out of Eliza's dubious expression and gave Violet the confidence to keep her head high at the other end of the breakfast table.

After breakfast, she went to see how many gifts were left to return, and busied herself there. When Eliza came in an hour later and told her that Rupert had come to call, Violet was surprised, to say the least.

"Do you want me to see to him?" Eliza asked, placing a firm but gentle hand upon her arm.

Violet patted those little fingers. Eliza might not be her true mother, but she had much of a mother's protectiveness—a fact Violet appreciated and loved her for. "No. I'll do it. I owe the poor man that much at least." She glanced around at the piles of gifts that had yet to be returned. "But perhaps in the parlor, where it won't be a constant reminder of my betrayal."

"He's already there." Eliza's grip tightened. "It would have been worse to marry him and betray yourself."

A truth Violet knew in her heart, but it made her happy to hear it said aloud all the same. She used that happiness to give her strength when, a few moments later, she entered the parlor where her former fiancé waited.

She straightened her shoulders at the sight of him. "Good morning, Rupert."

He looked surprisingly well for a man who had been jilted by his bride-to-be. "Violet. You look lovely."

"Thank you." She frowned. "To what do I owe the . . . pleasure of this visit?" Poor choice of words, but she was working with a befuddled brain at the moment.

Rupert glanced behind her at the closed door. "Is Mr. Carr here?"

"He's indisposed at the moment." And thankfully so, as the sunlight pouring into the room would kill him. "You needn't be afraid of him, Rupert." The moment she said the words Violet realized the light in Rupert's eyes wasn't fear at all. It was excitement—a glitter that formed a lump of unease in her stomach.

"I would like to speak to him," he said suddenly, turning on her with those spooky bright eyes. "I understand Mr. Carr's misgivings about my affiliation with the Silver Palm, but we'd like to assure him that the Order of today is nothing like the one he often fought."

"We?" The unease grew . . .

"Yes, the Order."

. . . and became a full blown brick of fear. "You told the order about Payen."

"Of course." He talked like it had been the most natural progression. How deep was he into the Order? Had he pretended his ignorance the night Payen arrived? Or had someone decided he deserved to know more once they heard of Payen's arrival? And dear God, what did modern men know about a seven-century-old vampire?

"Why would you tell them about Mr. Carr, Rupert?"

He gave her a sly look. "You know what he is, Violet, don't play coy with me. I saw him leave your room this morning. Very impressive. Shocked me at first, but afterward I realized what a marvel he is."

How had Payen left her room? By the balcony. Oh

God. Violet pressed a hand to her churning stomach. He had flown, and Rupert had seen him.

"Were you spying on me?" It hardly mattered, but it was something to channel her anger into rather than the fear that Payen was in danger.

"Of course." His smile faded a little. "Didn't take you long to let the vampire into your bed did it?"

Oh no. Now was not the time for weakness. She had to think of Payen. She forced an expression of confusion. "The what?"

He came toward her, that patient smile on his lips once more. It was all she could do to flinch backward, away from his touch. "I don't blame you. I imagine he can be very seductive. Masterful even."

Now, that was just unsettling. "He's none of your business. This is between you and I, Rupert."

"Yes. And I think it would be of benefit to all of us if we remained friends."

I think you should be committed to Bedlam. "Regardless of my infidelity?"

Light fingers stroked her arms. "I can forgive your indiscretion."

"Why would you want to?" Then it hit her. "You want to get closer to Payen. Why?"

He didn't bother to pretend. "My fellows in the Order would love to talk to him, study him. He's a walking encyclopedia of historical knowledge, Violet. Imagine what we could learn."

Academic curiosity did not put such a predatory gleam in the eyes of a man who used to shudder at anything scholarly, Violet knew that much. She also knew better than to underestimate a member of the Order of the Silver Palm. Regardless of her own opinion of Rupert, she knew Payen's history with the sect, and she knew how much he hated them. They had to hate him almost as much. Rupert's interest was predatory and she would protect her lover at any cost.

"You and I don't have to be friends for you to talk to Payen, Rupert."

"No, but I think it would help him to trust me. And it would quiet all those ugly rumors about you, my dear." His fingers tightened slightly on her arms. "I adore you, Vi. I hate to see you injured in anyway."

He had certainly changed his tune since the other night when he accused her of practically being a slut. There was a glimmer of truth in his eyes—enough to make Violet feel like dirt. And just enough lie to make her spine tingle with fear. Was he threatening her, or was it just her wild imagination?

"I'm sorry, Rupert. Truly I am, but I think you should go now."

Not one to give up easily, he gave her arms another squeeze before releasing her. "Trust me, Violet. Think of Lord and Lady Wolfram. I want what is best for you."

And for himself, she suspected. He had been badly hurt the night their wedding plans were destroyed, and she knew him well enough to know that he hadn't reconciled with it at all. He hadn't forgiven her. He never would. He was driven by what he felt she could do for him, rather than what he felt for her. Just as she had been when she agreed to marry him. She had given up hope for Payen even though she dreamed of him coming for her.

What Rupert was doing now wasn't for her, and perhaps it wasn't even truly for himself, but it was for the Order of the Silver Palm. They wanted Payen.

Oh God.

"I'll think about it." It was a lie, but it seemed the easiest way to get rid of him.

Rupert smiled, obviously believing her. "Good." He leaned in for a kiss. She turned her head, giving him her cheek.

"We'll talk later," he said as he moved toward the door.

"Of course." But as she saw him out, Violet's head was filled with one thought alone.

Getting Payen the hell out of England.

Payen was in the bath, shoulder deep in hot, sandalwood-scented water when Violet slipped into his room. The sun had barely slipped over the horizon on its long, late summer descent when he caught the subtle scent of her perfume, heard the not-so-subtle pounding of her heart.

"Checking to make sure I'm still here?" He called out with a touch more annoyance than he meant. "Did you think I would run away?"

She barged into the bath with a rustle of skirts and shallow breath. It was the fear radiating off of her that had him sitting up, sloshing water over the sides of the tub. "What is it?"

"You have to leave." This would have been amusing after all her talk of chasing him if he ran were it not for the insistence in her voice, the wide appeal in her eyes. She fell to her knees beside the bath, heedless of the water that would soak her pretty gown.

He caught one of her cold hands in his. "Easy, pet."

She stared at him, hazel eyes huge and round. "Rupert. He knows what you are. He says he wants to be friends now. Payen, I think you're in danger."

"From Rupert Villiers? Not likely." The words were more for her peace of mind than his own. Rupert Villiers might not be a threat on his own, but in the company of several other men skilled in combat who knew a vampire's weaknesses . . .

Her other hand clutched at his shoulder, her fingers digging into the muscle beneath his wet flesh. "You have to leave. Tonight."

She was afraid for him. More than that, she was terrified. When had anyone been concerned with his well being? Decades at the very least. Most people assumed he was indestructible, or at the very least nigh on impossible to kill. Not his Violet. Perhaps he should be insulted that she thought so little of his abilities, but he wasn't that stupid. With an odd clarity he knew that her concern sprang from her feelings for him, and not any doubt as to his physical prowess.

The realization was as humbling as it was arousing, and he rose from the tub with a heart full of an emotion he couldn't name, and a cock so hard he could use it as a battering ram.

Violet noticed it, of course. How could she not? She stood as well, her hand still in his.

"I don't think you're taking my concerns seriously at all," she informed him with a tight jaw, but her gaze slipped back to his erection with an interest that had the damn thing twitching in anticipation.

"On the contrary," Payen replied, stepping out of the tub and pulling her tight against him. "I take everything about you seriously. You're like a sword hanging over my head."

She glared at him. "What a lovely compliment."

He wrapped his fingers around the thick knot of hair coiled on the back of her head, holding her so she couldn't turn away. "I can't get away from you, and I know it's just a matter of time before you cleave my heart." As far as compliments went, he knew it wasn't a pretty one, but Violet understood. She always understood, damn her.

Warmth shone in her face, but there was sadness in her eyes. "You could just let me have it, you know. Then I wouldn't have to cut it out of you."

He smiled. "Where's the fun in that?"

She didn't return the smile. "I don't have time to wear you down."

He swallowed against a strange lump that was forming in his throat. "I thought you were going to chase me."

"Until I died. I'm going to die someday, Payen. Do you really want to live with that regret?"

He had forced himself not to think about it, but here it was, tossed in his face like last night's wash water.

Violet and death was not something he thought about if he could help it. She was so young, how could he think of her ending? And yet, he knew it would come. He had seen it so much in the past.

No more Violet. No more hazel eyes and sweet lips. No more driving him insane with questions and demands. No more sword above his head.

He couldn't breathe.

Soft fingers brushed his cheek. Violet's fingers came away damp. "I'll take that as a no," she whispered.

Then she was up on her toes and her lips claimed his with an urgency that eased the ache in his chest and directed it south. He was hard with wanting her, and if she let him, he was going to have her.

But when he was on his back on his bed, Violet straddling him with her skirts billowing around them, Payen realized that it was she who was going to have him. He guided himself between her spread thighs, to the slit in her thin drawers where the fabric was damp with her juices. Her body accepted him readily, slick and hot as she took him inside, tightly sliding down the entire length of him, so that her buttocks rested on the top of his thighs.

It was quick and urgent, with her grinding herself against him as he clung to her hips beneath the mountain of petticoats and gown. All he could do was arch his hips and groan, beg her to take him all the way, to let him come inside her as she came for him.

And when it happened, it was sharp and intense, almost violent as they climaxed together, voices mingling as they cried out in joy.

Afterward, with Violet collapsed on top of him, Payen realized that he was lost. He would have to find some kind of compromise within himself, between the vows he took and his feelings for this woman, because there was no way he could let her go again.

She stroked his jaw with her fingers, her chest pressed against his. He could feel the beating of her heart, even through the layers she wore. It tripped in time with his own.

"Promise me you'll leave," she whispered. "Just this once, do what I ask of you and run."

The tightness in his throat returned, but he ignored it. He didn't want to leave her. Didn't know if it was safe, but she would be in more danger with him there. "Only if you promise to chase me as soon as you can."

Violet's head lifted. An expression of wonder softened her lovely, round face. Tears shone in her eyes. "I'll chase you."

He kissed her. "I'll make sure you catch me."

And that was all he could allow himself to give her for now.

Chapter 7

 Letting Payen go took all the trust Violet had and then some. She trusted him with her very life, but trusting him to allow himself to love her was another story.

She loved him, but after his sudden departure five years ago she was reluctant to trust him with her heart again. Knowing him, he'd run somewhere she couldn't follow, and claim it was for her own good.

His belongings were packed and already sent on to London where he would board a ship for the continent. Once it was safe, Henry, Eliza, and Violet would leave as well, dodging the scandal Violet had brought down upon them. Payen would come for her in Italy. Eliza was sure to disapprove, but Violet had to follow her heart.

They said their good-byes in the library, where the french doors opened onto the garden. They had no close neighbors, but the seclusion of the garden would help ensure that no one happened to see Payen leap into the sky like a giant bat—that was how rumors got started.

"I don't like running like a coward," Payen said. "I want to stay and fight."

Henry clapped him on the shoulder. "I know you want to protect us, my friend, but we've agreed that it's safer for all of us if you go. Neither Eliza nor I want to see anything happen to you, and I know how you would feel should anything happen to either of us." His gaze skipped to Violet. "Or someone else."

Violet blushed under the knowing stare of both her guardians, but most of all she blushed because Payen was looking at her the way she had always wanted him to—like a woman he didn't want to leave.

"Stay away from Villiers," Payen warned her—as though she hadn't planned to do just that. "He may think you know where I am and use you to get to me."

Violet swallowed. Before she wouldn't have thought Rupert capable of such underhandedness, but his visit earlier had shown her a man different from the one she thought she had known.

And it made her wonder—had he or someone close to him known of her connection to Payen before this? Was Payen the reason Rupert proposed to her in the first place? How ironic that would be, since spite against Payen was the reason she'd accepted Rupert's suit.

"Are you certain it's safer with you gone?" Even though it had been her idea, she was having second thoughts.

Payen took one of her cold hands in his much larger warm one. "Yes. Villiers and the Order would most certainly use you against me if I remained."

"I thought you said there wasn't much of the Order left."

"I've heard there are still little pockets here and there

across Europe. But all it takes is one person to rekindle interest in the old ways, the old beliefs. One person to say they've found a Templar vampire and then all Hell breaks loose."

"What do they want from you?"

"Revenge. Power. Revenge for the Templars interfering centuries ago, and the power they believe is their right."

Violet watched as something darkened Payen's sherry eyes. His face tightened as his head came up, turned toward the door. She followed his gaze. The doorway, which had been empty, now had a figure standing at its threshold. Several figures actually, but it was the one up front that caught her attention.

"Rupert." Damnit. They hadn't been fast enough.

Her former fiancé smiled coolly. "Going somewhere, Carr?"

Payen shrugged, appearing nonchalant, but the hand that kept Violet at his side was anything but relaxed. "I did what I came to do."

"Ah yes." The younger man pressed his hands together as he placed one booted foot inside the door. "You ruined my wedding."

"Happy to have done it," came the smooth, taunting reply. "Violet deserves better than your kind."

Rupert laughed. "I'm not sure the vicar would agree with you."

Payen held his gaze. His face was void of emotion—Violet had never seen him so shut down, so empty. "The Vicar knows only his own ignorance. True evil often wears a human face."

"Monsters always say that." Rupert shook his head. "You know, before you showed up, I had no idea about the history of the Silver Palm? I owe you a great debt in regards to my education. If you hadn't spouted off as you had, I would have assumed you and Violet had been lovers and nothing more. Imagine my surprise when I told several friends in the Order what you had said."

For the first time a frown creased Payen's brow. He blamed himself for this, that was obvious. "I would imagine they were more than eager to 'educate' you."

"Oh they were. They were." Rupert chuckled. "I almost didn't believe the fantastic tale they told me. In fact, I came here to discuss it with you last evening—and then I saw you leaving Violet's bedroom." He shot a condemning glance at her, but it was the surprise on Eliza's face that cut more. "I saw you fly, and I knew then that my brothers had been right."

Payen's jaw tightened. Violet could almost hear him cursing himself for being so careless. She wrapped her fingers around the tight fist he held clenched at his side and squeezed. He spared her the briefest of glances, but the warmth there was all she needed.

"What do you want, Villiers?" It was Henry who asked. Stern, brave Henry.

Rupert kept his attention on Payen. "The Blood Grail. Where is it?"

So that was it, Payen realized as he tried putting Violet's body behind his. They wanted the chalice of eternal life—a cup imbued with the essence of Lilith, demoness and the mother of all vampires. He could only suppose that Villiers wished a taste of immortality for himself.

"I have no idea." That was only half a lie. He knew the Grail to be in the possession of the men who stole it from the Templars on the fateful October day more than six hundred years earlier, but beyond that he knew nothing except that it was safe. His friend Father Molyneux, a young French priest, had been chosen by the few remaining Templars to watch over the vampires and the Grail, though the young man knew little more than he had to. He wasn't about to tell this little miscreant who those men—vampires—were.

"Well then," Villiers began, lifting a pistol. "I shall just have to take you instead, Mr. Carr."

Payen laughed out loud. "You think so, little man?"

Villiers scowled. "I have silver bullets in this pistol." He nodded at the men behind him. "Go."

Payen tensed but the men didn't come for him. They went for Eliza and Henry instead, and when Payen moved to help them, the barrel of Villiers' pistol drifted to point at Violet. Two men came to take her as well. He could smell her fear as they flanked her.

They all had pistols—pistols trained on him, his friends, and on Violet. Being shot would hurt him, but even he wasn't fast enough to save the other three. At least one of them would die.

God help him, he would save Violet if he could, sacrificing his friends to do it.

A shot rang out. Payen jerked to the left and felt the hot metal whiz past his ear. He could tell from the smell of it exactly what it was. Silver shot. Villiers hadn't lied. Silver could be fatal to a vampire if it pierced the right organ—like the brain or the heart.

Villliers was grinning. "Consider that a warning shot. Will you come peacefully, Carr? Or do I have to get the nets?" Behind him was a man holding what appeared to be a large sheet of silver mesh.

Jesus Christ.

"We don't want to hurt Lord and Lady Wolfram, or Miss Wynston-Jones," Villiers said. "But we will if you don't cooperate."

"Good lord, man!" Henry cried. "What the devil are you doing? You'll be hanged for this!"

And for a moment there was a flicker of indecision in Villiers' eyes. "Not if they don't catch me, my lord. What do you say, vampire?"

Payen glanced at his friends. Eliza and Henry were pale, pistols aimed at their temples. Violet watched him with eyes as big as saucers, begging him not to give in.

It was for her and her safety that he turned back to Villiers with a sigh of defeat. "I'll come willingly."

"No!" Violet cried. She reached for him, but Payen side-stepped her hands. His heart was heavy with an ache he couldn't name, but he knew he was doing the right thing. This would ensure that Violet was safe once and for all. Once they were out of the house he could attempt his escape—he would kill Villiers for certain—but he couldn't risk any more harm coming to those he loved.

He should have known that Violet wouldn't let it end that way. He should have known that love of hers transcended good sense. Should have known she would never sit quietly while he walked away from her, when he swore he wouldn't.

He strode quickly toward Villiers. The barrel of the pistol trained on him barely wavered. Oh yes, the Order had chosen well with this one. "What did they promise you?" He asked.

Villiers smiled. "Money. Power. Everything."

"Still won't get you Violet."

For a moment, Villiers pleasure faded. "I can find someone who will make a better wife than a fat vampire fucker."

Payen would have ripped his throat out if it hadn't been for the note of hurt in the young man's voice. He smiled instead, dimly registering that someone had snapped a shackle onto his wrist. Judging from the heat and fact that it seemed to sap his strength, he'd wager it was silver. "It must kill you knowing I got there before you, and that I've had her again since."

Villiers' jaw tightened. "You've ruined her. In every way." He raised the pistol. "Maybe I should just kill you—let her live with the image of your pretty face splattered all over the parlor wall."

Payen didn't fear death, but he didn't want Violet to see that. "Your superiors wouldn't like that."

"Don't be so sure. I'll be the first of the Order to have killed a vampire in centuries. I'm sure your blood would be very useful in our experiments."

Their gazes locked. "And you call me a monster."

Villiers pulled back the hammer with a look that resigned Payen to his fate. This little boy was too excited, too full of power and fear and his own importance. He was going to pull the trigger.

And then Payen was knocked off balance. He pitched forward little more than a couple of steps, but it was enough to send him into Villiers. There was a tug on his arm as the man trying to shackle him let go of the irons, and an explosion near his ear as Villiers fired his weapon.

Eliza screamed and the world stopped. He could smell, taste blood on the air. He had heard the bullet strike flesh, heard a strangled gurgle, and then a body struck the floor in a rustle of skirts. His head turned and he saw her.

His Violet, lying on the floor, blood gushing from a gaping hole in her throat. Had she tried to push him out of harm's way?

Beside him, Villiers gasped in shock, trembling like

a fool. It would have been so easy to kill him then, to rip his throat apart with two fingers and watch the life drain from his eyes.

But it was the life draining from Violet's eyes that kept him from doing just that. He ran to her, fell to his knees beside her with a howl of rage that shook the entire house. Out of the corner of his eye he saw Villiers and his remaining men escape, and he didn't care.

He'd find them later.

Blood spread out on the floor beneath Violet, soaking through her gown and oozing into her hair. Awful gurgling noises came from her throat as her mouth worked.

"Don't talk," Payen demanded when he realized just what she was trying to do. "Jesus, Vi. Don't talk."

Eliza and Henry were suddenly there beside him; both of them began to weep when they saw the severity of their ward's wound. There was nothing they could do. Violet was going to die.

"No," Payen whispered. That couldn't happen. A world without Violet would be gray and lifeless, just like the photograph Lady Verge had shown him. There would be no music, no pleasure, no laughter without Violet to bring it. The idea of it, the certainty of never seeing her again, never holding her again, struck him in the chest like a cannon blast.

And he knew with total certainty, and without shame, that he could not live in a world where there was no Violet. He would not live without her.

He loved her.

And that was why, even though Eliza and Henry were right there, he looked into the eyes of the woman he loved and said, "I'm going to chase you, Violet Wynston-Jones."

Hazel eyes, dulled with shock, met his, and for a second brightened as his meaning sank in. She nodded—so slightly he would have missed it were he not watching so closely for just such a sign.

And then, hearing the slowing of her heart and knowing there wasn't much time left, Payen lowered his head to the wound in her throat, where the silver had tore her flesh, and drank. He didn't want to cause her further pain, so he took only what he needed as Eliza and Henry cursed and demanded to know what he was doing—had he no respect?

He didn't look at them and he certainly didn't ask their permission as he lifted his head long enough to bite his own wrist and offer the blood there to Violet. The pulls of her lips were tentative and weak at first, but they grew in strength and suction. He let her drink her fill, until his own head grew light and woozy. He wanted to make sure she had enough.

Finally, he broke away. With Eliza and Henry watching him in horror, he pulled the cravat from around his neck and wrapped it around Violet's to help slow the bleeding.

"My God, man," Henry's voice was raw with disbelief. "What have you done?"

Payen turned weary eyes to his friend. "I hope I just saved the woman I love."

Chapter 8

 The wedding was held at eight o'clock two nights later on the deck of a ship bound for France.

The bride wore violet—the groom's favorite color—instead of white. And on her finger, the smiling groom placed a ring that had belonged to another Carr bride almost eight centuries earlier—his mother.

"Do you take this woman to be your wife?" The captain asked.

Since he had broken his vows to the Templars, Payen decided that it was only right that he take the most important vows of his life with Violet, the woman he had turned into a vampire.

The woman who wouldn't let him run away even if he wanted to.

He grinned at the woman beside him, showing just a hint of fang. "I do."

Henry and Eliza bore witness to the ceremony. Neither one had fully forgiven him for making their former ward a vampire and cursing her to a life only at night, but neither could they contain their joy at having her alive once more.

"I now pronounce you man and wife."

Violet practically leapt into his arms, every sweet inch of her. He loved being able to hold her and not worry that she might break. He loved her strength and softness, every hollow and every round curve. He loved her.

Rupert Villiers had left England the same night of the attack. No one seemed to know for sure where he had gone and for now Payen was all right with that. Eventually, once Violet had settled into her new life, and the two of them together had settled into their new life together, he would start hunting for the little bastard. But he wasn't going to think about that on his wedding night.

They shared a light supper with Henry and Eliza and then retired to their cabin. Payen was thankful for the privacy.

"I couldn't stand one more minute with Eliza frowning at me."

Violet chuckled as she presented him her back. "She'll be fine. Unbutton me, will you?"

He kissed the side of her neck. "With pleasure."

"Any regrets?" She asked as his fingers raced down the row of tiny pearl buttons along her spine. He wanted her naked. Now.

The back of her gown gaping, sagging at her shoulders, he turned her to face him, so that he could look into those big eyes of hers and let her see the truth there. "I regret leaving you five years ago, but I could never regret being with you now."

"Are you sure?"

Sure uncertainty was strange in her. Did she doubt his reasons for changing her? "I regret cutting through Lady Verge's china plate more."

Her eyes widened. "You cut through a plate?"

"When I heard you were engaged, yes."

She chuckled so beautifully that he didn't mind admitting the embarrassing incident. "I have many regrets in my life, Violet Wynston-Jones Carr, but loving you isn't one of them."

"You love me?"

His hands came up to cup her cheeks. "Of course I do. And I'm an ass not to have convinced you of it before this. You are the color in my world, Violet. Every night is brighter with you in it."

Tears clung to the gold-tipped sable of her lashes as she smiled. "I knew you loved me, but after . . . what happened," she still wasn't able to speak plainly about the attack on them, "I thought you might have done it out of guilt."

"I did it for purely selfish reasons," Payen replied, tugging the gown from her shoulders so that it fell to her feet in a soft silky heap. "To keep you with me for eternity."

She wrapped long, strong arms around his neck. "No more running?"

"Not unless it's around the bedroom. But I'll chase you, my love. No matter where you go, I'll find you."

Violet smiled. "And I'll find you."

Payen would have made love to her right there, standing in the middle of the floor on a ship that swayed unevenly beneath their feet, but his wife deserved a bed on her wedding night, and so once he removed the rest of her clothes and his, the bed was where he placed her.

She lay beneath him, spread and open to his gaze and touch like a pagan offering to the gods. An offering to him.

He cupped the fullness of her breasts in his hands, lightly dragging his thumbs across the tight pink peaks. Violet gasped in pleasure, her hands coming up to cover his own, a sight that sent a surge of desire straight to his already throbbing cock. Her nipples were so sensitive, so incredibly receptive to his slightest touch. Payen took one between his lips, whipping it with his tongue before he nipped it gently with his teeth. She writhed beneath him, lifting her hips in silent invitation— one he accepted, sliding between her full thighs to push the eager length of him against her hot dampness.

He loved the feel of her. Loved her taste, the texture, the way she moaned. He loved the way she smelled, all heat and moist female, sweet and delicious.

He sucked and pulled at her nipple until it stood red and distended, and her fingers pulled at his hair, then he turned his attentions to the other breast. When he had her grinding herself against him, the slick little cove of her sex beckoning, he knew it was time to move on.

He moved down, planting kisses along the undersides of her breasts, the soft flesh of her rib cage. He swirled his tongue around the small pool of her navel and nuzzled her soft, round belly with his jaw. She shivered against the rasp of his stubble, gasped when he grazed her with his fangs.

Payen knelt between her legs as her hands clutched at his shoulders. The warm, salty scent of her arousal filled his nostrils, flooding him with a longing so great it took all his will to control it.

He parted the lips of her sex with gentle fingers. The first pass of his tongue was a quick lick just to lift her hips off the bed. The second was firmer, had more purpose. Violet moaned her approval, digging her heels into the mattress as she lifted her mons to his mouth. Payen licked again, this time coming in closer so that the light beard on his lip and chin brushed her sensitive skin, so that he could use both his lips and tongue on her.

He laved his tongue relentlessly against her little hooded friend until she was fairly sobbing with pleasure. Then, he slid two fingers into her slick pussy, curving them upward to stroke the tiny ridged wall there. Violet's hips lifted as her moans intensified, then, Payen pressed his lips against the sweet flesh of her inner thigh and bit.

She came so hard she soaked his fingers as her muscles clamped around them like a vise. Her cries echoed throughout the room and his male pride preened knowing that at least one crewman had to have heard the effects of his prowess. There wasn't a man alive who was worth his salt who didn't understand what it was to make a woman scream with pleasure.

Payen's smugness was short-lived, for the next thing he knew he was on his back and Violet was on top of him, straddling his hips and plunging the wet heat of her down onto his aching cock with such abandon that soon the sheets were tearing under the force of his fists and he was shouting out his own release as Violet sang out for a second time. Just as the tremors began to subside, Violet lowered herself over him so that she could sink her fangs into his shoulder and he into hers, sending another wave after wave of pleasure through each other.

"That was nice," she said later, tucked into his shoulder as they lay together on the torn and damp sheets.

Payen laughed. "Nice? Woman, you'll be the death of me."

Rolling toward him, she lifted herself up onto her elbow. A thick curtain of sable hair fell over her shoulder to pool on his chest. "The death of you? Hardly. I think I'm the *life* of you, Payen Carr."

He had to agree, but he pressed anyway. "I lived for centuries before you, you impertinent little chit."

"You existed," she corrected arrogantly. "You didn't start living until that first night with me. Admit it. That's why you ran away."

He stared at her. She never failed to amaze him. Lifting a finger, he trailed it down the satiny curve of her cheek. "You're right. And I almost died when I thought I lost you. I would have followed you into death, Violet. I was so stupid not to see it before, but I would have ended my own life just to find you in another."

Tears dripped down her cheeks, and Payen's own eyes burned as well as dampness threatened to spill over.

"You don't have to turn your back on the Templars," she told him. "I won't stand in the way of keeping your promises to them."

Pulling her close he kissed her. "I love you."

Violet opened her mouth, but Payen silenced her words with his own. She didn't have to say she loved him. He felt it in his bones, just as he knew that he could indeed keep his promises to the Templars. In fact, he planned to. But those vows would come a far and distant second to the vows he made to his wife.

Kathryn Smith

My husband says I have the best job in the world. The only thing that could top being paid to do what I love is if Avon Books decided that all their authors had to be hand-fed chocolate by Hugh Jackman, Gerard Butler, or John Cusack. But my husband probably wouldn't think so much of my job then, so instead I'll let him feed me chocolate and go on being forever thankful that I have the best job—and husband—in the world.

Photo by Jennifer Berry / Studio 16

www.maggieshayne.com

Photo by Jinger Benson

www.jeanienefrost.com

Photo by Bella Portraits

www.tgarey.com

Photo by Sarah Kolej

www.kathryn-smith.com

ISBN 978-0-06-147268-8

Some marriages
are made in heaven . . .
Some are not.

What happens when "the happiest day of your life"
turns into a nightmare? Forget the drunken best man or
the bridesmaid dresses from the '80s . . . none of these
wedding day disasters can compare to a cursed bride
determined to make it down the aisle, or a vampire
who is about to disrupt your wedding.

Join *New York Times* bestselling authors
MAGGIE SHAYNE and JEANIENE FROST,
USA Today bestseller KATHRYN SMITH, as well as
TERRI GAREY in four unforgettable tales of unholy
matrimony . . . where the grooms are dark,
dangerous, and mostly dead, and to love and cherish
till death takes on a whole new meaning.

www.harpercollins.com

Fiction

ISBN 978-0-06-147268-8

5 0 7 9 9

EAN

9 780061 472688

USA $7.99 Canada $8.99

S

0608